KACHINA

by
J. R. Rada

OTHER BOOKS BY J. R. RADA

The Man Who Killed Edgar Allan Poe

A Byte-Sized Friend (Hackers #1)

Welcome to Peaceful Journey (e-book)

Kuskurza (e-book)

KACHINA

by
J. R. Rada

AIM
PUBLISHING GROUP

KACHINA

Published by AIM Publishing.
Gettysburg, Pennsylvania.
Copyright © 2017 by James Rada, Jr.
Printed in the United States of America.
First printing: January 2017.

ISBN 978-0-9985542-0-4

PUBLISHING GROUP

315 Oak Lane • Gettysburg, Pennsylvania 17325

PART 1

Tu´waqachi

"The name of this Fourth World is Tu´waqachi, World Complete. You will find out why. It is not all beautiful and easy like the previous ones. It has height and depth, heat and cold, beauty and barrenness; it has everything for you to choose from. What you choose will determine if this time you can carry out the plan of Creation on it or whether it must in time be destroyed too."

So´tuknang to the Hopi
from *Book of the Hopi*

"(Of whom the world was not worthy :) they wandered in deserts, and in mountains, and in dens and caves of the earth."

Hebrews 11:38

CHAPTER 1

David Purcell raced south in his Camaro along Highway 191. He figured that if he ignored the angry rumblings from his car now, he would be able to avoid the angry rumblings from Terrie later. She would be fuming if he wasn't standing on her doorstep at seven o'clock to take her to dinner.

Light gray smoke seeped around the edges of the hood of the Camaro and blew back against the sides of the car. Water drops splattered against the windshield. David glanced at the sky. It wasn't raining. As usual, there wasn't a cloud anywhere in sight. His eyes were drawn next to the temperature gauge. The needle was in the red zone and quickly climbing.

David slapped his hands against the top of the steering wheel. "No, not now," he whined as he shook his head.

It wasn't smoke he was seeing; it was steam. He hoped the problem was only a busted hose and not something major like his radiator or water pump. However, with his history with the car, he doubted it.

"Come on, just a little bit longer. *Please*," he said.

David had bought his red dream car in St. George a year ago. It had cost him less than five-thousand dollars, and he thought it had been a bargain at the time. Most used-car dealers were selling the same car for a thousand to fifteen-hundred dollars more than the man from whom he bought this car. Now David knew why he had gotten such a good deal. Since last year, it had cost him another ten-thousand dollars to keep the car running. A month after he bought the car, the carburetor had blown up on him. Five months after that, he had two flat tires. Two months ago, it had been the shocks and the brakes. Last month had been the crowning glory. He had cracked the engine block while sitting at a traffic light in Salt Lake City.

And now this.

He wasn't sure what was left under the hood for him to replace.

David wondered if he could make it to Blanding and the Shell station there. Stuart, the mechanic, and David were becoming good friends. Any why not? With all the work David was bringing him, Stuart and wife could take a nice long cruise or send one of their kids to college.

The temperature gauge needle edged up another sixteenth of an inch, which meant the temperature of the engine probably jumped another twenty to thirty degrees.

David pressed the brake pedal and pulled the Camaro over onto the shoulder of the highway. He heard the sharp pings of gravel flying off the tires and hitting the car, and he groaned. The only thing that hadn't needed

3

repairs so far was the body of the car. He hoped the gravel wasn't putting dings in his doors. If the car looked good, he had a better chance of selling it to some young guy like himself who fell so in love with how the Camaro looked that he wouldn't take it for a long test drive.

David turned off the engine and jumped out of the car, slamming the door behind him. Wrapping his hand in his handkerchief so that he wouldn't burn it, he popped the hood. He backed away as a large cloud of steam billowed up from under the hood. If any Navajos were watching the sky in his direction, they probably thought David was sending up smoke signals. The smoke probably said something like, "White idiot bought hunk of junk from man who speaks with forked tongue."

While David waited for the steam to clear so he could see the engine, he checked the sides of the car by running his hands over the doors and fenders. The fenders and doors felt smooth. No dings. And no paint chips missing either. He smiled. Good, at least something was going right for him tonight.

Once the steam cleared from under the hood, he moved closer to the car to look at the engine. It only took him a moment to spot the trouble. The top radiator hose had a three-inch split on the side that steadily dribbled water onto the engine block. The *new* engine block. The heat from the engine vaporized the water into steam. David considered cutting off the rotten end of the hose and reconnecting it, but the cut hose would have been about two inches too short to reconnect. The split was near the middle along the length of the hose. He didn't even have any duct tape in his tool box to make a temporary patch. It looked like he was going to have to hitch a ride into Blanding and buy a new hose. Stuart could bring him back here with it.

David pulled his smartphone out to call Terrie and let her know that he would be late, but he wasn't getting a signal out here in the middle of nowhere.

He slammed the hood shut. This was the last straw! He would sell the heap of scrap metal as soon as it was fixed. Of course, he had said the same thing when he replaced the carburetor, and again, when he saw the bill for the new engine block. He hadn't. If he had, he wouldn't be standing on the side of Highway 191 wondering how he was going to get into town. David kicked the side of the car, and his hard-soled shoe not only left a scuff on the fender, but it left a small dent.

David threw his hands up in the air. He couldn't win.

I might as well lie down in the middle of the road and let an eighteen wheeler run over me. It would be less painful.

He looked at his watch. When he saw what time it was, he rolled his eyes. At this rate, he wouldn't even make it to Terrie's today. At least she would really have something to complain about. She was already mad at him because he had been out of town for her birthday last week. Not that he could blame her. He had gotten tied up with a purchasing agent at the University of

Arizona and hadn't gotten back to Blanding until eleven o'clock. He had gone to Terrie's trailer with flowers and her birthday present. She had opened the door wearing a red bathrobe and a film of cold cream on her face. When she saw him, she slammed the door in his face.

Their dinner tonight at Stromsted's Inn was supposed to be his late birthday present to her. David actually hoped it would be a new beginning for them.

Supposed to.

He was beginning to think that his relationship with Terrie was a lot like the one he had with his car. Both had enchanted him with their looks but were a lot different under the hood.

Terrie was beautiful, no doubt about that. David had flipped for her the first time he saw her waiting tables at the Double T Diner where she worked. She had smiled at him in such a way that he thought about her all the way through his meal. He had barely even tasted it. He had asked her for her phone number when he paid his bill.

He looked up and down the highway, praying he would see a car coming toward him from one direction or the other, but the road was empty. He couldn't be lucky enough to have a ride stop for him right after he'd broken down. It was six-thirty now, and he was still twenty miles outside of Blanding and even further away from Monticello where he lived. If someone didn't drive by and pick him up soon, he wouldn't be in time to get to the Shell station before it closed.

What's worse, he would be alone in the dark. The skin on the back of David's neck tingled, and he rubbed it with his hand.

"It won't be completely dark," he told himself out loud. "The stars will be out, and you have a flashlight under the driver's seat. You've got nothing to worry about so stop being a sissy."

Easy for you to say, David thought.

He reached inside the car behind the driver's seat and pulled out his olive-drab army cap he wore when he was doing his weekend duty for the Army Reserves. He knew he looked foolish dressed in a navy-blue suit and a green camouflage cap, but he didn't want the sun beating down on his head for the next hour or two until it set. He pulled the cap on over his dirty-blond hair and scanned the highway again. Still nothing.

No choice now but to start hoofing it.

An hour later, he was still walking. He had seen only one car in all that time, and it had passed him by without even slowing. He didn't blame the driver, though. People just didn't pick up hitchhikers in this day and age; not if they wanted to live. It was just too dangerous. You never knew when a hitchhiker might be someone like Rutger Hauer in *The Hitcher*.

There wasn't much to look at along the highway, either. No buildings. No animals. The brown landscape was broken only occasionally by some color from desert flowers.

Seven-thirty. Boy, would Terrie be fuming! At this rate, he wouldn't reach Blanding until eleven o'clock, and that was if he didn't stop walking. If only there was an emergency phone along the highway so that he could call for help.

He took off his hat and wiped the sweat from his forehead. Forget the phone. What he wanted right now was a large, shady oak tree to sit under so he could cool off. He wished the shimmering mirages of water he saw in the distance on the highway were real. A splash of cold water on his face would wash away some of the gritty, dried sweat.

David moved off the edge of the road and walked in the short desert grass. The ground, although it was hard, was gentler on his feet than the unyielding asphalt, and the dirt and grass didn't reflect back the day's heat like the road did.

Glancing to the right, he saw the bottom of the sun had just touched the top of the mountains. Once it went down completely, the ninety-degree temperatures of the day would drop quickly into the seventies. He had already noticed a difference for the better in the last hour. If only it would cool off without getting any darker, he would be happy. He didn't relish the thought of walking along Highway 191 in the dark. There were no streetlights, no town lights, and only a slight amount of starlight to see by. With his luck, he'd probably wind up getting lost as well as stranded in the middle of nowhere.

The thought sent a chill down his back.

In the distance, David saw a small speck racing toward him along the highway. It shimmered as it passed through the heat radiating off the road. He stopped walking and watched the speck as it drew closer. He moved back onto the edge of the highway and raised his thumb. For a moment, he considered jumping out into the middle of the lane so that the pickup truck would have to stop. The ways things were going today, the truck would run him over without even slowing down. He took off his camouflage cap and held it behind his back so that he wouldn't look too odd.

David smiled at how stupid it was to think whether he was wearing a hat or not would make a difference. He could see a pair of people in the truck and imagined what they might be saying to each other:

"Look, Horace, there's a hitchhiker on the side of the road, and he's wearing a suit."

"He sure stands out wearing that dark suit."

"Are you going to pick him up?"

"Well, I suppose so. A fella wearin' a suit can't be too bad, but if he'd been wearin' an Army cap too, I would have locked my doors. Them type's crazy."

The pickup truck passed David. He dropped his arm; another driver afraid of the big, bad hitchhiker. Maybe he should have worn his cap. As David watched the truck pass him, he saw brake lights go on.

Yes! Now he could get into town by eight o'clock.

He jogged toward the truck with renewed energy. Three feet from the rear of the truck, the brake lights disappeared. David thought the driver had turned off the motor. The rear wheels started spinning, spraying gravel into David's face. He felt like he had been caught in a hail storm.

"Hey! Watch it!" David yelled as he raised his arms to protect his face.

He dove to the side of the road away from the gravel spray, and he grabbed for the nearest rock. The driver of the pickup popped the clutch, and the truck jumped forward with a loud squeal and smoke from the tires. David rose up on his knees and heaved the rock at the truck hoping it would go through the rear window.

It missed and landed harmlessly on the highway. Could he expect any less on a day like today?

David threw his cap to the ground. His suit was filthy, but he tried to dust it off anyway. It was too expensive not to try and salvage. He noticed his hands were shaking as if he had a severe nervous tic. He did the best he could and picked up his cap, slapping it back on his head. He slung his suit jacket over his shoulder. It would come in handy when the sun set, and the temperature dropped, but it was still too hot to wear it now. He was already sweating as if it was midday. At least the Camaro's air conditioner had worked. Not that it did him any good now. He took a deep breath to calm himself as he looked down the highway.

He still had sixteen miles to go.

He moved back into the grass to avoid anyone else who might want to drive by and spray him with gravel. He walked about twenty feet away from the edge of the road. He figured that would be far enough away to avoid gravel sprays, but close enough to get to the road if somebody stopped.

Each time one of his feet touched the ground, the blisters forming on his heels warned him that if he walked all the way to Blanding, he would regret it. He was wearing his brown-leather dress shoes. Unfortunately, they were not designed for hiking. His shins already ached, but he ignored the pain and continued tromping through the foot-high grass.

David wished he had thought to read the practical joker's license-plate number. It was probably 666, the Number of the Beast.

He slammed his foot down again, but this time it hit the ground and kept going. The ground beneath his foot collapsed into a hole, and David's leg swung in the open air. Pinwheeling his arms, David tried to keep himself from falling into the new hole below his foot. He shifted his weight quickly to his rear leg, but it was too late. He saw the black pit under his feet come closer as he fell into it.

Screaming, he tried to avoid the hole. It was only about three feet in diameter, but at the moment, it looked like it was as wide as the Grand Canyon. If he fell into it, he had no doubt with the way his luck had been running today that he'd break his legs. And it would be hard for a salesman to drive from state to state with one or both of his legs in casts.

David's suit jacket flew out of his hand as he spun his arms around throwing him even more off balance. The jacket landed somewhere behind him, but he wasn't too concerned where at the moment.

He fell forward onto his chest and hit the ground in front of the hole. All his breath went out of him in a loud "whoosh." He expected to feel pain in his legs from broken bones, but he lay still. His legs were sore but unbroken.

He was safe! Only his legs were hanging inside of the hole. He had managed to keep the number of bones in his body to two-hundred and six. No more. No less.

David rolled onto his side so that he would be able to pull his legs out of the hole. As his weight shifted slightly, he started sliding into the hole.

"No!"

He grabbed for something, anything, to stop his slide. There was nothing. He caught a handful of grass, and he stopped.

It lasted long enough for him to take a breath. The blades of grass broke off just below his clenched fist. He tried to dig his fingers into the dirt, but it was too hard. One of his fingernails snagged on a small rock and tore in half. The sharp pain caused him to yell again. His finger started bleeding leaving a thin trail of blood toward the hole.

David's body tipped into the hole, and he fell. His left hand struck the edge of the hole and held. He tried to raise his right hand up, but just as he was about to grab the edge, a cramp hit his left hand.

He suddenly realized he was hanging in the hole and his feet still weren't touching the bottom. How deep was this hole? Not that he wanted to find out. It was too dark in there for him.

As David brought his left hand up to grab the edge again, the ground crumbled under his right fingers. He had only a brief moment to realize what had happened, and then he was falling.

CHAPTER 2

Adam Maho climbed down the ladder into the kiva, feeling a little pain in his knees. He wondered which was creaking more: his knees or the wooden rungs of the ladder that were lashed to the wooden poles? Nothing to complain about, mind you. A cup of snakeweed tea when he went home would ease the aches. It was just another of the trials of old age he had faced during the past few years. Only now it seemed he faced them every day instead of once in a while.

When he had climbed far enough down the ladder, he pulled the nuta, the thatched covering, over the opening of the kiva to keep the sunlight out.

The kiva was a circular room built below the ground. This particular kiva was about eighteen feet in diameter, although it was slightly longer on the north and south sides. Unlike many of the other kivas in Oraibi, or throughout the Hopi reservation for that matter, no woman or white man had ever set foot in this sacred room. It was even more sacred than the other ceremonial kivas. In the center of the room, the coals of a near-dead fire throbbed with a red-orange glow giving almost no light.

Though he could only see a few feet in front of himself, Adam knew he was not alone in the room, which was not unusual. Someone was seated against the far wall hidden in the darkness of the shadows. As Adam passed by the fire, he tossed a handful of small juniper branches on the sheep dung and charcoal coals. The coals flared with small flames, then settled down to the familiar red-orange glow. White smoke billowed up from the fire into the room.

He stopped next to the sipapu, the ceremonial emergence hole into this world, and looked down at the massive stone plugging the four-foot-wide hole. Other kivas had smaller sipapus, and they were left open as this one had once been. The stone had been placed in this sipapu long ago when Chief Raymond's grandfather's grandfather had lived. Very few Hopis knew of the reason for this break in tradition if they even knew of it at all, but they did not question the wisdom of Those-Who-Had-Lived-Before. Adam knew the reason, for it was the responsibility of his clan, the Sun Clan, to protect this kiva. That was the reason he chose to come to this sacred place to receive his visions. There were two kivas closer to his home, but none such as this one. The magic was strong here; the mystery overpowering.

No gaps showed around the edges. That was as it should be. It was better that no kachina, good or otherwise, be able to use this kiva to enter the Fourth World.

9

He pressed one foot on the stone to make sure it was still wedged tightly within the sipapu. The stone trembled beneath his foot. Startled, Adam jumped backward hitting one of the roof-supporting pillars. The stone had moved! But that was impossible.

Was it?

Yes! Just because he had received visions of a sipapu opening from Kuskurza, the Third World, did not mean that this sipapu would open. Those-Who-Had-Lived-Before had made sure of that. He touched his foot to the stone again. This time he felt nothing. Satisfied, he removed his foot from the rock.

Adam walked to the far wall and sat down on the stone bench built along the curving wall. He leaned back against the clay and stone wall allowing its coolness to spread through his body. He could see the man in the shadows now. It was Peter Kwa´ni. The older man sat silently to Adam's left, deep in his own meditation.

Adam leaned his head forward and closed his eyes to meditate. He did not know if the visions would come once more, but he had to learn why the harmony between the Third and Fourth Worlds, Kuskurza, and Tu´waqachi, was now unbalanced. Since the Fourth World was his own, Adam had a stake in seeing that it thrived.

Holding a deep breath of smoke from the fire, Adam tried to relax his body. The smoke was thick and foul-smelling. He blew the air out slowly between his pursed lips. One of the juniper branches crackled in the fire. Beside him, he heard Peter take a deep breath and hold it. The kiva seemed to be filling with smoke, but Adam knew that was impossible. The ventilation hole allowed the smoke to escape into the sky. Yet, Adam's eyes teared up as the smoke stung them.

He continued to try and relax because he wanted to be prepared to receive a vision.

He coughed from the smoke. The ventilation hole must be blocked because the air in the kiva was filled with smoke. Why was it darkening? The burning juniper gave off a white smoke.

Adam looked over at Peter, whom he could barely see through the dark smoke. The medicine man didn't seem bothered. His head was slumped back against the wall, his eyes closed. His arms were folded across his chest. Had Peter eaten herbs that would keep the smoke from choking him? Was there a poultice that the medicine man had rubbed on the eyes to keep them from tearing? Adam had never heard of such a treatment or herbs, but he was not a medicine man. Peter was. He knew many things about the medicinal properties of plants that most Hopis did not, and he seemed unaffected by the thick, dark smoke.

Again Adam concentrated on relaxing his body. His body had to be receptive if his mind was to pierce the veil between the Third and Fourth Worlds. He had determined after his second vision a week ago that he had actually seen the mythical Third World, which legend said was destroyed because of its evil. But Kuskurza hadn't been destroyed. At least not if Adam's visions were real. Kuskurza still existed or at least a portion of it still existed and continued to breed the same evil that had supposedly led to its original destruction. Only now it threatened to destroy both Kuskurza and Tu'waqachi.

Adam straightened his back so that his head was upright. The very top of his head tingled like an annoying itch as his ko'pavi opened to receive a vision from Taiowa, the Creator. The ko'pavi was the doorway through which life entered the body of a baby. As the baby grew older, the doorway hardened and closed. In adulthood, the ko'pavi only opened when a Hopi communicated with the Creator.

Images flooded into Adam's mind too fast for him to comprehend. He glimpsed pueblos eight-stories tall and with at least fifteen-hundred rooms, flat-sided mountains of stone even larger than the pueblos, a war among a pale-skinned race of people with skins even whiter than the white man's, pale-skinned warriors flying on shields of scaly, feathered skins, and other images. They flashed in his mind so quickly that he barely had time to register he had seen anything let alone understand them. The images finally slowed, and Adam saw a lone man, a white man, not one of the pale people. The man ran through the darkness. He wore a filthy and ragged suit. Some distance behind the white man, Adam saw five members of the Bow Clan chasing him.

Pahana. The white savior of the Hopi. Could it be?

The pursuers did not look the same as the Hopis, although they were of the same people. The members of the Bow Clan had pale-white skin the color of snow at the tops of the mountains. Their eyes were large and round but had sharp corners on the sides. Their hair was not black, but as white as their skin. The Bow Clan were short, thin men with long fingers. Perhaps the most obvious difference was not physical. The members of the Bow Clan were warriors who ruled the Third World brutally in a way that pitted the Ancient Ones against one another. They inspired distrust, fear and hatred among the Ancient Ones. When the other clans had fled Kuskurza and emerged through the sipapu into Tu'waqachi, they had left behind the Bow Clan. Adam was not sure how he knew the pale-skinned men were of the Bow Clan, but he did not question the insights given to him by the Creator.

The Bow Clan warriors closed the gap between themselves and the white man. The white man knew he was being pursued, but he could not move as quickly in the darkness as the Bow Clan warriors. Adam knew the warriors must not kill the white man, though that is what they planned to do if they caught him. If the white man died, then Adam's world, Tu'waqachi, would be destroyed and So'tuknang, the nephew of Taiowa, would not create another world as he had done in the past. This was the last chance for the Hopis to prove themselves worthy of Taiowa. But if the white man died, the dark kachinas would rule everything and everyone in the Third and Fourth Worlds rather than just controlling the Bow Clan in Kuskurza.

Adam heard a whisper in his head. It was too faint to understand. He concentrated on hearing the words, for it might be Taiowa advising him on what he must do to save the white man. As Adam heard and understood the whisper, his vision faded from his mind. No longer could he see Kuskurza. He sat in the kiva. Peter's hand was on his shoulder. The thick smoke had vanished, and the kiva looked as it should.

"Are you well?" Peter asked.

Adam stared at him blankly. Peter was a medicine man. He knew how to cure the problems of the body, but this was a problem of the spirit.

"Don't you feel it?" Adam said.

Peter thought for a moment. "I've felt an uneasiness here today, but I don't know what it is."

Adam remembered his vision and interpreted it. "Someone from this world has gone to Kuskurza."

Peter smiled and patted Adam on the shoulder. "The Third World is gone, my friend. So'tuknang destroyed it when he created the Fourth World for our people. You know that as well as I do." He paused and stared closely at Adam's face. Peter reached out with a finger and wiped the tears from Adam's cheek. "Even if it weren't so, who would be so foolish as to venture below where evil thrives?"

"A white man."

"A white man?" Peter said sharply. "Pahana?"

Adam thought about it. "I don't think so, but I'm not sure. I only know he went from the Fourth World to the Third World."

"But no white man knows the path to Kuskurza. It is a sacred place among the Hopi. Very few know that it even exists. Certainly, no white man could know how to find it. No white has ever set foot in this kiva. The stone is still in place."

Peter pointed to the plugged sipapu.

"I don't know this man's name. Only that I have seen him in my visions recently. This is the fourth vision. He has found another sipapu ... somewhere, not here ... and it has led him to Kuskurza."

Peter nodded his head. "So that's why you have visited this kiva while your crops cry out for water. People have been saying that your visions have made you sick in the head."

Peter tapped his finger against Adam's forehead. Adam pushed his friend's hand away.

"I'm not sick. It is distress and fear that you see." Adam recalled all that he had learned from his previous visions and told Peter. "The dark kachinas were imprisoned because they are spirits, and spirits cannot be killed. They would have only waited for the destroying flood So´tuknang sent to recede and then they would have followed the clans through the sipapu to the Fourth World. They have not been punished with death as we believe. So´tuknang spared a small portion of Kuskurza from the flood and imprisoned the dark kachinas with bright light in mountains of stone, but the light that holds them in their prison is dimming. When it fades enough, it won't be strong enough to hold the dark kachinas in the mountains of stone, and they will be free. They will leave the Third World and spill over this land like the flood that destroyed Kuskurza, and they will destroy this world just as thoroughly, unless..."

"Unless what?" Peter asked.

Help him. That is what the whispering voice in his head had said over and over, but how do you help a stranger who was somewhere unknown?

Adam sighed. His shoulders slumped forward and he bowed his head as if in prayer. "I don't know."

Peter rubbed his chin. "You're my friend, Adam, and because of this, I believe you. However, what you have seen is important to all our people. Chief Raymond should be told. It's up to him to decide what should be done to protect Tu´waqachi."

Adam stood up quickly. "No. It is not up to him. It is up to Taiowa to decide. If the Creator wants Raymond to act, he will give Raymond his own vision. Otherwise, Taiowa has given me the responsibility. I must find a way to protect this white man I have seen in my visions."

Adam knew Peter was not convinced, but he would say nothing...at least for now. Adam walked toward the ladder holding to the edge of the round wall so that he would not have to look at or touch the sipapu stone once again.

He climbed out of the kiva and left Peter alone to meditate. Though Adam doubted the medicine man would find much peace in the kiva now. Adam knew he wouldn't.

Standing on the ground above the kiva, Adam squinted his eyes against the bright midday sun. When he could see without squinting, he stared out over the sparse fields below the Third Mesa of the Hopi Reservation. He admired the order among the fields, straight lines of plants that were carefully tended and cultivated by the men of Oraibi. This was the view he preferred to see before he entered and as he exited the kiva. It was a sight that showed him the faith of the Hopis and the power of Taiowa. Together, they had brought forth life upon the barren land.

Adam turned slowly to face the village. He walked toward his pueblo trying not to let Oraibi's decay upset him. For nearly a millennia, the Hopis had lived in Oraibi. It was the oldest, continuously inhabited town in the United States. The Hopis had thrived in Oraibi centuries before the white Europeans had even set foot on this land.

The white anthropologists who studied Hopi ancient artifacts thought Oraibi had been built to defend the Hopis of the Third Mesa against attacking Navajo and Sioux war parties. They were wrong, as they usually were in matters concerning the Hopis. Oraibi had been built to protect the Navajo and Sioux from the Hopis, or rather from those from whom the Hopis had fled. Those-Who-Had-Lived-Before had felt a responsibility not to spread their evil over their new world. Oraibi had been built as a shelter for the families of the men who guarded the sipapu to make sure it remained closed.

As Adam walked down the main street of Oraibi past the two-storied pueblos, he noticed the cracked and missing clay from the pueblo walls that left the stones beneath exposed. Some of the roofs on the lowest rooms had caved in. Roofs on the higher rooms threatened to do the same. On other pueblos, entire walls had fallen leaving the rooms behind them exposed to the elements. Stone stairways were nothing more than slanted ledges, the steps worn down to nothing.

Such decay had not existed before the Great Division. It was only afterward, when Oraibi was controlled by those who wanted change that the slow death of the village began. During the Great Division, the Hopis who welcomed the changes the white men offered drove those who felt it was unwise to forget the old ways from Oraibi. The Hopis who left had built the villages of Hotevilla and Bacabi on the Third Mesa, or they had gone to the other villages on the First and Second Mesas. The Great Division left only a few in Oraibi who remembered why the village had originally been built. The Hopis who welcomed the white man's changes didn't recall the purpose of Oraibi, or if they did, they did not believe it. They allowed the old things to fall into disrepair as they were abandoned for the white man's things.

Adam nodded to those people he passed. Because the day was warm and the sun was high, he saw mostly women sitting in front of their rooms shaping or painting pottery. While the men worked in the fields below the mesa, the women formed the clay pots by coiling strings of clay on top of each other with the same symmetry a pottery wheel could create. Some of the women prepared piki or other foods by grinding corn, seeds, and herbs into meal with a metate and mano, a mortar and pestle. These were the ones who still believed, who did not go to McDonald's for a Big Mac or Albertson's for canned vegetables.

Adam turned left at an intersection and walked to the second pueblo, one of the older pueblos that made up a wall of the plaza. The wooden door to his rooms was open, allowing whatever breeze there might be to blow through.

Adam had built the chairs, stools, and table in the main room. He had bought the cabinet standing in the back corner in Winslow for his wife, Connie. A shallow pit for cooking fires was dug into the floor near one wall. Most of the wooden floor was covered by a large, colorful Navajo rug for which Adam had traded two silver bracelets and a turquoise necklace.

His granddaughter, Sarah, sat on a mat in the middle of the main room. She hummed to herself as she shaped balls of cornmeal dough to make pik'ami, a sweet cornbread that would be cooked in the pit. She did not look up when Adam entered. She hummed and patted more meal into dough balls.

Adam crossed the room to where the wash basin sat on a small table. Using a pitcher Sarah had made when she was a child, Adam filled the basin with water. The Hopi reservation had no indoor plumbing, except at the Hopi Cultural Center where the white tourists stayed.

He removed the red bandeau wrapped around his head and dipped it into the water. Wiping his face with it, he tried not to think about his visions, which was impossible. He had seen things more horrible than any nightmare he might have dreamed. He had to act. It was his responsibility. Taiowa had given him this duty; he must not fail.

"You have been to the kiva again. The smell of smoke follows you," Sarah said from behind him.

Adam turned to face her. She had set the dough ball on the mat and was standing only a few feet away from him.

"Have you decided to give up your crops? They must be dying now. They have been a week without water," she said.

Adam could tell how upset she was. As he watched her nostrils flare and the shaking of her head that appeared to be nothing more than a twitch, Adam could have sworn that he was looking at Connie. Granddaughter and grandmother shared the same delicate features. On occasion, Adam thought even their voices sounded alike. How he wished his wife had lived long enough to know her granddaughter as a woman.

"I feel that if the things I have seen come to pass, the crops will not matter," Adam told her after a moment.

He imagined what the world would look like if the dark kachinas were free. He shook at the image of the pale-skinned Bow Clan overrunning his beloved Fourth World.

Adam sat down on the small stool next to the basin and held his head in his hands. Sarah stood at his side stroking his hair.

"Are you all right, Grandfather? Should I get Peter?" Sarah asked.

She started to move away, but Adam grabbed her arm and motioned for her to stay.

"I've already seen Peter in the kiva. He can't help me."

"Then tell me why you are so afraid. What has driven you away from the fields and into the kiva?" Sarah said to him.

"I cannot."

Sarah turned. "Then I'll find Peter."

Adam held up his hand. "Wait. Don't go to Peter. He already thinks I am crazy."

Sarah crossed her arms over her chest. "He's not the only one."

"Then you've heard the talk, too?" Sarah nodded. "Why didn't you tell me?"

"It would have only added to the sorrows that you're holding inside yourself. But you don't need to keep your sorrows inside. I'm not my grandmother, but I love you too. I would share your sorrows with you to lighten the burden you carry." Sarah pressed her grandfather's hand against her cheek.

So compassionate. It was odd, thought Adam, that his own daughter, Patricia, who had been a full-blooded Hopi, looked and acted less like Connie, than his granddaughter, who was half-white, and had her mother's dark skin and straight black hair and her father's blue eyes and narrower face. Even though she was only half-Hopi by birth, in many ways, Sarah was more Hopi than Patricia had ever been or ever would be.

Adam motioned to the chair by the window. "Sit, and we will talk of visions and beliefs and which is correct."

Sarah sat down on the wooden chair and waited for her grandfather to begin.

CHAPTER 3

Darkness.

It was dark, so dark.

Why did it have to be dark? David hated the dark. Ever since he was a kid and learned the dangers that could hide in impenetrable shadows.

It swirled around him rolling like a wave. He could feel it moving between his legs and over his chest, chilling his body like cold water. It poured into his mouth and nostrils choking him until he swallowed. He reached out his hand for nothing in particular and touched the darkness. It passed through his fingers like water.

He shivered, not from the chill of the darkness, but from his fear of it. This was the ultimate night. To David, it meant danger. His mind would not tell him why it was dangerous, only that he should fear it.

This was all he could remember and all he could see. Where was he? How long had it been since he had seen the light?

A flash of light. A clap of thunder.

For a moment, David saw a pale-skinned man lying in front of him. The man wore a yellow-and-black robe, but most of it was missing. Most of the center of the man's body was nothing more than a charred, black hole.

Was this a dream? Some sort of disjointed nightmare trying to destroy his sleep? He couldn't be sure, but it had to be a dream.

Didn't it?

Had he fallen asleep or passed out? Time must be passing, but he couldn't be sure. There was no way to tell. He couldn't even see the luminous hands on his watch when he held it up close to his face, and he had no idea where his smartphone was. There was no trace of light, not even a lighter area among the pitch-black darkness.

Something unseen grabbed his ankles and yanked his legs. David screamed. He felt a pain in his legs that seared his entire body as if someone had lit his legs on fire, but he saw no light to mark that a fire was near.

Something hard and ridged covered his mouth and muffled his scream. David jerked his head back and forth, but the covering moved with him. It loosened itself briefly, and something that tasted like gritty pudding was pushed inside his mouth. David tried to spit out the foul-tasting mix, but two fingers pinched his nose shut, and a hand covered his mouth until he swallowed the gritty pudding. Almost immediately the pain in his body subsided. His head buzzed, but it did not ache.

17

David relaxed. He knew he was in danger, but his body felt so light. He thought he would float away to the top of the darkness and into the light where it was safe.

When David became aware again, he was running as fast as he could, but he wasn't moving forward. He thrust his arms out in front of him to feel his way along the passage. It was only when his fingertips grazed the rough surface of the walls that he realized he was moving forward. His legs pumped up and down, and his breath came in ragged gasps, which tore at his throat.

What was he running from?

He stopped to catch his breath. Leaning forward, he placed his forearms on his thighs and inhaled deeply. His legs ached, but not because of the running. This was a deeper pain, one that resided in the core of his legs. He massaged them, but the pain did not subside.

How long had he been running?

Why was it so dark? He wanted to see the light. It didn't have to be much light, just something that would...

Would what?

Protect you.

The thought was spoken in his head but not in his voice. The monotone voice he heard spoke with an unnatural precision. Did the conscience have a different voice than the body?

The air smelled slightly musty. David wished he could see where he was, but he could see nothing except the total darkness that surrounded him. How was he able to run in the darkness without continually running into walls? Was he on an immense, dark plain?

David glanced over his shoulder out of habit. He didn't know what he expected to see behind him. A monster, glowing in the dark, closing the gap between them, perhaps?

There was only the black darkness. Never had he seen a darkness so impenetrable.

No. That wasn't right.

Long ago he had seen such a darkness. He couldn't remember it clearly, but he knew that this was not the first time he had been in utter darkness. He tried unsuccessfully not to tremble. How could such darkness swallow up all the light?

David guessed he was in a tunnel, but even in a tunnel, there was always some light that his eyes could adjust to using. Even the night vision goggles his Army Reserves platoon used on maneuvers wouldn't be able to find enough ambient light to illuminate this area.

Whatever was behind him was getting closer. He didn't know what it was or how it could see him in the darkness. Even animals with eyes that were adapted to night couldn't see in total darkness. He wasn't even sure how he knew whatever was out there was coming for him, but he did.

Although he was tired, he started jogging again.

How long had he been running?

He couldn't remember.

Where was he running to?

He couldn't remember.

He couldn't remember anything, could he? What was wrong with him? He tried to tell himself there was nothing behind him, but he wasn't entirely convinced. Something had to have started him running in the first place. So what had it been?

And where was he?

David glanced behind himself again, wondering if he was moving. Whatever he thought was behind him had moved even closer. Somehow he could sense it. If only he could see it. Maybe it was nothing more dangerous than a bat.

No, it wasn't a bat, it was...

He couldn't remember.

He screamed at having to tell himself those three words again.

As he ran faster, his legs cried out in pain. Though he couldn't remember how long he had been running, he knew it had been too long. His thighs and calves burned and shook, and his pace began to slow.

He was too tired.

He should stop and rest again. There was nothing behind him. He was sure of it. So why was he so afraid to stop running?

Disembodied voices spoke all around him. He couldn't understand their words, but he could tell there was more than one voice. One of the voices was higher pitched than others. Another one spoke faster than the other two.

They had found him again.

Again?

He couldn't remember ever hearing these voices before, so why did he think he was hearing them again?

He couldn't even understand what they were saying. They murmured amongst themselves, but he was sure they were talking about him.

Had he died? Had whatever he was running from caught up with him and killed him? Was he hearing the voices of angels coming to lead him to God?

David twisted his head to the side to see if any of the voices had a body, but he couldn't see anything in the darkness.

To his left, a voice said, "He's coming out of it."

English. The voice spoke English! Someone had found him and rescued him. He would be safe.

Off to his right, another voice mumbled its response. The voice was low and distorted, but he was sure it was female. It was not deep enough to be a male voice.

Ahead of him, David heard someone walking away. Whoever was making the sounds moved away fast. Had he scared them off? Were these voices what he had felt following him? Had he been running from the help he had been looking for?

Suddenly, he felt the need to reach out and touch the body that belonged to one of the voices. Did angels have human bodies? The one voice he had understood had sounded human. He stretched out his left hand toward the voice that he had understood. He just wanted to touch the person to know that it had a body and he wasn't alone in the darkness.

A pair of hands pushed him back against a wall made of something soft. But they had been hands! Human hands. He was not alone. David tried to move forward, but the hands kept him pressed tightly against the wall.

"His pulse is thready," a voice on his left said.

He wanted to tell them he was friendly. He didn't want to cause them any trouble. He just wanted to find his way out of the darkness because he would die without the light. He wanted to wake up in his bed and discover he had dreamed everything. He wanted to tell them all of this, but when he opened his mouth to speak to them, nothing came out. He knew the words he wanted to say, but he couldn't form them. It was as if he had forgotten how to speak.

He tried to move forward again, but the hands still held him back. A screeching whistle sounded above his head. Why didn't someone turn it off? The noise hurt his ears. He tried to clap his hands over his ears, but he couldn't move his arms. They lay numb at his side.

There was a sharp pain in his right arm near the elbow. He tried to scream, and this time the sound did come out. He could hear himself screaming even above the noise of the whistle. Then his scream began to fade. As it did, the whistle stopped, and the mumbling voices faded, too.

All that was left was the darkness.

Always the darkness.

The light appeared slowly like a sunrise taking place over hours instead of a few minutes. It had been so long since David had seen any light, he did not recognize it at first. When he did, he cried with joy. He moved toward the light wanting to be immersed in its brightness. He never seemed to get any closer to it, though. It always stayed just beyond his reach. He stretched his arms out toward it wanting to grab it, hold it, embrace it.

It wasn't really a light, but more of a haze with no real color or boundaries. What had once been black slowly turned to gray, and the gray just as slowly increased in intensity. Still, he had never seen anything quite so beautiful. David didn't know how long he watched the light appear, but there was nothing else he could do or wanted to do. Even so, there was not enough light from the spreading gray area to reveal where he was. Maybe it would come later.

A darker blob of gray moved into his line of vision from the right side, eclipsing his newfound light. The hazy lines marking the edge of the blob changed, giving it a defined form. The blob was a man. David looked at his face as if he had never seen another person before. The man had brown hair and a brown beard and mustache. He wore wire-frame glasses with circular lenses. David thought the man's face looked young, but his eyes were much older. They were tired and sad and filled with doubt and triumph at the same time.

Tears ran down David's cheeks. He could feel their moist trail on his face. He didn't want the darkness to return. He wanted the light. Please, let the light return. If this man could keep the darkness from returning, David would be forever in his debt.

He smelled onions. Onions and steak with an antiseptic smell lingering behind the scents. His stomach rumbled at the thought of food. How long had it been since he had eaten? He couldn't remember.

A blinding light flashed across his eyes as the man flicked a small pen-light back and forth in front of his eyes. David wanted to laugh at the bright light. This man had found him. He had saved David from the darkness.

"David? Mr. Purcell? Can you hear me?" the man asked.

David. That was his name. How long had it been since he had heard it spoken?

Too long.

David nodded his response to the question. His neck was stiff, and it hurt him to make even the slightest nod. It was worth the pain, though. Someone was speaking to him.

"David?" the man asked, "Can you speak?"

David's gaze turned toward the woman who stood facing the brown-haired man. He hadn't noticed her at first, but his field of vision seemed to be widening. At that moment, she was the most beautiful woman he had ever seen. Perhaps he would think her plain later on, but for now, he was happy to stare at her as if she were Venus incarnate.

"David, can you say something?" the man said again.

David tried to say "yes," but it only came out as a hoarse rasp more like a cough. He was surprised his mouth was so dry. It felt like someone had stuffed a handful of cotton into it.

The woman pressed a glass against his lips. Cool water spilled over David's lips and inside his mouth. He savored the moistness it brought. The cottony feeling faded, and he swallowed the water with a loud gulp.

"More," David whispered.

The woman took the glass away. Her fingertips brushed against his chin as she moved the cup. How long had it been since he felt the touch of another person?

"Later," she said. She had a lovely voice that reminded David of silk rubbing against his skin.

"But I'm thirsty," David pleaded.

"I know you are, but too much, too soon, might make you vomit. I don't want your system shaken up any more than necessary." Her voice made even the unpleasant words sound melodic.

"Am I in a hospital?" David asked, suddenly placing the antiseptic smell behind the steak and onions.

The man spoke. "Yes, this is Blanding Community Hospital. I'm Dr. Haskell, your doctor for the time being." David noticed for the first time that both the man and the woman were wearing white outfits. The angels he had thought he heard.

"What happened to me?"

There was a break in the conversation that lasted forever. Now that David finally had someone to talk to, he missed the sound of Dr. Haskell's voice when he was quiet. He wanted the doctor to talk to him. David wanted to keep talking forever.

Just when he thought the doctor wasn't going to answer him, the bearded man said, "What do you remember?"

Now it was David's turn to break the flow of conversation as he tried to remember what might have happened that would have caused him to be in the hospital. At first, when he tried to remember, all he saw was the blackness that he had seen in his dreams. At least he thought they had been dreams. They had to have been dreams or rather nightmares.

What had happened before the nightmares?

"I fell into a deep hole," David said, his voice only sounding like a whisper. Why couldn't he speak in a normal tone?

"And?" the doctor urged him.

"That's all I remember. Did I pass out?" David answered.

"Nothing else?"

"What's the matter? Did I break my legs, too?" David remembered the pain he had felt in his legs during one of his dreams and how he had been afraid he would break a bone when he fell.

"No. Do your legs hurt?" Dr. Haskell asked.

The doctor ran his hands along David's legs, occasionally pressing to check for any deformity that might mark a broken bone.

David shook his head even though it didn't want to move. His neck felt like an old hinge that had rusted shut and was being forced open. He even thought he could hear popping and creaking sounds from his neck when he shook his head.

"David, you didn't just fall into a hole. You fell into a cavern. An immense large cavern if the newspaper stories are right. The sheriff had an emergency rescue team looking for you down there."

"Why?" David asked. "I couldn't have been too difficult to find. I didn't move...I don't think." When he tried to remember what had happened after the fall, all he saw was the darkness, in which case, he would rather not think about it. Maybe the darkness hadn't been a nightmare.

Dr. Haskell was silent as if he didn't know what to say next. David could hear his shoes squeaking against the floor as he shifted his weight from one foot to the other. What was he afraid to say?

"David, you were missing in the cavern for five weeks."

CHAPTER 4

"Five weeks!" David shouted. His voice rose to a normal pitch, which, in his condition, was his equivalent to a scream, then fell back to a whisper. "No way! I've been out of town for three days." He tried to hold up three fingers to emphasize the point, but his arm felt stiff and achy. "I just got back in last night, but my car broke down on Highway 191. I was hitchhiking to Blanding and fell into that stupid hole. I probably knocked myself out for five hours, not five weeks."

With an exhausting effort, David pushed himself up in bed, but Dr. Haskell put his hands on David's shoulders to push him back down. David remembered how the hands in his dreams had held him against a soft wall, and he realized it hadn't been a dream—at least not that part of it. The hands in his dream hadn't been holding him against a wall. They had been pushing him down onto a bed. David tried to knock Dr. Haskell's hands off his shoulders, but his arms were as weak as a child's arms.

"Mr. Purcell, if you don't calm down, I'll have to have the nurse sedate you. I'd rather not have to do that. You've already forgotten the past five weeks; do you want to add a few more hours to that?" Dr. Haskell warned him.

David relaxed and lay back on the bed. He was actually glad he didn't have to try and get out of bed. His entire body felt as if he had just gone ten rounds with Anthony Joshua. The fall must have really banged him up. It was a wonder he didn't have any broken bones.

"You can't be right. I would remember being in a cave for that long," David insisted, slowly shaking his head.

Dr. Haskell pushed his glasses up on top of his head and rubbed his eyes with one hand.

"The search-and-rescue team didn't find you until this morning, which, for your information is August fourth."

"No," David objected, "It's only July first." He shook his head. His neck didn't feel quite as stiff as it had before.

Dr. Haskell let the comment pass. "From what I've been told, you were conscious when a county deputy found you in the cave, but you were delirious. You apparently passed out as the deputy approached you, and you've been unconscious since then. Except for a brief moment when you went into cardiac arrest."

"I had a heart attack?" David asked.

"Yes, only an hour after you were admitted. There's no physical cause that we've been able to determine so far. You're in good health, and your body wasn't under any type of physical stress. However, you were having some ex-

24

tremely violent dreams when you arrested. The nurse," Dr. Haskell nodded toward Venus' twin sister, "observed your body twitching and very quick eye movements just a few minutes before you arrested. So it may be that your body could not keep up with what your mind was telling it you were seeing."

"You mean a bad dream caused me to have a heart attack?"

Dr. Haskell shrugged. "It's unlikely, but for now it is the only possibility we have."

David tried to think of what he could have imagined that would have scared him so badly. It must have been a horrible nightmare. But horrible enough to cause a heart attack? He doubted it. He remembered the whine of a heart monitor in his dreams. Had that been when he had his heart attack? That was another part of his dreams he realized wasn't a dream. What about the other parts? Had something been waiting for him in the dark? Had he been running from something? Would that have been enough to cause him to have a heart attack? David shivered and tried to think of something else besides the dark.

"Other than the heart attack, am I all right?" David asked almost afraid of what the answer would be.

Dr. Haskell smiled broadly. "You're in excellent health. That in itself is a small miracle."

"Why?"

"It's not uncommon for someone who has been in complete darkness for as long as you have to temporarily lose their sight. The complications result when a person spends a month or more in that darkness. Then the blindness can become permanent."

"I was in the cave for over a month," David interrupted. His voice revealed his anxiety. "Does that mean I'll lose my sight?"

Dr. Haskell shook his head, and his glasses slipped down onto his face. He straightened them and said, "If you were going to lose your sight, it would have happened in the cave. You would be blind right now. The fact that you can see is amazing. I would have expected you to have at least some blurry vision until your eyes adjusted to the light again. It's almost as if there was some light down in the cave that your eyes adjusted to using so the muscles that control your irises wouldn't atrophy."

"I can't remember much about being in the cave except snatches of what might have been dreams or they may have been real. Either way, I don't remember any light. Everything was pitch black," David added quickly.

Dr. Haskell patted him on the shoulder. "The other factor besides your eyesight which surprises me is your general health. You've just spent five weeks in a cave, David. You had no food or water. You had no way to see where you were going. And yet, even after all that, you don't appear dehydrated or emaciated. You don't even seem to have any wounds from your initial fall or from stumbling around in the dark. It's remarkable."

But David did remember light. At least he had seen light in his dreams when he saw the dead man.

Dr. Haskell continued talking, "We took x-rays of your entire body while you were in the emergency room. We were looking for broken bones or cranial pressure, which might have been caused by your fall. Except for some recently healed breaks in your legs and an old break in your arm, your bones are perfect. I may get cocky about my own ability to heal someone, but not enough to not recognize God's work. The only reason you're alive, David, is because God wanted you to live. By every medical standard, you should be dead or at least in critical condition, but you're not. That's divine intervention in my book. If you're a praying man, you should thank him."

David guessed that Dr. Haskell was Mormon, which wasn't unusual to find in Utah. David was also Mormon.

"Why would God step in on my behalf when so many other people die every day?" David asked.

"I'm a doctor, not your bishop. I can't tell you why. I can only say you ought to be grateful."

David nodded. "Don't get me wrong. I'm grateful. I'm very grateful. Not only to God but to you, too. I'm sure you helped him a bit."

Dr. Haskell's eyes looked younger for a few moments as he accepted the compliment. "I did my best."

David shifted his weight trying to find a slightly more comfortable position on the bed. Something the doctor said suddenly struck David as odd.

"What did you mean before when you said I had recently healed breaks in my legs?"

"Didn't you have casts removed from your legs around February?"

David shook his head. Shaking his head hurt him more than nodding. He guessed he would have to agree with everything everyone said until he worked the kinks out of his body. "I've never had any broken bones in my life except for my right arm, but that was when I was thirteen."

Dr. Haskell was quiet. David knew what the doctor was thinking because he was thinking the same thing, too. What if he had forgotten more than just his five weeks in the cave? What if he had broken his legs and simply couldn't remember doing it? But how could he not remember hobbling around in a cast for at least eight weeks, which was how long he had had to wear the cast when he broke his arm? Then again, how could he forget walking around in a cave for five weeks?

Dr. Haskell chewed on his lower lip as he thought. "Nurse, can you bring me Mr. Purcell's x-rays?" he said finally.

The red-headed nurse left the room. David watched her go, wondering if she was as beautiful as he thought, or if he thought she was beautiful because he hadn't seen a woman, beautiful or otherwise, in five weeks.

Five weeks!

He had lost over a month of his life. What had happened to him? What had gone on in the world while he was underground wandering around? His mother must be in a state of panic if she hadn't already given him up for dead. She would have been the last person to give up on him. After five weeks, though, everyone might have given up.

"Where did you break your arm?" Dr. Haskell asked.

"I fractured one of my forearm bones in my right arm. I couldn't play in the summer baseball league that year because I had to wear a cast for eight weeks," David told him.

The nurse came back in the room and handed the doctor a set of x-rays. David heard the sound of soft thunder as the x-rays buckled when Dr. Haskell held them up to the light. The sound scared him for some unknown reason. It sounded like something else, something dangerous.

Dr. Haskell studied the first x-ray and quickly exchanged it for a second film. He studied this second x-ray more carefully.

"David, I see the old fracture of the radius that you mentioned. It was on the first x-ray." He brought the second x-ray over to the bed and held it in front of David's face between David and the ceiling light. "I can also see three, no four, fracture points on your legs." He pointed out the breaks as he spoke, and David saw them for himself. The areas Dr. Haskell pointed to looked like thin, white scars running across the entire width of the bone. "These were not hairline fractures either. You must have been in a lot of pain when you broke your legs. Judging by this x-ray, I would say the breaks are probably four- or five-months old. It probably happened in early March or late February."

"It can't be, doctor," David insisted. "I can remember what I was doing five months ago and even further back than that. I don't remember ever wearing casts on my legs."

"These x-rays are labeled with your name." He pointed out the name in the corner of the x-ray film.

David could hear the doubt in Dr. Haskell's voice. "Well, wouldn't I remember if I broke my legs?" Dr. Haskell said nothing. "And it's not the amnesia, either. I can remember everything, everything, except for those five weeks in the cave."

Dr. Haskell stepped away from the bed and handed the nurse the x-rays. She took them and left the room. "Okay, don't get yourself worked up, David. I believe you. I'll check around and see if your x-rays somehow got mixed up with someone else's. If I can't find anything out, we'll just retake them. I'll develop them myself if I have to."

"Thanks." David paused. "Doctor, does my girlfriend know I'm here?"

What did Terrie think about all this? Would she still be mad at him for missing their dinner date? It was bad enough to be an hour late, but five weeks late? He had a good reason for missing, of course. But there had been other times he'd had good reasons to be late or cancel dates, and Terrie had liked none of them.

"She's the reason you're still not down in the cave. Apparently, you had a date with her five weeks ago. When you didn't show up or call, she tried to call you at your apartment. Obviously, she didn't reach you, so she called the police later that night when she still hadn't heard from you. One of the sheriff's deputies found your car on the highway, and he began searching for you starting at that point. The next day, searchers found your sports coat only a foot or so away from the hole you fell into."

"Will you bring my girlfriend up to my room when she shows up?"

"Of course. What's her name? I'll have the nurse at the front desk keep an eye out for her."

"Terrie McNee."

Dr. Haskell smiled. "Okay. When Terrie comes in, someone will make sure she gets up here." David thanked the doctor. "I'm going to leave now, but I'll be in to see you tomorrow. We'll give you a complete physical to verify you're as healthy as you look."

David raised his arms over his head to stretch. It felt like an alien motion to him as if the pathway from thought to motion had slowed down.

"Doctor, can you leave my light on?" he asked.

Dr. Haskell paused at the door and turned to face David. "Are you a little leery of the dark after all this?"

David hesitated unsure if telling the truth would make him look foolish or not. "I've always had a problem with the dark. The cave probably only made it worse."

"We have a staff psychiatrist here. If you want, I can have him come up to talk with you while you're here. After the ordeal you've been through, it is almost a standard practice."

David shook his head quickly even though it hurt. "No. I'll get over it. I'd rather not talk to a psychiatrist."

"Well, if you change your mind, he's always here. I'll leave the lights on for you." Dr. Haskell opened the door and then stopped again. "Oh, for your information, you made the national news while you were missing. Like the woman who broke her leg in Carlsbad Caverns years ago. Just about every newspaper and radio station in the country must have picked up on the story about the search for you. There's been a pack of reporters in the lobby ever since word went out that the rescue team found you. They are all waiting for the chance to talk with you. What do you want to do about them?"

David nodded slowly. "I'd like not to have to talk to them. I don't want to be famous for being a klutz. However, if they want to get in, they'll probably find a way. I guess I might as well get it over with. Would you tell them I'll meet with them tomorrow? Today I just want to rest and catch up with the world."

Dr. Haskell smiled. "I understand. I'll let them know."

The doctor left the room, and David was alone. But at least there was light. He could see what was around him. Not that there was much to see in the sparse hospital room, but it was more than he had seen in a long time.

He tried to remember the past five weeks of his life. Where had he been? In a cave, obviously. A huge cave since it had taken the rescue team so long to find him. He remembered the ground collapsing under his weight and falling into the hole near the highway. Dr. Haskell said the police had found him in the cave. But between David's final memory and the police finding him, what had he done?

Five weeks.

Thirty-five days.

He heard thunder outside and shivered. It was unusual to get rain in Blanding, but it was always nice to have water. The thunderclap raised the hair on the back of his neck.

Was he afraid of thunder?

He had never been afraid of it before. In fact, he usually enjoyed the rain since it was so rare in this part of the Four Corners area.

The rumbling sounded like something else, though. Something he couldn't remember like x-rays rippling. He tried to recall it, but the sound was buried somewhere in his memory. Maybe he did have amnesia about other things besides being in the cave.

David gave up trying to remember and lay back on the bed.

Other sounds came to him even through his closed door. He could hear the nurses at the nurses' station mumbling to themselves. As someone passed by his door, he heard the rubber soles of the nurse's shoes squeak slightly against the tiled floor. From the room next door, he could hear Jimmy Kimmel interviewing an actress whom David didn't recognize.

If he closed his eyes, the darkness would return. He didn't want the dark to return now that he could see light, no matter how unattractive his surroundings. At least he could see that they were unattractive. The solution was simple: He wouldn't close his eyes. There was something in the darkness that meant to hurt him. He had been lucky and escaped it once. He didn't want to give it a second chance.

CHAPTER 5

It was ta´supi, twilight, before Adam returned to the rooms in the pueblo. According to tradition, the three living rooms and one storage room Sarah and her grandfather lived in belonged to her. Unlike the white world, the Hopi world was matrilinear. Children belonged to the clan of their mothers rather than their fathers.

Having lived most of her life outside the reservation and growing up in a white man's world, this was something with which Sarah had never been comfortable. Adam had been living in these rooms for nearly sixty years. He had been living in the rooms before Sarah, or even her mother had been born. Sarah had only lived on the reservation for the ten years since her mother had brought her to Oraibi and left her with her grandparents, whom she had never met before that day. When her grandmother Connie had died two years later, the ownership of the rooms had passed to the next woman, sixteen-year-old Sarah.

As the sun set, it cast long shadows surrounded by a luxurious, red light across the sides of the pueblo. Sarah lit the oil lamp on the small square table next to the chair and continued painting the clay pot sitting on the board across her lap. Not having been brought up on the reservation, her curving designs and bright colors differed from the traditional style. However, the quality and attractiveness of the finished piece was just as good as any full-blooded Hopi's.

Occasionally, Sarah glanced out the window hoping to catch sight of her grandfather walking up the street. He had been in the sacred kiva since the rising of the sun. He had eaten a little before he left this morning, but he hadn't been out of the kiva all day.

It didn't matter to her that Adam was a Hopi and that Hopi men were active into their eighties and nineties. When Sarah looked at Adam, she saw an old man. It did not matter to her that he could climb down the steep trail leading from Third Mesa to his field in the wash, work all day, and make the return climb up to the mesa. Adam was at least eighty-four years old. He could not continue to bypass the effects of old age by ignoring time itself.

Though Adam said he didn't know his age in the white man's years, Sarah had some idea of how old her grandfather was. Adam's father had been born during the year of the Great Division, which had been in 1906. Adam had been born twenty-seven summers after that. That meant her grandfather was eighty-four years old.

A white man would not have believed it. Though Sarah had not made a habit of checking the ages of white men who died, she knew it was commonly in the seventy- to eighty-year-old range. When white men grew old, they grew frail and weak. Hopi men had no calendars to remind them how old they were. They continued working the same as they had when they were young men. However, Adam had not been himself the past five weeks. His visions drained him of the strength and energy that he normally possessed. For the first time in his life, her grandfather looked and acted his age.

Sarah heard footsteps outside and turned to look out the window. She saw her grandfather slowly shuffling up the street. She closed her eyes and sighed. Thank goodness! Quickly turning back to her painting, she didn't want her grandfather to think his granddaughter thought him frail. It would shame him.

It seemed an eternity until Adam opened the door. It opened slowly under his touch as if it were too great a weight for him to push. He stepped into the room and pushed the door closed behind himself. Leaning with his back against the door, Adam slid slowly to the floor.

Sarah put her clay pot on the table and rushed to her grandfather's side. She tried to help him to his feet, but he weakly pushed her away.

"I'll be all right. I just need to rest for a time," Adam told her.

Sarah went to the table and poured a cup of water from the pitcher. She carried it to her grandfather. He held it between his shaking hands and drank it greedily.

"I've had nothing to eat or drink since early this morning," he said when he had drained the cup.

Sarah knew as much, but she said nothing. Adam's visions diminished his appetite until he ate no more than a frog might have eaten even on the days he did not go to the kiva.

Turning up the flame on the oil lamp, Sarah leaned close to her grandfather. His eyes had sunk so far into his head that they seemed to be two hollow holes. His skin had tightened so that many of his wrinkles had disappeared. If he had not been so ill, he would have appeared thirty years younger. As it was, he looked like a corpse dead five days.

"This is not right, Grandfather. You haven't slept in four nights. You eat barely enough to live. You stagger like a drunk as you walk down the street. People now truly believe you are crazy."

Adam raised his left hand and rested it on Sarah's shoulder. His sad eyes, looking larger than usual, met hers. "Do you believe I am crazy?"

"No," she said without hesitation.

"Then that is enough for now."

Sarah's voice trembled, and a tear slipped from her eye. "But your visions are killing you. Why must you continually seek them out?"

Adam frowned. "The visions are finished. I have seen what I needed to see."

"What did you need to see?"

Adam nodded toward the bedroom. "Help me to the bed first. It's time for me to sleep finally."

His body trembled in Sarah's arms as she tried to help him stand. He would not have been able to do it under his own power. Sarah swung his right arm over her shoulder and half-walked, half-carried him into the bedroom, the second of the three rooms they lived in. It was not difficult to carry her grandfather. At five-feet six-inches tall and one-hundred-and-ten pounds, he was scarcely larger than Sarah.

Adam fell back onto the thin mattress on the bed and smiled. He moaned contently and then lay silent.

Sarah thought he had gone to sleep until he said, "I must find this white man who has visited Kuskurza. We must talk together, he and I, of how we can aid the Sun Clan."

"The Sun Clan? Your clan?" Sarah asked.

"This Sun Clan is not the same as our clan. The Sun Clan that I must help is the children of Ma'saw, the guardian of Kuskurza. They are his children by ideals, not blood. Among the members of the Bow Clan, there are still some who believe in the teachings of So'tuknang. These people have humbled themselves hoping to find favor in the eyes of Taiowa so that Pahana might lead them to freedom. They follow Ma'saw and help him fight the Bow Clan to keep the dark kachinas imprisoned," Adam explained.

Sarah wasn't sure what he was talking about, so she focused on the part that she did. "How will you find the white man?"

"To find a white man, you must use the white man's ways." Adam took Sarah's hand in his. "Find me a newspaper. Someone in Oraibi must have one. I need to borrow it for a day. If you cannot find one in Oraibi, go to Hotevilla and Bacabi. Someone will have one. When you have found one, wake me. Then we will find the white man."

Adam closed his eyes and sighed.

It took Sarah over two hours to find a newspaper somewhere in the village. She went from room to room throughout Oraibi asking at each home if those inside had a newspaper she might borrow. Each person would shake his or her head "no." Sarah would offer thanks and move onto the next door. After knocking on over sixty doors, Ethan Ta'bo, a young Hopi who had yet to take a wife, told her he had a newspaper. He had found it on a bench in Winslow when he went to sell some pieces of jewelry he had made.

"Is this for Adam and his visions?" Ethan asked as he handed the newspaper to Sarah.

She glanced at the date. It was a two-week-old copy of *The Arizona Republic*, but it would have to do. No one else in Oraibi seemed to have another newspaper, let alone one more recent.

"This is for Adam only. He wants information on a white man," Sarah told Ethan.

Ethan smiled at her. She tried not to feel uncomfortable as he stared at her.

"I hope he gets better soon," Ethan said after a moment. Sarah thanked him and turned to go back to her own rooms. "Wait. I have something else. Please come in while I find it."

Ethan was Sarah's age and a full-blooded Hopi. He had the typical round face of Hopis and black hair and eyes. Ethan always seemed to have a broad, friendly smile that made his face not look so round. Slightly taller than Sarah, he had muscular shoulders and powerful legs. Ethan was a skilled silversmith who sold most of the jewelry he made to shops in Winslow and Tuba City. In fact, from what Sarah had been told, his work was in high demand throughout Arizona.

She stepped into a larger room than the main room she and her grandfather shared. Ethan disappeared into another room – he had four – to get what he wanted to give to Sarah. He returned in a moment holding a silver-and-turquoise bracelet.

Sarah took it and studied the intricate details Ethan had carved into the silver. Birds flying over tall stalks of corn. The turquoise had a deep color showing its high quality. It was cut with extreme precision to fit into small areas. Looking at the bracelet, Sarah understood why his work was in such demand. Ethan watched Sarah as she turned the bracelet over to look at it from every angle.

Then she handed it back to a surprised Ethan.

"It's beautiful, but I can't accept this. You could get three-hundred dollars or more for this in the city."

Ethan nodded. He stepped closer to Sarah and slid the bracelet onto her arm. "I did not make this bracelet for money. I made it for love and for you."

Sarah shook her head. "Then I know I can't accept this. I like you, Ethan. I have since you defended me against that man in Hotevilla who called me a white man's folly. But friendship and love are not the same." Ethan's head tilted forward so he would not have to look at her. "It's not you, Ethan. You are a handsome man. It's not just me speaking, either. I have heard the girls in the village talk about you. One of them should receive this bracelet."

Ethan slid the bracelet onto Sarah's arm again. She started to protest, but he said, "This bracelet was made to be worn by only you. For anyone else to wear it would be a lie. I shaped the silver and turquoise with an image of you in my mind. My hands worked according to what would best suit you."

"I have never seen anything so lovely."

Ethan smiled. "Take it, please. It is still a symbol of my love. Perhaps, one day you will feel the same. I am not in a rush."

Sarah ran her finger around the edges of the turquoise. She had not lied when she had said she hadn't seen anything quite so beautiful. It did seem to have a special appeal to her. "Thank you. I will cherish it as I do you." She kissed him on the cheek before she left with the bracelet and the newspaper.

Adam was sleeping so peacefully when Sarah got back to the rooms, she decided to let him rest until morning. She set the newspaper on the chest of drawers in the far corner of the room and lay down on her own bed to sleep.

She laid her arm near her head so that she could look at the bracelet as she went to sleep. Although she hoped Ethan would find someone who would return all the love that he had to offer, she did not think it would be her. Perhaps she would give Ethan's bride this bracelet as a wedding gift.

Sarah wasn't sure when she awoke, but the first thing she realized was that it was still dark outside. The room was lit by a flame from an oil lamp, not sunlight. A drawer shut behind her. She rolled over and saw her grandfather stuffing his clothes into a canvas bag.

"Grandfather, what are you doing?" she asked.

Adam stopped working. "I asked you to wake me when you returned."

His voice was weak but agitated. He still looked tired, but he acted like he had more energy.

"But you needed the sleep. You couldn't even stand when you came home from the kiva."

"My health is not for you to judge."

He tossed the newspaper onto her bed. Sarah lit the oil lamp next to her bed to add to the light in the room. She picked up the newspaper and leaned close to the light. Scanning each story's headline, she finally found the one that had undoubtedly caught her grandfather's attention: Rescue Team Cannot Find Man Lost in Cavern. The story explained that the search-and-rescue team had been searching for David Purcell for three weeks. It had been assumed they would find him near the hole he fell into, but that had not been the case. Now as they widened their search, they were also exploring a new, large, cave system. They didn't hold much hope of finding him alive.

"Is this the man your visions told you about?" she asked when she finished the article.

Adam nodded.

"They say they think he is dead." She glanced at the paper again. There was a picture of David Purcell. His hair was blond. It had been a long time since she had seen anyone with blond hair. She tended to stay indoors when there were tourists in town, and no Hopi had blond hair.

"Yes, he's the man, but he is not dead. He accidentally found Kuskurza. My visions have shown me the search team has found him now and have taken him out of the caverns, but he is not yet out of danger. The dark kachinas want him dead." Adam started filling the bag again.

"How will you get to him? He is in Utah," Sarah wanted to know as she stood up from her bed.

"Paul agreed to let me use his truck. I've promised him my crops this season."

"Your entire crop?"

"Yes, if someone does not tend the fields, they will die anyway. Paul has agreed to tend my crops and lend me his truck. In exchange, whatever he harvests from my fields he may have."

"But what will we do for food this winter?"

"We have a full supply to carry us easily through the winter. We won't starve, but if I don't go north to talk to David Purcell, we may not need any food."

Sarah climbed out of bed and walked over next to her grandfather. "I'm going with you. You are in no shape to drive."

Adam did not argue. He simply said, "Then help me prepare what we will need. Pack enough food for two, and I will pack your clothes."

"How long will we be gone?"

"A week, maybe two. There is much David Purcell, and I must talk about."

CHAPTER 6

Smack!

David closed his eyes, unsuccessfully keeping them from tearing. The blow felt like it had knocked his head from his shoulders. As the pain in his right cheek faded, he opened his eyes. His cheek still stung from the slap, but the pain was not nearly as intense as it had been the time before or the time before that.

Smack!

David slapped himself across the left cheek this time. Pain rushed to his brain, but it was not enough. He was falling asleep.

He wondered if he should pinch himself again. Until an hour ago, he had kept himself awake with sharp pinches that nearly drew blood. He had pinched his arms so many times that they were both covered with small, red welts. Anyone looking at his arms would have thought he was a junkie.

His body had deadened itself to that pain just as it was deadening itself to his slaps now. Sleep was creeping up on him, and it was getting too close. His eyelids drooped lower and lower no matter how much he fought to keep them open.

David wasn't sure why he was afraid to fall asleep. All he knew was that he would be in danger if he did. Anytime he thought about sleeping or felt sleepy a black wave of fear washed over him.

But why? he asked himself once again.

Bed rest would help him recuperate faster. His joints and muscles ached with exhaustion. He must have pushed himself to his limits while he was in the cave. Not that he remembered to what limits he had been driven or what had caused him to push them. He only knew his body needed time to rest. He was so tired. If he could just close his eyes for a little bit.

David shook his head. No! He couldn't sleep.

Could he actually have been lost in a cave, in total darkness, for over a month? He sluggishly shook his head. How could he simply forget about five weeks of his life no matter how horrible they had been? It was impossible. The memories were in his head. He was just too tired to think about them. Every time he tried to recall the missing time, a massive headache formed at his temples and he saw nothing. Was his body telling him not to try and remember?

No, he was just tired. He needed to sleep.

Anything but that. David couldn't let himself sleep. He couldn't...

His eyelids began to slide closed despite his efforts to force them open.

David tried to raise his hand to a bare spot on his arm so he could pinch himself, but his body was too relaxed. His arms felt like they were buried in cement. It took focused concentration for him to even wiggle his fingers. His body was too exhausted to fight off his fatigue anymore.

He managed to raise his left arm a few inches off his bed, and he reached for his right arm. His concentration broke, and his hand fell limp on his stomach.

He tried once again to will his eyelids to open wide. The opposite happened, and the bright light of the room became a thin, white line.

No! The lights couldn't go out again. Dr. Haskell said he wouldn't lose his eyesight. David didn't want to be in the dark. He had to open his eyes.

He had to...

David tried to remember if his eyes had closed entirely or not. His head felt fuzzy, and he couldn't think clearly. Something massaged his brain. That couldn't be, could it? His brain was stored safely inside his skull. So what was he feeling inside his head?

Ko'pavi. The foreign word filled his mind and then vanished.

Suddenly, his field of vision exploded into a bright, yellow light. The light was so bright that David squinted as well as threw his arms up to shield his face. Even through his arms and eyelids, he still saw the blinding brightness. He felt no heat from the light, which surprised him. Anything that could generate that bright a light should be throwing out a lot of heat.

The light slowly faded. David lowered his arms, but he still squinted at the light. He tried to turn away from it, but there was no source for it. It came from everywhere at once. No matter where he looked, he was blinded by the brightness.

Was there something out there? And where was "there"?

There seemed to be an area where the light wasn't as bright. David stared at that because it didn't hurt his eyes as much to look in that direction. The light continued to dim, and eventually, David opened his eyes fully without too much pain.

As the light faded, David saw a massive mountain of stone. It resembled an Egyptian pyramid, but this was more ornate. There were steep steps carved into the side, which led to doorways at the very top of the pyramid. Surrounding the larger pyramid were four smaller pyramids, one on each side.

The light seemed to be fading faster now.

The larger pyramid shook slightly, and David thought he heard thunder. One of the stones on the side of the pyramid edged out of place disturbing the smooth face.

It was no brighter than nightfall now and still growing dimmer.

The pyramid shook fiercely. One of the stones popped out like a cork being shot from a champagne bottle. Others shifted out of place.

Only a faint hint of light remained. As it faded, David saw the largest pyramid explode without making any noise. Stones flew in all directions, many of them toward him. Before he could shield himself from flying debris, darkness filled his vision. The final bit of light faded, and David saw nothing.

He knew he had dreamed the incident, but it seemed so real that he couldn't help but react to it. He tried to outrun the darkness. At least he tried to run from it in his dreams. He didn't know if his body physically reacted while he was asleep, though.

His head throbbed, and then burned. If this kept up, he would need an aspirin tablet the size of a golf ball.

David saw a stone wall in front of him. It was smooth and straight as if it had been chiseled. On the wall, he saw paintings. There were heads painted on the wall. He counted them. Seventy-three intricate paintings. Each painting was about a foot tall. The faces were painted with much attention to detail. Each one was a different person with its own unique personality. Some of the faces seemed solemn, others smiled, two looked bored, and one was laughing. They all shared two distinguishing characteristics, though. They all had white hair, and their skins were pale white.

David reached out to touch the nearest face, but as his hand neared the wall, a pale-skinned hand came from behind him and grabbed his wrist. David screamed, and the memory went black.

He woke up breathing hard. The blackness from his dream faded to gray as the light from his room tried to penetrate his sleep. He took a deep breath, held it for a moment, and then released it slowly through pursed lips. He did it again and then again until he had calmed down.

David sat up straight in his bed. He had had enough sleep for tonight. In fact, he'd had enough sleep to last him for a while. He didn't think he would be going back to sleep anytime soon.

As he pressed the button to raise the head of the bed so that he would have some support for his back, he had the nagging thought that he needed to do something but he couldn't remember what. It must have something to do with the five weeks he couldn't remember. It was lost in that big, black hole of a memory he had.

CHAPTER 7

Gary Morse watched the white police sedan pull off Highway 191 in front of him. He steered the large Winnebago he was driving off the road following the police car. Sheriff Harding of the San Juan County Sheriff's Department was leading the way to Gary's next job site. Gary and his team had been hired by the State of Utah to map out a new cave system and make recommendations as to the commercial possibilities of the caverns. He was so excited about this opportunity that he had taken a leave of absence from the University of Tennessee where he taught geology.

"Looks like we're just about there," Gary said to Jared Chapman as the tall black man settled into the passenger seat beside Gary.

Jared nodded and opened the can of Hawaiian Punch he had taken from the refrigerator in the back of the Winnebago only a few moments before. "Not much in the way of scenic beauty around here. Be nice to see some green grass or a beautiful big oak or maple."

"We're not concerned with what's up here. Our job's in the cavern. There'll be plenty to see down there."

Gary had known Jared for nine years since they had both started teaching at the University of Tennessee. Together, they had explored over fifty caves throughout the world, including the Mammoth Caves in Kentucky and Carlsbad Caverns in Arizona. They had also authored two books on caving; one on mastering the basics and the other on mapping caves. Among spelunkers, they were considered two of the best, which is why the Utah Bureau of Recreation and Parks had hired them for this particular job.

The sheriff's sedan kicked up so much dust that Gary almost lost sight of it. He slowed the Winnebago to a crawl so that he wouldn't rear end the sheriff's car accidentally.

"Do you really think it's as big as they say?" Jared asked after a moment of silence. "It's hard to imagine there being enough water running through this country to carve a cavern that's the size they've described."

Gary grinned. "It's that big. I can feel it. The search and rescue teams explored it for five weeks, and they still didn't explore it fully. I bet it's even bigger than they think."

He leaned forward in his seat hoping to see a little better. The dust in front of the Winnebago settled. He was thankful for that. It probably meant the sheriff had stopped. They were at the cave entrance.

"The search-and-rescue team that pulled out David Purcell said they explored fifteen chambers, but they also said there were more, a lot more,"

Gary added.

Gary saw the police car in front of him. The sheriff had stopped. Pulling up beside the car, Gary turned off the engine. About half a dozen yards in front of the Winnebago was a small area surrounded by metal poles driven into the ground and yellow tape running between them that read, "Police Line. Do Not Cross."

Gary stepped out of the RV as Lou Montgomery's red Jeep Cherokee pulled up on the other side of the sheriff's car. He waved to the two men in the Jeep and walked over to the sheriff.

Sheriff Harding rolled down his window. He was an overweight man in his mid-fifties. Gary could tell the man had no intention of getting out in the ninety-degree heat unless he had to.

"Well, this is the place, Mr. Morse." The sheriff pointed over to the taped-off area. "Unless you need me for anything else, I've got to head down to Bluff for the day."

Gary shook the sheriff's hand. "Thanks for the escort out here. Even with the yellow tape marking it, it's an easy place to miss."

Sheriff Harding nodded. "I know. If my deputy hadn't found Purcell's sports coat, we might never have seen the hole ourselves. Without it, we probably wouldn't have thought to explore off the highway. I can radio into town for one of my deputies to escort the other two members of your team out here when they get into town."

Christine and Alex still hadn't arrived this morning. Their flight out of Louisville had been delayed, but Gary had been so anxious to get out to the cave site that he had decided to leave Blanding without them. They would catch up later. When all six spelunkers got together, the team would be complete, and they could begin their work. Meanwhile, the rest of the team could start preparing to go down.

Gary shook his head. "That's not necessary. They know what highway we're on and approximately how far from Blanding we are. It's a lot easier to see the Winnebago than the yellow tape. I don't think they'll have any trouble finding us."

Sheriff Harding shrugged. "Suit yourself. Good luck. And be careful down there. I don't want to have to send another search-and-rescue team in after you."

The sheriff laughed as he rolled up his window. Gary laughed politely, but he didn't think the comment was amusing. Not that he would need someone to come and find him. He hadn't written a book on cave mapping because he got lost all the time.

Gary stepped away from the car as the sheriff backed up, stirring up the dust again. He held one hand to his mouth to try and keep from swallowing the swirling cloud of dust and waved with the other hand. The car pulled out onto the highway and within a few moments was lost within the shimmering heat waves bouncing off the asphalt.

Gary wiped his hands over himself trying to brush some of the dust from his University of Tennessee t-shirt and blue jeans. The problem was the dirt turned into mud when it mixed with the sweat on his arms and face.

He walked over to the Jeep. Lou Montgomery and Billy Joe Nash were sitting inside. Both men were friends of his from Knoxville. Lou was another professor of geology and Billy Joe was a graduate student studying botany. They were also both experienced spelunkers, which was why Gary had asked them along on this job. They would get paid for exploring and mapping a new cave system, something both of them would have probably done for fun.

The Cherokee's engine was still running so they could keep the air conditioner on. Billy Joe, sitting on the passenger side, rolled down his window. He was twenty-seven-years old with long, blond hair that he tied back in a short ponytail. He had the lean, hard body of a gymnast, which came from the hours of working out on gymnastics equipment at the university. Women were attracted to him, but most of them did not share his notion that exploring a cave was an ideal weekend getaway.

Billy Joe pointed to the marked-off area. "That's not the natural entrance, is it?"

"Sure doesn't look like it. However, it's our only entrance for the time being," Gary replied. "Why don't you and Lou come on over to the RV? Jared has the air conditioner on, and he's in there sipping a Hawaiian Punch."

Lou turned the engine off and jumped out of the truck. At forty-five, he was the oldest person in the group. In contrast to Billy Joe, Lou wore his black hair trimmed short. He was two inches taller than Gary's five feet, six inches, and he was just beginning to show the bulging belly that most men usually got before his age. Lou started toward the RV detouring to look down into the hole David Purcell had fallen five weeks ago. Then he jogged over to the Winnebago and entered it with his two friends.

Jared was sitting on the cushioned bench flipping through the television channels on the small television. He turned to the three men as they came in.

"Close that door. I just got it down to a comfortable temperature in here." He slapped the television with his palm. "I can't get a single station in on this thing. I guess I'll have to set up the satellite antennae later."

Gary motioned to Lou and Billy Joe. "You guys grab yourselves something to drink and then start setting up the tripod and the winch over the hole." He opened a closet and took out a long ball of thick twine that had a weight tied on one end of it from the shelf. "Jared, let's you and I see how deep this hole is."

"Not even going to let us catch our breaths, are you?" Jared joked.

Gary shook his head. "I'm anxious to see what's down there. This will be a totally new system."

Jared gulped down the rest of his fruit punch, tossed the can in the recycling bin, and headed out the door behind Gary.

"Don't you want to wait for Christine and Alex before you head down?"

"Of course I'll wait for them, Jared, but at least when they get here, we'll be ready to head down."

Lou and Billy Joe walked back to the Cherokee, each with a beer in his hand. Jared and Gary pulled up the metal poles that held the yellow-tape police line around the hole. When they had finished, they laid the poles off to the side and sat down near the edge of the hole.

"You're kind of anxious to get started, aren't you?" Jared asked.

Gary smiled. "Is it that obvious?"

Jared nodded. He turned on a powerful flashlight and shined it into the hole. He whistled when he saw that the light didn't reach the bottom.

"This chamber's deep," Jared commented. "And you say that David Purcell didn't break any bones falling through here?"

"That's what I was told," Gary answered.

"Lucky man."

Gary tossed one end of the weighted string over the edge and began to gradually play out the rest of it. Each foot of the white string was marked with a black line to make it easier to count off the feet. Gary had initially thought the chamber might be fifteen-feet deep. However, the fifteen-foot mark disappeared over the edge and was lost in the darkness. The slack in the line appeared between the twenty-six-foot mark and the twenty-seven-foot mark.

Gary lifted and lowered the string to find the point when the slack began. He grabbed the string between his fingers and held it out to Jared. Jared pulled out a small tape measure and measured the distance from the twenty-six-foot mark to Gary's finger.

"Four and a quarter inches. Twenty-six feet, four and a quarter inches," Jared said.

"Lucky man," Gary said, repeating Jared's earlier comment.

Jared nodded. "The bottom of the cave must be made of sponge for him not to have broken any bones in the fall. Either that or his bones must be made of steel."

Gary leaned over the edge. "The roof looks to be about four-feet thick. That would make the actual chamber height about twenty-two feet plus a few inches."

Jared shook his head slowly. "A two-story-tall chamber. I wonder how wide it is."

"We'd better not bring the truck and RV in any closer. We don't want to find another weak spot in the roof like David Purcell did."

Billy Joe and Lou walked over to the hole with the metal tripod. It was used to hold the winch line over the cavern so the cavers could easily be lowered and raised from the chamber without a danger of fraying the nylon cord. By using the tripod and winch, they wouldn't have to struggle to climb up a shaky nylon ladder when they were exhausted from a day of exploring. Billy Joe anchored the six-foot high tripod over the hole and ran the winch line through the pulley that hung from the intersection of the three tripod legs.

Gary told Lou and Billy Joe how high the chamber was. Billy Joe looked over the edge and whistled just as Jared had done.

Then he looked at the others and said, "I can't wait to get down there. This is going to be quite an adventure."

CHAPTER 8

Watching the reporters file into his room reminded David of the clowns at the circus. A small car, which looked just big enough for one clown, would stop in the center of one of the circus rings. The door would open, and a clown would climb out, then another and another and another. More clowns than could ever physically fit inside the car. Every time David thought the line of reporters would end, another walked through the door.

Dr. Haskell had said that Blanding Community Hospital didn't have a conference room so David would have to talk to the reporters from his bed in his room. He preferred that anyway. His legs were sore, and he didn't want to walk if he didn't have to. A nurse had come in right after breakfast to wash and cut his hair. David also shaved his face, which was a slow-going process, but at least he looked presentable for the reporters.

He tried to smile as half a dozen photographers snapped his picture. Blue-dotted visions of flashbulbs blinded his view so that he could see little else besides bright splotches of light. He had wanted to see light, but not that bright. He ran his hand over his cheeks to make sure he hadn't gouged his face with the razor. Although David was a man who had been lost for five weeks in a cave, he didn't want to look it.

He felt the heat from a bright light being used by a television reporter. The brightness hurt his eyes even more than the flashbulbs. The intensity of the light reminded him of the bright light he had seen in his dream, but unlike his dream, this light was not fading. It was also not all-encompassing like the light in his dream. Wouldn't the light make him look pale? The thought of appearing pale white to the people who saw him disturbed him for some reason. He supposed it was because looking so pale under the light would make him look ill.

The smell of different colognes and perfumes in the room combined to form one noxious odor that made David feel like heaving up his breakfast, which he hadn't cared much for anyway. At least seven reporters, six photographers, and a cameraman were in the room with him, which was about six people too many for the small room. He wasn't sure who was with what newspaper or television station, but that probably didn't matter much. They were all going to share the same information.

David waved his hands in front of himself to tell the reporters that he was ready to begin.

"I'm not sure how press conferences are usually conducted. I don't usually fall into deep holes to get the media's attention," he explained as he

44

raised the end of his bed so he could easily sit up. "If you want to ask your questions one at a time, I'll try to answer them as well as I can."

"How are you feeling, David? The country is anxious to hear," an older woman asked. David almost laughed. What did the country care about him? All his family lived in Utah and Idaho. Probably very few people outside of those two states even knew his name.

Was this the fifteen minutes of fame Andy Warhol had promised everyone in the country?

David tried to answer the woman's question seriously. "Fine. I'm feeling fine. Actually, according to Dr. Haskell, I'm better than expected considering I've spent the last five weeks of my life in a cave. The doctor says I show no signs of dehydration or starvation."

"What happened to you? How did you fall into the cave?" a male reporter asked with a thick western accent. He wore thick glasses and a thin mustache. David guessed the man was definitely a newspaperman. He didn't fit the television reporter image.

"I was hitchhiking to Blanding because my car blew a radiator hose. I was walking in the grass because it was easier on my feet and it wasn't as hot as the road. The ground caved in under my feet, and I fell into the hole. Unfortunately, the hole led into the cave."

"What did you eat while you were in the cave?" a woman asked.

David shrugged. "Who knows? I certainly don't."

"Are you saying you don't know because you couldn't see it in the dark?" the reporter continued.

David shook his head. "No, I'm saying I don't know because I can't remember."

"Do you have amnesia?" the male reporter with the western accent asked. He had a high-pitched voice, which David found annoying. Even a radio station couldn't have used him as a reporter.

"That's what it looks like. I can't remember anything after falling into the cave. Dr. Haskell says the amnesia could be a result of the fall. He said there are some unexplained bruises on my head. I'm lucky I'm not blind as well. It's not unusual for someone exposed to total darkness for such a long time to become blind for a short time until their eyes get used to the light again, or worse yet, to become blind permanently. Dr. Haskell wants to take x-rays of me later to make sure I don't have any hidden broken bones." Actually, the x-rays were being taken because Dr. Haskell hadn't been able to confirm that his previous x-rays had gotten mixed up with someone else's.

"So why aren't you blind? Was there light in the cave you could see by?" a young female reporter asked. She had a sultry sounding voice and the face to match. Definitely a television reporter. She was even more attractive than the red-headed nurse David had seen when he first woke up in the hospital.

"Like I said, I can't remember much about my time down there. But I can remember that it was pitch dark. So I'm not sure of why I'm not blind. I guess I'm just lucky. Dr. Haskell thinks I must have seen some light down there to keep my eye muscles from atrophying."

"Do you remember moving around at all down there? I mean, the search-and-rescue team took five weeks to find you. They thought they were going to find a dead body, not a live person. You surprised them, but you apparently didn't stay where you had fallen into the cave," the older female reporter asked. She stood waiting with her mini-recorder aimed at him. To David, it seemed the reporters were waiting for him to make a confession.

He shrugged. "I guess I must have moved, but I don't know why. One of the things they taught me in Boy Scouts was if you are lost, you should stay at the point where you realized you were lost. If you were with a group, someone would find you," he said.

David's mouth felt so cottony he picked up the glass of water next to the bed and sipped it.

"Mr. Purcell, you've said you showed no signs of dehydration or starvation. Looking at you, I would say that's true. Since you were hitchhiking into Blanding after your car broke down, I doubt you were carrying a knapsack full of food. How could you not be at least a little underweight? Caves aren't known for their abundance of food."

David was felt hot in the crowded room. He wished this press conference was over with already.

"I really don't know," David said. "I don't remember anything. To prevent dehydration, I might have found some water in the cave, but I truly don't know what I ate while I was lost. I must have found something, though. I'm hoping I'll remember when I recover from my amnesia."

"Will you recover?"

David nodded his head vigorously. "Certainly. It's just like in those old movies. I need to get a brick dropped on my head or get hit in the head with a hammer." The reporters laughed. "Unfortunately, I'm not able to say how long it will take. I hope I remember everything that happened to me during the last five weeks by the time I leave the hospital." he paused. "Listen, I hate to be rude, but I'm about done in for the day. I'm sure Dr. Haskell can answer any other questions you might have."

"Thanks for talking with us," the reporter with the thick western accent said.

"I hope you're feeling well soon," the older woman said.

"Me, too," David replied.

The young, sexy reporter moved close to him. "When you do remember everything that happened to you, I hope you'll let me interview you again. Maybe we can meet in more pleasant surroundings."

David felt himself blush. It was almost like he was cheating on Terrie. He wondered where she was.

He smiled sheepishly. "I'd like that very much," he told her. He wondered if she was toying with him or if she was attracted to him.

He watched the reporters shuffle out of the room. When the last of them had gone, he felt as if the temperature in the room dropped ten degrees. He lay back on his bed and sighed.

"Mr. Purcell?"

David sat up quickly. He thought everyone had left. This didn't sound like one of the reporters, though. It was an older voice; it had a hesitancy of speech that David associated with senior citizens. Sitting in a chair in a corner of the room was an old Indian dressed in blue jeans and a red and black, short-sleeved shirt. Beside the old Indian stood a younger woman about David's age. She was quite attractive. Almost as attractive as the sexy television reporter.

"Who are you?" David asked a bit too sharply. He didn't like being taken by surprise.

"My name is Adam Maho, but most white men just call me Adam. I'm a Hopi. I live in Oraibi on Third Mesa in Arizona. This is my granddaughter, Sarah." He motioned to the woman. "We've come a long way to speak with you."

"Your granddaughter doesn't have a second Hopi name?" David asked out of curiosity.

"No," Adam said.

"My mother didn't have me go through the naming ceremony," Sarah said. She had a lyrical voice that was quite pleasant to listen to, although, there was a hint of hardness to her words.

"I'm not sure why you've come all the way from Arizona to see me, but I don't feel much up to company right now. So if you don't mind, I'd like to rest. The press conference was more draining than I thought it would be."

Adam stood up and moved closer to him. "What I've come to speak with you about is more important than the questions you answered for the reporters."

David crossed his arms over his chest. "I don't know about that. Those guys thought their stories were pretty important."

He tried to smile and be pleasant, but all he really wanted was to lie down and rest.

"I must speak to you about Kuskurza," Adam said in a loud whisper.

Pain shot through David's temples, and he grabbed his head.

"Are you all right?" Sarah asked.

David nodded. "I'll be fine. I just need some rest."

He felt a hand on his shoulder and jerked away from it.

"I just wanted to help you," Adam said.

"Well, you're no doctor. I don't even know you."

"But I must speak to you about Kuskurza," Adam insisted.

The pain shot through David's temples again. Was it that Indian word that was making his head hurt?

"I don't know what you're talking about. Now please leave before I have the nurse call security," David warned them.

"But I cannot. You have found a sipapu, and it must be closed."

"Sipapu...an emergence hole," David murmured to himself.

Adam's face brightened. "Yes! You know of it then."

"No I don't," David said quickly.

"But you just said..." Sarah started to say.

"I know what I just said, but I've never heard the word before you said it," David snapped. He was confused as to how he knew what a sipapu was because he had never heard the word before the old man said it.

David grabbed for the nurse call button and held it out toward them as a threat. It didn't take much to bring the kooks crawling out of the woodwork. They heard he fell into a cave and suddenly they wanted to share their life experiences with him.

"I asked you nicely before, but now I'm going to have to get a nurse in here to lead you out."

Sarah grabbed her grandfather by the arm. "Come on, Grandfather. He's just another white man. There's nothing special about him. He won't be able to help us."

Adam sighed. He stared at David and shook his head slowly. Then he turned and walked out of the room with his granddaughter. He paused at the door and cast one more sorrowful glance in David's direction. Then the door closed.

David relaxed his grip on the nurse call button and lay back. His head didn't hurt anymore. What had made it hurt in the first place? Could a single Indian word have caused the pain? He didn't think so, but his temples had only hurt when Adam said Kuskurza.

David wondered what the word meant. Probably nothing important. He turned on the television to watch a rerun of Bonanza.

CHAPTER 9

Centuries ago, a small rock slide crashed onto the narrow ledge on the side of the Woodenshoe Buttes and settled in a pile in the crevice between the butte and the ledge. It had remained undisturbed ever since. In front of the pile of tightly packed rocks, lilies grew up between cracks in the ledge. The ledge offered a seldom-seen view of the surrounding country because of the difficulty involved in climbing up to the rock shelf from the ground.

A rock in the middle of the pile moved slightly. Just a wiggle, an imperceptible shift that caused a few pebbles to tumble down the exterior of the pile. After a moment of stillness, it moved again. The distance of the movement was no more than a half an inch, but there was no apparent cause for it.

Suddenly, the rock disappeared into the pile leaving a black hole in its place. The two rocks that formed one side of the border of the black hole vanished next. It looked as if the small rockfall was collapsing in on itself. When the collapse was complete, all of the rocks had vanished, and in their place was a three-foot wide hole.

A pale, white hand with six-inch-long fingers appeared at the edge of the darkness created by the hole. It slid forward along the shelf of rock until it reached the edge of the shadow caused by the butte blocking the sun. The hand remained motionless inside the edge of the shadow for about ten seconds and then retreated back into the darkness of the hole.

A pale, white face filled the space. His white hair was tied in a long braid, which hung down his back. His large eyes were closed. Kel'hoya took a deep breath and then opened his eyes wide. He quickly squinted as he looked at the sun, but he refused to close his eyes. He blinked away the tears. His eyes were dark brown and only intensified the paleness of his skin.

"The sun," Kel'hoya whispered. His words were not English, but of a language that had not been spoken on the surface for centuries.

Never had he seen anything so bright. The small pieces of the sun that So'tuknang had left behind to light Kuskurza and imprison the dark kachinas were nothing in comparison to this. Even the sunbeams that the dark kachinas sometimes gave the Bow Clan to use to see in the dark tunnels were not this bright.

Legends talked of the sun as the giver of light far beyond the power of darkness. If the legends spoke the truth about the sun, what else might they speak the truth about?

Kel'hoya thought of the stories told by the dark kachinas about the Outlanders, the people who lived in this world outside of Kuskurza. It was said death awaited any from Kuskurza who ventured to the surface. Taiowa had forbidden the members of the Bow Clan to leave Kuskurza because they had used their creative powers to follow the dark kachinas and rebel against the teachings of Taiowa.

But how could something so beautiful be so deadly? He reached out and touched the petals of the nearest lily. The colors were so vibrant! Bright yellow, red, and green. The flowers and plants in Kuskurza were so pale it was difficult to say if they had any color.

The dark kachinas had warned Kel'hoya and his companion, To'chi, of the dangers of the surface. Their journey would be dangerous, and they could not allow themselves to be lured into a feeling of security by the beauty of the place. The dark kachinas had told them they would die before they could ever return to Kuskurza, but before they died, they must kill the one the Sun Clan called Pahana, their lost brother. He could tell other Outlanders of the existence of Kuskurza and that the dark kachinas still lived. If that happened, Taiowa might return to strengthen the weakening prisons that held the dark kachinas. All that had been gained over the centuries of waiting would be lost in moments.

Kel'hoya looked over his shoulder and said, "If we leave the protection of the sipapu, we will be killed as the ancient ones were."

He chose to speak to To'chi, rather than think his words. He had been told to do so by the dark kachinas, even though it was not the way of the Bow Clan. The Bow Clan communicated by sending their thoughts to each other. By doing that, the mighty Bow Clan could act as the body of the dark kachinas in their war against the Sun Clan, the children of Ma'saw. By speaking to To'chi, Kel'hoya ensured that the rest of the Bow Clan would not hear his thoughts and grow curious about the surface.

Kel'hoya was glad the other members of the Bow Clan did not know his thoughts for another reason. For the first time in his life, he knew fear. To venture beyond Kuskurza was to venture into lands he knew only through legend. The Fourth World was unknown. No one from Kuskurza had ventured to the surface in centuries. No one would have had to come now if the Outlanders hadn't sent Pahana to spy on the dark kachinas. Pahana had seen Kuskurza and inspired the Sun Clan and the slaves to continue their rebellion against the Bow Clan and the dark kachinas. Already the slaves were rallying to the cause of the Sun Clan. To those who were foolish enough to believe that life was better in Tu'waqachi, Pahana was a symbol from Taiowa that they would be allowed to leave Kuskurza for the Fourth World to dwell with Taiowa.

Now that Kel'hoya had seen Tu'waqachi, he wondered who the real fool was. The Sun Clan and the slaves who believed they would see this world or the Bow Clan and the dark kachinas who tried not to believe this world existed? It was a thought that would mean his death in Kuskurza.

Kel'hoya had no desire to leave the safety of the sipapu, and he was not alone in his feeling, either. To'chi had grown continually nervous and more silent as they made their way from the safety of Kuskurza where the dark kachinas ruled to their current position just inside the sipapu. It did not take a telepath to understand those emotions. In front of them was Tu'waqachi, the Fourth World. Kel'hoya could not blame his companion for his nervousness. He felt it too.

This was the sipapu of the ancient ones. This was the passage taken by The People to the surface during the great exodus. All but the members of the Bow Clan had been allowed to leave Kuskurza. The Bow Clan had been forced to stay below with the dark kachinas. The flood waters sent by So'tuknang had killed most of the Bow Clan, but a few managed to survive. The strong and determined had climbed to the tops of the great stone mountains where the dark kachinas were imprisoned by Taiowa the Creator. The destroying waters did not reach the tops of the stone mountains, and the Bow Clan had dwelt there for many days. When the waters receded, the few remaining Bow Clansmen had been left alone to serve and care for the dark kachinas in the small area that was all that remained of Kuskurza.

This world Kel'hoya was seeing now was what the Sun Clan still sought to find. The dark kachinas had told the Bow Clan and the slaves that the sipapu did not exist; Tu'waqachi did not exist. And yet, here was the proof. The Sun Clan was right. Kel'hoya now realized why the dark kachinas ordered the Bow Clan to kill anyone who ventured too close to the sipapu. This world would lure anyone who saw it away from Kuskurza leaving the dark kachinas alone. Even if they were free, the dark kachinas would not be able to remain long in the Fourth World. They would always have to return to Kuskurza and to the safety of the darkness.

"We are protected by the power of the dark kachinas," To'chi said from behind him. "As long as we do their will, we will not die."

Kel'hoya was tempted to remind his companion of the dark kachinas' warning that they would die before they reached Kuskurza again, even if they did carry out their mission.

"Look at this world, To'chi. It is even larger than Kuskurza. How can we find Pahana within this world where we are the Outlanders?"

Kel'hoya withdrew into the hole. His pale face was replaced by the equally pale face of his companion. To'chi stuck his face out of the hole and stared at the blue sky. He took a deep breath of the mountain air and coughed. He quickly withdrew into the shelter of the sipapu.

"The air is poison. It makes me dizzy," To'chi said between coughs.

"Here, Kuskurza ends," Kel'hoya said.

"How will we know where to go to find Pahana?"

Kel'hoya remembered the commands of the dark kachinas. "We will wait until the sun sleeps as the dark kachinas have told us it will. We will rest, and the dark kachinas will have to show us where we must go if we are to succeed. When they have shown us, we will go there on the pa'tuwvotas and complete our mission."

"And the air?" To'chi asked.

"It is not poison, only different."

The two white forms retreated deeper into the shadows of the cavern. When the dark kachinas showed their power and vanquished the sun from the sky, the Bow Clan would venture onto the surface to kill Pahana.

CHAPTER 10

David lay on his bed staring out the large window in his hospital room. He wondered what it had been like lying in utter darkness for five weeks. With no light at all. Darkness so dark that there were fish that lived in caves with no eyes because they had nothing to see. Their eyes had atrophied from non-use until the fish became genetically eyeless. He wondered why the reporters hadn't asked him that question. What was it like living in total darkness for five weeks? If they had, they might have gotten a good look at his fear.

Of course, he had been in a situation that might have led to his total blindness, but he couldn't remember anything about it. He knew he must have had some sort of light; otherwise, he would be blind now and living in permanent darkness.

An overweight woman opened the door to his room enough to stick her head inside. "David?" she said cautiously.

David smiled. "Mom."

Marcy Purcell pushed open the door and rushed to her son, her large body rippled like a wave beneath her pink-striped dress. She grabbed hold of David's shoulders, kissed him once on the cheek, and then buried his face in a smothering hug against her breast.

"Oh, Davey."

Lewis Purcell silently followed his wife into the room. He stood on the opposite side of the bed across from his wife. David stared at his parents wondering why they looked different. Then he realized they looked tired. How long it had been since they had had a good night's sleep? What had they done while the search-and-rescue team was looking for him? Worry. Wait for the bad news that his body had been found.

His parents' contrasting sizes reminded David of the old-time comedy teams he enjoyed watching on television. Laurel and Hardy. Abbott and Costello. Gleason and Carney. And now Mom and Dad.

"Oh, Davey! I was so relieved when the police called and said they had found you. I knew you weren't dead. People were beginning to say that after five weeks, you would have had to have died. Oh, they didn't say it to my face, but I could tell what they were whispering when I wasn't around. I knew differently, though. And you showed 'em, Davey. You showed 'em. I knew you would. Didn't I, Lew?" She looked across the bed at her husband.

Lewis nodded his head. "Yes, you did, but I didn't believe he was dead, either," Lewis said in his own defense. "I know my boy's a tough scrapper."

He lightly punched David on the shoulder. "Besides, he was a Boy Scout. He was trained to know how to handle himself in that type of situation." Lewis leaned closer to his son. "Do you remember that time your troop went caving and your flashlight..."

"Lewis!" Marcy said sharply. "He just came out of that pit! Do you think he wants to be reminded of another time when he was in one?"

His mother was right. He would rather not remember that caving trip with the Boy Scouts, but now that his father had mentioned it, David couldn't help but remember. He and sixteen other boys had made up Troop 558. David had been a Life Scout before he quit in his junior year of high school. His friends had thought the Boy Scouts were for little boys, and at sixteen years old, they were too old to dress in khaki uniforms. Someone should have reminded them that the army did the same thing and no one called them "babies." His troop liked doing outdoor activities. He could remember rafting down the Colorado River, hiking to the Phantom Ranch in the Grand Canyon, and rappelling off a cliff in the Wasatch Mountains.

Then there was the caving trip. He had been twelve years old when his troop decided to go caving. They chose a cave the scoutmaster knew in Glen Canyon. Ten boys and four adults had gone on the trip. About halfway through the trip, David had heard a sound like thunder inside the cave. He stopped to listen, and the next thing David remembered was that he had been alone in the darkness of the cave, and then...

And then what?

He couldn't remember. That whole experience in the cave was the reason why at the age of twenty-six, he still slept with a nightlight on. That cave and the darkness had terrified him for some reason, yet he had never been afraid of the dark before that time in the cave. So it had to be something more than the darkness and the cave.

What?

David patted his mother's arm. "Mom, you can let me go now. I'm all right."

Marcy loosened her grip and straightened up. David reached up and wiped away a tear that was hanging off the tip of her nose.

"I think we should move you back into the house as soon as possible," she said. "I don't like the way the doctors at this hospital think they are so important. They wouldn't let us in to see you until visiting hours began this morning. And all that after we spent most of yesterday trying to see you. No one would let us in! Imagine keeping parents away from their son!"

David looked closely at his mother's face. The past five weeks had aged her at least a decade. The wrinkles in the corners of her eyes had deepened. The corners of her mouth seemed to turn downward in a perpetual frown. Dark circles had formed under her eyes. She had tried to comb her hair, but she still looked slightly disheveled.

He hoped that the fact he had been found alive and well would change some of that. Ease the wrinkles. Bring the smile back.

David was the youngest of his five siblings and the only boy. When it came to raising a son, his mother had drawn on the only experience in child rearing she knew. She had tried to raise him the same way she had done with her daughters. But David was not a girl, and the open affection that had raised his five sisters had nearly smothered him.

His mother had gradually given David the room he needed to grow. She had surrendered her time with him so that he could spend more time with his father and learn what he needed to know to grow into a man. Fishing. Boy Scouts. Cars. Now it was as if his mother had forgotten all that. She was once again playing David's over-protective mother, and no one was going to stop her. She was going to take care of him whether he wanted her to or not.

How could he tell her he didn't need his mommy without hurting her feelings?

Marcy finally gave in to her emotions and started crying again. The tears rolled down her cheeks and fell onto David's blankets.

"I prayed every night that God would bring you back to me, and he did. He did," Marcy said.

David stroked his mother's head trying to calm her down. He looked in his father's direction for help. He noticed his father's clothes were wrinkled, and he wondered if his father had slept in them last night. Lewis walked around the foot of the bed and took his wife by the shoulders. He led her to the plastic chair with vinyl cushions in the corner of the room. Marcy's hips barely fit between the arms of the chair.

"How do you feel son?" Lewis asked after he had helped his wife sit down.

"Fine," David answered.

"I can give you a blessing if you want. I have my oil with me." Lewis held up the small vial on his keychain.

David shook his head. "I'm all right, Dad."

But he really wasn't. He still couldn't remember what had happened after the fall into the cavern, and he got a headache that felt like someone dropped a stick of dynamite in his ear and it exploded in his head whenever he tried to remember. If his mother hadn't been in the room, David might have told his father about the headaches. Since his mother was nearby, he chose to keep silent. He didn't want to give her another reason to cry. He had worried her enough to last the rest of his life.

"Despite what Mom thinks, they're treating me really well here," David said. He patted his stomach. "It's already hard to tell I was near starvation two days ago, isn't it?"

Lewis Purcell nodded. "Now that you mention it, you don't look like you lost any weight. How'd you manage that?"

David had no answer, so he shrugged. The movement caused a twinge of pain because his shoulders were still stiff.

"You know, I think your mom is right about inviting you back to the house for a few weeks. Nothing permanent. Just until you're well again. You're not going to be working with a full head of steam for the next couple of weeks, and you're going to need some help. So why don't you come home with us, son? We can make up your room, and you can stay as long as you need to," Lewis offered enthusiastically.

David smiled as he remembered the rancher home on the north shore of Utah Lake. He wondered if the fish were biting this summer. He tried to remember what his room looked like. At first, he saw nothing but a bare room. Then the details began to fill in. He saw his twin bed with the Speed Racer sheets and blanket. From the ceiling, hung an air force of model airplanes. The small desk in front of the window looked out over the lake. It was a boy's room, and to return to it, he would have to become a boy again for his parents. David didn't think he could do that or if he was even willing to try. He had been on his own for four years now, and he wasn't all that anxious to return to living under someone else's rules.

"Thanks, but I'll be able to manage on my own," David said.

"But you're sick, Davey..." his mother whined.

David tried not to wince at his mother's insistent use of "Davey." He hadn't gone by that name since he turned thirteen, but to his mother, he still seemed to be only twelve. He didn't want to be a boy again. Something had happened to that boy that shouldn't have.

David leaned toward his mother and held out his hand to her. She put her hand in his, and he placed her hand on his forehead.

"Do I feel sick to you, Mom?" he asked.

"No," she reluctantly admitted. "But a fever is only one way to tell if you're sick."

David took his mother's hand from his forehead and patted it. "I'm fine, Mom. Really. Just relax. I tell you what; the first weekend after I get out of here, I'll drive up to see you in Provo so that you can see that I'm fine. You and Dad can baby me all you want then."

"I never baby..." Marcy started to say.

David squeezed his mother's hand slightly. "You do, Mom, but when I come up to the house, you can do it, and I won't even complain. Dad and I will just sit out back on the pier and catch a few fish. Maybe even eat a few." David smiled in his father's direction.

His mother stood and smoothed his hair down like she was petting a dog, but David didn't complain. His mother's touch brought an odd sense of security. Maybe he should consider going back to Provo for a few days, not weeks. He wouldn't mind eating a few home-cooked meals instead of the TV dinners that were in his apartment freezer.

"It must have been horrible for you to be trapped down there for all that time," his mother said.

David didn't know if it had been horrible or not. He couldn't remember any of it. All he remembered was the blackness.

"I'd rather not talk about it," David said tactfully, but he didn't say that he couldn't talk about it because he couldn't remember it.

"I understand."

She tried her best to smile, but David could tell she was still worried. *Oh, well,* David thought, *I guess that's part of a mom's job description.* He put his hands behind his head and tried to enjoy his mother's company.

CHAPTER 11

David rolled onto his side trying to remember what had happened to him in the cave. His parents had left an hour ago leaving him alone with what few memories he had of the past five weeks. What had he been doing? How had he stayed alive?

He closed his eyes and pictured his hike from his car in his mind. He saw the ground crumbling beneath his feet in slow motion and the black hole opening up under him. He saw the area around him quickly fading to a small dot as he fell into the hole, and then there was darkness. He focused on trying to remember what had happened immediately after the fall. If he could remember even a little bit past the point where his amnesia began...

A sharp pain stabbed the center of his head, and David winced. It was the same pain he had felt when the Hopis had said "Kuskurza." But they were nowhere around this time, and he hadn't said the word. He had only tried to remember.

He was no glutton for punishment, so he quickly gave up trying to remember. His memory would return at its own pace and without any pain. Or so he hoped. To help ease his headache, he grabbed the remote control and turned on the television. Watching the news on CNN took his mind off of thinking about the cave.

The pain in his temples receded to an annoying throb as he drifted into a fitful sleep filled with dreams of the darkness in the cavern he couldn't fully remember. He wanted his memory to return. He had to know what had happened to him in the cave. It was important that he remember. He had lived for five weeks under near-impossible conditions but couldn't remember any of the time. If he couldn't remember it, there was always the possibility it wasn't true.

What wasn't true? David puzzled over the thought until he began to dream.

He dreamed the same dream he had last night. The bright light gradually dimmed. The stone mountain quivered, and finally exploded throwing pieces of rock in every direction. But it wasn't the stone shards that scared him. It was the absolute blackness he saw spreading out from where the stone mountain had stood. Something had been freed because the light had gotten too dim, and it was something that shouldn't be free.

The scene abruptly switched and David saw a white-skinned man sleeping in front of him. The man looked human, except that his skin was white like David might have looked under the bright light of the television reporter who had been at the press conference. This man looked like an albino except his fingers were longer than normal human fingers. David noticed the charred, black hole in the man's chest. He wasn't sleeping at all. He was dead.

Who was he?

David could see a stone wall behind the man and assumed he was in a cave. Had David seen a dead albino in the cave?

The headache returned, and David tried to fight it off. He had to remember. He was so close! He had to remember. Why did his head hurt every time he tried?

Had David stumbled on a murder victim in the cave? The pain intensified making him want to cry.

He woke at three o'clock in the afternoon with a throbbing headache. The red-haired nurse who David had seen when he first woke up in the hospital came into his room a few minutes later with his medicine. After seeing the sexy television reporter and the beautiful Hopi woman, this woman did not look as attractive to David as she had looked at first. She was older than he would have thought yesterday, and heavier, too. David asked her for some aspirin, and she left his pills on the bed tray and went into the hallway to get the aspirin.

David swallowed the tablets and followed it up with a swig of water.

"How are you feeling?" the nurse asked as she took his temperature. "You certainly look better than you did yesterday."

"I feel okay, I guess, but I keep getting a painful headache," David told her hoping she might be able to explain it. "I'm hungry, too."

The nurse cocked her head to the side. "You ate lunch only a couple of hours ago when your parents were here. You'd better be careful how much you eat, Mr. Purcell. Dr. Haskell doesn't want you to upset your system any more than necessary. If you throw up, the doctor may put you on a liquid diet," the nurse warned him.

David knew she was right, but he couldn't help it. He was hungry. Besides, he didn't feel sick at all.

The nurse cast a curious glance in his direction just before she left the room as if she expected David to start eating the sheets or something.

David leaned back in his bed and stared out the window. He thought about how good it was to see the sun again, and how close Dr. Haskell said he had come to losing his sight. Why wasn't he even temporarily blind like the doctor expected him to be? There hadn't been any light in the caves.

Or had there been?

He thought about the dimming light surrounding the stone mountain. That pyramid hadn't been above ground. The first time he dreamed about it, David had thought it had been on the surface because of the bright light, but as the light dimmed, hadn't he seen rock walls further away on the other side of the pyramids? He tried to remember, but his temples throbbed.

Sooner or later he would remember, but he wasn't sure he was going to like it when he did.

CHAPTER 12

Sarah sat down in the shade of the tent and wiped the sweat from her neck with a bandeau. Her grandfather sat outside the tent in the direct sunlight, yet he was not sweating. He sat cross-legged on the hard ground staring at a small stone he held in his hand. He kept turning the stone over and over as if it was some sort of talisman.

She reached into the canvas bag that was sitting on the ground inside the tent, pulled out a piece of jerked beef, and she held it out to her grandfather. Adam acted as if he didn't see it.

"I never thought of you as a sulker," she said trying to trick him into saying something.

It didn't work. He sat and stared at the small stone. It turned over and over between his fingertips. She looked at the stone wondering if that was what held his concentration or if he was simply lost in his thoughts. She decided he was probably thinking about David Purcell.

Sarah shook her head in frustration. Why he would waste his time thinking about an impolite white man was beyond her.

She scooted back deeper into the tent to get out of the heat of the sun. Picking up the canteen, she sloshed around the contents. She hoped Adam would hear the sound and come in from out of the sun for a drink. When he didn't move, Sarah unscrewed the cap and took a gulp of the cool water from the canteen, then tossed it back on the ground.

She couldn't understand it. They had given up a season's crops to sit in the middle of the desert and meditate. They had driven 200 miles on her grandfather's crusade to save the Fourth World, and the object of their journey had thrown them out of his room.

They should be on their way back to Oraibi now. If it had been up to Sarah, they would never have come in the first place. She could have told her grandfather that David Purcell wouldn't believe a story about Kuskurza and the Bow Clan. Adam hadn't seen it that way, though. He thought David already knew what Adam wanted to tell him, and he only needed to talk to David to fill in the gaps in his visions.

Her grandfather insisted on staying until he could talk to David. She and Adam had driven out of town and made camp about half a mile off of Highway 191. She had thought they might stay in a hotel in Blanding, but they didn't have enough money to pay for a hotel room. Even though it might not be the most comfortable place to sleep, at least there weren't white men here to stare at her and Adam.

"He's a white man. What do you expect him to do? He doesn't believe in the legends of our people," Sarah said sharply.

Adam turned slowly and stared at her. His features were frozen in a stone mask, and for a moment, Sarah could see every wrinkle etched in his face. He looked furious, and Sarah thought he was mad at her. Then his face softened, and he smiled.

"He acted as if he didn't know what I was talking about," Adam said finally.

"Maybe he didn't."

Sarah crawled toward the front of the tent to talk to her grandfather, but she still didn't want to sit outside in the hot sun.

"But he was there. I saw him in my visions. He was the white man running from the Bow Clan. The one I told you about. It was him."

"Are you sure you couldn't have been mistaken?"

Adam shook his head fiercely. "No! It is him. I'm sure of it. As soon as I saw him in the hospital, I recognized him from my vision."

Sarah reached out and took one of his wrinkled hands in hers. "It may have been him, but what if it wasn't a literal vision you saw? What if it was something that needs to be interpreted?"

Adam thought for a moment and then said, "David Purcell would still be involved."

"Yes, but he might not necessarily know that he is involved. The chase you saw might be symbolic of a struggle between the Bow Clan and the whites," Sarah told him. "Maybe he never saw the Bow Clan in the caves. Maybe he is a symbol Taiowa used to represent a white man."

Adam slowly shook his head. "He knew what the sipapu was."

Sarah sighed. "Grandfather, we tried to talk to him, but he won't listen. If he knows what's down there, he can't remember it. You heard what he told those reporters. He has amnesia. Let's go home. Maybe you can get part of your crop back from Paul."

Adam held up his hand to silence Sarah. "No. We have come to learn what David Purcell knows about Kuskurza, and we must find out."

"But he knows nothing," she insisted.

"You are wrong, young one. He knows much. He just does not know he knows it. We must help him remember."

Sarah knew his use of the words "young one" were meant as a mild rebuke. A warning that she should respect her elders, but she ignored it. She was tired of watching her grandfather humiliate himself.

"You're not going to be able to convince him, you know. The next time he sees you coming, he'll call hospital security and have you thrown out," Sarah warned him.

"Nevertheless..."

Sarah slapped the ground hard with both her hands and a small cloud of dust puffed up. She stared into Adam's eyes and yelled, "You're crazy! Do you know that? Why are you walking into a situation like that? Do you like letting white men humiliate you? If your roles were reversed and David Purcell needed to warn you, do you think he would have come to Oraibi? No. He would have shrugged and said, 'Oh, well. What's the loss of another Injun?'"

"Sarah," Adam said calmly.

She continued her tirade. "He'll just use you, and when he's gotten what he wants from you, he'll leave you without anything. That's the kind of man he is. You can't trust him. Hopis and whites can't live together or work together."

"Are you speaking from personal experience?" Adam asked calmly.

Sarah buried her face in her hands and started crying. Adam slowly stroked the back of her head as she leaned forward against his shoulder. She didn't want to cry in front of him, but she couldn't seem to stop herself.

"I'm sorry, but you can't judge a race by a single man," Adam explained to her.

Sarah raised her head. "I'm not."

"You are. You don't know David Purcell. Taiowa has chosen him to help the Hopis."

"He's not special. He's just like any other white man," Sarah argued.

Adam arched his eyebrows. "And you know this to be true?"

Sarah nodded. "Yes."

"So then, you have talked to every white man there is? I find this hard to believe when you don't even leave your rooms when there are tourists in town." Sarah blushed so that she almost looked like a full-blooded Hopi. "I would not want to be judged on the impression a white man got from meeting one Hopi. If the white man happened to meet Ralph Tawanimp'tewa, he might think I am also a drunk. Or, if the white man met Ethan Ta'bo, he might think I am skilled with silver. I'm neither. I am my own person. Just as David Purcell is his own person."

"Oh, grandfather," Sarah moaned and fell forward again softly sobbing.

Adam held her by the shoulders and lifted her up until she faced him. "I can't say I know why you feel this way. It's not because of anything that was done to you by a Hopi. We've accepted you as our own, which you are. If something happened to you before you came to Oraibi, then you must decide if it is important enough to allow it to scar your life."

Sarah sniffled. She felt like a little girl tagging along with her grandfather as he worked his fields.

"I know one side of you, but you hide another side even from me. I would hate to see the side I know and love destroyed by the side you hide and hate," her grandfather added.

"I'll try to keep it from happening," she said.

Adam nodded once that he accepted that. "It's all I can ask." He smiled and wiped away a tear from her cheek.

"How will you get in to see David Purcell?" Sarah asked. "He won't want to see you."

"I've thought about that, and I have thought of a way. But it requires your help."

Sarah straightened her back and met Adam's stare. "I'll help you the best I can."

"Good. I knew you would." He paused. "And Sarah?"

"Yes?"

"I am not a sulker."

Sarah smiled and then giggled.

CHAPTER 13

David's stomach rumbled, even though he had eaten just a few hours ago. He had devoured a ham-and-cheese sandwich on stale bread, a bowl of fruit, and watered-down orange juice as if it were a feast. It had stayed down, too, without any hint of nausea. Now he was hungry again. He might not look like a man who hadn't eaten in five weeks, but he ate like one.

The red-haired nurse, Nurse Montgomery, came in for a short time to make him swallow another pair of bitter pills. David was tempted to chew on them just to have something to eat.

The nurse talked incessantly about how her daughter had just had a baby boy and was staying up on the third floor. And, oh, wasn't her grandson the most handsome baby in the maternity ward; everyone said so. And wasn't he the most well-behaved baby up there? He didn't cry or mess his diaper every five minutes like all the other babies.

David tried to tell the woman he was tired, but when he opened his mouth to speak, she stuck a thermometer under his tongue. She continued talking as she flicked a small penlight in his eyes to measure their response to the light. Then she tilted his head back and administered eye drops.

Kel'hoya saw the white-uniformed female and tried to roll to the side before she could kill him with whatever weapon she was holding. Realizing he couldn't move out of the way, he screamed curses at the woman for imprisoning him only to kill him. He stared at the woman as she aimed the short stick at his face. A blinding light seared his eyes. He tried to cover his face with his hands, but his arms wouldn't respond to his movement. Kel'hoya braced himself for whatever pain would follow.

The woman lowered the short stick. She tilted his head back and dripped a liquid into his eyes. The liquid burned and Kel'hoya wanted to scream, but he would not give her the satisfaction. When the woman realized Kel'hoya would not cry out in pain no matter what sort of torture she devised, she turned and left the room.

Room?

He was not in a room. He was resting in a cave behind the sipapu. He must be seeing Pahana's room. It had to be. The dark kachinas were sending him a message. Where was Pahana? He could not see Pahana in the room, but why else would the dark kachinas show him such a vision? And who was the woman he thought was trying to kill him?

Kel'hoya saw a hand rise from his lap to rub his eyes, but it was not his own hand. This hand had the cream-colored skin of the Outlanders. Why did his skin appear like that of the Outlanders? Had the air of the Fourth World changed his skin color?

Then he saw the fingers. They were short, not long and slender like the fingers of the Bow Clan. This was not his arm at all. It was the arm of an Outlander. He was seeing through an Outlander's eyes.

Pahana's eyes!

He was being shown where Pahana was by being able to see what he saw. This was the way the Bow Clan would track Pahana and kill him. Now if only the darkness would come.

When the nurse finally left, David tried to nap. He was surprised he felt so tired all the time. It was like he hadn't slept in the five weeks he was in the caves. As he fell asleep, he wondered if he still had a job to go back to.

That final thought must have influenced his dream because he saw himself as a new employee standing in front of his boss's desk. Jared Abbott, sales director for Hayden Laboratories, was a balding man in his late forties. Though David hadn't known it when he stood nervously in front of Jared's desk three years ago, his new boss was two months away from a fatal heart attack. David would be the one who watched his boss crumple to the floor as he fumbled with the lock on his office door trying to open it. David would be the one who administered CPR, and he would be the one to feel the man's heart stop just as the paramedics arrived.

But all those things were sixty-two days into the future from this dream. On this particular day, Jared was still in fair health, and he was welcoming David to the company as Hayden Laboratories' newest regional sales representative. David would bring the latest products for cell-culture research to medical-research labs in Utah, Colorado, New Mexico, and Arizona.

Jared recited the usual rhetoric concerning the company workings. David had company-paid medical coverage. He could take vacations whenever he wished because he was working on straight commission rather than salary. He had a sample account from which the cost of client samples would be deducted. If he overspent from the account, the difference would be deducted from his commission check.

His new boss didn't even maintain eye contact with David. Jared just leaned his 275-pound bulk over his desk and read down his prepared list of notes like a computer repeating programmed commands. David wondered how someone with such an impersonal manner could have ever made a life in sales, especially as the leader of salesmen.

David was only listening to Jared's (he insisted on being called Jared, not Mr. Abbott) talk with half an ear. Most of his attention was focused on the bald man's head. Jared's skin was pale and unblemished except for a single brown mole just off center at the top of his head. He hadn't noticed it when Jared had actually been talking to him three years ago. He had been too anxious to start his new job, but now that he was only an observer and not a participant, David had time to study the small details. The mole looked like a little eye staring at David. A thin film of sweat covered the top of Jared's head and reflected the fluorescent light from above. It gave the pale skin on top of Jared's head a slightly luminescent glow.

David tried to readjust his position without having Jared look up at him, but the shine seemed to follow him no matter where he moved. Suddenly, Jared looked up. David thought he had been caught, but his new boss thrust out his hand.

"Welcome to Hayden Labs, son. You've joined a great company," Jared said with only the bare trace of a smile.

Taking hold of Jared's hand was like grabbing a dead fish that had been out of water for two hours. It was clammy and limp, definitely not the handshake of a salesman.

"Thank you, sir," David replied as he let go of Jared's hand. "I'm happy to be here."

David wanted to wipe his hand off on his pants, but Jared was watching.

"Call me Jared, please," his new boss said.

David heard a door open and turned to see who was coming into Jared's office. Instead of seeing someone standing in the doorway to Jared's office, he saw his hospital room.

He opened his eyes and was granted a beautiful sight. Terrie was wearing the polyester uniform that she wore when she worked at the diner. It hugged her hips and showed off her figure. David hated the uniform, but he had to admit it accentuated Terrie's body in a flattering way. Her brown hair was tied in a shoulder-length ponytail. He would have expected to see a smile on her face, but instead, he saw only uncertainty.

"Hello, David."

A soft voice with a hint of sexiness and a lot of charm. He knew he had missed her, but he hadn't known just how much until now.

Terrie came closer, holding her purse in front of her as if for protection. She didn't rush to hug him like David hoped she would do.

Was she mad at him for some reason?

Could she be mad at him for falling into the cave? Even Terrie couldn't hold that against him.

"I won't break you know," he said and held out his arms.

She finally came forward and hugged him. It was a light hug; the type of hug David would have given his grandmother. It was definitely not the kind of hug he expected from a woman who wanted to marry him. He didn't say anything about it. He was just happy to be holding her.

It had been a long time since he had touched anyone. True, the doctors had moved him and prodded him, but they had not touched his skin. Or if they had touched his skin, they had been wearing gloves to protect themselves. David detected the hint of a scented soap on her skin. He touched her cheek and slid his fingers down to her lips.

Terrie pulled away and said, "I'm glad to see you're all right."

"Thanks to you. Dr. Haskell told me you're the one who reported me missing and got the police looking for me."

"When you didn't show up for our date or call to cancel, I knew something must be wrong. I was worried," she explained.

"That's not all you were."

"What do you mean?"

"Terrie, I've been dating you for over a year now. I've learned how you react to different things. You were probably mad at me for not showing up before you ever got worried."

David thought he detected more tenseness in Terrie's voice when she spoke again. "Okay. I was a little bit angry, but what girl wouldn't be when she thinks she's been stood up? Besides, I had something important I wanted to talk to you about." Her voice edged up a notch in volume, and David could tell she was getting frustrated with him. Why did they always seem to get on each other's nerves lately?

"Don't get upset. You've got my attention now. What did you want to talk about?" he said. He held out his hand hoping she would take it. She didn't. He laid his hand on the bed.

Terrie hesitated. "I can't talk about it here. When you get out of the hospital, we'll talk about it." She backed away from the bed and leaned against the window sill. She took a deep breath. "How are you feeling?"

"I'm a little sore, but the doctor says it's amazing how well I came through the whole thing. I think they should release me in a day or two."

"I'm glad you're all right."

"Thank you."

David was puzzled. Something was different. Before the accident, the one thing he and Terrie never had trouble doing was talking, but today their conversation seemed forced and phony. If David hadn't known better, he would have thought he was talking with a total stranger, maybe a volunteer who went from room to room trying to cheer up the patients by impersonating their loved ones. His feeling could have come from Terrie if she felt uneasy about seeing David in the hospital, but he didn't think so. That sort of feeling should have faded after a few minutes, especially when she saw he was in good spirits.

"David," Terrie said, "I have to leave now. They're expecting me at work." Terrie was a waitress at the Blanding Inn.

David wanted to ask her why she hadn't come earlier if she knew she had to go to work, but he decided against it. Besides, he already suspected the answer. This visit was only a formality; something she felt she had to do. To question Terrie about it would only put her on the defensive and make her angry. Of course, he thought he might prefer her anger to the cold shoulder he was getting now.

"I'll see you later," Terrie said.

David waited for her to kiss him goodbye, but the kiss never came. She turned and walked out the door. Seeing her leave as she did, depressed David. He had been looking forward to seeing Terrie since he had awakened. It had been so long since he had seen her. Now that she was gone, he almost wished she had never come.

He remembered the last time he had seen Terrie. It had been the weekend before he had fallen into the cave. He remembered holding her hand as they walked out onto the dance floor of the St. George Hilton during Terrie's sister's, Rose's, wedding reception. Two chandeliers dimly lit the Hilton ballroom. Off to David's left, the band started playing a slow song that David didn't recognize. They weren't very good, but Terrie's sister had liked them, and it was her wedding.

Terrie looked gorgeous in her maid-of-honor dress. It was peach taffeta with a long skirt and off-the-shoulder sleeves. Her hair was pulled up in a bun showing her bare neck. David admired the gentle slope of her neck and her flawless, tan skin. He found it slightly arousing.

She turned to face him. Sliding his free arm around her waist, David pulled Terrie close to him. She laid her head on his shoulder, and they began to turn in time with the music. The sweet scent of Obsession perfume drifted past his nose. He applied the slightest pressure on her lower back, and she responded by moving even closer to him.

That was one of the good memories, but now David was wondering if it hadn't been the last of the good memories. Was he too late to make up with Terrie this time?

Terrie climbed into the BMW on the passenger side. A blond-haired man was sitting behind the steering wheel listening to the Box Tops sing about how a soldier's girlfriend had written him a "Dear John" letter. He turned to Terrie as she sat down, and she leaned over and kissed him. He pulled her closer and held her tightly for a moment before breaking the kiss.

"So how did he take it?" the man asked.

Terrie turned away from him.

"I didn't tell him."

The man slapped his hand against the steering wheel. "What? That was the whole reason you came today."

Terrie nodded quickly. "I know. I know. And I was going to tell him, but when I saw him looking so helpless in the hospital bed, I couldn't do it. I want to let him recover from his accident first before I drop another bombshell on him. He's going to hate me," Terrie said.

"That's wonderful," the man said sarcastically as he crossed his arms over his chest. "So what do we do until then?"

Terrie touched the man's left cheek and turned his face toward hers. "Randy, I love you. You've helped open my heart up more than it ever has been. But just because I love you, doesn't mean I should be cruel to David. After all, he didn't hurt me. True, he was not as attentive as I would have liked, but he was never mean."

Randy kissed her quickly. "Okay. I'll let you handle it your way, but for some reason, I feel like we're going behind his back. I don't like feeling like a scoundrel."

"You're not. As far as I'm concerned, David and I were through over a month ago, and if he had shown up at my apartment instead of falling into that stupid hole, I would have told him." She patted Randy's hand. "Don't worry. I'll talk to him soon. He said he gets out of the hospital next week."

CHAPTER 14

Sarah hurried through the sliding glass doors into Blanding Community Hospital leading Adam. He clutched at his chest and walked with his eyes closed. His breaths were short and stopped abruptly with each inhale. Sarah's brown eyes were wide and darting around the lobby.

She helped her grandfather sit down in one of the hard, orange plastic chairs in the lobby of the emergency room. His head slumped forward onto his chest, and he groaned.

When he was seated, Sarah said, "I'll only be a minute."

He barely nodded, and she ran to the emergency room desk wiping the tears from her eyes.

"Please help us. My grandfather...his chest hurts. We were driving to Salt Lake City, and he suddenly grabbed his chest and yelled," she told the nurse behind the desk. "He's eighty-four-years old. I'm afraid the strain may kill him."

The woman looked over at Adam. "How are you feeling now?" she asked.

"I'm dizzy, and my chest still hurts," Adam said weakly. He started to wobble back and forth in the chair and had to steady himself by grabbing the arm of the woman sitting in the chair next to him.

She looked surprised and then patted his hand. "He tries to do the same things younger men do. He doesn't want to admit he's an old man," Sarah told the nurse.

"I do what I can. If I can walk, I walk. If I can tend a garden, I tend. That's our way," Adam said behind Sarah.

Sarah looked over her shoulder. "But you have to know what you can safely do. You've been pushing yourself too hard lately."

"I have not!" Adam snapped.

The nurse put her hand on Sarah's arm. "Try not to upset him. It may only make things worse. Wait right here. I'll get a doctor," the nurse explained to her.

The nurse disappeared through the emergency room doors and returned a few minutes later leading an older doctor. The doctor ran over to Adam and kneeled down next to him.

"I'm Dr. Brady," the bespectacled man said, "I need to examine you to see how urgent your condition is."

Adam nodded. The doctor put the earpieces of his stethoscope in his ears. The cone end he put under Adam's faded red shirt to listen to the old Indian's heart. The doctor listened for a few seconds and then wrinkled his forehead.

"Your heart sounds strong and regular," the doctor said as he pulled his hand out from under Adam's shirt.

"But he's in pain," Sarah said as she stood behind the doctor. "He screamed in the truck when it began."

The doctor stared at Adam and rubbed his chin. "I can admit him for observation and run some tests on him. Meanwhile, I can put an EKG on him to monitor his heart. I can't really advise any medicine or other treatment for him until I know how severe his problem is."

Sarah nodded frantically. "Yes, please do that. He's the only family I have left. I don't know what I'd do without him," Sarah said. "I don't want him to die."

"Don't worry, miss. We take good care of our patients." Dr. Brady turned to the admitting nurse. "Call an orderly and admit this man," the doctor told her.

The nurse picked up the phone and punched an extension. "I'm admitting a patient, and I need an orderly to take him up to the cardiac wing." When the nurse hung up, she told Sarah, "I'll need you to fill the admission forms."

Sarah nodded and sat down in front of the desk. The nurse opened a metal file drawer and took out some forms and passed them across the desk to Sarah. Sarah picked up a pen off the desk and began answering the questions on the forms. There weren't too many she could answer, particularly the ones about insurance and family medical history. She and her grandfather had no health insurance, and Sarah knew little about her family medical history.

A minute later an orderly came into the waiting area pushing a wheelchair. The nurse snapped a plastic bracelet on Adam's wrist. The young orderly helped Adam into the wheelchair and wheeled him into the hospital. Sarah watched her grandfather disappear and tried to keep from smiling.

Her grandfather was in.

CHAPTER 15

When Kel'hoya opened his eyes, he was immediately cautious. He was the Outlander in the Fourth World. Although he and To'chi lay in the shadows and darkness of the cave, it was still brighter than the brightest chamber in Kuskurza. He had only seen forbidden places this bright in his dreams, and when he looked through the sipapu into the Fourth World, he saw a land of brightness that was beyond his dreams.

Legend said there had been a time when the light in Kuskurza had been as bright as the sun in the Fourth World. It had been an ancient time when the dark kachinas had little power. The light in the Third World had faded much since that time, and the places of light had become the places forbidden by the dark kachinas. Anyone from Kuskurza who tried to venture to the surface was killed by the Bow Clan.

Yet now, the dark kachinas had sent him, a member of the Bow Clan, to a place of light; a place he had been told by the dark kachinas did not exist. He had been sent here, and he would die here. He and To'chi had accepted the conditions of their mission to the Fourth World because they would be serving the dark kachinas. Without the dark kachinas to protect it, Kuskurza would have been destroyed by Taiowa, and all the Bow Clan would have perished in the great flood. It was only the power of the dark kachinas that kept the Third World functioning.

Now Kel'hoya knew that even if he did successfully complete his mission and return to the sipapu, the dark kachinas would kill him and To'chi. They could not be allowed to go back to Kuskurza, where they might tell others of the beauty of the Fourth World. Such a discovery would inspire the Sun Clan even more to find the path to the sipapu and the fact that the Fourth World had been seen by the Bow Clan would cause a destroying dissension among the guardians of the dark kachinas. The knowledge that Kel'hoya and To'chi possessed would destroy the way of life in Kuskurza.

But Kel'hoya wanted to return to Kuskurza. He did not like the cream-colored skin of the Outlanders or their stubby fingers. The bright sunlight hurt his eyes and burned his face. No wonder the Outlanders wore such elaborate body coverings. The only thing he liked about the Outlanders was their women. It aroused Kel'hoya to see such exotic-looking women. They had beautiful dark hair on their heads, and their bodies were more rounded than those of the women of the Third World. The woman he had seen in his vision of David's room was the type of woman seen in the Bow Clan's collective dreams.

72

Kel'hoya sat up and looked at To'chi to assure himself he was not alone. He needed to know this was not a dream from which he would wake. To'chi was still asleep curled into a tight ball. It was the shape that all those who lived in Kuskurza assumed when they slept. It kept the body warmer. His companion's body reflected the small amount of light that made its way into the sipapu, and he glowed like a small sun.

Kel'hoya wondered if To'chi was as awed by the Fourth World and the Outlander women as he was. The women, perhaps, but never the land, Kel'hoya decided. He had never realized how different he was from To'chi until they came to the surface. Though they looked the same and were from the same clan, they were as different from each other as the Bow Clan was different from the Outlanders.

For the first time, Kel'hoya wondered if the dark kachinas controlled the thoughts of the Bow Clan. If the dark kachinas could direct the Bow Clan's attacks against the Sun Clan, might they not control the thoughts of the Bow Clan to suppress any rebellious murmurings among the clansmen and minimize the personality differences between the individual members of the Bow Clan?

Was he nothing but a tool for the dark kachinas like a langher? Were the feelings he felt now his true feelings? Was Kel'hoya the individual a warrior or was the warrior aspect of his personality created by the dark kachinas? Did Kel'hoya the man want to return to Kuskurza or explore the Fourth World?

There was no end to the land. He could spend the rest of his life exploring it. The surface was varied in shape, and there was no ceiling of stone above his head threatening to fall. The Fourth World was so different from Kuskurza. How could To'chi not wonder how such a land could contain the great evil they had been told it held?

Unless To'chi told him, Kel'hoya would not know. He could no longer read To'chi's thoughts. Nor could he read any of the Bow Clan's thoughts.

While he had slept, Kel'hoya had let his mind wander beyond the confines of the sipapu. He did not try to stop himself. He doubted he could have even if he had wanted to stop. He experienced too much pleasure when he was released from the confines of his body. He had been isolated from the minds of his brothers since leaving Kuskurza. He needed to hear their thoughts again and feel as if he were a part of the mighty Bow Clan, a physical manifestation of the dark kachinas. So Kel'hoya's mind had reached out for them, and he had let it. He thought that if he could once again feel the strength of the Bow Clan and speak with the dark kachinas, he might be able to ask for guidance as to how he would complete his mission. Their minds would strengthen his and chase the weakness from him.

But in reaching out for the dark kachinas, Kel'hoya had not found the guidance he sought. Either they had blocked his thoughts from reaching

Kuskurza, or perhaps the earth itself kept his thoughts from reaching below to the Third World as it kept the thoughts of the Outlanders reaching the Bow Clan.

What Kel'hoya had found was Pahana, or Pahana's mind to be more precise. He had seen Pahana's room in the white pueblo from behind Pahana's eyes. What amazed Kel'hoya was that Pahana felt no fear of the Bow Clan although the Bow Clan had nearly killed him in Kuskurza. How could Pahana know the Bow Clan pursued him and wanted to kill him and not be afraid? Was his protection that powerful that it could protect him from death?

Kel'hoya wondered if he could reestablish his contact with Pahana. As long as he could enter Pahana's mind, he would be able to find the enemy of the dark kachinas.

Kel'hoya laid his hand on To'chi's shoulder and shook him awake. To'chi jumped to his feet as if expecting an attack. He would never have slept so soundly in Kuskurza. The Fourth World air was like a drug on their ability to function. It made them sleepy and sluggish in their movements. If they weren't careful, they might sleep and never wake.

"What is it? I heard nothing," To'chi said.

"That's because there was nothing to hear. The sun is retreating. It is time to find Pahana."

To'chi wrinkled his nose at the sound of the name. "Pahana. Not only is he an enemy of the dark kachinas, but his name leaves a sour taste on my tongue. It is nearly as bad as Ma'saw. He would kill the dark kachinas and free the Sun Clan."

"The Sun Clan reveres Pahana's name almost as much as Ma'saw's," Kel'hoya said.

To'chi wrinkled his nose again. "I need something to eat to get this taste out of my mouth."

He picked up the bag of provisions he and Kel'hoya had brought with them from Kuskurza. He reached in and pulled a piece of white fruit from the bag and bit into it.

"The only way to get rid of a sour taste is with something sweet," To'chi said.

Kel'hoya crept closer to the sipapu and looked out. Through the opening, Kel'hoya saw that the ledge fell away steeply a few feet beyond the sipapu. It was a good thing they had brought the pa'tuwvotas with them otherwise there would have been no way to climb down the side of the mountain and find Pahana before the sun rose again.

To'chi came up behind Kel'hoya and looked out at the darkened land outside the cave. "Why doesn't the sun burn the ground in the way a fire would? With such heat, you would think the land would be in flames."

"I don't know, and I don't care," Kel'hoya lied. Actually, he was wondering the same thing, but he was not sure he wanted To'chi to know his thoughts now that he could keep his thoughts to himself.

Kel'hoya looked to his side where To'chi still stared at the landscape. The dark kachinas had reclaimed the surface gradually and chased away the sun. Kel'hoya slipped through the entrance of the sipapu and stood on the narrow ledge above the canyon. He felt a cool breeze blow across his face, and he lifted his chin high. He took a deep breath.

"Tonight, we will kill Pahana," Kel'hoya shouted. "We will watch a legend die."

"What if Pahana has already gathered a force to attack Kuskurza?" To'chi said from inside the sipapu.

Kel'hoya shook his head. "He hasn't. I have seen through his eyes. He still feels the pain we inflicted on him while he was in our land and continually lays down. He isn't ready to attack us yet."

Kel'hoya did not add that though Pahana felt the pain, he showed no fear of the Bow Clan. That fact disturbed Kel'hoya more than knowing he would die before seeing Kuskurza again. For a man to show no fear and yet know he was being hunted, the man was either a fool or a powerful man. Kel'hoya knew from the short time Pahana was in Kuskurza that the Outlander was no fool, which left only a choice Kel'hoya hoped was not true.

Kel'hoya reached inside the sipapu and pulled out his pa'tuwvota. It was a saucer, the size of a shield, made of the hide of the tangjar, a feathered serpent. He set it on the ledge and then sat cross-legged on top of it. He closed his eyes and concentrated. The pa'tuwvota rose from the ledge and moved away from the side of the mountain.

Kel'hoya opened his eyes. "Come, To'chi," he ordered.

As he spoke, the pa'tuwvota dropped from beneath him. He panicked for only a moment before he closed his eyes and stabilized the saucer. He would have to be more careful. Controlling a pa'tuwvota in the Fourth World required more concentration than he was used to needing.

To'chi put a second pa'tuwvota on the ledge and sat on it. After a moment, he hovered next to Kel'hoya.

"Which way do we go to reach Pahana?" To'chi asked.

"Follow me," Kel'hoya told him. He pictured the white pueblo in his mind and commanded the pa'tuwvota to fly in the direction of his thoughts.

He could traverse Kuskurza from one end to the other in fifteen minutes. That was how quick the pa'tuwvota moved, but the trip to the white pueblo took half an hour. They traveled more than twice the length of Kuskurza and still there was still no end to Tu'waqachi in sight.

Kel'hoya commanded the pa'tuwvota to hover outside Pahana's window. Through the window, he could see Pahana sleeping. This mission would be easy to complete. Maybe a successful mission would convince the dark kachinas of their worth. Perhaps the dark kachinas would even allow Kel´hoya and To´chi to return to Kuskurza.

The path seemed to be open to fly into Pahana's room, but when Kel´hoya held out his hand, he touched an invisible wall. Part of Pahana's protection undoubtedly. However, while part of the window was covered with a hard wall that would be difficult to penetrate, another part of the opening was covered with a mesh that was easily opened.

Kel´hoya smiled. The dark kachinas were with them.

Kel´hoya pressed on the screen with his long fingers until he had poked five holes in the screen. He pulled hard on the screen and ripped a large hole in it.

Kel´hoya motioned to To´chi. "Hold onto my pa´tuwvota. Don't let it fall while I am in the room."

To´chi nodded his understanding. He grabbed onto the edge of Kel´hoya's pa´tuwvota with one hand. Kel´hoya stood up on the shield and stepped onto the ledge in front of the invisible wall. As his body lost contact with the pa´tuwvota, it fell, but To´chi held onto it and pulled it onto his lap.

Kel´hoya crawled into the room through the hole. It was bright inside the room, brighter than the night outside. Pahana was using light to protect himself from the dark kachinas. Though Kel´hoya would have preferred to work in the darkness, he was not a dark kachina. He could function in the light. He squinted and started toward the bed where David lay sleeping.

It was time to complete his mission.

CHAPTER 16

The nurse took Adam's dinner tray off the rolling countertop. The young woman had dark skin and black hair, and Adam wondered if she were a Navajo girl.

"Well, it looks like you ate everything but the plastic plates," the nurse said. "If you weren't sick before, you probably will be now."

The nurse laughed at her own joke. Adam wondered what the young woman found so humorous. He thought the food tasted quite good. Not as good as Connie's, of course, but it was certainly better than Sarah's meals. Unfortunately, Sarah had not inherited her grandmother's ability to cook delicious foods. Hers usually wound up tasting dry or bland.

"I'm feeling tired. May I go to sleep now?" Adam asked.

The young woman turned from her cart full of dirty, plastic dinner dishes. Adam got a good look at her face. Definitely a Navajo. She seemed nice enough, though. Adam wouldn't hold her heritage against her.

"If you can go to sleep, sure."

"No, I mean if I go to sleep, another nurse isn't going to come in and wake me up to give me medication or take my temperature, is she?"

The nurse walked to the foot of the bed and looked at the chart that hung there. She flipped through the sheets on the clipboard and read the notations written on the sheets.

When she finished, she hung the board back on the bed, and said, "It doesn't look like you're scheduled for any medication, just observation. So I don't think anyone will be coming in tonight. You can get a good night's sleep."

Adam smiled. "Thank you." That was just what he wanted to hear.

He laid back and fell asleep. It was only a short nap. That seemed to be all he could take nowadays. Even when he was exhausted from a full day of working hard in the fields at harvest time, he slept only three hours at most. This nap had been even shorter than that.

When he awoke, it was dark outside. He figured it was late enough that there wouldn't be many people in the halls. The fewer people who saw him, the fewer there were who might stop him.

He climbed out of bed holding his gown closed behind him. He hadn't wanted to put it on, but the nurse had told him it was hospital policy. Adam had given in because he didn't want to attract too much attention to himself. Talking to David Purcell was more important than his modesty. He wished he had something to cover himself with so his butt wasn't exposed to the wind, though.

Adam opened his door so that a small gap of light showed in the room. Because his line of sight was not the best, he could only see a short distance down the hallway and nothing in the opposite direction. He didn't see anyone so he would have to take the chance.

Opening the door wider, Adam stepped into the hallway. David Purcell was on the same floor, but Adam would have to walk to the other end of the hall to get to David's room. A pair of nurses talked at the nurses' station to his left, but he was going to the right and wouldn't have to pass them. If they didn't look in his direction, he would be able to go by unnoticed.

He found room 203 easily enough. Adam considered knocking on the door, but it would only attract undo attention. Better to walk right in and start talking quickly and hope David Purcell would listen to him and not call the nurse, at least not before Adam finished speaking.

Adam pushed open the door and froze. A pale, white-skinned man was standing next to David's bed choking him. David struggled, but the Bow Clansman had his hands wrapped tightly around David's neck. The insight Adam's vision had given him came back: If the Bow Clan killed David Purcell, the Fourth World would be destroyed.

Adam reacted quickly. Grabbing the chair next to the door, he pushed it across the tiled floor. It slid easily enough and struck the Bow Clansman in the legs, behind the knees. The man staggered, but didn't fall. However, his grip faltered, and David rolled to the side. Before the Bow Clansman could regain his grip, David punched him in the mouth. The man stumbled backward holding a split lip.

"Taiowa, rid us of this evil," Adam prayed loudly.

At the sound of the Creator's name, the Bow Clansman stopped. He bared his teeth at Adam and then turned to look at David again. Instead of charging, he crawled through the window onto the ledge.

That was when Adam noticed the other Bow Clansman floating on a saucer outside the window. The clansman who had attacked David climbed onto another saucer, and the two pale-skinned men flew off into the night.

Adam hurried to the window to watch them go. It was hard to believe that people such as these had given birth to the Hopi. When the Bow Clansmen had disappeared in the darkness, he mumbled to himself, "Pa´tuwvotas."

He turned back to face David Purcell. The man who Adam had seen in Kuskurza was sitting up rubbing his throat.

"Thank you. He caught me while I was asleep." David paused. "Was his skin really as white as I thought it was or was that just the sleep affecting my senses?"

Adam shook his head. "No, his skin was white."

David stared at Adam. "You're that Indian who was in here this morning."

Adam nodded. "I came back because we need to talk."

"I told you this morning. I don't know what you're talking about. I can't remember anything that happened in the cave."

Adam moved closer to the bed. "You're right. You know, but you can't remember. I'm sure of it now. If you will talk with me, I can help you. I can explain who those men were." He waved his hand toward the window.

David stared out the window.

A nurse opened the door. She glanced from David to Adam and started to back out of the room. "Excuse me. I thought I heard a noise and wondered if you had fallen," she said.

David smiled. "I guess you thought I was like that old woman in those commercials for the personal emergency call boxes; the one who says, 'Help me, I've fallen and I can't get up.'" The nurse laughed. "I'm fine as you can see, but thank you for being concerned."

The young nurse blushed and looked at Adam. "Is this your room, sir?"

David answered before Adam could say anything. "He's a friend of mine who was admitted to the hospital this afternoon. When he found out I was here too, he came down to see me." Adam nodded his agreement.

"Okay, but don't stay here long, sir. I'm sure you both need rest." The nurse turned and left the room leaving Adam and David alone.

David turned to Adam. "Okay. Pull up a chair. Let's talk."

CHAPTER 17

David swung his legs over the side of the bed so that he could look at the old Indian without straining his still-stiff neck. He had a feeling he wasn't going to like what Adam had to tell him. Sitting up uncovered David's legs, and he pulled the blanket over them because, for some reason, he felt embarrassed having Adam see his naked legs. The Indian couldn't ever see him more exposed than when that...that man had tried to strangle him.

What was happening to him? What had he gotten himself into?

If only he could remember what had happened to him during the forgotten five weeks in the cave, then he wouldn't feel quite so defenseless. He hoped that this Hopi he had never met might somehow be able to fill in the blank spots in his memory.

Adam repositioned the orange plastic chair near the window so that when he sat down in it, his back wouldn't be toward the window. David wondered if Adam thought the pale men would return again.

Adam stared at David with a poker face that a Las Vegas dealer couldn't have read. He didn't look nervous, but David knew he would have been as jumpy as a cat in a roomful of rockers if he had even been sitting near the window. What if those pale-skinned men decided to make a second attack? The one who had attacked David had been very strong, and neither David or Adam was in the best of shape right now.

"Obviously you know something about what just happened to me. You probably know more than I do coming in here in time to save me from whoever or whatever tried to choke me. That was more than I could do." David rubbed his throat. The skin was tender, but at least his throat seemed undamaged. It was painful to touch, but he felt sure it would be even worse tomorrow. "That guy looked like the type of alien you might see on *Star Trek*. I've never seen anything like him before."

"He's a person," Adam said.

"But his skin was that pale-white color like a piece of paper or a bed sheet." David grabbed a handful of the bed sheet and shook it. "People don't have skin that white, not even albinos."

"Your skin is white."

"Not that white."

"Your skin is cream colored, then. Mine is red. Others have yellow skin or brown. Because my skin is not the color of your skin, does that make me something other than a person?"

David sighed. That last thing he felt like was being lectured to by an In-

80

dian who wanted to wax philosophical. He wanted to know why he had been attacked and who had attacked him.

"Cream, red, brown, and yellow are skins tones that are expected. The world has been explored, and no one has ever reported a race of people with white skin. Albinos are still an oddity in the world."

Adam nodded. "He is not of this world. He is as my people once were and maybe your people, too. He's one of the Bow Clan," Adam explained.

Adam seemed to expect the title "Bow Clan" to evoke some sort of response from David, but David had never heard of the Bow Clan before. The words meant nothing to him.

"Does he have something to do with my being lost in the caverns?" David asked.

Adam considered his response, and David began to doubt. He wondered if the Indian knew what was going on or if he was making up things as he went along.

But Adam hadn't made up those pale-skinned men, had he? And Adam hadn't invented those floating saucers they had flown away on either. Those saucers were another good reason that David thought those men had been aliens. No technology like that existed on earth.

Adam finally answered. "He and his people live underground. For some reason, he feels that killing you is important enough to him and his companion to come to Tu'waqachi."

"Tu'waqachi?"

"It's a Hopi word. It means the Fourth World."

David hoped Adam didn't use many Hopi words. He had barely passed English a couple of semesters in high school, and that was his native language. How well could he be expected to understand Hopi?

"The Hopi believe this is not the first world in which we have lived. There have been three others. Tokpela was the First World. It is where life was created by Taiowa the Creator, and his nephew, So'tuknang. Men and animals lived in peace together in Tokpela. They could communicate with each other without speaking. It was a perfect world."

"It sounds like the Garden of Eden," David commented. In fact, Taiowa and So'tuknang reminded him of God and Jesus Christ. David wondered if the Hopi were Christians without even knowing it.

Adam shrugged. "I haven't heard of that place."

"It is part of Christian religion."

"It's not surprising they are similar then. Truth may be disguised, but it is always recognized no matter what disguise is used.

"The First World became evil when Mochni, the bird, talked to the people and the animals about the differences between them. The people gradually grew away from each other and from the animals. Then came Ka'to'ya, the snake with the big head. He also talked and created an even greater division between men and animals."

David thought Ka´to´ya sounded an awful lot like the serpent who had beguiled Eve in the Garden of Eden. Maybe Adam was right about truth taking on many disguises. David wondered if anyone had ever tried to compare the Hopi beliefs to Christian beliefs.

Adam continued talking, "However, there were still those who tried to follow the teachings of Taiowa and So´tuknang. These people followed their ko´pavis through a sipapu..."

"An emergence hole," David blurted out happy to have recognized a word. Saying it caused him only a twinge of pain this time.

Adam nodded and smiled. "Yes, they left the First World by going through an emergence hole into Tokpa, the Second World. Because the Fire Clan had been the leaders of the troublemakers in the First World, So´tuknang destroyed Tokpela by fire.

"Tokpa was also a beautiful world, but So´tuknang kept animals and man apart in this world. Men prospered and began to barter and trade for things. This created greed and pride among the people, and again, they drew away from the teachings of Taiowa. Not all the people were evil. The good were led through another sipapu to the Third World, Kuskurza, and the Second World was destroyed by earthquakes and an ice age.

"In Kuskurza, the people again prospered until they began to forget Taiowa's teachings as they had done before. The Bow Clan, in particular, became greedy and war-like, which was not the way of our people. We are a peaceful people. This has always been and will always be. Instead of following the teachings of Taiowa, the Bow Clan heeded the talk of a group of the dark kachinas."

David interrupted once more. He felt like a small child who kept interrupting his father during a bedtime story. "What are kachinas? Another Hopi word?"

Adam nodded. "They are spirits. Each kachina performs a special duty for our people. One brings rain, one makes a woman fertile, and one causes the corn to grow. There are over 250 different kachinas, and they are all more or less good. However, the kachinas the Bow Clan chose to follow were evil. Before Taiowa and So´tuknang destroyed Kuskurza, they imprisoned the dark kachinas in a large mountain of stone. They gave a powerful man named Ma´saw the duty of guarding the dark kachinas and keeping them imprisoned in the stone mountain."

A mountain of stone. A pyramid! Just like he had seen in his dreams. But that pyramid had exploded. What did that mean? Had Ma´saw failed in his duty? Had the dark kachinas escaped?

"Why didn't Taiowa just destroy the kachinas instead of the whole world?" David asked.

"Spirits cannot be killed. Only with the aid of the bright light in Kuskurza were Taiowa and So'tuknang able to imprison the dark kachinas. The bright light subdues them and makes them hide within the darkness of the stone mountains.

"The people who continued to believe in Taiowa were once again led by So'tuknang through a sipapu into this world, and Kuskurza was destroyed by a great flood.

"For many centuries, my people have believed that all of Kuskurza was destroyed by a flood. I now know this is not so. I've seen the truth in visions I've had in the sacred kiva. Most of Kuskurza was destroyed, but the flood waters did not entirely cover Kuskurza. The top of the stone mountain remained dry. A handful of Bow Clansmen were able to find safety there until the waters receded enough for them to begin rebuilding their world."

"Why wasn't the world totally flooded?"

"I don't know. Either Taiowa did not want to risk extinguishing the bright light and destroying the stone mountain, or the dark kachinas had enough power to save themselves and their followers from the flood."

Recalling the exploding mountain of rock, David said, "There's a problem down there now, isn't there? The light that's keeping the dark kachinas imprisoned is fading, and when it dims enough, the dark kachinas will be able to escape their prisons."

Adam nodded. "That's what I have seen in my visions."

"It's what I have dreamed." David paused. "What would happen if the dark kachinas were freed?"

"This world would be lost, and my people do not believe there would be another to replace it. For the Bow Clan to fear you enough to try and kill you at a time when the dark kachinas are continually growing stronger, means you must threaten them somehow," Adam explained.

"You said the white guy who attacked me was one of the Bow Clan. Is he still living in that little portion of Kuskurza that wasn't flooded?" David wanted to know.

Adam nodded. "The Bow Clan serves the dark kachinas. They act as the eyes, ears, voice, and hands of the dark kachinas. However, I've seen others who fight the Bow Clan. They look like the Bow Clan, but they are not evil."

"The Sun Clan," David said without pause.

Adam stared amazed at David, his poker face dissolved. David suddenly realized what he had said and that there was more to say.

"They are called the Sun Clan because they still follow the teachings of Taiowa. They want to live in the Fourth World in the sun," he added.

Adam nodded numbly.

David was overjoyed that he had remembered something. After all the energy he had expended trying to remember, he had recalled something without trying at all. Was that the key? Would he not remember unless he allowed to it come naturally?

Adam said, "My clan is also the Sun Clan. It is my clan's duty to guard the true sipapu we know of and keep it sealed."

"Then you should feel a kinship with those people in Kuskurza."

Adam nodded slowly.

"Can you help me remember everything that happened?" David asked.

Adam shook his head. "I don't know why you have forgotten your memories to know how to make you remember them. As you recall bits and pieces, I may be able to interpret them for you. Together, we can understand what is happening in Kuskurza and how you are connected to it," Adam offered.

David felt no immediate danger from the Bow Clan. They might attack again but not tonight. There was another danger, though, and he was not sure how much time remained to prevent this one. If the dark kachinas escaped from the stone mountain, the world, his world, would be destroyed. David knew it was going to happen if something didn't change to stop it.

Adam had said David had somehow threatened the Bow Clan and the dark kachinas. If that was so, didn't he have a responsibility to try and stop the dark kachinas from escaping if he could? After all, it was his world the dark kachinas would destroy if they escaped. If he could ever remember how to do it, he had to stop the Bow Clan.

CHAPTER 18

When he woke up in the morning, David wondered if he had dreamed everything that had happened the previous night. Maybe the pale men and the old Indian had all been a part of another one of the weird dreams he had been having lately. Then he saw the torn screen in his window and knew everything had really happened.

He decided it was time for him to get out of bed before he got bedsores. Holding onto the side rail to keep from falling, he swung his legs over the side of the bed and slowly stood up. David thought he could feel himself swaying when he stood still. When he finally stopped rocking, he felt like he was standing on stilts and the unsteady sensation that went with it. This was the first time he had been on his feet for at least two days, but judging by how unstable he felt, it could just as easily have been two months.

Feeling like a feeble old man, he slowly shuffled to the closet and took out the clothes his mother had brought him. A pair of blue jeans and a Brigham Young University T-shirt hung on a pair of hangers.

Halfway across the room, he stopped. His legs ached. Sharp pains pinched his thighs and calves. He fell to his knees, which only caused him more pain as he hit the floor, but he managed to keep from falling on his face by putting out his hands to catch himself.

What was wrong with his legs? Why couldn't he walk like a normal person? Had he hurt his legs in his fall into the cave?

David crawled to the bed and used it to support his weight as he struggled to his feet. Sitting down on the edge of his bed, he tried to keep himself from shaking.

He slammed his hand onto the bed. If he could only remember what had happened to him, he might know what other surprises to expect from the Bow Clan. What else would happen to him? Would he go blind while he was driving and send his car off the road and into a building or telephone pole? Would his arms fail to move the next time he was attacked by one of the Bow Clan? David didn't like the unexpected especially when it came from his own body. He had enough things to worry about now without wondering if his body would work when he needed it to.

He dressed, happy that nothing more happened to him. When he finished, he stared at the torn window screen through the closed window. It was the only testament that he hadn't dreamed everything that had happened last night. The Bow Clan had been real, and they had tried to attack him. Adam wasn't around to reassure David, and thankfully, the Bow Clan wasn't around to attack him.

Someone from another world wanted to kill him, and he didn't know why.

"Davey, you look so much better."

David turned from the window and saw his mother walking into the room. For a second, David thought she might be alone. Then she was through the door and moving off to the side toward him. David had a moment to see his father dressed in a short-sleeved, white shirt and blue tie before his mother filled his vision.

Marcy hugged her son tightly. "You look so thin. I could get you back up to a decent weight if you would come home and let me feed you. I could even find a place that sells gyro meat if you want."

David sighed. Now she was trying to tempt him with his favorite foods. He had been through this same conversation with her yesterday. Why couldn't she just let him grow up?

"Marcy, let the boy be. You can't baby him anymore. He's a man, now," Lewis said, echoing David's thoughts. He had opened the small overnight bag he had carried into the room and was filling it with the few things David had accumulated during his stay in the hospital.

Marcy turned to face her husband. "I know he's a man. But he's also very sick. He's just spent two days in the hospital. He needs someone to help him until he feels like himself again. He needs his mother," Marcy argued.

"But Mom! I can take care of myself," David insisted.

Marcy put her hands on her hips. "Oh, really?"

"Yes, I'll manage. I've been on my own for eight years now," David said, avoiding his mother's stare.

"Marcy, leave him alone. He's over twenty-one. He can make his own decisions," Lewis said as he zipped the overnight bag shut. David was glad that at least his father seemed to understand him.

Marcy swung her arms around the hospital room. "Look where his decisions have gotten him so far."

"I didn't decide to fall into that cavern, Mom," David said in his own defense.

"Maybe not, but you bought that fancy car, instead of a dependable one. If you had bought a good car, it wouldn't have broken down out there."

David could have pointed out the fault in his mother's logic, but it would only have made her even madder. He could have said if he hadn't had to visit Brigham Young University's College of Science to make a presentation he wouldn't have been on Highway 191 when his car broke down. If he hadn't taken the job with Hayden Laboratories, he wouldn't have had to go to BYU. If, if, if, if. The unique combination of a thousand variables had caused him to fall into the cave.

Or maybe it was just unavoidable fate.

Was doing something about Kuskurza also unavoidable fate?

David turned back to the window. The sun looked higher. It felt good to squint while he looked into the sun. It told him that his eyes were sensitive to bright light once again. He tried to imagine what the world would look like without the sun. Was that how Kuskurza looked? Was that the world he had been in for five weeks?

He still hadn't made any decisions as to what to do. He had tossed around his options in his mind last night because he hadn't been able to go back to sleep after Adam left. He wanted to think about it a little more and maybe do some research into the Hopi legends. It might jog his memory some more like Adam's story had helped him remember the name of the Sun Clan.

He was glad that he was getting out of the hospital, though. Being cooped up in a room made him feel like a sitting duck for the Bow Clan. Now maybe that he was going home his life would become normal again.

You're kidding yourself, and you know it.

He still had two loose ends to tie up. One was to find out what had happened to him for the five weeks in the cave. David had to know. He would never be comfortable having a blank spot in his life. He was so desperate, he had even considered going to a hypnotist. Then he remembered that not trying to remember seemed the best way for him to remember. Any other way gave him a splitting headache.

The second loose end he had to tie up was what do about what Adam had told him about Kuskurza. Was he really so important to the dark kachinas that they wanted him dead? He didn't like feeling that the Sun Clan was counting on his help when he couldn't even remember them. He might not do what they wanted him to do if he couldn't remember in time. That was why he needed to remember. He felt it was important if the dark kachinas were to be stopped.

David jumped as a nurse pushed the door open to roll in the wheelchair to take him down to his parents' car. His mother gave him a strange look but said nothing.

She stood on his left side as his father on his right to help him into the wheelchair. If he swayed in the slightest, he felt his parents' hands on his arms or back supporting him. David settled into the wheelchair with a sigh.

It was time to face the world again. Both of them.

CHAPTER 19

When Kel'hoya saw the Outlanders in front of him, he knew he was having another vision. Even so, there was a moment he wanted to reach forward and strangle the two Outlanders. They sat in front of him and all of them seemed to be enclosed within invisible walls. The Outlanders' backs were toward him, and they were talking between themselves, but he could not understand their words. If he had indeed been seated behind the Outlanders, they wouldn't have turned their backs to him. They would not have trusted him to do nothing.

Kel'hoya suddenly felt Pahana stiffen and at the same time sink lower in his seat. Pahana was afraid! But of what?

Kel'hoya could see through Pahana's eyes, but he didn't see what caused the Outlander's terror. If the Bow Clan didn't cause Pahana fear, then Kel'hoya wanted to know what did make him afraid. He might be able to use it to the Bow Clan's advantage.

He could see nothing. The land sped by the vehicle too quickly. It moved much faster than a pa'tuvwota. If the Bow Clan had such a vehicle in Kuskurza, they could obliterate the Sun Clan. Pahana stared out over the bright land. He saw some vehicles off to the side of the road. They were positioned around what looked like a sipapu. If that were so, then Pahana wouldn't be afraid, but Kel'hoya would. If the Outlanders had found the same sipapu Pahana had, then Kel'hoya's mission was a failure. He had failed the dark kachinas, and he deserved to die.

The vehicle passed the open hole, and the fear faded from Pahana's mind. It had been the sipapu that he was afraid of. This was useful. Kel'hoya did not know how he would use it, but he knew he would.

As Lewis Purcell drove his Cavalier along Highway 191 on the way back to Monticello, Marcy chattered incessantly about how nice Provo was this summer and how David should reconsider coming home for a few weeks. He would enjoy it; she knew he would.

David sat quietly in the back seat. His eyes were closed, and his head was leaning back against the seat. Despite not wanting to close his eyes, it was the only way to clearly review the past three days of his life.

How could he begin to remember what had happened to him before that, though?

If he had lost his keys, he would try to retrace his movements until he found where he had left the keys. Could he do the same thing with time? If he replayed the past five weeks in his mind, would he naturally slip past his amnesia and remember everything?

The first thing David remembered after the missing five weeks was waking up in the hospital. Before that, he had obviously been brought to the hospital, probably by an ambulance.

And before that?

He couldn't remember anything. There were only scattered memories that could just have easily been dreams. It was like continually running into a brick wall that had bricks missing. He could see small pieces of the world beyond the wall, but he couldn't get over the wall. So he kept running into it. He wasn't hurting anyone but himself.

David had been rescued from the cave. Had he been conscious when the search-and-rescue team found him? Had he said anything? Had anyone in the search-and-rescue team seen anything?

Talking to the person who had found him would be his first step in remembering. And – he shuddered at the thought – he would have to go back to the cave. It might stir up some memories of what had happened to him. He wouldn't go alone, this time, and he would take a powerful flashlight with him to keep the darkness at bay.

David opened his eyes. His mother was staring at him.

"You know you should have told us you couldn't remember the awful time you had, Davey," his mother said from the front seat.

He hadn't meant to tell her at all. She had read about his amnesia in the newspaper yesterday.

Through the gap between the front seats, David watched the highway approach and disappear beneath the car. In another twenty miles or so, his father would turn the car onto the Center Street exit and drive into Monticello.

David looked forward to walking into the small two-bedroom apartment he rented on the west side of town. Only then, when he could touch his furniture and sleep in his own bed, would he know that at least part of his nightmare was over. He was finally going home after having been away more than a month.

"What good would it have done if I had told you, Mom?" David asked.

"It would have eased my mind."

Lewis stifled a laugh. Marcy heard him and hit him on the arm. The car swerved slightly to the left as Lewis jerked away from his wife's punch.

"Well, it would have," she said.

"What you don't know won't hurt you, Marcy," Lewis replied.

What you don't know won't hurt you. The old saying repeated itself in David's head like an echo. What you don't know. What you can't see you don't know. Does that mean the dark can't hurt me? But why would the dark want to hurt me?

His head suddenly throbbed painfully, and he rubbed his temples.

"Dad's right," he said. "The fact that you didn't know I had amnesia at first eased your mind. I didn't see any reason to tell you because Dr. Haskell told me it was probably only a temporary condition. If he had been wrong for some reason, I would have told you."

"You still should have told me," Marcy grumbled but not as forcefully. She knew she was wrong. David had won an argument with his mother, and he savored the rare moment.

The mountain foothills were closer now. They were close enough so that David could see the brown grass that covered the slopes. Occasionally, the grass would part and make way for a clump of brown brush. But there was not much more than that on the mountains.

"Dad, remember when you mentioned the Boy Scout caving trip in the hospital?" David asked.

"I'm sorry I brought that up, son. Your mother was right. It was not an appropriate topic at the time."

"Well, I think it is now. How long was I lost in the cave?" David asked.

Lewis cast a sidelong glance at his wife, but she was looking at David. Lewis thought for a moment. "About two hours. We noticed you were missing within a few minutes after you got separated from the troop, but you must have gotten disoriented and wandered deeper into the cave."

It seemed to David that he never sat still long enough in any cave for someone to find him easily.

"Was there anything odd about me when you found me?" David asked.

Lewis shook his head. "You were crying, but as soon as I got to you, you started wiping your tears away so that none of the other boys would see that you had been crying. You made me promise not to tell anyone that I found you crying."

"There's no shame in crying, Davey," his mother said. "You were scared. Anyone would have been."

"Did I say anything weird?" David asked his father.

"Well, you were muttering something over and over. It didn't make any sense, though," Lewis recalled.

David leaned forward in the seat so that he was looking over his father's shoulder. "What was I saying?"

"Something like 'For low the path to the fourth world' or 'Follow the path to the fort word.' Neither one makes much sense."

David sat back. *Fourth World. Follow the path to the Fourth World.* Now that his father had reminded him, David was sure that was what he had been saying. Especially considering what he had learned the last few days. His father was wrong about one thing, though. It did make sense if you knew Hopi creation stories.

And it made even more sense if you had seen a dying member of the Sun Clan when you were twelve years old. In a flash of insight, David remembered why he had wandered off in the cave. He had heard a sound like thunder, and he was curious as to what had caused the sound. So he had gone to investigate. Instead of some odd phenomena, he found a pale-skinned man. The man's skin was so white, it had seemed to glow in the light from David's flashlight. The man was wearing a yellow tunic with black trim, and in the center of it was a gaping hole in the man's chest.

Come closer. The voice startled David because it had been spoken inside his head, and it wasn't his own voice.

David moved closer and stared at the man. The man's fingers waved David toward him.

"What happened to you? I should go get my father," David said.

The man reached out laid his hand over David's. The man patted his hand in the same way his mother did when she talked to him sometimes.

No. It is too late. I have failed, but I came close. You are from the Fourth World, aren't you? Ma'saw was right. The Bow Clansmen are fools. The dark kachinas are wrong. If only I could return to Kuskurza and tell them how to follow the path to the Fourth World.

The man coughed, and his body shook violently. His eyes rolled back in his head, and he grabbed at his chest with his free hand. The hand that was covering David's tightened in a vise-like grip, then the man lay still. When David saw a dead man's hand was holding his, he shook his hand free and ran away. He had never seen a dead man before, especially one who had been so horribly wounded. That must have been why his twelve-year-old mind blocked the memory. He hadn't wanted to remember the horror.

Even now he felt there was more to remember, but he had run into the wall again. He couldn't finish the memory.

"Davey, why did you want to hear about all that again?" Marcy asked looking over the top of her seat.

David shrugged. What would his mom say if he told her that he had watched a man die in the cave, a man who hadn't even been from this world? She would probably think he had brain damage from his fall into the cavern. He could see his mother forcing his father to turn the car around to drive back to Blanding Community Hospital so that she could make the hospital give him a CAT scan.

He said, "You know how they say, 'History repeats itself.' I think it's interesting that I've been lost in a cave twice. What are the odds of that happening? If I'm smart, I'll stay away from caves from now on." Even as he said it, he knew David would have to go back to the cave at least once more if he wanted to find out the truth.

"Well, I would hope so."

His mother turned and faced forward again.

A cold lump formed in the small of David's back. He looked at his parents. They had fallen into talking about the drought that western farmers were having to deal with this year. They weren't cold at all. No chills. No white-vapor breath spewing from their mouths as they talked.

David looked out the car window and saw only the hills. But he knew it was something outside that was causing the chill. Then he saw a car and a Jeep parked along the side of the road next to a large RV. He didn't see the drivers anywhere around. They were probably in the RV keeping out of the sun.

There was something familiar about the area. He had seen it before, but without the truck and the RV. If it were deserted, it would look like...

Where he fell into the cave!

"This is it," David whispered.

Marcy looked over her shoulder and saw her son's pale face and wide eyes.

"Davey, are you all right?" she asked.

David nodded slowly. "This is where I fell into the cave, isn't it?" he asked.

"Yes. The state wants to map out the interior since they own the land. They'll probably turn it into a state park and sell tickets to people who want to tour it."

David shuddered and lay back against the seat. He couldn't imagine anybody paying to go down into the darkness of the cave. It was probably the same impulse that drove people to parachute out of airplanes or stay in a nuclear submarine for three-month stretches.

The cold lump eventually melted and released its grip on David's spine once he had passed the small camp, but he watched the area out the back window until he couldn't see it any longer.

He sighed as he turned forward. Settling into the seat, he saw he wasn't looking at the back of his parents' head. He was staring at the back of a pale-skinned Bow Clansman. He knew the man was a Bow Clansman because he wore a black tunic with red trim. All Bow Clansmen wore the same colored tunic. It was a symbol of the power of the dark kachinas just as the yellow-and-red tunic of the Sun Clan symbolized the power of the sun. The man was staring out of a cave shielding his face against the bright morning light.

How could David be seeing this? He was sitting in his father's Cavalier driving towards Monticello, not in a cave.

Adam had spoken of visions. Was this some sort of psychic vision? David almost laughed until he realized it wasn't very funny. Was he actually seeing through someone else's eyes?

Whose?

He could only see one of the Bow Clansmen, but there had been two Bow Clansmen last night. Was he seeing through the eyes of one of the Bow Clansmen? The thought chilled his spine again.

What would Adam think about this vision?

David didn't really believe it was a vision. If he could read people's minds, wouldn't he know how to handle Terrie better?

Then David remembered how when he was younger, and his mother had misplaced a gold bracelet with intricate carvings. He had been the one who knew where the bracelet was. He had seen the bracelet in his mind even if he couldn't actually see the jewelry with his eyes. There had been other times like that, too. He had known the exact grades his friends got on their tests before the teachers had handed them back. Once he had known lightning was going to strike a tree by Utah Lake. Dozens of little things he hadn't associated with psychic experiences until now suddenly seemed connected.

But they had all been a long time ago. Nothing like that had happened since he was twelve. Since he was lost in the cave as a Boy Scout. David also remembered how he had seen the pale-skinned man sleeping in the cave before the Bow Clan had attacked him. At the time, he had thought it was part of his dream, now he knew differently. David had started having psychic visions again after he was rescued from a cave the second time.

David didn't like coincidences. Loose threads were tying themselves together around him, but they were in a knot he couldn't unravel. He didn't seem to be in control of his life.

Why hadn't he had any psychic visions in the time between the two instances he was lost in the caves?

Why had he had them at all?

CHAPTER 20

David's legs tingled as if they had been asleep, but rather than fade, the tingling became an ache. He climbed the stairs to his apartment lifting each leg as if he were trying to balance an egg on the top of his foot, then set his foot down on the next step and gradually shifted his weight onto it. The pain wasn't so great when his legs slowly took on his weight. He also had to make sure his legs would support his weight. If his mother saw him fall, David would never be able to get his parents to leave.

He couldn't have them around when the Bow Clan came back for him.

His pulse quickened as he slipped his key into the lock and turned the doorknob. His giddy feeling was his excitement to be out of the hospital. He swung open the door and wanted to run across the floor. He probably would have wound up lying on his back listening to his mother scold him if he had tried it.

"Davey, I could take care of you here at your apartment," Marcy Purcell offered as she watched David walk across the floor.

David stopped walking and closed his eyes. There must be a gene in a mother's chromosomes that made her worry about her children. He drew in a deep breath and let it out slowly. Time to say "no" for the one-hundred-and-first time.

"Then who would take care of Dad, Mom? You know he can't live without you." David turned to his father and winked. Lewis smiled and settled into the armchair on the far side of the living room.

Marcy wasn't amused. "Your father can take care of himself. You can't," she snapped.

"I don't know, Marcy. Who would tell me to take out the garbage or to get ready for church or to take the car in to get the oil changed or to bring in the groceries?" Lewis said.

David laughed, which only made his mother madder.

"Keep that up, and we'll see what else I'll be telling you when we get home," Marcy warned her husband.

"I already told you that I would manage fine by myself, Mom," David said.

He moved over to the couch and sat down. As long as he was sitting, he wouldn't have to worry about falling on his butt.

Marcy walked into the kitchen, which was no bigger than the master closet in her house in Provo. As it was, she barely had room to turn around in it. She opened the door to the refrigerator and pulled out a half-filled jug of milk. She opened the jug, rolled her eyes, and began to pour the lumpy, spoiled milk down the drain. After the milk, she removed a rotten cucumber, a wilted head of lettuce, and a green block of what had once been cheddar cheese.

"Looks like you need to go grocery shopping. How are you going to fill this refrigerator? You can't drive. You don't have a car. It's still at the sheriff's office. If you try to walk, you will fall before you got a quarter of a mile away." David turned and looked at her over his shoulder. "Did you think I didn't notice how carefully you were walking?"

His mother put her hands on her hips and smiled her smug smile. It was the smile of a woman who had no doubts she was right. The reason David hated it was because he knew she was right. Until he could walk with ease again, he was helpless at least regarding defending himself against the Bow Clan.

It was odd that his legs were giving him so much trouble. Could Dr. Haskell have been right about the recently healed breaks in his legs? David hadn't believed him even when he saw the x-rays, but now he wondered if that was what was causing his pain.

"I'll manage," was all he could think to say.

Marcy grabbed his hand and held it between the two of hers. "Davey, I'm not trying to restrict your freedom or run your life. I just want to help you, and despite what you think, you need it."

Why was he holding her back? He knew she was right, but something inside of him kept telling him not to let her stay. The Bow Clan would come after him again. If they had been willing to risk exposure and come to the surface to kill him, they wouldn't stop until they were successful or dead. When they came after him, David didn't want his parents anywhere around him.

"Mom, I need to get back to doing things on my own. If I depend on you now, it's going to be all that much harder to be on my own later. It's not that I don't want you around. It's just that's it's better for me if you aren't. I need to get used to looking out for myself again."

"But..."

"Mom, please. I promise I'll come see you next weekend. Really."

Marcy let go of his hand and shook her head. "I'm not sure why you're fighting me, but I can't make you do anything you don't want to do." She glanced at Lewis for a moment, then back at David. "We'll pick up some of the basics for you at the store before we go home. You can call us if you change your mind about needing help."

David kissed his mother on the cheek. "Thanks. You're an angel. You know I love you."

Marcy pushed herself to her feet. "If I'm such an angel, then why do I have a little devil for a son? You had better keep your word and come home this weekend, if you don't, you'll never hear the end of it," she warned.

David crossed his heart and held his hand up. "I promise."

Marcy nodded but didn't say anything.

After his parents had left to go to the store, David collapsed onto the couch again. He put his feet up on his coffee table. It was good to be home. It was comfortable. The food may have spoiled, and there may have been a layer of dust an inch deep on the furniture, but it was familiar. It was home. Not like the hospital. If he was going to have to defend himself, it was better that he do it in his own territory. A home-field advantage as it were.

The red light on the answering machine next to the couch blinked furiously. He tried to count all his calls, but the light was blinking too fast. There must have been at least twenty messages.

He leaned over and hit the button to listen to the messages.

"David, this is Terrie. Where are you? You were supposed to be here an hour ago. Is this my birthday present, my late birthday present? Or did you forget again? The least you could do is be on time. I have something important to talk to you about. Call me if you stop home before coming to my trailer."

She had probably figured he was on his way to her house when the answering machine picked up. She just wanted to yell at him about being late, but he hadn't been around to yell at.

No, at that time, he had been somewhere under Highway 191.

Doing what?

All he remembered was the utter blackness. There was no light at all, but they didn't need it.

They?

Who was the "they"? The Bow Clan? The Sun Clan? The dark kachinas?

The answering machine continued playing through the messages marking the end of each one with a beep. His parents had called three times. His boss had called twice. Various friends and clients had called about a dozen times. Four reporters had called. But only one call had been from Terrie, and that one had been to complain.

With all the calls that had been waiting for him, David wondered what the inside of his mailbox looked like. As he sat on the couch, he realized the point his mother had been trying to make. Going out to the road to retrieve his mail had been a task that involved no more than a minute or two of his time. Now, it would take considerably longer, and there was no guarantee he wouldn't fall down the stairs.

For at least the next day, he would be severely limited in mobility.

That thought made him uncomfortable. He didn't want to be a sitting duck for the Bow Clan. It was important that he walk now.

It was time he learned to stand on his own two feet, pun intended. David pushed himself to his feet. His shins, knees, and thighs hurt, but he was not nearly as unstable as he had been in the hospital. He was already getting used to the pain. Either that or the pain was fading.

David walked towards the door, his steps no longer than a foot apart. He moved more easily now, which he took as a good sign.

As he stepped onto the outside landing, his toe caught on the metal strip that ran across the floor beneath the door. He started to fall but managed to catch himself against the door frame before he hit the floor. He could understand why so many old people fell and broke bones now. The slightest bulge in the ground was a mountain to someone who couldn't walk well.

David smiled at his small success and continued onward.

He looked down the stairs that ran along the side of the house and stopped. He faced a full flight of stairs down to the driveway of the house whose top floor he rented. The mailboxes were at the end of the driveway next to the road. He might as well have been standing on top of a mesa looking down at the San Juan River.

David took a stranglehold on the stair railing. He wasn't sure if he would be able to walk back up the stairs without holding onto the railing, but he would worry about that when the time came. Right now, he just wanted to reach the bottom of the stairs standing on his feet and not lying on his face. He took a tentative step down the stairs and was surprised he felt confident.

How could he have broken his legs and not remember it? Dr. Haskell had to have been wrong. He could remember running through the darkness. He could also remember the pain in his legs when he felt himself rising. If he had broken his legs, how had they healed so quickly? Or had all those memories just been dreams?

David stepped onto the cement driveway and sighed. He had made it. Maybe he was getting better.

He slid his foot across the cement as he edged toward the mailboxes. He noticed the oil spots on the driveway. Quite a contrast from the clean look of the hospital floors. He didn't let himself become so enamored with the driveway, though, that he fell over.

David reached the pair of mailboxes and opened the one with his name on it. The mailbox was about six inches tall, four inches wide, and a foot deep, and it was overflowing.

Steadying himself against the mailbox, he pulled out the letters and junk mail that had been crammed into the metal box. He noticed bills that should have been paid weeks ago, junk mail, a commission check from work, three magazines, and half-a-dozen letters from people whose names he didn't recognize.

David bundled up the pile and jammed it under his right arm so he would be able to hold onto the railing with his left hand. Going up the stairs back to the apartment seemed much less of a struggle than it had been coming down. He would force himself to be walking normally by tonight. No later.

He would manage.

He had to.

The Bow Clan was coming for him.

CHAPTER 21

Sheriff Harding settled into the wobbly chair behind his desk. It creaked under his heavy weight. He spun the chair around so that he was looking out the window and his back was facing David. The sheriff's hair was so thin at the back David could easily see his scalp.

David squirmed in his own seat trying to find a comfortable position on the hard, wooden chair.

He had managed to walk the mile to the sheriff's office in Monticello to get his car. It had been towed from the Blanding office to Monticello a few weeks ago. The walk helped David regain some of his mobility, and getting his car back would help him even more. While he was filling out the forms to get his car, he saw Sheriff Harding walk in and asked him if it was possible to talk to the man who had found David in the cave. Sheriff Harding agreed and called Officer John Peterson into his office to speak with David.

The young officer shifted his weight from his left foot to his right foot, then back again as he stood in front of Sheriff Harding's desk. His eyes kept darting back and forth between Sheriff Harding and David. John acted like he was delivering bad news to the state police chief instead of accepting someone's thanks. David wondered if he were the cause of the police officer's nervousness or if the man was just that way naturally.

"Sit down, John," Sheriff Harding said motioning to the chair next to David. The young officer did. "Loosen up, John. Mr. Purcell just wants to talk to you about the search and rescue."

John looked at David and David nodded.

"So you're the officer who found me in the cave?" was David's first question.

"Yes sir," John answered stiffly.

David noted that he was no older than John. In fact, John was probably three or four years older, in his early thirties. In the same circumstances, most people would not have addressed David as "sir." The police officer almost seemed afraid of David.

"Where was I?" David asked.

John's eyebrows arched, then drew together as he considered the question. "You were in one of the cave chambers about a half a mile from where you fell in."

David sat up straighter. "A half a mile?"

John nodded. "That cave you were in is probably as big as a small town. Maybe bigger. At least that's the way it seemed to me. It's filled with pits and tunnels, almost like a giant ant farm," John explained.

David shivered. He imagined the cave as a set for a 1950s B-grade horror movie. Something with a campy title like "Radioactive Ants from the Underworld." Ants the size of dinosaurs living beneath the earth until one man accidentally opens up their world to the surface. And that man had been him. Only it wasn't ants he had released but the Bow Clan.

"Were you working with the search-and-rescue team the entire five weeks I was missing?" David asked.

"No, sir. I came in for the last two weeks. Brian Dalton was working with the search team, but he twisted his ankle something fierce when he fell into a small hole down there. His ankle swelled up to the size of a football, and the doctor told him to stay off of it for a week. Anyway, by that time they had cut the search teams down to three men. Two would search, and one would stay on top to listen to the radio, make reports, and keep people out. When Brian couldn't do it anymore, they needed someone else to fill in for him."

David nodded, but he wasn't looking at John. He was staring out the window over John's left shoulder. What was he hoping to learn from drilling this scared officer?

"I assume you had plenty of lighting while you were down in the cave?" David asked after a moment.

John nodded and said, "Yes, sir. It's pitch black down there without lights."

No one had to tell David that. It was one of the few things he remembered about the cave.

"Everyone was probably calling my name, too?"

"Yes, sir."

David looked away from the window and stared at John. "And I never answered any of the calls, and no one saw me for five weeks?"

John looked at his shoes as if he were afraid to meet David's glance. "It would have been easy not to see you inside that cave. There were so many tiny tunnels all over the place I'm still not sure how many we missed. Even so, we were as careful as we could because we didn't want anyone else to get lost or hurt."

"Well, how did I look when you found me?"

"You looked exhausted," John said. "When I passed my flashlight over you, you looked sick. There was a moment when..."

John paused.

Sheriff Harding leaned forward in his chair. It tilted forward on a short leg and made a loud thud on the white-tiled floor. John looked across the desk at his boss and sighed.

"There was a moment when I first saw you that you seemed to glow,"

John finally said.

"Glow?" David repeated in a strained voice.

John glanced nervously at the sheriff as if expecting him to back up his story. Then he looked at David.

"Maybe 'glow' is the wrong word. It's hard to say. I only glimpsed you for a second, and I wasn't expecting to find you at that time. You sort of surprised me," John explained.

"What do you mean you weren't expecting to find me? You were part of a group looking for me."

"But you were in chamber four." John let the statement stand as if it were self-explanatory.

"Chamber four. What's that mean?" David asked.

"The room you fell into we called chamber one. From that chamber, the search team did a radial search going north and southwest of the chamber following the cave. The next chamber we searched we called chamber two, the third chamber was chamber three, and so on. We even marked the walls by the entrances and exits with the numbers. That way if anyone became lost all they would have to do would be to find out which chamber they were in, then find the next-lower-numbered chamber, and then the next, until they got back to chamber one. Anyway, the search team was exploring the chamber fifteen when I found you. I wasn't searching. Howie Ply had just relieved me, and I was walking back to chamber one to get pulled out of the cave because my shift was over."

David's lips drew together in a thin line. "So if I was in chamber four, why didn't the search party find me when they originally explored it? It sounds like your search was not as thorough as you thought." David regretted the sharp tone of voice, but if the search team had found him quicker, he might not have to be coming to term with Hopi legends now.

John rolled his eyes. David knew the young officer probably thought he was the most ungrateful person on earth, but if David was going to understand what was happening to him now, he had to first figure out what had happened to him in the cave.

"But we were thorough," John said when he looked back at David. "You weren't in chamber four when we explored it."

David slammed his hand against the arm of the chair. "Are you saying I was deliberately avoiding your search? That's stupid! I wanted to get out of the cave!" David shouted.

John closed his eyes and took a deep breath. David admired the man's patience. He wasn't sure he would have been so patient if someone who should have been grateful to him started yelling at him. He kept telling himself to calm down, but the thought that all this might somehow have been avoided kept nagging at him.

"Calm down, Mr. Purcell. There's no need to get angry. Why don't you let the officer explain?" Sheriff Harding said.

David nodded and tried to relax. "I'm sorry. It's just that I'm trying to understand this whole ordeal and not having much luck."

John opened his green eyes and said, "I didn't say you were avoiding the search, Mr. Purcell, but you were making it difficult for us. For instance, why didn't you answer our calls?" John didn't give David a chance to answer. "Why didn't you approach our search parties? You had to have seen them at some point during the five weeks. And why did you run when I shined my flashlight on you?"

David started to say something and then stopped. He glanced toward the window then back at John.

His voice was weak when he spoke, barely above a whisper. "I don't re-member. I can't remember anything after falling into the cave. I can't tell you why I did anything. All I know is that I wanted out of the cave. I was scared. That much I do remember. That's why I'm here talking to you now. I was hoping that you would be able to fill in the missing time."

John took a deep breath before he spoke again. "If you can't remember any of the time you spent in the cave, how can you be sure you wanted out?"

David rested his face in his hand. "What do you mean?"

"Well, if you have amnesia, maybe it did more to you than just cause you to forget," John suggested.

David looked up. His full attention was focused on John. "What else could have happened?"

John took a step to the side and ran his hand through his hair. "I'm no psychiatrist. I just know what I've learned at college. There are different ways amnesia could affect you. The one way you always seem to hear about is simply forgetting who you are because of some sort of head trauma, but amnesia can also be self-induced. The body can react to extreme fear by throwing up a mental block so that you can't remember anything. It's the mind's way of protecting itself from a breakdown."

David leaned back in his chair and considered what the officer was say-ing. It was much the same thing he had thought about why he had forgotten about the first time he was lost in a cave. Could he have blocked out the sec-ond experience too? Or did his mind block out any memories he might have of caves no matter how far apart they were.

"So you think I was so afraid of the time I spent in the cave that my mind created a mental block to make me forget what happened, and that same fear is also what made me run from you when you shone your flashlight on me?" David asked.

John shrugged, "I'm not saying that's what I think. It's just a possibility to explain what happened to you."

"I can accept that as a possible reason, but what did you mean when you said I glowed?"

John was obviously embarrassed about the comment. His face flushed, and he looked at his feet again. "I was walking through chamber four on my way out. I had my flashlight shining on the floor of the cave so I wouldn't fall into a hole like Brian. I heard something moving off to my right, so I stopped and shined my flashlight in that direction. I certainly didn't think I would find you, but I did. I saw a man, a very pale man, run out of the circle of light. His entire body seemed to glow in the light, like cat's eyes do."

"Why did you call me a man? Why don't you just say you saw me?" David asked.

"Because if I had to swear to it, I couldn't be sure it was you. I assumed it was you because I didn't know who else it might have been. But there were a few seconds when the glowing man was outside my flashlight beam before I shined it on you. The second time I was sure it was you I saw, but it wasn't until the day after we got you out of the cave that I thought you looked more normal the second time I saw you. You still looked sick, but at least I hadn't thought you glowed the second time I saw you."

"Did I say anything to you?" David asked remembering what his father had said he had mumbled in the cave when he was younger.

John shook his head. "Not a word. I walked up to you and said your name. Your eyes were open, but they were blank. You didn't even blink when I shined the flashlight directly into your eyes. I reached out and touched your shoulder, and you collapsed into my arms."

"Then you brought me out of the cave," David added.

"Then I brought you out. I'm sorry I can't tell you anymore to fill in that missing gap."

"While you were looking around down there, did you see any water or food that I might have drunk or eaten to stay alive?"

"No. There was nothing. From what I was told, there had to be water down there at some time to form the cave, but it's not down there now. At least not where we looked. It's a dry cave system."

David held out his right hand. John lightly shook David's hand. He still seemed a little afraid of David.

"Thank you for your time, Officer Peterson, and thank you for taking me out of the cave." David thanked Sheriff Harding for allowing him to take up his time as well.

David stood and started out of the office. He paused at the door and said, "I have one more question if you don't mind. Did you see anything else down there? Any life?"

"Only you and the other searchers," Officer Peterson replied.

"What about the first time you saw me? What did that 'man' look like?

Why did you think he might not be me?"

John looked at Sheriff Harding with a pleading look in his eyes, then back to David. "Have you seen the movie, *Close Encounters of the Third Kind*?" David nodded. "At the end of the movie, when the alien ship has lands, everyone finally sees the alien. He's human shaped but just barely. He's very white and has long fingers and large eyes. The lights from the ship are backlighting him so that he seems to glow. That's what I thought of when I saw you the first time in the cave."

David suppressed a shudder. The Bow Clan had nearly killed him in the cave before he had even been rescued.

CHAPTER 22

David slowed his Camaro when the green light switched to yellow instead of flooring the gas pedal and shooting through the traffic light, which he would have done six weeks ago. When he looked in his rear-view mirror, he could see the teenager in the pickup truck behind him angrily gesturing about having to wait the thirty seconds for the light to change back to green.

Unconcerned, David settled into the seat and waited. Why should he rush through the light? What were thirty seconds of waiting to a man who couldn't remember five weeks of his life? For once, he wasn't hurrying to meet a client or to see Terrie. He just wanted to get the car home before it broke down again.

Besides, it would take him a little time to get used to driving again. It had been over a month since he had driven, and the last time had not been the best experience for him.

Five minutes ago, he had driven away from the sheriff's office delighted that someone in the department had replaced the split radiator hose for him. At least something good had come out of the trip. The information Officer Peterson had been able to give him certainly was not comforting. How long had the Bow Clan been after him? A week? Two? Five? How long would his luck hold out before they were finally successful?

When David drove his car off the sheriff's department lot, he realized he had nothing to do for the rest of the day. His parents had brought him three bags of groceries before they left yesterday. He was on short-term disability with Hayden Laboratories until the end of the month, so he didn't have to make appointments and pitch scientists for their business. Of course, he could start calling them again just to reopen the lines of communication, so he didn't have to start from scratch when he went back to work.

The light turned green, and David started down Center Street at a leisurely twenty-five miles per hour. Barely through the intersection, the pickup truck came up behind him and roared past. David shrugged and kept right on driving the speed limit.

At the corner of 400 East, he pulled his car into the parking lot of the Dairy Queen and climbed out. He walked up to the carry-out window and ordered a chocolate-dipped cone, one of his favorite sweet indulgences. The teenage cashier stared at him from behind the Dairy Queen carry-out window, and David tried not to meet her stare. He wouldn't have minded her watching him so much if her gaze had been a "What a hunk!" stare, but it was more of a There's-something-weird-about-you stare.

When she returned to the window to hand David his cone, she said, "Are you David Purcell?" When David nodded, she said, "I saw you on the news a couple of nights ago. I hope you get better. You look better."

David took a bite out of his cone and then wiped his mouth with a napkin. "You saw me on the news?"

"Yeah, the woman reporter, Brenda...somebody. I don't remember her last name. Anyway, she showed a tape of you in the hospital. You look a lot better now, though."

He remembered talking with Brenda Jennings in the hospital. She had been the sexy one in the form-fitting red dress.

David pocketed his change and walked back to his car. Suddenly, the Camaro no longer looked like a fancy sports car, as it had a year ago. It seemed like a death trap. He was tempted to kick it, but with his luck with the car, he would probably break his toe. At least now he knew what he could do this afternoon.

He drove up to the corner of 300 East and 500 North and parked the Camaro in Framer's Toyota parking lot. By the time he left the dealership three hours later, he was driving a new Corolla. It wasn't as sporty as the Camaro, but it was dependable. And new. Hopefully, those two facts would mean he wouldn't find himself hitchhiking on the highway anymore or signing over his paycheck to the repair shop. His mother would certainly be pleased, but David had no doubt she would still worry about him.

The Corolla was navy blue and got ten more miles to the gallon than the Camaro had. The salesman had even given him $1,500 as his trade-in for the Camaro. That, with the factory rebates and a single-digit finance rate, put the monthly payments right in his price range.

David's first thought when he drove off the lot was to ride down to Blanding to see Terrie, but she would still be working. She never spent much time talking to anyone when she was working. Her belief was that if she wasn't working, she wasn't earning any tips. Besides, David wondered if he really wanted to see her. Their last meeting hadn't been the romantic reunion he had hoped for. She had acted like she hadn't even wanted to see him. If he saw her today, they would probably get into a fight over something petty because neither of them wanted to talk about the real problem in their relationship. David didn't want to get married right now, and Terrie did.

Maybe it was time for him to step back and see the forest without the interference of the trees. Sure, he and Terrie had shared some beautiful, loving moments, but the important word in that thought was "had." Those times were in the past, and the wonderful times they shared nowadays were few and far between.

Terrie was one of those people who was born, lived, and died in the same town. She would have been happy never setting foot outside of Blanding or at least San Juan County.

David could trace the problems between Terrie and him back to his job with Hayden Laboratories. His traveling had taken him out of Terrie's small world more and more often, and she simply couldn't handle the change. At first, she had gone with him on his trips around the region, and she had enjoyed traveling. Then he had taken her with him on an overnight trip to Denver. She had awakened him at three in the morning crying and asking to go home. That was the last time she had traveled with him out of state.

Maybe it was time he and Terrie sat down and hashed out their problems to see if any part of their relationship was left when it was over. It certainly wouldn't be a pleasant conversation, but not many of their conversations nowadays were. At least there was a chance that they could salvage their relationship. Maybe if they could start over, things would be better.

With an afternoon to kill before Terrie would be home from work, he decided he might as well visit the cave and get it over with. Hopefully, a few more bits of memory would return to him if he actually set foot in the place again. He wondered if Adam and Sarah would want to visit the cave with him. He hoped they would. He didn't want to go out there alone, and he couldn't put it off. That would only make it harder to go.

If he went, he would be in a place that the Bow Clan knew. They would have the home-field advantage. He didn't want to give them anymore of an advantage than they already had since he couldn't remember what he had done to anger the Bow Clan and the dark kachinas in the first place.

He drove back down Center Street and headed for the highway.

CHAPTER 23

David pulled his new car off the side of the road and reread the directions Adam had given him two days ago. They said to turn off the road at this point, but there was no road to turn onto. David checked the trip odometer and saw that he was at the correct point so he drove off the highway into the desert. The car pulled to the right slightly when the right front tire slid off the asphalt into the dirt and grass.

In his rear-view mirror, David could see a large, brown dust cloud obscuring the pickup truck that had been tailgating him since he had crossed the median to turn around. He hoped that the redneck driver choked on the dust especially if it was the same guy who could have picked David up five weeks ago and hadn't.

David stopped beside the beat-up, white pickup that he assumed was Adam's. Who else would be camped out in the desert? Climbing out of his car, David stared at the tent Adam, and Sarah had set up. Adam was sitting in the open under the sun. Sarah stepped out of the tent when she heard David turn off his engine.

"I thought Indians lived in tepees," David joked.

Neither Adam or Sarah laughed. David held up his hands. "I'm sorry. I've just never seen an Indian sleeping in a tent. Do you have something against hotel rooms?"

"We can't afford them. We're not rich," Sarah said.

"Well, don't look at me like I'm a long, lost Rockefeller. I'm not rich myself."

"By comparison you are," Adam said. "What brings you out here? Have you remembered something else?"

David shrugged. "Maybe. I've been talking to the man who found me in the cave. He said a couple of interesting things. I was thinking about driving out to the cave where I fell in. If you and Sarah want to come along, I'll tell you all about my conversation with Officer Peterson."

Adam nodded. "Yes, I would like to see this cave. It is a true sipapu. We thought there was only one, but we were mistaken."

Ten minutes later, Adam, Sarah, and David were standing outside an RV as David knocked on the door. Adam had listened to his story without comment. Sarah had said the police officer must have been blind to think that a Bow Clansman and David looked alike.

A tall, black man in dirty overalls opened the door to the RV.

"Are you in charge of the caving team?" David asked as he felt a rush of cool air from inside. He lifted his chin slightly to catch some of the cool air on the underside of his chin.

The man laughed. "Not quite. I'm Jared Chapman. Gary Morse is the group leader. He's not around right now, though. Can I help you? You don't look like a reporter."

David hesitated. "I'm not. My name is David Purcell, and I..."

The man's eyes widened slightly. "You're the one who was lost down in the caves for all that time, aren't you?"

David blushed. "Well, yes..."

The man grabbed his hand and shook it as he pulled David inside the RV. "Come in, David. Come in."

Jared ushered David, Adam, and Sarah into the RV. The three of them sat down on the bench seats around the table. Jared went to the front of the RV and came back with another man. This man was young, and he had his hair tied in a ponytail.

"This is Alex Parton," Jared said as an introduction.

"What brings you back here, David?" Alex asked.

David shrugged. "I'm not sure. I guess I wanted to find out what it was like down there."

Alex glanced at Jared then back to David. "You don't remember?"

David glanced at the floor as he blushed again. "Actually, no. Before I woke up in the hospital, the last thing I remember is falling into the hole. After that, I draw a blank."

"You're one lucky man, David, in more ways than one," Jared added.

David doubted the truth of that statement. What would they say if David told them he was being pursued by hit men from the underworld?

"How so?" he asked.

"Well, there aren't many people who could fall twenty-three feet without breaking any bones, and since you aren't wearing a cast, I guess you're one of them. Also, you've discovered what may be the largest cave system in the United States, even bigger than the Mammoth Caves in Kentucky. It should be commercially profitable, too. These caves are filled with unusual formations that people love to see, and we've been having a ball naming them. We've also found a number of unique features that will attract geologists and spelunkers as well as tourists," Alex said.

"In other words, it's a gold mine," Jared added.

"So you've explored most of the caverns?" Sarah asked.

Jared arched his eyebrows and tilted his head to the side. "Well, that's hard to say. We've mapped about two miles of passages, but we have yet to find the natural entrance. In fact, we seem to be going deeper."

"Have you ... I mean is there anything alive down there?" David asked.

Jared paused for a moment. He looked back at David and said, "There are various cave insects. Because of the absence of light and lack of food, nothing too large could live in the deepest portions of the cavern, especially not at the point we're at."

"So men can't live in the caves?" David proposed hopefully. He didn't want to believe in the Bow Clan even though he had seen him with his own eyes.

Jared nodded his head. "Impossible. Not even animals can live that deep in a cave. There's not enough food to support large life. Because there is absolutely no light down there, no plants will grow."

"There's no light at the bottom of the ocean, but there are plants there...and fish, too," David countered.

"That's different. The oceans are still vastly unexplored, so anything could happen down there. But most of the world's caves have been explored at many different sizes and depths. If there were life, animal or plant, we would have seen the signs. Even when man was called a cave man, he only lived in the openings of the caves. Some Native American tribes used to bury their dead further back in the caves, but not miles from the entrances."

David glanced at Adam as if to say, "See, there is no underworld. Men can't live down there." Adam seemed undisturbed by the conversation.

"You said there were insects in the cave," David said.

Jared nodded. "Very small insects. They have adapted to life in the caves. They don't need much food. They are blind, and their skins lack any pigments because none are needed in complete darkness."

"Lack pigment?" David repeated. "Do you mean that they are colorless?"

Jared nodded, and David glanced over at Adam and Sarah. Adam nodded that he understood. David thought he even detected the hint of an "I told you so" smile.

"Why would the Indians be so fascinated with an underground world and coming through emergence holes if there wasn't some truth connected with their beliefs? There usually is a grain of truth associated with most legends," David continued.

Alex agreed and then said, "I can only guess at what that truth might be, though. I'm no theologian. Neither is Jared. The underworld myths may just be the Native American way to explain the existence of caves, or death, or birth. All I know is what is not the truth. Men cannot live deep in caves."

David heard Adam grunt slightly in disagreement, but the old Indian didn't say anything.

"People have been fascinated with death since the beginning of time. There is always that mystery of what happens to someone after he dies. But science has proved the Indian legends about other worlds where the dead go wrong just as it proved the earth is not flat," Jared said.

"Would you like to go back down into the caverns, David? With a light, you can see why humans can't live in complete darkness. I'm sure Gary would love to meet and talk with you. I'm working as one of the top men for Gary and the others today," Alex offered.

"How do we get down there to talk to him?" David asked.

"Jared can show you the way. I'll be top man by myself for a while," Alex said.

Jared grabbed a jacket and stepped out onto the grass, closing the door behind himself. The cool air from inside the Winnebago disappeared much to David's dismay.

Jared saw his disappointed expression and said, "Don't worry, after an hour or two downstairs, you'll learn to appreciate the heat."

"How cold is it in the caves?" Sarah asked.

"About fifty-two degrees. It varies a little here and there. Chamber one is the warmest since it's directly beneath the entrance. Warm air and light can get inside."

Jared walked over to a pickup truck parked a few yards in front of the RV. Leaning over the truck bed, he pulled out three miner's helmets. They were yellow hard hats with flashlights built into the crown. Jared tested the light on the first hat by cupping his hand over the face of the light to see if it lit up. Satisfied, he passed the helmet to Sarah.

"You'll need to wear this while you're down there. We don't have any lighting other than what we take in," Jared explained.

He tested two more helmets and handed them to Adam and David. The fourth helmet he put on his own head.

"Have any of you ever been caving before?" Jared asked.

Adam and Sarah shook their heads. David said, "Years ago I went when I was a Boy Scout."

Jared laughed. It was a deep, throaty sound. "My, my. You are in for a surprise then."

He walked over to a large pulley hanging over an open hole.

Jared ran his hand over his curly, black hair and smiled. "This is it. It's also the only entrance to the cave we can find so far. We know there has to be a natural entrance because the river that formed the cave had to enter and exit somehow. Our best guess is the natural entrance is probably in the foot-hills near the San Juan, but we haven't been able to locate it so far."

"But the river is three miles away," Sarah noted.

Jared nodded. "It's one hell of a cave."

David looked over the edge into the hole. He had to steady herself on the tripod frame of the pulley to keep from falling in.

Jared grabbed the nylon cord threaded through the pulley. On the end of the cord was a loop.

"Put one foot in this loop and hold on. I'll operate the winch on the truck to lower you down."

Adam took one step back and lowered his hands. "Not me. I don't feel up to making this journey. Please, the three of you go."

David looked at him with surprise. Was Adam scared of the cave? The man who had charged into his room and saved him from the Bow Clan?

David walked over beside him. "Are you all right, Adam? Before we got here, you wanted to see the cave," David whispered.

Adam put his hand on David's shoulder. "I'm an old man, David. I have seen the underworld in my visions, and that nearly killed me. I don't have the ability to recover as quickly as one your age. Besides, I have found my answers. It is your answers that lie beneath the ground," Adam told him.

David walked back to the tripod.

Jared handed David the rope. "Test it out. That's a mountain climber's rope. It's made of nylon so that it will be fray resistant. It may not look like much, but it could hold you, me, and Sarah."

David arched his eyebrows. He wasn't too anxious to find out if something made out of what women wore on their legs would keep him from falling.

Sarah laughed. "You're such a coward. Just like a white man. I'll go down first, you big baby."

"I've already fallen in there once. I don't want to do it again."

"What if the ground gives way like it did with David?" Adam asked.

"The surrounding ground is sturdy. But, we've taken precautions if we happen to be wrong. The winch is hooked to the truck, which we parked far enough away so that if the ground collapsed, you'd fall no further than a few feet."

Sarah took the nylon rope from Jared. "Okay, I'm convinced. Let's get going."

She stepped into the loop and hung suspended over the black hole. David watched her spin around in a slow circle as Jared walked back to the red Jeep Cherokee. He opened the door and slid behind the wheel.

"Ready?" he asked.

Sarah waved her hand. David unconsciously held his breath as she started to descend into the hole. He wondered if he would chicken out when the time came.

As if reading his mind, Sarah looked up at David. "Chicken," she said right before her head disappeared below the surface.

CHAPTER 24

A four-foot wall of rock surrounded Sarah at first. Then the rock disappeared, and she was in total darkness. The light from the hole above her head extended only three or four feet into the chamber. As she waited for her eyes to adjust, she expected to see vague shapes come into view like she would if she walked from a lighted room into the night. Instead, she saw nothing. Her eyes had no light available to adjust to.

Sarah had never been in utter blackness before. Even in the kivas, fires cast a yellow-and-orange glow over the room. If this had been a month ago, the darkness wouldn't have bothered her, but now, knowing that Kuskurza and the dark kachinas actually existed, it made her uncomfortable. The years she had spent living with her mother in Phoenix had given her her mother's skepticism of Hopi beliefs. Her grandfather had softened her somewhat towards the Hopi way; at least enough so that she could live among them, unlike her mother. Sarah had always hung onto her doubts about the legends. Now she wasn't so sure.

"Switch on your headlamp so I can see where you are," David called out from the edge of the hole.

Sarah looked up and saw the round circle of light that was the hole Jared had lowered her through. It looked only as big as a plate. Part of the hole was blocked out by David's head as he leaned over the edge. How far into the cave was she?

Sarah reached up on the side of her helmet and pushed the button to turn on the battery-powered light. The small amount of light extended her vision to about ten feet.

"How's that?" she called to David.

"Better."

Not much, Sarah thought.

She touched the bottom of the cave floor. The cord slackened suddenly, and she almost lost her balance because she had been leaning on it.

"I'm down!" she yelled once she had steadied herself. She heard David relay her comment to Jared.

"Tell me when you're out of the loop," David said.

Sarah pulled her foot free from the loop at the bottom of the cord. "Okay. I'm out."

She watched as the orange nylon cord disappeared into the darkness above her. She was stuck now...trapped. If for some reason, they couldn't get the rope back down into the cave...

Sarah slowly spun around in a circle trying to see if there was a wall or a rock formation nearby she could use to orient herself with, but there was nothing within her small area of sight. The light from her helmet didn't penetrate the darkness far enough, and she was not inclined to move from her spot unless she had someone to guide her.

She stopped turning.

Had she seen something moving at the edges of the light?

Were there animals in caves besides bats? She knew it hadn't been a bat. Bats would have flown through the passage. Whatever she had seen had been moving closer to the ground.

The Bow Clan?

Had the dark kachinas sent more members of the Bow Clan after David? Was it that important that David be killed? He didn't seem like anything particularly special. Just another white man like her father had been. And just as likely to run off leaving her and her grandfather holding the bag if the Bow Clan came after him again.

Sarah shivered even though the temperature in the cavern was comfortable—about sixty degrees. When David touched down on the cave floor a minute later, she was still shivering.

"Are you cold? It's cooler down here, but it certainly isn't cold," he said.

Sarah shook her head. "Is Jared on his way down? I'd like to get out of here as soon as possible."

"Now who's the chicken?" David said without any humor in his voice.

Sarah glanced at him and saw that he was just as tense as she was. His eyes darted around the cavern. It was if he expected the Bow Clan to attack him again.

Jared came down two minutes later shining a powerful flashlight around the cavern that illuminated the walls as he descended. The chamber was not as large in the light as it felt in the dark. Sarah guessed it was ten-feet wide at its greatest width and maybe fifteen-feet long.

"This is chamber one," Jared explained, "but it is by no means the largest. Chamber three has that distinction so far. It's 110-feet long, thirty-two-feet wide, and twenty-three-feet high. My guess is we'll find some even larger chambers the deeper we go."

Jared started walking, and David and Sarah fell in behind him. Sarah positioned herself between the two men so that she wouldn't have to see the scurrying shadows behind and in front of her. They reminded her that anything could be hiding in the darkness ready to attack her.

Jared pointed out the different features of the passages by shining his flashlight on them. He also illuminated holes and rocks to avoid. Despite the light from the three miner's helmets and Jared's flashlight, Sarah still had the feeling that she was being suffocated in a small tunnel. She wondered if she was claustrophobic, but she had been in smaller rooms before and hadn't been bothered. It was not the size of the caverns that bothered her; it was the darkness.

As they passed into chamber three, she saw a bright light in the center of the room.

Gary Morse was not the sort of man Sarah had expected to meet. In her mind, she had thought he would be more like David. Medium height, broad-shouldered, strongly muscled. Gary Morse was only as tall as her. His skin was pale and appeared almost white under the lights, but still not as white as the Bow Clan's skin. His dark hair was cut short, and he wore round wire-rimmed glasses. The one thing he did share with David was his muscles. Because of his shorter height, he looked even more muscular than David.

After Jared had introduced Sarah and David, he excused himself and made his way back to chamber one. For a moment, Sarah thought David would follow him. He took a step toward Jared but then stopped.

Gary motioned to toward one of the tunnels. "Come on, I'll take you to meet the rest of the team." He glanced at Sarah. "Are you claustrophobic?"

"No," she snapped a bit too forcefully.

"I'm sorry if I've offended you. I just thought you looked a bit uncomfortable. I don't love my work enough to force you and Mr. Purcell to stay down here if you are," he explained.

Sarah took a deep breath. "Please don't apologize. It's just a little unsettling. I feel like I'm sitting in the very center of a dark kiva. I don't know whether the walls are a foot away or a mile, but I know they're there."

Gary's eyebrows knitted together. "Really? I've never seen it that way. To me, it's like sitting in my backyard on a starless night or sitting in a large cathedral with only candles for light. Maybe that's what separates spelunkers from the rest of the world."

"Spelunkers?" David said.

"Cave explorers. I'm not sure myself as to how the term came about or why. It's just something that people who explore caves are called. Maybe the first person who fell into a cave made a sound like 'spelunk!' when he hit." Sarah and David laughed. "Well it is good to know all the time I've spent down here hasn't dulled my sense of humor."

David asked. "I was told that the state hired you to explore this cave for commercial possibilities. What do you think so far?"

"This is a magnificent cavern system. My team has mapped a little over two miles of passages and chambers so far. We think that it's only the beginning of this system, though. We're hoping for a lot more."

"Five miles?"

Gary shook his head. "More like fifty."

David shuddered.

"It's almost like a small underground city under Blanding," Sarah said.

"Sort of redefines the way you look at the world, doesn't it?" Gary said. "Don't judge a book by its cover as they say."

Sarah nodded. "So this is longer than the Carlsbad Caverns?"

Gary shook his head. "At least not yet, but I think it will be. This cavern was more than likely formed when the Great Salt Lake was still part of the ocean. When the water receded, it carved its way through the ground leaving this behind. For all we know, there may be a small line of caverns that runs all the way to the ocean. There hasn't been much water in here since then unless there's a water source we haven't found yet, which is entirely possible."

Sarah liked the sound of Gary's voice. It was warm and friendly. It sounded like the voice of the old storytellers in Oraibi who would sit on the edge of the pueblo and tell the children the legends of the Hopi. It was a voice that young men tried to copy but never duplicated. It could only be earned through experience.

"How deep under the surface are we?" David asked.

Gary turned toward him. "I'm not sure, but it is deep, and will get even deeper. I'd say right now we're about 150 feet below the surface."

"Oh," David said weakly.

"Are you going to recommend that this cave be developed for tourists to visit?" Sarah asked.

Gary shrugged. "It hasn't been decided yet. It seems large enough to attract people. Right now we're mapping the caverns in detail so we can see if there are any 'touristy' features. Since this system is fairly dry, the stalagmites and stalactites are small, so we're looking for other features. We've found a few of those and have been giving them fancy names. After we finish our exploration, we'll need to compare our maps of the caverns to the state land maps and see if the state actually owns all of the property. If not, we may have a bit of problem, especially if the natural entrance turns out to be on private property."

Gary walked into a low tunnel, and Sarah and David followed. From chamber three, the trio entered a low passage. To pass through it, they had to duck-walk through a low, wide tunnel. Gary stopped in chamber four and shined the flashlight on four different exits from the chamber, not including the one they had come through.

"This seems to be unique to this cave system," Gary explained. "Up until the point my team entered this chamber, we thought we were in the common chamber-type cave. Now we're not so sure."

"Why not?" David asked.

"Chamber caves are just what the name says. Chambers. A series of them usually along one main route. Such as the series of chambers we walked through to get here. There is only one line of travel. In this room, though, there are four choices, not one. We have already explored one passage and discovered it was a dead end, but that still leaves three exits. It certainly is not typical for a chamber cave."

Gary walked toward the gaping hole on his left. At least in this passage, they were able to walk upright.

"If this isn't a chamber cave, what is it?" Sarah asked. She looked over her shoulder and saw David was still standing near the entrance to the passageway.

"The other choice would be a catacomb cave. Those types of caves are more like mazes or spider webs. Of the 170 developed caves in the United States, only two are catacombs and both of them are east of Mississippi. I know of five more wild caves that are catacombs, and except for one, they are also all in the East. None of the other caves in this area are catacombs, so I don't expect this one to be either, which makes this cave that much more impressive at least to spelunkers like me." He stopped walking and looked over his shoulder at Sarah. "If just one or two of the exits from chamber four continue in different directions, we may have some sort of new cave, which would definitely make this cavern unique. That alone might not make it a tourist attraction, but it would make it a scientific attraction."

And that attraction would be disastrous, Sarah thought.

Sarah could tell when they entered chamber five without being told by Gary. The lights that had been reflecting off the rock walls in the passage suddenly stretched itself out to its limits and found nothing to reflect back from.

In front of the group, three circles of light bobbed, and then pointed at the three of them. Sarah panicked for a second when she saw the lights. She couldn't see the people behind the lights, and she thought it might be members of the Bow Clan coming for David.

"There's the rest of my team," Gary said.

Sarah relaxed.

As Sarah came closer to the other members of Gary's group, the light from all the lanterns and flashlights merged creating a small bubble of light within the cavern about twenty feet in diameter.

The first impression Sarah had about the three people was they were utterly filthy. Each of them reminded Sarah of Pig Pen, the Peanuts character who always had a cloud of dust following him no matter where he went. She had always enjoyed watching the Peanuts cartoon specials when she was a little girl. This group's resemblance to Pig Pen was because their sweat had mixed with the dirt on them to form a film of mud on each person. One man was so covered in mud that he looked like a black man.

"This is the rest of my team," Gary said. "This is Billy Joe Nash, Lou Montgomery, and Christine Stills."

Sarah was surprised to see a woman among the group. She was even more surprised that she hadn't recognized the woman because she was covered in mud and had on thick coveralls.

"Between these three people, there's fifty-two years of caving experience," Gary continued. "This is David Purcell and his friend, Sarah," Gary said to his team.

Sarah started to reach out her hand to shake theirs but decided against it and said, "Nice to meet you all. So you four do all the dirty work while Jared and Alex sit up on top?"

Billy Joe wiped some of the mud off his face and said, "If it was always like that, we'd probably revolt. We alternate in pairs two days upstairs and four days down. We need to get a little sun every now and then."

Even with all the people around her, Sarah still felt like something was moving outside the range of the flashlights and lanterns. She concentrated on listening to the group talk. She made eye contact as often as possible and never looked over their shoulders to the edge of the light.

She was afraid of what she might see out there.

CHAPTER 25

After leaving the caverns with Sarah, David still didn't feel as if he knew anything more about what had happened to him than he had before he went in. He hadn't had any startling revelations as he stood in the dark with Sarah and the spelunkers. If anything, he was more convinced it had all been a nightmare. How could anything live in a cave? Without light, it was entirely dark. There was no food, and at least in this cave, there was little water.

It did him a little good, though, to walk around in the chambers and see how quickly the spelunkers moved around. They weren't scared of the place; they were fascinated by it. They were mapping the passages he had been lost in, and those maps would take the mystery out of the cave. It would be a less-scary place once it was mapped out and there were no more unknown areas.

It was true that he had seen the pale men, but did they come from the caves? And if not from the caves, then from where?

It was after seven o'clock when he dropped Sarah and Adam off at their campsite. He felt a little guilty going home to his air-conditioned apartment when he knew they were sleeping a half a mile from the highway in the stifling heat. But he hadn't forced them to camp there. They had chosen it themselves.

David went home, took a shower, and changed into clean clothes. Now he had to do something that made him just as uneasy as going into the cave had made him feel.

He had to talk to Terrie.

He drove his new car out to Terrie's mobile home. It was on two acres of property at the east edge of Blanding, but she had no immediate neighbors, so it looked like she owned more like sixty acres. David had always thought it was odd that she lived in a mobile home, but had never moved out of town. Terrie had planted a garden behind the trailer and had a concrete patio laid in front of the trailer. There were no shade trees on her property, but she did have sod laid out on it and an automatic watering system to keep it thriving. Her yard was a patch of green in an oasis of brown. If there had been a way for her to make the trailer a permanent fixture to the land, she would have done it.

He glanced at his car and thought he could still leave. He hadn't knocked on her door yet. Somehow he knew what he would find when he knocked.

He should have called her first. Then he wouldn't have to put himself in this embarrassing situation now, but maybe this was just what he needed to shake himself to his senses. Glancing at the driveway for the hundredth time, he noted there were three cars in it. His Corolla, Terrie's Geo Metro, and a BMW 325i. He didn't recognize the BMW, and he had a feeling he didn't want to know who owned it. It certainly wasn't Terrie's.

He hadn't knocked on the door he reminded himself once again. Terrie might not know he was here. He could...

He knocked.

He heard movement from inside the trailer. When Terrie opened the door, he had to catch his breath. She looked beautiful, as always. Her brown hair hung loosely across her shoulders. She was wearing a pink T-shirt, which hugged the curves of her body, and her white shorts showed off her sleek runner's legs of which she was so proud.

When Terrie saw it was David at the door, she quickly closed the door until it was only a narrow slit. She hadn't wanted him to see into her trailer, but she'd been too slow.

"David, I didn't expect you tonight," she said quickly.

David looked at his feet. "I know. I'm sorry I didn't call, but I didn't want to be put off. We really need to talk. I can see you're busy, though. I guess this means we don't have anything to talk about after all." There was no anger in his voice, only sadness.

The smile on Terrie's face fell. "Oh." She opened the door wider, and David saw the blond-haired man in a navy-blue suit sitting on the couch in Terrie's living room. He lifted his hand as if to wave to David.

"Do you want to come in?" Terrie asked.

David shook his head. "Sorry to have barged in."

He spun around quickly and headed for his car. He wasn't sure if he was going to cry. He hoped not. It would only add to his embarrassment. No wonder things had gotten so bad between him and Terrie! She'd been dating another guy.

For how long?

David felt a hand on his arm. "David, wait."

He jerked his arm away and then felt he was acting like a child. He stopped and turned around. Terrie looked like she was about to cry, too.

"I was going to tell you. Really I was. The night you fell in the cave and the other day when I came to see you in the hospital. I didn't want you to find out like this," she tried to explain.

"How did you want me to find out?"

"Slowly. I wanted to break up first, and then when you were used to that, I was going to tell you about Randy."

"How kind of you." He paused. "You've got a thing for guys in suits with fancy cars, I see." David could see the comment hurt her and in a way, he was glad. He doubted it hurt one-tenth as bad as he hurt at that moment.

"You got a new car," Terrie said glancing over his shoulder.

David nodded. "The Camaro let me down one too many times. It was time for a change."

"Oh."

Kel'hoya opened his mind and waited. He called out to Pahana. He hoped the Outlander would still be in his room in the white pueblo. The pueblo was a good place to kill Pahana. To slay an enemy where he felt safest would inspire fear in the other Outlanders who sought to destroy the dark kachinas.

When his mind met Pahana's, he saw the lost white brother was not in his room at the pueblo. He was outdoors beside a small dwelling. It looked to be a solitary room, not like the pueblo where Pahana had stayed the night before. Perhaps, Pahana thought that the female he was staring at would protect him from the Bow Clan as the old Outlander had done. Pahana did not realize how lucky the old Outlander had been. He did not know the true power of the Bow Clan. That was the reason why Pahana did not fear.

But tonight, he would learn fear.

Fear first, then death.

Kel'hoya opened his eyes. To'chi was already awake and pacing the cave. Kel'hoya wondered if this impatience he saw in To'chi was part of To'chi's real personality, uncontrolled by the dark kachinas.

"Tonight we will kill Pahana," his companion said. "We will carry his head with us back to Kuskurza for all the Sun Clan to see."

Kel'hoya stood up and stretched. "He is with a female."

"A female? We should capture her. She would bear healthy slaves for the dark kachinas. Now that the Sun Clan has stolen our women, we need all we can get even if they are Outlanders," the younger Bow Clansman said out loud.

Kel'hoya shook his head. "We will be lucky if we can return to Kuskurza ourselves. This female is Pahana's current protector. We will make him fear the Bow Clan first before he dies. If we are able to return to Kuskurza, we can tell the dark kachinas of the rich source of slaves that could be ours for the taking if the Bow Clan attacked the Fourth World with their weapons.

"But first, Pahana must die and all those he might have told the secrets of Kuskurza to. We have already failed once, and the Bow Clan does not fail. We must kill him tonight so we can return to Kuskurza before our judgment has completely deteriorated."

Terrie rubbed her thigh nervously. "I'm sorry about this, David, but you need to know how I feel," Terrie tried to explain.

The sky was dark enough now that she was only a vague shape to David. "So tell me."

Terrie touched David's arm. He didn't pull away this time, but he realized her touch no longer excited him as it once had.

"I really don't feel like I've been cheating on you," she began.

David laughed. "Funny how I don't remember us breaking up. I thought I was still your boyfriend."

"You haven't been my boyfriend in months."

"Now that's not true," David said as he shook his finger in her face. "I've always been concerned about you. Don't I call you when I'm out of town?"

"But calls don't take the place of seeing you. Don't you understand that I wanted to be with you?"

"I suppose, but I have a job to do, and it takes me out of town sometimes."

"Too often," Terrie added.

"That's the way you see things, but it's not the way I see them. And that is the heart of our problem, isn't it?"

Terrie paused, and then said, "Maybe you're right."

"I love you, Terrie. I was willing to try and work things out. I hoped they could work out. I didn't turn to the nearest female the first time things got tough for us."

"I didn't turn to the nearest male, either. Randy has been a friend of mine from the diner for years. He saw I was upset one day and we started talking, and then one thing led to the next..."

"And you both wound up in bed," David interrupted.

Terrie slapped him hard across the face. "That's a lie! Just because things didn't work out for us, doesn't mean I'm sleeping around."

David realized he had overstepped his limits. Terrie didn't believe in sleeping around. The only man she would go to bed with would be the man she married. Having dated her for a year, David knew that as well as anyone. But he had wanted to make her mad to make his break from her complete. He had, and now he was sorrier for having done it. "You're right. I'm just angry."

"If you had wanted things to work out between us, you could have gotten a job that didn't take you out of town three nights a week," Terrie said.

"I could have, but no job around here would pay me as much as I can make with Hayden."

"Money's not everything," Terrie insisted.

David nodded. "I agree, but the point of the matter is, I don't mind being out of town three nights a week. It's not like we saw each other every night, anyway. Before you start laying the fault for our failure on me, look at yourself. We could have moved to Salt Lake City. That way I'd have been close enough to the airport that I could turn most of my overnighters into day trips. Then, if things had smoothed out between us, we could have gotten married."

Terrie snorted. "Married? Do you think I'd leave my life just because you finally mentioned the M word? What if I didn't want to live in the city?

What would I have done for work?"

"Probably the same thing you do here, but you'd have gotten paid better for it."

Terrie waved her hand around the yard. "This is my home."

"People move all the time, Terrie. Why couldn't you?"

"Because I like living here. My family lives here, and so do all my friends. This is the only place and way I know how to live. Randy accepts that. Why can't you?"

"Because I'm not Randy. I'm David. David Purcell. Remember me? I used to be your boyfriend. Besides, you just told me money isn't everything, well, either is location." David turned away from Terrie. "Goodbye, Terrie. Good luck with Randy. I hope he wants the same things you want."

The Bow Clansmen moved through the darkness without saying a word. Kel'hoya searched for the landmarks he had chosen while he had watched the world through Pahana's eyes. He had chosen ones that would keep To'chi and him away from any of the Outlanders. Kel'hoya wanted to keep his companion's thoughts on killing Pahana and not returning to Kuskurza. He did not want to think that he would die soon.

As they approached the dwelling of the female protector, Kel'hoya saw no one outside the pueblo now. They must have gone inside, and Kel'hoya thought he knew how to get inside. He had seen how Outlanders worked the doorways in his visions.

Pahana had been too careless this time. He took too many risks because he did not fear the Bow Clan. Now he would learn that lesson, but it would be too late for him to apply it.

Kel'hoya paused by the entrance to the metal pueblo. To'chi sunk to a crouch ready to launch himself through the doorway onto Pahana. Kel'hoya reached out and grabbed the door handle. Then he turned it as he had seen the Outlanders do. He pushed the door open.

As soon as To'chi saw that his companion was successful, he gave a war cry and charged through the doorway.

Terrie screamed, but Kel'hoya clamped his hand over her mouth quickly to silence her. He did not want any interference this time.

To'chi jumped on Pahana's back as he turned to run toward the door to the pueblo. To'chi grabbed a handful of Pahana's blond hair and yanked his head back. Pahana fell face forward onto the floor. To'chi maintained his hold and saw Pahana's exposed neck.

To'chi's hand found Pahana's neck and tightened its grip.

"To'chi, no!" Kel'hoya yelled.

The Bow Clansman reacted instantly as he had been trained to do. He released his grip.

"Why? With his death, our mission will be complete," the younger man said.

"Yes, but not yet. Have you not realized that he does not fear us? The Bow Clan means nothing to him."

To´chi rolled Pahana over onto his back. Pahana's eyes were closed, and his lower lip trembled. To´chi tugged at the lip with his long fingers and wondered how they would taste. Pahana whimpered at the touch of To´chi's hand.

"He looks afraid to me," To´chi said to his leader.

Kel´hoya stared at the man on the floor. "That is not Pahana."

"How do you know?"

"I saw Pahana close up when I attacked him in the white pueblo. I know what he looks like."

To´chi screamed and pounded his fists on Randy's chest. "We have failed again. He has escaped us once more. This world has made us weak and powerless."

"At least we have his protectors now. He is also powerless," Kel´hoya said.

"You said that Pahana would be here. We should kill the man and take the woman as a breeder for when we return to Kuskurza!"

Kel´hoya thought for a moment and said, "No! I am the leader, and I will command! Make the male face me now. We will leave Pahana a message."

CHAPTER 26

David pushed the Corolla's accelerator all the way to the floor. The car jumped forward and gradually gained speed. Too slowly for David's sake. At least the Camaro had been quick to accelerate. The Corolla's speed topped out at eighty miles per hour. Luckily, Highway 191 wasn't too busy.

He had put up so much resistance to his mother's idea of coming to Provo, and now he was racing there at eighty miles per hour. He hoped his parents would be happier to see him than Terrie had been. He needed to be pampered a little bit and loved a lot.

He would never have thought Terrie would cheat on him. She was right about one thing. He could have handled a breakup, but not this.

Moab was still half an hour away. He would have to get gas there, and then he should be able to make it all the way to Provo.

Forget Terrie. Forget the Bow Clan. Forget Adam and Sarah. If Adam wanted a hero, let him find someone among his own people. David had lost five weeks of his life in that cave. He didn't intend on losing it completely.

A trailer appeared in front of him suddenly. David swerved to avoid it, but it followed him across the road. He slammed on his brakes and was thrown against his seat belt.

The trailer disappeared, and David saw an empty highway in front of him. He glanced in his rear-view mirror and saw a set of headlights far behind him that couldn't possibly be the trailer.

David slowed his car down to forty miles per hour in case something strange happened again.

The trailer appeared out of nowhere again. He realized this trailer wasn't on the road, though. It sat in a yard that he could see right in front of him.

He was seeing through one of the Bow Clansman's eyes again. The Bow Clansmen were after someone.

David turned his car into a hard 180-dgree turn. The tires screamed against the road, throwing David hard against his seat belt again. He would probably have a diagonal bruise across his chest tomorrow, but he didn't care. He knew who the Bow Clan was going after this time. They had been looking at Terrie's trailer.

David's brief vision that told him he would not make it back to Blanding in time to help Terrie. The Bow Clan was already at Terrie's trailer. David saw her face in front of him. She did not look beautiful any longer. Her eyes were red from crying and a thin, white hand was clamped over her mouth.

David blinked and pulled out his cell phone and dialed 9-1-1. When the dispatcher came on the line, he yelled, "There's a woman in trouble in Blanding. Her name's Terrie McNee, and she lives on County Road 323, Box 2. You've got to send someone out there quick. She's in terrible danger."

The operator started to ask him something, but David hung up the phone before she could even finish her question. He wouldn't have been able to answer any of the woman's questions. He only hoped she relayed the message to the Sheriff Harding or one of his deputies. Maybe someone was close enough to get to Terrie's in time to help her before the Bow Clan killed her.

The younger pale-skinned man spun Randy Houser around on his knees so that he was facing in the direction of Kel'hoya and Terrie. Randy's head drooped, and To'chi grabbed another handful of hair and pulled Randy's head back. To'chi whispered something in Randy's ear. Even though Randy did not understand the Bow Clan's language, he understood the tone. He started to cry, but he kept his eyes closed.

The younger Bow Clansman touched one of Randy's eyes with his long finger, and Randy clenched his eyes shut even tighter. Finally, To'chi hit him across the side of the head. Randy opened his eyes.

Kel'hoya held Terrie only a few inches from Randy's face so that her boyfriend could see her tears. She tried to yell something to him, but it sounded muffled through Kel'hoya's hand.

"It is hard to believe Pahana would consider you two his protectors. You are weak and afraid," Kel'hoya said.

He doubted whether the Outlanders could understand his words, but he wanted them to understand his anger. He did not like being cheated out of his prize.

With the hand that covered Terrie's mouth, Kel'hoya pressed her head against his body. His free hand moved up from her shoulder and traced an invisible line up the side of her mouth, across her cheekbone, and next to her eye. Terrie tried to pull away, but Kel'hoya's other hand kept her head steady. She cried instead.

David pushed the Corolla up to ninety-five miles per hour. It shimmied a little, but it held constant at its top speed. He pressed his foot down even harder hoping that he might somehow get a few more miles per hour out of the car. He kept his eyes on the road ahead hoping to spot any police waiting in hiding before they saw him. The last thing he needed now was to be pulled over by a state trooper and have to wait twenty minutes while the cop wrote him out a speeding ticket. David kept his hands clenched tightly around the steering wheel so that he wouldn't shake or lean over in his seat and throw up.

An image of Terrie leaped into his mind. She was dressed in the same clothes she had been wearing tonight. However, in this vision, she was dying as a long, white, skeletal finger dug into her eye socket. Her right eye silently popped from the socket. He was glad he couldn't hear it or else he might have thrown up right then. Her eye hung against her cheek by a few strands of red flesh.

The horrifying image surprised David so much that he lost control of his car for a moment. The car passed over the center line, and he pulled it back into his lane just as a car coming from the opposite direction beeped its horn at him.

Stomach churning violently, he knew he wouldn't be able to control himself much longer. He rolled down his window as he pulled the car over onto the side of the road. He had barely put the car in park when he felt a massive constricting in his stomach. He leaned out his window and coughed. Only a thin line of spittle dripped from his mouth, but his empty stomach still continued to constrict violently.

When his stomach finally stilled, David wiped his mouth with the back of his hand. Although he hadn't vomited, he still had a bad taste in his mouth from the bile that had come up. He sat back in the car and leaned his head against the headrest.

What was happening to him? His world was coming apart at the seams.

David shook his head in frustration. If he could only remember what had happened in the cave. Why couldn't he remember? Had something so terrible happened that he wouldn't let himself remember it like Officer Peterson had suggested? Why did he suddenly have a psychic connection with the Bow Clan?

David leaned his head against the steering wheel and cried.

Randy fainted when he saw Terrie die. To'chi released his grip on the man and let him fall back to the floor.

"You failed to bring us to Pahana," To'chi said.

"He was here. I saw him," Kel'hoya defended himself.

Why had the dark kachinas given him the vision is he wasn't going to be able to reach Pahana in time?

"You what?"

"I saw him. The dark kachinas have given me visions since we have arrived on the surface. I have seen through Pahana's eyes. That is why we have been able to follow him."

"Your vision was wrong this time."

"No. He was here. We have his protectors. We were just too long getting here. Tu'waqachi is too large to travel as quickly as we do in Kuskurza," Kel'hoya said.

"We have been too long on the surface. The dark kachinas warned us our senses would be dulled. We should return to Kuskurza and admit defeat. The dark kachinas can send others more capable than us to kill the hero of the Sun Clan."

As Kel'hoya approached his companion, he kicked the unconscious body on the floor. "Are you that anxious to die, To'chi? The dark kachinas said we would never live to see Kuskurza again. Do you want to die a failure? Because if we start back to Kuskurza without having killed Pahana, we will never have a chance to redeem ourselves."

To'chi looked at Randy's body. "You are right. We must not fail the dark kachinas."

Kel'hoya nodded. To'chi squatted down beside Randy as his companion watched. It was time to leave Pahana the second half of his message.

CHAPTER 27

David wasn't sure how he made it back to Blanding without wrecking his car. He kept catching flashes of what the Bow Clansman was seeing. Terrie's dead body laying sprawled on the floor of her trailer. Luckily, she lay face down. All David could see was a pool of blood beneath her head. During another vision, he saw Randy strangled by the Bow Clansman whose face he could see. Though David had not liked Randy because Terrie had chosen him over David, seeing Randy choked wrenched David's stomach. It reminded him too much of how close the Bow Clansman had come to strangling him in the hospital.

David cruised slowly down the road that led past Terrie's house. Three police cars sat in the driveway with their lights flashing. A state police car and a county police car were parked next to the trailer. The third car was parked at the end of the driveway to keep unwanted cars from getting too close to the trailer. A deputy was standing on the side of the road signaling the slow-moving cars to keep moving.

A crowd of people had already formed along the opposite side of the street where the deputy herded them. It looked like everyone who lived within a mile of Terrie's trailer was standing along the road looking across at the police cars. It wasn't often a murder happened in San Juan County, let alone a double murder. How had everyone found out so fast? And why would they want to be here to see two dead bodies being rolled into a morgue wagon? This wasn't a movie. Terrie and Randy weren't being wheeled into make-up where their fake blood and putty wounds would be removed. They were dead. Cut. Print it.

How long would it be before David wound up the same way?

He was tempted to yell at the deputy who was keeping the crowd back. Why hadn't the police gotten here faster? It was their fault. They knew Terrie was in danger, and they had failed. They might as well go back into town now. The killers were far away, and Terrie and her boyfriend were dead. They couldn't do any good now.

David kept his control because he knew he shared the blame with the police. He had been careful not to let his parents stay in his apartment after dark. Why hadn't he taken the same care with Terrie? He had led the Bow Clan right to her front door.

As he passed by the driveway, David saw two paramedics wheel a covered body out of the trailer on a gurney. He couldn't tell whether it was Terrie's or Randy's. That gave him little comfort since he knew both of them were dead. His stomach was already beginning to feel queasy again.

When would all this end?

He drove home slowly. He went through the motions of driving without really seeing the road. In fact, he was surprised when he realized he was sitting in his driveway.

He thought he wouldn't be able to sleep, but as soon as he fell into his bed, he was asleep within moments.

David woke up the next morning with a fog of uncertainty surrounding his brain. He raked his fingers through his hair and tried to push the vision of Terrie being tortured and killed out of his mind, but it seemed to be permanently etched in his mind. He could remember waking up in the middle of the night, but just barely. Somehow, he was sure his mind had been replaying his visions in his head throughout the night. Terrie. Randy. How many more people would die?

David wiped the tears away from his eyes as he started crying. Helpless. He was helpless. If only he knew how to find the Bow Clan. Even if he could, what could he do? He didn't seem to be able to influence the Bow Clansman's actions when their thoughts were connected. He had tried to when he realized the man was going to kill Terrie. Although he had kept sending the thought to run away, the man had murdered Terrie and then Randy anyway.

David had to know what had happened to him in the caverns. That was the key to ending this madness. When he knew all that had happened to him, then he would know how to defend himself.

He finally got control of his crying and took a hot shower and shave. He wiped his hand over the glass in the mirror to clear it of the steam fog. Seeing his reflection in the mirror, David asked himself, "Would she have died if I had been there to help her? Could I have stopped the Bow Clan by myself?"

His reflection had no answer. It just disappeared behind the glass as the mirror clouded over again.

David skipped breakfast because his stomach was so tied up in knots there was no room left for any food. Besides, he still had a bad taste in his mouth from the night before.

It was time to find some answers, but where could he start?

CHAPTER 28

Gary, Jared, Christine, and Billy Joe squatted in a tight circle in the center of chamber six about half a mile from where David had fallen into the cave system. Their headlamps created a bubble of light around them as they stared at their map of the newly-named San Juan Caverns.

It was the name the group had given this particular cave system. They had voted on it the night before. Anasazi Caves, Utah Caverns, and the Big Hole had all been in the running. San Juan Caverns had been chosen because it seemed fitting to name a child after its father. These caves had been formed by the either the San Juan River or a dried-up tributary. Gary had even speculated that the ocean when it made its way inland to form the Great Salt Lake, might have contributed to creating the caves.

Jared laid the map out so that everyone was able to study it. It was a plan-view map that showed the width and length of the passages and chambers in the cavern. Of the fifteen explored chambers, eleven had been mapped. The outlines of the passages and chambers had been drawn to scale on the art pad. With a scale of one inch equal to one-thousand feet, the map was four-pages long and two-pages wide so far. The open lines at various points on the map showed where there were still passages to be explored. The heights of the different chambers and the depth underground had been noted on the maps. Within the open areas were rough drawings of the various features. If the feature had been given a name, it was written beside the drawing. Of the eleven mapped chambers, ten roughly lined up on a northeast to southwest axis. The eleventh chamber was not along the main axis but off a passageway beginning in chamber four.

"So any guesses as to what we have here, guys and gal?" Gary asked, pointing to the rogue chamber on the map.

Jared tapped his finger on the lone chamber. "I still think this is a fluke chamber on an otherwise typical chamber system. A small tributary probably ran off and swirled around there until it found its way back to the main route."

"But the open routes from the rogue run away from the main route," Christine said.

"But these caves are not made of siliceous limestone. It can't be a catacomb system," Jared argued. Of the known catacomb caves, all were made of a water-soluble siliceous limestone.

A white millipede, one of the few types of creatures that had adapted itself to living its life in a cave, walked across the map. Gary picked up the page it was on, held the page off to the side, and gently brushed the millipede off. Cave creatures were too unique to squash like common bugs. They resembled their surface cousins but also had striking differences. All white because no pigmentation is needed below the surface, skin color was their most noticeable difference. There were other differences, too. For instance, cave fish have no eyes and cave crickets have extra-long antennae.

"What if it's some sort of hybrid?" Gary asked excitedly looking away from the millipede. "We could be exploring an entirely new type of cave system. Part chamber-style and part catacomb-style."

Jared shook his head. "That would be great, but I think you are letting your imagination get away with you. There's just too much information that has been gathered about caves all over the world, and the idea of a hybrid cave has never been seen or suggested."

"That doesn't mean it doesn't exist. Gary could be right," Billy Joe said in defense of the idea.

"He could be, but the odds are against it."

"Besides, a cave isn't an animal. It can't crossbreed to form a hybrid," Christine pointed out.

"I know that," Gary said defensively. "A cave is living, though. As long as water runs through it, it is changing. Maybe two different water sources formed this cave. The Great Salt Lake could have formed the original chamber line, then the San Juan River came through and created the cross line." Gary ran his fingers over the map to visually demonstrate his point. "This cave could be the child of an ocean and a river. That is what I would call a hybrid."

Christine stood up and stretched. "Why don't we see what the rest of this place looks like before we start guessing at what type of cave system it is? After all, we've only explored about six-and-a-half miles worth of passages. Now, I'm guessing we'll get at least fifty miles before we've finished."

The three men nodded their agreement.

"I bet there's even more than fifty," Gary mumbled.

"Any preferences on which way to go?" Billy Joe asked Christine.

She stared at the map for a moment, and said, "Let's explore the two passages off the rogue since that's what we're all curious about. We may dead end or wind up back on the main line. Then all our questions would be answered."

When she finished speaking, she looked up and smiled at Gary. Even with half an inch of dirt covering her, Gary thought she was beautiful.

"Or we may find something entirely new," Billy Joe added.

Christine turned from Gary and gave Billy Joe a quick nod as if the say, "Maybe."

Jared stacked the numbered map pages and tucked them into his knapsack. They would use small notepads to draw rough sketches and make notes about the passages they explored today. Tonight, they would incorporate the notes into the main map.

The passageway between chamber four and chamber eleven started out at six-feet high, but within minutes the ceiling had dropped two feet, and the group was forced to bear walk. Gary occasionally paused to take height and width measurements. He also readjusted his pedometer to account for the shorter steps he took when he walked bent over.

As he moved through the passage behind Christine, he watched her hips sway enticingly in front of his face. He wondered if anything would ever come of his feelings for her. He doubted it. If something were going to happen, she would have to set them in motion. He was too afraid. There were too many failed marriages in the country. Gary was happy exploring caves and having an occasional non-committal date with Christine. Safety first whether in a cave or in a relationship.

Gary taught a geology course at the University of Tennessee and lived up to the stuffy professor image. He had explored the many Tennessee and Kentucky caves on weekends during the semesters. Bigger caves like this one, he spent his vacations exploring.

When the group reached chamber eleven, they headed toward the passageway on the left. It was only about two-and-a-half feet wide. Everyone, even Christine with her small body, had to walk sideways for the first hundred yards. After the first narrow section, the passage widened, and everyone was able to walk normally.

Gary stopped when the passage widened and drew the length and width into his notepad. When he had mapped out the new section of passage, he took a reading on the compass and started walking behind Christine again.

Billy Joe led the way to chamber eleven. The light from his lamp penetrated only about fifteen feet into the darkness. Gary didn't bother trying to look over Billy Joe's shoulder to see ahead of him. He knew that all he would see beyond the light of the lamp was blackness.

The four spelunkers fell into a silent shuffle through the passage. It was one of the few times that no one felt like talking. Instead, they preferred to listen to the stillness of the cavern. They heard no sounds in the tunnel other than those they made themselves, and on level ground that wasn't much. Within the cave, no crickets chirped. No traffic roared down nearby roads. No electricity buzzed through power lines, no wind rustled through the leaves in the trees. This was a world where the blind and the sighted and the deaf and the hearing could be nearly equal.

Gary loved the strangeness of it all. In his twenty-one years of exploring caves, he had seen things very few people ever saw. He had even seen things that he would like to think he was the first to see, like this cave system. On the surface, there were very few still-unexplored areas. The only true frontiers lay in the water, in space, and below the surface. He felt like one of the members of the cast of Star Trek whose mission it was "to go where no man has gone before."

Christine suddenly stopped in front of him, and Gary almost ran into her because he had been lost in his own thoughts.

"What's wrong? Is the tunnel blocked?" he called to Billy Joe.

Billy Joe stepped forward and turned around to face the others. "Look at this," he said pointing at the ground.

"What is it?" Jared wanted to know.

On the floor was a small wooden doll. It was covered with multi-colored disks, and there were corn husks around its eyes and mouth. The teeth were squash seeds. The legs were painted red with black spots, and the torso was covered with a small, fur robe. Hanging around its neck was a necklace of what looked to Gary to be bones.

"It's an old doll," Gary said as he reached down to pick it up.

"Be careful," Billy Joe warned. "It may be fragile."

Gary nodded as he lifted the doll and passed it to Christine and Jared.

"This is a kachina doll. I've seen Hopi and Pueblo children with them. It's supposed to represent one of their gods or spirits," Christine said. She taught archeology at the same university as Gary.

"Well, what's it doing down here?" Jared asked.

"Maybe we're near the natural entrance," Gary suggested.

Billy Joe gave him a look that said, "What are you stupid or something?" At 333 feet below the surface, it was doubtful they were near the natural entrance.

"Do you think we may be near a burial ground? You know some of the Indians buried their dead deep inside caves," Christine suggested.

Gary shrugged. "Could be, but without knowing where the natural entrance is, we've got no way to know unless we start running across bodies. Personally, I don't relish the thought."

Christine passed him the doll and he looked at it carefully. It was ten-inches long and obviously hand carved. Someone had invested a lot of time in making this doll, so why had it been left behind? And which god did it represent?

"Do you think we'll find a mummified body?" Billy Joe asked. "This cave is dry enough for it."

Gary didn't answer him because he wasn't sure. All he knew was that this cave system had a lot of hidden secrets, from the formation of its tunnels to how an ancient kachina doll could have found its way over 300 feet below the surface. Even Indians who buried their dead in caves didn't travel far past the twilight zone in a cave.

Gary took a waterproof bag from his knapsack and gently wrapped the doll in it. When he had placed it in his knapsack, he looked at the blackness over Billy Joe's shoulder and wondered what other surprises the caves held for them.

CHAPTER 29

When David saw Adam and Sarah step out of the tent, he should have felt a sense of relief. After all, it was Adam who David had come to see. He felt the old Indian was probably the only person in the world who could help him make sense out of what was going on in his life. Adam had already helped him understand some of what David had gotten involved in during his missing time in the cave. Maybe Adam could help him discover the part of his life he still could not remember.

So why did he climb out of his car feeling angry towards the two Hopi Indians? They weren't responsible for Terrie's death. They didn't control the Bow Clan any more than he had been able to control them.

But it's their legends that are coming to life, he thought irrationally. It wasn't Paul Bunyan or Pecos Bill who had killed Terrie. It was a pale-skinned Indian who lived in an underground world that only the Hopi Indians seemed to know.

Adam stopped in front of David and waited for him to say something.

David counted to ten slowly to keep control of his anger. Finally, he said, "The Bow Clan killed my girlfriend and another man."

Adam would have been a great poker player because his face showed no expression. David wondered if he would ever be able to distance himself so well from the murders.

"I'm sorry this has happened, but you were lucky to escape," Adam said as he sat down on the ground.

"I wasn't there. I tried to help, but I got there too late."

"Then how do you know the Bow Clan is to blame? The Bow Clan has a single purpose for being in this world and that is to kill you. Though they probably hate all those who live in the Fourth World, they must keep focused on a single goal here. I'm sure they do not want to be discovered. That's why they are trying to kill you. The Bow Clan must kill you and return to the Third World as quickly as possible if they are to keep their world a secret. If you were not with your girlfriend when she was killed, I am not sure it was the Bow Clan that killed her."

"It was. I saw them."

"But you just said you weren't there," Sarah interrupted as she moved to stand behind her grandfather.

David turned to her and controlled his urge to yell. "I'm seeing things through one of the Bow Clansman's eyes. I saw them attack Terrie in my mind." He tapped his head with his finger. "When I went to her trailer she was dead just as I had seen in my mind."

"Then you've had a vision," Adam said.

"If so, it's not the first one. I've seen odd things I couldn't explain a couple of times since I got out of the cave."

"Then Taiowa has given you a great gift."

David scowled. "I don't think being able to watch someone murder two people is such a great gift."

Adam was unconvinced. "But if you can see into their minds, you might be able to figure out how to defeat them."

"I don't want to defeat them," David snapped. "I just want them to go away and leave me alone. I want my life back."

Adam took hold of David's arm and pulled him down to the ground beside him. David reluctantly sat down on the dirt in front of Adam.

"The Bow Clan will not leave unless they complete what they came here to do. The dark kachinas fear you. Locked inside your head, must be the secret to their defeat. It's the only reason they would risk exposure," Adam told him.

David tapped his finger against his temple. "Well, if it's locked inside my head, then it's going to stay there because I don't seem to be remembering anything about those five weeks I was in your Third World."

"You must. It's the only way to stop the dark kachinas."

David was surprised to hear Adam raise his voice. It must be important to the old man to stop the dark kachinas. Of course, it was important, David corrected himself. Adam believed the dark kachinas were going to destroy the world. Something like that would be important to anyone. It should have been important to David, but all he could think about was how the Bow Clan had killed Terrie.

"But at what cost? They killed my girlfriend because they saw her through my eyes when I went to visit her. If I don't remember what happened soon, who will they kill next trying to get to me? My parents? My boss? I don't want any more deaths on my conscience."

Adam frowned. "You may not be able to avoid it."

David jumped to his feet and dusted his backside off.

"Yes, I can. If I can figure out why I see things through the Bow Clan's eyes, and why they see things through my eyes."

"I can't tell you why or even how. I only know that it is."

"You're a psychic," Sarah said suddenly.

"I am not," David snapped.

"But that would explain why you see things through their eyes. It's like you are reading their minds. You even called what's happened to you psychic visions."

David shook his head furiously as if he were trying to shake the words out of his head. "If I were psychic, why would I only be able to see things through their minds? Wouldn't I also be able to read other people's minds?"

"Do you?"

"No," David snapped.

"Maybe you can. Try and see if you can read my mind."

David laughed. "That's stupid."

"Do you have any other ideas?"

David closed his eyes and rubbed his temples. He tried to connect with Sarah's mind, but he didn't see anything.

He opened his eyes and shrugged his shoulders.

Sarah sighed and walked back to the tent.

Suddenly, David saw an image in his mind of a dog. For a moment, he thought it might be an actual stray that had wandered into the camp. It was an ugly black-and-white mutt. It sat looking at David with its head cocked and tongue hanging out. Although the dog was right next to Adam, he didn't seem to see it. David wanted to tell the dog to get away. He opened his mouth to call out to the dog.

"Tagalong," was what came out of his mouth.

Sarah stopped and turned around. "What did you say?"

David shrugged. "I don't know. I saw this dog and called out to him."

"You said, 'Tagalong.'"

"Did I?" He wasn't sure what he said, but he knew it wasn't what he meant to say.

"Tagalong was a dog I had when I lived in Phoenix. I was thinking about him."

"Was he an ugly black-and-white dog?"

"He was black and white, but I never thought he was ugly," Sarah answered with some hurt in her voice.

"You have to admit he was mangy."

Sarah's eyes widened. "You did see my thoughts."

Kel´hoya saw the woman and wanted to reach out to her, but he realized she was only an image in his mind. So Pahana had chosen to have another woman protect him. Didn't he know it was futile to resist the power of the dark kachinas and the Bow Clan? Sooner or later he would be caught and killed, and when he was, his death would not be pleasant.

Pahana turned, and Kel´hoya saw the old man. This was the one who had knocked Kel´hoya away from Pahana in the white pueblo. If it had not been for him, Kel´hoya would have been able to kill Pahana the first night. He could have returned to Kuskurza by now without having had to suffer the embarrassment of failure in front of To´chi.

If Pahana thought he could find protection with this old man again, he was wrong. He would pay for his defiance.

136

CHAPTER 30

David drove back to his apartment amazed at what Sarah's experiment had shown him. He was a psychic. He had suspected it ever since he realized he could see through one of the Bow Clansmen's eyes, but why couldn't he remember any other psychic incidents? Were the psychic urgings so subtle that David hadn't realized what they were?

He parked his car in front of his apartment and got out. As he started up the stairs toward the front door, he heard someone speak his name.

David turned and saw Sheriff Harding leaning against the hood of his police cruiser. His stomach strained the buttons on his light-brown shirt. David held out his hand to the law officer.

"Hello, sheriff. It's good to see you," David said as he approached the sheriff.

Sheriff Harding stared silently at him.

"I wasn't sure if you'd heard. I wanted to be the one to tell you," Sheriff Harding said.

"Tell me what?" David wondered for a moment if the sheriff was going to say that the Bow Clan had attacked his parents in Provo.

"Terrie McNee was murdered last night."

David tried to look shocked. He didn't want the sheriff to know he had driven by Terrie's trailer last night. The sheriff watched David's reaction carefully, and David wondered if he was successful.

"I wanted to go by and see her last night, but when I called, she said she was busy." It was a lie, but David was sure Terrie would have told him she was busy if he had called.

Sheriff Harding barely nodded keeping his eyes on David. "So what did you do last night?"

"I stayed home and rested. I've only been out of the hospital a couple of days. I'm still not quite myself."

"That's interesting. I tried calling you last night, and I didn't get an answer."

David thought for a moment and then said, "Well, you must have called when I took the trash out to the curb or when I went to the store for some milk and bread. I guess you didn't leave a message on my answering machine because I checked both times I came back in."

David didn't like lying to the sheriff. His mother had taught him when he was younger that a man's lies always come back to haunt him, but David couldn't very well say he was having psychic visions. The sheriff would never believe him. It was hard enough for David to believe it himself.

"Did you know a man named Randy Houser?" the sheriff asked.

David shook his head.

"It seems your girlfriend might have known him. He was with her in the trailer when she was killed."

David tried not to react. Houser. So that was Randy's last name. Not that it mattered much now.

"I'm sorry to hear that, sheriff. I guess it might have been me if Terrie had told me to come over."

"How was your relationship with Terrie, Mr. Purcell?" Sheriff Harding asked suddenly.

The sheriff suspected him! How could he think David would kill anyone? But why not? Hadn't David unknowingly led the Bow Clan to Terrie and Randy? Didn't that make him an accomplice?

"Things haven't been great for the last couple of months. We both discovered we wanted different things out of life and those wants had started leading us in different directions. If she thought I had died in the caves, she might have been seeing someone else if that's what you're getting at."

Sheriff Harding pushed himself off the hood of the car and stood face to face with David.

"That's part of what I was wondering about. The other part is: If she was seeing someone else, how would you feel about it?"

David thought about his answer. If he didn't phrase it quite right, the sheriff would surely suspect him. If he outright lied, he might be too obvious or unconvincing.

"Well, if things had been great between us, I would have been very upset. As it was, I've been expecting a breakup. In fact, she hinted at it when I was in the hospital. I think she was just waiting for me to be released. So, if she had been seeing someone, I would have been upset, but I don't think I would have been surprised."

"Are you still on disability with your company, Mr. Purcell?"

David thought that was a strange question to ask amid all the others.

"Till the end of the month."

"Good. I hope to have some answers about this case by then, so until then I would like to ask that you not leave the county."

"Do you think I killed Terrie and Randy, Sheriff?"

Sheriff Harding had a poker face that rivaled Adam's.

"I'm not saying that at all, Mr. Purcell. It's just that I have a double homicide in my county, the first I've ever seen in my twenty years as a law officer. I don't mind telling you, I don't like it at all. And you happen to have known one of the victims quite well. If I have any questions about Terrie, I may need to talk to you. I don't want this murder to go unsolved for long. There's an election coming up, and people have a funny way of not reelecting a sheriff who can't solve the county's first murders in four years."

"What happens if I need to leave the county for some reason?"

"Why would you need to do that? You don't have to go to work."

Sheriff Harding sounded like an innocent boy, but David was beginning to feel led by the nose.

"I was supposed to see my parents in Provo this weekend," David said.

"Well, I can't keep you in the county, but it certainly wouldn't look good if you left. Do you know what I mean?"

David did. He was a suspect in Terrie's murder.

CHAPTER 32

The Bow Clansmen watched the Outlanders from their position behind the scrub brush. The dark kachinas had given them another night to help them hide, but their pa'tuwvotas and the scrub brush were still needed to shield the glow of their white skin from the Outlanders.

Kel'hoya watched the old man with particular interest. He knew To'chi wanted to make the woman a slave, and perhaps, his personal breeder in Kuskurza. This was all right with Kel'hoya. All he wanted was to kill the old man and avenge himself of his defeat and embarrassment two nights ago.

The deaths of the other two Outlanders last night had put the taste of murder in his mouth and a war cry in his heart. The murders had helped him align his wandering mind and focus himself on his purpose for being in the Fourth World. He was here to protect the dark kachinas from the Outlanders. In a few years when the light had faded enough, the dark kachinas would be all powerful once again. They would rise to the Fourth World and destroy the Outlanders in the same way Taiowa had destroyed the ancients in the First and Second Worlds.

Kel'hoya closed his eyes to narrow slits and watched the movement in front of him over the top of his pa'tuwvota. The female Outlander walked around the camp while the old man sat in front of the fire with his back toward it. He was facing away from Kel'hoya, so the Bow Clansman did not know if the old man was awake or asleep. He hoped he was awake. A man should always look death in the face before it took him.

Kel'hoya expected the old man to fight well. He had shown his spirit in the white pueblo. It would be an honor for Kel'hoya to face him now and kill him. To'chi thought the woman would be easy to take, but Kel'hoya did not underestimate her ability, either. He had thought the old man as useless as the old men of Kuskurza, but this one had a warrior's spirit. If the woman was his child, she might have inherited some of his spirit, which would make her a formidable opponent. The Sun Clan women were excellent warriors, and so was this one.

If they could kill the old man and subdue the woman for To'chi, then they could wait for Pahana to return to the camp and kill him.

Perhaps the woman would be the prize they needed to get the dark kachinas to spare their lives. The dark kachinas desperately needed women to breed with the Bow Clan now, and this woman would birth strong children...strong Bow Clansmen. The dark kachinas might even forgive Kel'hoya and To'chi for their partial failure if they could return with a woman for the

140

breeding chamber.

Kel´hoya smiled. Yes. Yes, they would forgive him. He would not have to die. He and To´chi would lead the Bow Clan to the Outlanders and destroy them all.

David sat on his couch and unsuccessfully tried to watch the ten o'clock news. Failing that, he stood up and paced around the well-lit room. He went to his back window and looked out into the back yard. He couldn't see anyone out there, but for some reason, he felt that Sheriff Harding or one of his deputies was parked in a car down the road watching and waiting for David to try and leave.

David was uncomfortable with the speed at which events were moving. The questions were coming at him very quickly, but the answers came much more slowly. There was no happy medium.

He turned back toward the television to hear the weather report and froze. He saw the desert in front of him. Then he saw the fire with the old man sitting in front of it. He knew it was Adam immediately. However, it took a few seconds for the fact that if he was seeing Adam sitting in front of the fire, David must be having another of what Adam called visions.

That meant the Bow Clan was watching the camp. The only way they could know where Sarah and Adam were staying would be if they had seen the camp through David's eyes this morning. He had led the Bow Clan to Adam and Sarah just like he had led them to Terrie and Randy.

David couldn't let them be killed. He didn't want two more deaths on his conscience.

He had to get out to the desert before the Bow Clansmen attacked Adam and Sarah. If the sheriff or one of his deputies wanted to follow, all the better. He didn't know what he would do when he got there, but at least if he had the sheriff with him, he could point out the Bow Clansmen and let the sheriff do what the people elected him to do.

He ran out of his apartment without even turning off the television.

Kel´hoya and To´chi screamed together as they flew from behind the scrub brush on their pa´tuwvotas. The female rushed into the tent, but the old man remained unmoved as if he had not heard the Bow Clan war cry.

To´chi's pa´tuwvota tilted away from Kel´hoya as the younger Bow Clansman ventured after the woman. As To´chi passed the old man, though, the Outlander suddenly came to life. His hand moved quickly grabbing onto the edge of the pa´tuwvota and flipped it over. To´chi went sprawling face first into the dust. Adam let go of the saucer and picked up a small log from the fire. He held onto it with both hands, and as To´chi started to rise off the ground, Adam hit him in the face with the burning end of the log. To´chi screamed falling back onto the ground.

Adam turned toward Kel'hoya, but then from behind the old Indian, To'chi started to move. He stood up swaying back and forth. Kel'hoya could see his companion was surprised at his instability. To'chi staggered toward the old man. Adam stood holding the burning log and faced To'chi. There was no fear on Adam's face, at least not yet. He waited patiently as To'chi approached, but To'chi never reached him. He fell on his face again and lay still.

David saw the pale-skinned warrior fall and smiled. At least Adam had a chance to defend himself. And if David was any judge of character, Sarah wouldn't be hiding waiting for someone to help her.

He looked in his rear-view mirror and was disappointed that he didn't see a deputy following him. He hoped that the fact he was speeding would also attract some attention, but there didn't seem to be anyone on the highway at all.

He was forced to slow up because he couldn't see the road clearly when a vision appeared. David pumped the brakes lightly as he waited for the image to fade. Just before it did, he saw the Bow Clansman whose eyes he saw his visions through move toward Adam.

And David was still two miles away from the camp.

Adam turned back to Kel'hoya. Kel'hoya could not believe the old man looked so relaxed. Did he have no fear of the Bow Clan at all? Pahana had chosen his protector wisely when he had chosen this one.

As he neared the old man, the woman rushed out from the tent and flipped over his pa'tuwvota spilling him hard onto the ground. Before he could stand, the woman kicked him in the side. She jumped on his back holding onto his braid with one hand and trying to scratch his eyes out with her other hand.

Kel'hoya swung his elbow backward and managed to knock her off his back. The woman grunted and fell away. He spun around with the intention of killing her, but it was not her he wanted to kill.

Adam advanced on the Bow Clansman with the burning log that had probably killed To'chi. Kel'hoya grabbed the woman and held her in front of him. The old man froze with his arm poised to swing the log.

Kel'hoya pushed the woman in front of him toward the old man. Adam's hand dropped slightly away from Kel'hoya as he tried to catch Sarah from falling.

Rushing forward, Kel'hoya tackled the old man in the chest. He grabbed for the log, but Adam would not relinquish his grip. Instead of trying to pull the log away from the old man's hand, Kel'hoya turned it inward and used his strength to control the force of the log. The old man was strong, but Kel'hoya was a member of the Bow Clan. He slammed the log into Adam's face, and the old man released his grip. Kel'hoya took hold of the log and pounded Adam's head until he heard bone break.

The old man gasped and then lay still. Kel'hoya rolled off the old man's body. The woman screamed. As he started toward her to silence her, he felt the ground tremble beneath him. Behind him, he saw one of the Outlander's vehicles approaching.

Should he stay and fight more Outlanders? He had managed to kill the old man, but the woman would fight him and so would the Outlanders in the vehicle.

He saw To'chi's body lying nearby. Should he hide the body so that the Outlanders wouldn't see it?

What would the dark kachinas have him do?

David slammed on the brakes of the Corolla. He threw open the door and jumped out of the car.

"Adam! Sarah!" he screamed.

He saw the Bow Clansman rise up and stare at him.

David wished he had some sort of a weapon to fight with. He didn't know how strong the Bow Clansmen were. As skinny as they were, they certainly didn't look too powerful, but that didn't mean anything.

David saw Sarah kneeling over Adam, and he wondered if he was too late again. He ran toward the Bow Clansman and dove at him as the pale-skinned man began to rise up. As he felt the man's fingers close around his throat, David punched him in the face.

Turning, he saw Sarah charging at the pale-skinned man with a knife in her hand. The Bow Clansman managed to roll out of the way just as she reached him. The remaining Bow Clansman hooked an arm under his dead companion's arm and pulled the body onto a saucer made of a reptilian skin covered with feathers. He sat next to the dead man as the saucer rose off the ground. It was the same type of flying saucer David had seen the Bow Clan fly on the night they attacked him in the hospital.

Before David could move toward it, it flew off with both of the Bow Clansmen on it.

David heard sobbing and spun around thinking Sarah might be in trouble. Sarah was kneeling over Adam. When David walked up beside her, he could see Adam's eyes were wide open staring at the night sky. Part of his skull was dented inward, and he was bleeding from his nose.

David had been too late again. Adam was dead.

PART II

Oraibi

"Many miles away in every direction, Oraibi now established shrines or altars marking the furthest limits of the land claimed by the Hopi."

Book of the Hopi

"Her house is the way to hell, going down to the chambers of death."

Proverbs 7:29

CHAPTER 32

The land on the reservation was flat and barren. If David hadn't known better, he would have sworn that nothing could have lived in the area. Yet, his headlights shined on rabbit brush and juniper scattered among the rocks that were near the highway. He knew there were animals he couldn't see, too. Most of them prowled and foraged far from the road for their evening meal. And then, there were the Hopis.

David saw their small tourist stands, not much more than wooden stalls with tables, spaced along the side of the road. The Hopis sold turquoise jewelry, pottery, and handwoven rugs to the tourists who stopped at the stands. They were bare now. Even the Hopi didn't do business in the night.

David saw the brake lights on the truck in front of him go on, and he slowed his car. He was following Sarah back to Oraibi. They had driven down Highway 191 until they hit Highway 160. Following that road to Tuba City, they had turned onto State Road 264. Now Sarah was starting up the side of Third Mesa on the Hopi Reservation. Oraibi was somewhere on top of the mesa.

How had he let Sarah talk him into coming with her? He was a fugitive from the law now. At least that was what Sheriff Harding had implied he would be if he left the county. Not only had he left the county, but he had left the state as well.

David started to blame Sarah for his troubles, but she had not charmed him into accompanying her at all. Liking white men was not one of her personality traits. David's own guilt and fear had forced him to risk making himself look like a suspect to come with Sarah back to Oraibi to bury Adam. He felt guilty because he had been unable to reach Adam in time to save him from the Bow Clansmen. He felt fear of being left alone while one more member of the Bow Clan still hunted him. So he had decided making Sheriff Harding angry would be safer than waiting for the Bow Clan to attack and kill him.

They passed through a town of pueblos without stopping. David hadn't even realized they were pueblos until he was inside the town. From a distance, and in the dark, the town looked like a part of the mesa.

David parked next to the truck and waited for Sarah to get out. She sat for at least five minutes in the truck just staring out the window over the edge of the mesa. She silently climbed out, glanced in the truck bed at the body of her grandfather wrapped in the tent they had been camping in, and walked into a nearby room.

David followed her through the open door. There were no curtains on the small windows of the house, and the front door was ill-fitted for the frame. Whenever it rained, the door probably swelled so much that it would be impossible for anyone to open it. Not that it rained much on the reservation.

The main room had a hand-made wooden bench against the far wall. To the right of the bench was a wooden rocking chair, also hand-made. Two small kegs with a plank laid across them served as a table. And, on the table was an eight-by-ten picture of Adam and a group who David assumed were Adam's wife and children. The little bit of light in the room came from the small window above the table. Only now that it was dark, the light came from an oil lamp, which Sarah had lit.

Sarah sat down in the rocking chair. The lamp light accentuated each small crevice and curve on her face making her look much older and tired. David sat down on the furthest end of the bench.

"You look like you need some sleep," David said. "I know I do."

Sarah shook her head. "I can't rest now. I must bury my grandfather before morning. Then I will need to sit with the body until the sun rises," Sarah said.

"You can bury him tomorrow. Right now you need rest. You've had a very rough night."

Sarah stood up and started for the door. "I can't. I have a responsibility to my grandfather. This is the Hopi way."

"It won't do him any good if you kill yourself in the process," David warned her.

Sarah smiled weakly at him. "Thank you for your concern, but I must do what my grandfather would do in my place. I just came here to show you where you can sleep tonight." She stood up and walked to the door. "I'll probably be back before you rise in the morning. We need to talk about the Bow Clan tomorrow."

She went out the door and left David sitting alone in the poorly lit room.

CHAPTER 33

Jared aimed the spotlight at Gary, Christine, and Lou as they checked the hoses and fittings on each other's dive gear. He called out each piece of equipment he wanted them to recheck. When he told Lou to check the seal on the waterproof flashlight for the third time, Lou scowled and flashed the light in Jared's eyes. Even Gary, who knew why Jared was so careful, was getting a little annoyed.

Among the six-person team, Jared was the only one who refused to dive within a cave. Five years ago, his primary and two secondary lights had gone out while he was diving, and he barely found his way back to the surface before his air had run out. He might not have made it back if Gary hadn't hung a light stick in the water to act as a beacon. The odds against all three light sources failing on a dive was high, but Jared had never been able to work up his nerve to make a cave dive after that, and Gary really couldn't blame him.

Gary looked at Jared's concerned face and immediately felt bad for feeling annoyed with his friend. He slapped Jared on the shoulder and said, "Don't worry. We each have two flashlights and a handful of light sticks."

Jared blushed. "Sorry, Gary." He pointed to the sump, a small pond about fifty feet in diameter, completely filling the downward-sloping tunnel. "I don't consider that part of the cave system. I think it's a death trap. You couldn't pay me enough to get me back in one of those."

Gary chuckled. "I've seen you hang over a two-hundred-foot chasm on a thin piece of nylon, any you're saying this is a death trap?"

Jared flashed a broad smile. "Well, I guess I ought to know, shouldn't I?"

He bent over and tied the lead line to the stake he had set into the ground. When the knot was tied, Jared gave it a hard tug and then leaned on it to see if the knot would slip. It didn't. As Gary watched Jared work, he thought at least he wouldn't have to worry about safety. Jared was fanatical about making sure every precaution had been taken to ensure the safety of the divers he supervised.

They had found the water-filled tunnel yesterday evening just before they went back to the RV for the night. It was the first source of water anyone had seen since they had started exploring the caverns. The first thing they did was drop a small amount of yellow dye into the water to see if there was any current in the water. If the dye had begun to move in one direction, it would have indicated an active stream, but there was no current. The dye spread out radially on the ripples the small splash had caused. The small pond appeared to be only a sump, a low section of tunnel that had flooded. It also happened to be the first source of water they had seen since entering the cave.

Gary cleaned out his mask and slipped it over his head. Lou and Christine did the same. As they moved toward the water's edge, Gary unclipped a flashlight from his belt and turned it on. When the light came on, he stepped into the water. He could stand in the water up to his waist by standing on a submerged ledge. Lou and Christine unhooked their own flashlights and joined Gary in the water. He bit down on his mouthpiece and turned on his air tanks.

"Check your pressure gauge!" Jared called from the shore.

Gary glanced at the gauge, noted that it was registering correctly, and waved to Jared. Gary turned to Lou and Christine and nodded to them. Then he rolled onto his back and sunk below the surface of the water.

When all three of them were in the water and had their flashlights turned on and aimed in the same direction, Gary could see about fifteen feet. He signaled to Lou and Christine and began to swim deeper. He needed to find the other side of the sump. The passage took a sharp drop for about seventy feet. It narrowed until Gary thought they would have to turn back because he wouldn't be able to fit through the passage. Just as he was about to give the signal to return, the passage widened enough for him to swim through.

Gary glanced at his pressure gauge. He still had plenty of air left.

He looked around himself and suppressed a chill. It was easy to get claustrophobia while cave diving, especially when he remembered there was no way to escape if he ran out of air. He didn't blame Jared for not wanting to dive. It was too easy to get trapped or get lost in the dark water. Too easy to die. But, if he wanted to see what lay beyond the sump and finished exploring the cave system, he needed to go through the water to the other side.

Gary rose gradually, and he turned to make sure that Lou and Christine were behind him. He saw Christine close to him, but he couldn't see Lou. Gary pointed behind Christine. She turned to look, and then she turned back and shrugged.

He started to swim back the way he had come following the guide wire Christine was holding. After a few moments, he saw Lou's light. When Gary swam closer, he saw that Lou had jammed himself in between two rocks while he was trying to go through the narrow passage at the bottom of the sump. Gary pushed on Lou's shoulders to dislodge him.

Once free, Lou moved backward and quickly checked his equipment to make sure he hadn't damaged his tanks or valves. When he was satisfied, he signaled OK to Gary. Gary nodded and watched as Lou carefully turned on his side and slid through the passage at the widest area he could find. He snagged himself again, but it lasted only momentarily and then he was through.

Lou would certainly hear some jokes about his weight when he got to the other side of the sump.

Gary swam with Lou back up to where Christine was waiting. Together, the three of them floated to the surface. As Gary's head broke the surface, the first thing that he saw was another tunnel that continued into the darkness.

Will it ever end? he thought to himself.

CHAPTER 34

Sarah woke up from her nap an hour after the sun went down. She had slept the entire day away after returning from burying her grandfather in the place he had shown her two years ago. She thought about what lay before her tonight and felt a heavy sense of sorrow at the duty she had to perform. She wished it could all be some sort of bad dream. She was alone now. Both her grandparents were dead. Her mother was off in some big city somewhere, which was as good as dead as far as Sarah was concerned, and she had never known her father.

She blinked and then rubbed her eyes. She could tell by looking out the window that the sun was down, but it still seemed very bright inside the bedroom. She looked at the doorway into the main room. It looked as bright as midday in there.

Sarah climbed out of bed and walked to the doorway. David had lit a large fire in the fireplace and all three oil lamps. He was sitting in the chair beside the window staring out into the dark.

The heat from the fire had warmed the small room to at least eighty degrees when the outside temperature was probably sixty.

"Why did you start a fire?" Sarah asked.

David jumped and spun around in the chair. He put his hand on his chest. "You startled me. I didn't hear you get up."

"Why did you start a fire? You're not cooking, and it's not cold enough to use it for heat." She waved her hand around the room. "And why do you have all three lamps burning? You're staring outside. You won't be able to see anything out there with all this light. Wood is scarce around here, as is money to buy oil for the lamps."

David looked at the ground. "I feel more comfortable this way."

Sarah put her hands on her hips. "Are you cold-blooded or something?"

David shook his head.

Sarah walked around to each of the lamps and turned the wicks down until the flames went out. As each flame was extinguished, Sarah thought she saw David shudder. Was it possible he was afraid of the dark? If that was so, he must have been terrified in the caves being in complete darkness.

David moved from the window and sat down in front of the fireplace.

"What were you staring at out there?" Sarah asked.

"I was just wondering if the last Bow Clansman would come after me here. I haven't received any more visions from him. Does that mean he hasn't received any from me? Am I out of range for this psychic thing to work?"

"I don't know, but I can't hide in here with you. I have work to do."

Sarah picked up her canteen and canvas bag filled with jerked beef and piki. Then she headed for the doorway.

"What work?"

"I have to make sure my grandfather reaches the spirit world."

Kel'hoya awoke disappointed. He had hoped the dark kachinas would show him another vision of where Pahana was. Kel'hoya had tried to let his mind travel outside his body, but there was nothing attracting it.

Had Pahana somehow shielded his mind?

No, that was impossible. It couldn't be done.

Perhaps after his failure and the death of To'chi, the dark kachinas felt he was no longer deserving of the visions.

To'chi's body lay in the corner of the cave already stiffened because his spirit had left his body. How could To'chi have been so foolish as to underestimate his enemy? His mistake had cost him his life.

Kel'hoya's stomach growled. He put his hand on it to quiet it. He had not eaten since he left the sipapu. If he did not eat soon, he would be too weak to kill Pahana.

Kel'hoya laid his pa'tuwvota flat on the ground and then sat on it. It was time to hunt for food. If he could eliminate the hunger that gnawed at his stomach and mind, he might receive a vision of where he might find Pahana and redeem himself. Besides, there were no supplies left. Their journey to Tu'waqachi was supposed to have been a short one.

The Bow Clan must survive at all costs. If To'chi had to die to continue the secrecy of Kuskurza, so be it. If Kel'hoya had to die to free the dark kachinas, he would.

The pa'tuwvota rose off the ground about a foot and moved toward the exit from the sipapu.

David stepped out onto the street and watched Sarah. She walked across the plaza to the truck and looked back at him.

"Are you coming with me?" she called.

As a reply, David jogged across the plaza toward her. Sarah had the truck started by the time he jumped into the cab beside her.

"Are we going to a cemetery?"

Sarah shook her head. "We're going to a canyon about half an hour away from here. I buried my grandfather on the Navajo reservation, but what they don't know won't hurt them."

"Why can't we go in the morning? What's this thing you have about doing stuff in the dead of night?" David asked.

"I have to watch the body for the next four nights. I can't let anything happen to it that might impede my grandfather's spirit getting into the spirit world."

They were silent for the rest of the drive. Not even the radio was playing. When Sarah pull off the highway onto a dirt road in the middle of nowhere, she turned her headlights off and navigated by starlight. She parked at the mouth of a small canyon her grandfather had shown her two years ago and got out of the truck.

David followed her as she walked into the canyon. Sarah climbed up a narrow trail that ran along the side of one of the mesas that bordered the canyon. About one-hundred feet up, she stopped and squatted down.

"You buried your grandfather here?" David said when he joined her.

Sarah nodded. She patted the rock at her back. "His body is behind here. I have to make sure it stays safe until Sunday morning at dawn."

David squatted down beside her and leaned against the mesa wall. He turned on his flashlight and let the beam play over the walls of the mesa. Sarah watched him.

"Try it without the light," she said.

David shook his head. "Not yet. Maybe when all this is over."

"They won't get you here, David."

"How do you know?"

Sarah shrugged. "I don't know. It's something I feel inside. Maybe I'm a little psychic, too."

A stone, dislodged by a passing animal, fell from high up the side of the mesa. David jumped to his feet and looked around in all directions. Sarah grabbed hold of his arm and pulled him back to the ground. Once he was seated, she continued to hold onto his arm.

"Thank you for coming tonight. I know this is probably the last place you want to be."

David nodded. His eyes still darted around looking for the source of the noise. "I liked Adam even though I only knew him a short time. He saved my life in the hospital. I owe him a lot. Right now, any understanding I have of this situation came from him. I only wished I could have helped him when he needed it," David said.

"My grandfather was an old man. He has seen the Hopi go through many changes. Some have even fallen away from their beliefs in the legends of our people. My grandfather always believed in the legends. He taught me to believe, and he tried to teach my mother to believe when she younger, which was probably why she rebelled. Dying answered his unknown question as to whether his faith had been correctly placed in the beliefs. He died knowing the legends were true. I don't think he would be sorry about that."

"That may be, but I think I'll still miss him."

Sarah leaned against David.

"I will too."

CHAPTER 35

Sarah and David drove back to Old Oraibi when the sun started to peek over the horizon. David staggered into the rooms in the pueblo and fell onto the bed that had been Adam's. He had only slept a few hours during the day yesterday and none at all last night. If he had been more awake, he might have felt uncomfortable about sleeping in a dead man's bed, but he was too tired to be choosy.

He dreamed of a great pueblo even larger than all of the small pueblos in Old Oraibi combined. It towered eight stories and was probably 200 yards wide. In his dream, he stood away from it in the twilight of a day. The pueblo was nestled into the crevice formed by the ground meeting a receding wall from the mountain. David tilted his head back to try and see where the mountain ended and the sky began.

It didn't.

There was no sky, only a stone ceiling. But then, where did the light come from? Was this Kuskurza?

Sarah woke him at eleven. He tried to push her away, but she kept shaking his arm.

"Come on. We've got to be in Hotevilla," she told him.

"Why?" David asked trying to pull a blanket over his head to keep the sunlight out of his eyes.

"There's a snake dance."

David finally surrendered to Sarah's urgings and rolled out of bed. He stood up and looked around the room.

"Where's the bathroom?"

"There is none," Sarah told him.

"Then where am I going to shower?"

"The only running water is at the cultural center, but you don't have time to go there. There's a pitcher filled with water and a basin in the main room. Wash yourself there."

David sighed and shook his head. He unbuttoned his shirt and walked into the living room. After pouring water into the basin, he splashed his face, which woke him up almost immediately. After that, he was able to wash quickly. It wasn't hard. He wanted as little of the cold water touching him as possible.

When he had changed into a clean shirt and jeans, he and Sarah drove north on the mesa to Hotevilla. This was the first town they had passed through when they came to Oraibi two nights ago. Hotevilla looked much newer than Oraibi. It wasn't in such dire need of repair as the older village. Then again it hadn't been inhabited for eight centuries like Oraibi had.

"Many of the traditionalists that used to live in Oraibi now live here," Sarah explained as they parked. "Many years ago, there was much controversy in Oraibi over whether to accept the white man's ways or not. When the controversy ended, the traditionalists left Oraibi and formed this village and Bakabi, which is next to it."

A crowd of people filled the edges of the central plaza. Cars were parked two or three abreast along the roads leading to the center of town. David noticed that many of the people in Hotevilla were white. They had come from outside the reservation to see the Hopi Snake Dance.

David and Sarah found an empty place to sit on the second level of one of the pueblos. The plaza was formed by the back walls of four pueblos built to create a square courtyard.

"Is this a dance put on for tourists?" David asked.

Sarah shook her head. "No, this is a dance for rain so that our crops will survive. The tourists are allowed to come, but they can't take pictures. This is a sacred dance."

The crowd around David suddenly fell silent. He heard chanting, but it wasn't coming from the crowd. A single line of costumed men shuffled into the plaza singing a solemn chant.

"Those are the antelope priests," Sarah whispered in David's ear.

The antelope priests circled the plaza and lined up along one side and waited. David found himself watching anxiously. The air seemed tense and exciting by the time the snake priests entered the plaza, opposing the antelope priests.

For the first time, David noticed a small bower made of cottonwood branches in the center of the plaza.

"That is the kisi. The snakes are kept there," Sarah told him when he pointed the bower out to her.

In front of the kisi was a wooden drum. Nothing more than a thick plank sitting across a pit in the ground.

"That," Sarah whispered pointing to the hole, "symbolizes the sipapu. The snake priests stomp on the drum to notify the gods of the underworld that the ceremony is beginning."

As the two groups of spectacularly attired and painted priests faced each other across the plaza, the gourd rattles tied to the priests' legs vibrated sounding like a giant rattlesnake. A deep, sonorous chorus reminded David of an approaching storm. As the song increased in volume, the lines of the priests swayed back and forth until, at a climax in the song, they separated.

The snake priests reformed themselves in groups of three men, and these groups danced with a strange leaping motion entirely different from any dance step David had ever seen.

As the first group of dancers passed the kisi, the first man in the trio reached in among the boughs of cottonwood with one arm. David wondered if their idea was to get bitten by the rattlesnakes inside.

"There's a snake priest hidden in the kisi. He hands each dancer a snake," Sarah said.

"He's sitting in there alone with a lot of snakes?" David couldn't believe it.

The dancer pulled out his arm, and he was holding a snake in his fist. He immediately placed the rattlesnake in his mouth, grasping it with his teeth and lips a few inches in back of the reptile's head. The snake writhed and rattled, but it did not turn and bite the man who held it in his mouth. The second man put his arm around the shoulder of the man carrying the snake, and the third man walked behind the other two.

"Why doesn't the snake bite the dancer?" David asked.

"The snake knows the dancer won't harm it. As long as the dancer remains pure of heart, the snake will sense it," Sarah told him.

"And the snakes always cooperate?"

"Not always. If a snake becomes unmanageable, the second dancer will distract it by stroking it with his snake whip."

The snake priests danced around in a circle with his snake four times, then he dropped it gently to the ground. The third man in the trio bent over and picked the snake up.

The nine other trios copied the process. Then the first dancer of the first trio took another snake from the kisi and danced again. Each trio did the dance five times until a total of fifty snakes were being held by various dancers.

David glanced away from the dance to look around, and he saw a tourist off to his left raising a camera to his face.

"Didn't you say that cameras aren't allowed here?" David asked.

"Yes."

David pointed to the tourist. Sarah's face flushed red for a moment. She stood up and walked over to the man.

"Sir, you aren't allowed to photograph this ceremony," Sarah told the young man.

"Don't worry, squaw lady, I won't steal their souls or anything. I just wanted to show some people back home how stupid those dancers are to hold the snakes in their mouths."

Sarah took a deep breath. "I'm sorry, but cameras are not allowed. Either you'll have to put the camera away or leave."

She stepped in front of the man to block his view of the plaza.

"Hey, get out of my way. They're just getting to the good part!" He reached forward to push Sarah out of the way.

David jumped up and grabbed the camera out of the man's hand. The man turned in his direction, and as he did, David opened the camera, popped out the data card, and crushed it on the ground. The man stood up on the roof of the pueblo.

"Hey, you can't do that," the man protested.

"The lady asked you to put the camera away. If you had, you might have saved the pictures you had already taken. Now you don't get any." David tossed the camera to the man.

"What are you? An Indian lover or something? Is this your squaw?" As the man spoke, David could smell alcohol on his breath.

David stepped forward surprised at the anger welling up in himself. Sarah stepped between them. He knew even as he prepared himself for a fight, it wasn't entirely this jerk's fault. Part of his anger came from his frustration at not being able to help save Terrie and Adam from the Bow Clan. Now he had a chance to help Sarah if only in a small way. He wasn't going to miss it.

"David, don't. Not here," Sarah pleaded. "This is a religious ceremony."

"But..."

"It won't bring Adam back. You stopped this man from taking the pictures. I'm sure everyone appreciates it, but don't hit him."

David backed away. "Okay."

The man laughed. "That's right, Indian lover, listen to your squaw."

David sat down and tried to tune the man's words out. Sarah sat down beside him and held his hand. David looked around and saw many of the people on the second level of the pueblo either staring at him or the man. He hadn't meant to draw their attention away from the ceremony.

"Thank you," Sarah whispered in his ear.

David looked at her and smiled. Then he turned his attention back to the dance.

During the dance, a priest who had preceded the dancers into the plaza sprinkled corn meal on both dancers and snakes. At one point in the dance, several women garbed in old-style Hopi costumes, entered the plaza. They held baskets in front of them containing finely ground corn meal. They also sprinkled the cornmeal on both the snakes and the dancers.

When all the snakes had been danced with and were being held by either the third men in the trios or an antelope priest, the priest with the corn meal used the last of his corn meal to draw a circular design upon the ground. The dancers tossed all of the snakes onto the design, and the women scattered the rest of their meal on the writhing snakes.

The Hopi spectators near the snakes added their spittle to the sprinkling of corn meal. Then it seemed everything suddenly went crazy. Snakes darted in all directions, and the dancers had a difficult time keeping them heaped on the cornmeal design.

David watched the rude man climb down the ladder all the way to the ground level so he could get a good look at the snakes in the cornmeal circle. David was glad to see him go.

David stood on the edge of pueblo so that he could see the pile of snakes clearly. He heard a group of women scream as three quick snakes darted toward them. The dancers picked them up before the snakes bit anyone and placed the reptiles back on the design.

A few moments later, David heard a man scream as another pair of snakes broke from the pile. David saw the rude man break from the crowd and run toward the parked cars.

"He must not like snakes," Sarah said.

David laughed.

After a few minutes, the snake priest dashed into the circle, seized handfuls of the writhing snakes, and rushed out of the village and down the steep trails of the mesa to the fields below.

"They'll thank the snakes and let them go now," Sarah said to David.

In the plaza, the antelope men circled the plaza a few times, stamped on the plank over the sipapu to tell the underworld that the ceremony was over. Then they marched back to the kiva.

"I still don't understand why the snakes don't bite. How could they tell whether someone was pure of heart?" David asked Sarah.

"The dancers have worked for many days to cleanse themselves of evil. The snakes know that no harm will come to them and so they don't bite. It's an animal instinct."

David wasn't sure if he believed her or not, but it certainly seemed to work. None of the snakes had bitten any of the dancers, and luckily, none of the spectators either, although he doubted that they were all so pure of heart.

He walked back down the stone stairs to the ground. As he started to walk toward the pickup truck, he felt someone touch his hand. He looked to his left and saw Sarah holding his hand. She smiled at him, and they walked to the truck together.

CHAPTER 36

Gary led the way as he, Lou, Christine, and Billy Joe worked their way through the tunnel leading from chamber twenty-three. It was a large tunnel with a seven-foot-high ceiling. He glanced at the pedometer on his hip. They had traveled a little under a mile so far in this tunnel. He would have expected it to open up into another chamber before this. None of the other chambers were more than a quarter of a mile apart.

His foot kicked something, and he heard it bounce along the floor of the cave. It had a hollow sound that made him stop.

"Something wrong?" Christine asked from behind him.

"I thought I just kicked a stone, but it didn't sound like a stone," Gary said.

He squatted down and looked in the direction he had kicked the rock. Only there was no stone. There was, however, a charred piece of wood. He grabbed it and stood up.

"What is it?" Lou asked as he came to the front of the line.

"A piece of wood," Gary said.

"Wood? But that's impossible," Billy Joe told him. "This is the center of a cave, not a forest."

Gary held up the six-inch piece of wood. "Not only is it possible, but this branch has also been burnt."

The group fell silent. Gary was thinking the same thing everyone else had to be thinking. How did a piece of wood wind up where there was no wood? How did a fire burn a piece of wood where there were no fires?

"It looks like it was part of a torch," Christine said.

"Then either we are close to the natural entrance, or some unprepared fool decided to go exploring and got himself lost," Gary said.

"There's one more explanation," Lou said. "What if it was part of a torch used by the Indians who left the kachina doll we found the day before yesterday?"

"There's still the problem of what Indians would be doing so deep in a cave."

Lou took the piece of wood from Gary's hand and stared at it in the light of his headlamp.

"One thing's for sure. We're not the first people down here," he told the others.

"Let's keep going," Billy Joe said. "I've waited long enough to find the next chamber."

160

The entrance to the next chamber came a few hundred yards later. The group suddenly found themselves standing on a ledge staring out over a dark chasm. Their flashlight beams could not reach the opposite side of the chamber let alone the ground at the bottom of the abyss.

Gary moved closer to the edge and peered over it. Nothing. Nothing but absolute darkness. He took off his backpack and fished a light stick from it. It was a plastic tube filled with chemicals that when shaken, threw off a dim light. Gary shook the stick until it glowed, then he tossed it over the edge.

It seemed to fall slowly as if it were falling through water and not air. As it passed out of the range of Gary's flashlight, he could still see a shrinking yellow line. That eventually disappeared, but Gary still hadn't seen the bottom of the chasm.

He straightened up and turned to the others.

"Can you see the bottom?" Christine asked.

Gary shook his head. "The light stick may still be falling as far as I know."

"Is it too far to rappel down?" Billy Joe asked.

Gary saw that the ledge behind Billy Joe continued to descend along the edge of the chasm.

"Yea, our lines wouldn't reach nearly far enough, but I think we may still be able to get down to the bottom," he said. He pointed to the trail. "The ledge may go all the way down. Even if it doesn't, it will get us a lot closer to the bottom than rappelling from here would get us."

"So you want to go down to the bottom?" Lou asked.

"Don't you? We're all here to explore and map this cave system, and that's part of it," Gary said.

"But we're not getting any closer to the natural entrance. We're just getting deeper."

"We can find the entrance later. Let's find out where this trail goes and how deep this cavern is."

Gary shouldered his pack and started toward the ledge.

CHAPTER 37

Sarah sat on the rock shelf with her back to the pile of stones that covered her grandfather's burial place. This was the third night of her vigil. She didn't think any animals would be able to get to her grandfather's body, but she was still obligated to watch over him and ensure her grandfather's safe passage to the spirit world.

"Take him to your heart, Taiowa," Sarah whispered to herself.

The watch was a tradition and tradition had suddenly become important to her. She had lived with her grandfather for ten years and had accepted his beliefs and his ways because it pleased him, but she had never really believed in the legends. That is, she never believed in them until she saw one of them kill her grandfather.

The Bow Clan lived.

If there was another world inside the earth, one of the worlds of creation, what did that mean about the Hopis? Were they a different race of humans or had all humans emerged into the Fourth World through their own sipapus?

The thought that she might not be the same as other people, even other Indian races upset her. She had spent her childhood as an outsider in the white man's world. She had always been different from them no matter how much she told herself otherwise. Now it seemed that perhaps she was different from other Indians as well.

Sarah heard a stone fall and for a moment, thought it might be her grandfather exiting from his body on his way to the spirit world. Instead, she saw David climbing the ledge toward her. When he reached where she was sitting on the ledge, he sat down next to her.

"I thought you were asleep back in town," she said.

"I was."

"How did you get out here?"

"I gave Ethan five dollars. He's a nice guy and talented, too. I saw some of the jewelry he made. He probably makes a killing on that stuff in Phoenix."

Sarah fingered her bracelet silently. David saw her and asked, "One of his?"

She nodded. David took her hand in his and brought the bracelet up closer to her face.

"Beautiful," he said.

Sarah looked at him and then quickly looked away.

They sat quietly for awhile. David leaned back and looked up at the stars in the sky. Sarah shifted her body so she was as close to him as she could get

162

without actually touching him.

"Thank you for what you did this afternoon at the snake dance," Sarah said unexpectedly.

"You mean the cameraman? I didn't do anything. You did. I just helped," David told her.

"But you didn't have to."

"Of course I did. You were right, and he was wrong. And besides, he was pretty rude. I may not understand your religion, but just because I don't understand it doesn't mean I shouldn't respect it. The same goes for him, too," David explained.

"Why did you come here tonight?"

"I thought you might want some company. I know I did. It's hard to explain, but even in that town full of people, I still feel alone. I keep expecting to see the second Bow Clansman come after me."

Sarah nodded. "I still feel that way, especially now. My grandfather was one person I didn't feel alone around, but with him gone..."

"You're alone again," David finished.

"Yes."

"Then I hate to tell you what I came to tell you." He paused, and Sarah looked up at him. "I have to go back to Utah tomorrow."

Sarah's anger flared for some reason she didn't understand. She felt as if David had just betrayed her in some way. But she had no hold on him, just as Ethan had no hold on her. David had come to Oraibi to honor Adam, not to be with her.

"Terrie's funeral is tomorrow," David was saying. "I should be there. It's my fault she died. I should tell her I'm sorry."

Sarah turned to David. "Why do you accept the responsibility of her death and my grandfather's death so quickly?"

"Because they are my fault. For some reason, I can't remember, the Bow Clan is after me, and one of them can see through my eyes. He sees what I see. He saw Terrie through my eyes and killed her because he probably thought I was at her trailer. He saw you and Adam through my eyes and the Bow Clan attacked your camp and killed your grandfather. If it hadn't been for me, both of them would still be alive."

"But you can't be held responsible for the actions of the Bow Clan. That's like saying if I gave you directions to someplace and then you got hit by a car while you were crossing the road on your way there, it would be my fault," Sarah told him.

"That's different."

Sarah crossed her arms over her chest. "How? You didn't send the Bow Clan to them on purpose. If you're going to martyr yourself, don't do it slowly. When you're back in Utah, wait around and let the Bow Clan get you.

The last one hasn't given up, you know. He just can't find you because you're too far away from him."

"Is that what you want me to do? To go back to Utah and fight him?"

Sarah turned away. "Of course not. But if you go back to Utah, the Bow Clansman will be able to find you again. He may come after you when you're unprepared."

"That's a chance I have to take. Terrie was my girlfriend. I can't be late for our last date."

"Did you love her?" Sarah asked suddenly.

David rubbed his chin. "At first, definitely. In the end, I'm not so sure. She definitely didn't love me." Sarah decided not to ask how he knew Terrie hadn't been in love with him when she died. "But you know how love is. It messes up your emotions when you're too close to it. You have to step back away from it to see things straight. And the straight truth is that Terrie and I were probably going through the motions for the last three or four months. We had reached a point in our relationship that we couldn't get past," David said.

"No, I don't," Sarah whispered.

"You don't what?"

"I don't know how love is."

David arched his eyebrows. "You've never had a boyfriend?"

"I didn't say that. I just said I don't know what love is."

"What's the difference?"

Sarah stared at him. She turned away from him when she felt the dirty feeling return. When she felt tears start to well in her eyes, she stood up and ran further up the side of the mesa. David quickly caught up with her and grabbed her by the shoulders.

"I'm sorry if I said something to upset you. I didn't mean to."

Sarah turned, leaned her head against his chest and started crying. David stood there and let her cry. She felt foolish doing it, but she was too tired to put up a front even for a white man. So she cried.

Besides, David wasn't like other white men. He had shown that this afternoon in the plaza. She had found what she had been looking for years ago, but now it was too late. This white man was going home to die.

David left her a few hours later around one in the morning. When Sarah got back to the pueblo just after sunrise and opened the door to her rooms, they were empty. David had gone. Her grandfather was gone.

She wondered if she would ever see him again. Or would the Bow Clan kill him?

CHAPTER 38

As the gray-steel coffin disappeared into the grave, David tilted his head back and stared at the bright afternoon sky. He could not stand to look into the dark hole where Terrie's body would rest. It was better to look at the light. The light hid nothing from his eyes. The darkness hid everything.

The grave reminded him of the hole he had fallen into. It looked like a large sipapu. However, for the Hopi, the sipapu was a place of emergence, of new birth. For Terrie, it was a place to be hidden away in and eventually forgotten.

Terrie's parents had chosen to bury their daughter in the Locksley Cemetery in Blanding. They had a large family plot filled with three generations of McNees. Terrie had never wanted to leave Monticello and now she never would.

Nearly a hundred people had turned out to pay their final respects to Terrie. That was one of the benefits of living one's entire life in a single town. Terrie had known a lot of people, and a lot of people knew her. David saw Terrie's old teachers, her old babysitters, and her school friends. Some came from Salt Lake City, Las Vegas, and Boulder, but others had chosen to remain in their hometown just as Terrie had done.

One person hadn't come to pay his respects to Terrie, but to watch David. Sheriff Harding stood on the opposite side of the grave staring across the dark chasm at him. David's parents had driven down from Provo to lend David their support and try to get him to return with them to Provo. He wasn't sure he needed their support and he definitely didn't want to go back to Provo. Terrie was dead because David had led the Bow Clan to her. He didn't want to do the same thing to his parents.

He missed Terrie, and he still felt guilty for leading the Bow Clan to her, but the hole she had left in his life wasn't as large as he thought it would be. Maybe she had been right when she said he was living for his job. Adam's death had left a larger hole in his life, which was odd since David had barely known the man.

As the coffin touched the bottom of the grave, Mrs. McNee sobbed loudly. Terrie's father put his arm around his wife's shoulders and held her tight. Mrs. McNee collapsed into the crook of his arm.

The Mormon bishop closed his Bible and bowed his head in prayer. When he said, "Amen," the people on the fringes of the crowd began to move toward their cars. Terrie's parents stood up and accepted the condolences of many of those leaving.

"Davey, do you want to go get some lunch with your father and me?"

David's mother asked.

David turned around to face his mother and shook his head. "No, thank you. I want to be alone for awhile."

Marcy Purcell hugged her son tightly. "I know it's a great loss, Davey, but you can't die just because she did. You have to go on living. Let's have lunch, and we can talk it over."

David looked over his mother's shoulder and saw Sheriff Harding still staring at him from the other side of the grave. The sheriff hadn't said anything or made any move to approach him.

David pushed himself away from his mother's embrace and said, "I know I have to go on living, Mom, and I will get over her. Just not yet." He glanced at the sheriff, then added, "I think I ought to stay in Monticello this weekend. I'm not in the mood for traveling."

Especially not after driving seven hours to get here, he thought.

"But Davey! I was counting on you coming home this weekend. You promised!" Marcy complained.

David held his mother's hands in his own. "I know that I promised, and I know I'm a lousy son to break that promise. But with everything that has happened lately with Terrie and Randy, I just wouldn't be good company."

"But being home would..."

David patted her hands. "No, Mom." He said it just firmly enough so that his mother would know his mind was made up, but not harshly enough to upset her. After all, he had already put her through, the last thing David wanted to do was upset her.

Marcy frowned. "Won't you at least come to lunch with us, then?"

David hated to keep putting her off, but it was for her own good. He didn't want to lead the Bow Clan to them. He purposely kept averting his eyes from his mother's face, so if the Bow Clansman was watching, he wouldn't see David focusing on any particular person. If his parents went home to Provo, they would be safe.

He turned and shook his father's hand. "I'll call you tonight," he told Lewis.

David walked off to his car without looking back at his parents. Sheriff Harding stopped him as he was about to climb in.

"I'm glad to see you back in town, Mr. Purcell."

David turned and held out his hand to the sheriff. "Hello, Sheriff. It's good to see you. I'd say 'It's good to see you again' except that your implications the last time we talked left me feeling pretty uncomfortable."

Sheriff Harding stared silently at him.

"It didn't seem to make you uncomfortable enough to stay in the county like I asked you to do."

"I had some things I needed to do outside the county, so I did them.

Since when did your request become an order?"

"It's not an order, just some sound advice."

The sheriff grabbed hold of his belt and pulled his pants higher up on his ample waist.

"I don't think so," David said. "You've got no right disrupting my life if you aren't going to charge me with anything. But you can't charge me, can you? You know I didn't kill her."

Sheriff Harding tapped his finger on David's chest.

"So you say, but this a small town, so I don't have a lot of choice in suspects do I? Whether you like it or not, you're my prime suspect. So until I find a murderer, you had better try to stay on my good side."

David ducked to get into his car. "Goodbye, Sheriff."

Sheriff Harding held the door open and leaned down close to David. "If I have to, Purcell, I'll arrest you. I'd be willing to risk a lawsuit if I thought it would keep a murderer off the street. If you're the one, believe me, you won't get away with it."

David pulled the door shut. Why had he come back? He had been safe in Oraibi. Safe from the Bow Clan and safe from the sheriff's suspicions. Now the sheriff was probably even more convinced he had murdered Terrie, and sooner or later the Bow Clan would come for him again.

CHAPTER 39

In the corner furthest away from the tall doors of his immense chamber, the darkest of the dark kachinas stirred at the intrusion of light into his sanctuary. Light was forbidden. He hated the light. It was deadly. This was a place of absolute darkness. Because of the light, the twin sons of Taiowa had driven him and the other eight kachinas into the chambers that had become their prisons. And now the light was invading his chamber.

Soon, though, very soon, there would be no light to hold him a prisoner in his world. The power of Taiowa would soon fade enough that the dark kachinas would be able to venture out into Kuskurza once again. Then the dark kachinas would quickly put an end to the Sun Clan and their leader who dared call himself Ma´saw.

The tall doors of the chamber swung inward just far enough for two Bow Clansmen to push the woman into the dark void. They screamed at the intrusion, and the Bow Clansman bowed quickly as they shut and sealed the tall door. The woman fell forward onto the stone floor, thrown into total darkness before she could stand.

She curled up in a small ball on the floor and cried. The darkest kachina ignored her for the moment. Let her taste the fear that came with failure to serve the dark kachinas. She was one of the women recaptured from the Sun Clan. If she would not bear children for the Bow Clan, then she would not bear children; she would not live. When he hungered, he would take her.

With the doors closed, no light came within the chamber to harm him in the slightest. It was as it should be once again. Kuskurza should have no light. It was needed only by the weak Outlanders. It was their shield, their protection, against the power of the dark kachinas. By bringing the sun into Kuskurza, the twin sons of Taiowa had imprisoned the dark kachinas within their temples for as long as the light was bright enough to keep them inside the temples. Even the weak light of Kuskurza could still hurt the dark kachinas, though it would not destroy them as it once would have. While the twins had imprisoned the essence of the dark kachinas, they could not imprison their thoughts. Though they could not sense anything within Kuskurza because of the cursed light, they could sense movement in the dark passages that lead to the Fourth World.

The dark kachinas had sought out the minds of those who were trapped in Kuskurza with them and commanded the people to rebuild Kuskurza once the flood waters had receded. From the handful of remaining Bow Clansmen, the dark kachinas had rebuilt their world. The weakest of the Bow Clan became slaves who performed the labors, and the stronger Bow Clansmen became the private guard of the dark kachinas and kept light away from the dark kachinas and the Sun Clan away from the Fourth World.

The Bow Clan had not been able to stop the Sun Clan from being reborn in Kuskurza. The original Ma´saw had planted his seed of rebellion among the slaves, and it had multiplied although the dark kachinas had commanded that the slaves be made sterile. Now that Pahana and the Sun Clan had freed most of the women, the Sun Clan might be able to breed them in the same way the dark kachinas had. Controlling the slaves would become nearly impossible. The Sun Clan might eventually even outnumber the Bow Clan.

The darkest kachina yelled at his frustration at not being able to end Ma´saw's control over the Sun Clan. The woman lying on the floor screamed at the sound and covered her ears. She could not see the darkest kachina in the darkness, but she would be his to take when he wanted.

The darkest kachina started forward and circled the woman waiting for her to sense his presence. She suddenly sat up and looked all around herself. He reached out to touch her face; to let the shadows move across her.

She screamed at his touch and scurried away from him. He smiled and moved forward again. Better to let her wonder what would happen next.

He stopped. Someone was in the caves. He could sense their presence as they chased away the darkness with their lights. They were still near the surface and not at all close to Kuskurza, but they were in the right passage. They had entered the chasm, and they might follow it to its end.

How had the Sun Clan gotten so far away from Kuskurza without the dark kachinas sensing them before now? No one had ever gotten this far from Kuskurza without the dark kachinas' knowledge. The darkest kachina paused and re-evaluated his information. His sense of the intruders was weak because of their distance from Kuskurza, but he decided the intruders he sensed were not of the Sun Clan. This was an Outlander. No, it was a group of Outlanders.

To´chi and Kel´hoya had failed to kill Pahana before he told other Outlanders of what lay below the surface. The darkest kachina had known they would fail, of course, but he had to send them after Pahana just the same. His vision was vague, at best, in predicting the future, and they might have succeeded.

He contacted the other seven dark kachinas with his thoughts.

Do you sense them? he asked in his mind.

There are three that have found the passage.

I think I sense one other on the far side of the passage, as well, thought another.

Yes, one dark kachina agreed. *There are four.*

They are leaving. Perhaps we should let them go. They have found nothing. It will be four cycles before the Bow Clan can reach the blockage. The

Outlanders will be gone by then.

But they will return. Send the Bow Clan quickly before the Outlanders return in greater numbers. We cannot risk more contact being made between the Outlanders and the Sun Clan. Such contact nearly destroyed us before when Pahana rallied them. We cannot allow it to do so this time.

Kill them all, another thought.

Kill them all, they all agreed as they sent the command to the Bow Clan.

The darkest kachina retreated back into his own thoughts hungry from his exertion. The woman's smell seemed stronger now in the midst of his hunger. He moved to her side and surrounded her. She screamed and tried to run, but he made the darkness around her solid and gave her no path to escape. She screamed and flung her arm ineffectually in the darkness. The darkest kachina watched the display with mild amusement, then he pressed in on her until her screams stopped and his appetite was quenched.

CHAPTER 40

The further the sun sunk below the horizon, the deeper David's stomach sunk. Much further and he would be wearing it for a shoe. He was glad his parents had left for Provo a little after seven o'clock while the sun was still up. If his mother had seen how shaky he was now, she would have insisted on staying, and that would have been a mistake. He must not endanger anyone else.

David turned on the television so that he wouldn't have to sit alone in his apartment and wait for the night to creep up on him. By the time the late news came on at ten o'clock, he was getting sleepy. The five cups of soda he drank weren't helping to keep him awake, but they weighed heavily on his bladder.

He had a choice. He could continue to sit on the couch and fall asleep, or he could get up, do his business, and go to bed. It wasn't a hard choice to make. His bladder hurt.

Why didn't you let your mother stay? he asked himself as he passed by the mirror over the sink in the bathroom.

He ignored the question and sat down.

She was only trying to help, you know, and you nearly bit her head off. A fine son you are.

"It's too dangerous for her to be here," David mumbled to himself.

Dangerous? If it's so dangerous, why are you here? You're no hero. Besides, you don't even know if you were seeing through someone else's eyes. You're taking Sarah's word for it and letting your imagination fill in the rest. You've never been psychic before. Does falling in a deep hole suddenly make you a god?

"I know what I saw."

David left the bathroom and crossed the hall into his bedroom. He fell backward onto his bed. This would be only the third night in over six weeks that he slept in his own bed.

Why did he think it was dangerous for his mother to be here, but not him? But he did believe that it was dangerous for him. However, he had no place he could run to escape the danger. If he was somehow psychically connected with one of the Bow Clan, and apparently he was, the Bow Clansman would find him wherever he went. David could possibly be tracked to Oraibi. It might take some time, but if the Bow Clansman was determined, he would find David. His mother and father could leave, and they would be safe. He couldn't. He might as well be comfortable because there was no place where

171

he could hide.

David rolled onto his side and switched off the lamp on his nightstand. He regretted his move almost immediately. The darkness that flooded the room reminded him too much of the cave. He started to turn the lamp back on, but he stopped himself. He couldn't give into his fear. He was acting like a five-year-old child. There was nothing to be afraid of in his dark room. There were no monsters in his closet waiting for the lights to be turned off.

He laid back on his pillows and tried to relax. It took over an hour, but gradually the tenseness faded from his muscles, and he fell asleep. It was far from a restful sleep, though. He was too afraid that he would see another murder in his dreams.

Instead, he saw something else.

In his dream, he was alone and walking in the dark when he was a Boy Scout. He thought he must be in the cave, but it was only a dream version of the cave he had fallen into he reminded himself.

He was lost.

Had he heard something? David waited wondering if he would hear it again.

He did. Far off to his right. Or was it behind him? He couldn't tell with the echo. It sounded like a rock striking another rock.

What had caused it?

He waited to see if it would happen again. It did. Only this time he thought it sounded slightly closer.

He had heard stories about the type of animals that lived in caves. Blood-sucking bats. Bears with claws three inches long. Snakes as thick as his arm. It could be any one of those things.

Or it could be something else.

What was he hearing? A bat or a snake wouldn't knock over rocks, and he didn't think a bear would venture this far back into a cave. That left the something else. Another dying man like the pale man he had seen earlier?

Where was his father?

The temperature in the cave was cool, but he was sweating. David wiped away the sweat that had beaded up on his forehead with the back of his hand.

Something was out there, and it was moving closer to him.

David turned and moved in the opposite direction hoping to get away from whatever was out there. If he could get far enough away, whatever it was might pass him by. It had to be just as blind in the cave as he was.

His hand slid into a crevice in the wall hoping it was a way out. It was only a foot wide and maybe five feet high. He shoved his hand further back into it. His fingers touched rock about two feet in.

What if he hid in the crevice? Would it do any good or could whatever was making the noise sense him in a way David didn't realize? He heard a scratching sound a few yards behind him and made his decision.

David bent his knees slightly and slid sideways into the crevice. He kept his eyes open and staring out into the cave. He didn't know why he was doing it. He certainly couldn't see anything. Even when he held his hand up in front of his face, David couldn't see it. It was just too dark.

He tried to slow his breathing so he wouldn't make so much noise. He wanted whatever was out there to pass him by. Whatever it was, David was sure it wasn't friendly.

There was no sound at all in the cave for two minutes, then he heard something scraping along the wall of the cave. Closer. It was definitely closer. But how could it be following him? Did it smell him? Was it an animal like a wolf or coyote with an acute sense of smell?

He wanted to scream. He wanted to yell as loud as he could and run for the exit. But which way was the exit? And how fast was whatever was out there? David bit his tongue and waited.

David saw the beam of light first and thought it was someone from his troop who had found him. Just as he was about to call out, he saw the pale man behind the light. The man almost seemed to glow in the dark. The pale man turned, and his light fell upon David.

The man moved closer.

David pawed in his pockets hoping to find something that would help him. A compass, a kerchief, his canteen. He didn't have anything he could use. Wasn't a Boy Scout always supposed to be prepared? David was going to have to tell them they needed to come up with a Get-Away-Monster Spray.

David found a whistle and blew it as loudly as he could. The shrill sound echoed through the caverns and the pale man grabbed his ears. When the sound died away, the man came at David again. David blew the whistle. Not surprised, this time the man kept coming.

David shined his flashlight in the man's eyes. The pale man blinked but kept coming. He yelled and charged David.

Instinctively, David raised his hands to protect himself. With his hands, came his walking stick he had been using on the hike. The pale man impaled himself on the end of the wooden stick.

The pale man screamed.

David screamed.

He sat straight up in his bed. As he did, he pulled a muscle in his lower back. He was so frightened that he wouldn't notice the pain until later in the morning.

The first thought that went through his mind was that he was still dreaming. He was still twelve-years old and lost in the dark. He realized he was clutching his blanket and not the crevices of a cave wall. And he could see shapes. His bed. The window. The bureau. And...

He couldn't place the shape against the wall off to his right. It wasn't furniture. That area of his wall should have been bare.

The shadow moved.

David rolled onto his side and reached for his lamp. He switched it on and washed the room in 100-watt light.

The shadow disappeared.

Had it even been there? David wondered if his imagination had gone into overdrive. He leaned back against the headboard and sighed. It was because of his amnesia. Something was wrong with his mind. His mind was making him see things that weren't there and believe things that weren't true. Until he was able to remember what had happened to him in the cave – both times – he would never be normal. He hoped that when he remembered his time in the caves, he would somehow learn through whose eyes he was seeing.

David threw back his top sheet and swung his feet over the floor. He hesitated just before his feet touched the floor.

Boogeymen under the bed?

Now he knew he was in trouble. He was imagining the same things a child imagined. He chuckled nervously and set his feet on the floor. The cold floor shocked him.

Nothing else happened.

He walked into the living room and made sure the front door was locked. To be certain it would stay locked, he flipped the deadbolt down, which was something he rarely did. Before he went back to his bedroom, he also made sure his patio door was locked, and the aluminum bar was down.

Hobbling back into his bedroom, David closed and locked the door behind himself, again something he had never done before. Since he lived alone in the apartment, there had never been any need.

Even with the precautions he had taken, he still felt he needed to do something more. What could he do though against someone who could read his thoughts?

He climbed back in his bed without turning off the lights this time. If he woke up, he wanted to know where he was immediately.

David had nearly fallen asleep when he heard something scratching at his window. He rolled onto his side and looked at the window. With his lamp on, his window was a mirror of the room. He couldn't see outside.

The scratching stopped, and David continued to stare outside. He couldn't get over the fact that something was watching him from outside the window. He might have turned off the light so that he could see whether he was right or not, but he was too afraid to be in the dark.

He was too afraid of what he might see outside the window. David laid back in the bed.

His window shattered inward spraying glass over David. The remaining

Bow Clansman flew through the hole on his feathered-hide saucer. David threw his blanket at his attacker and rolled out of his bed.

He hit the floor on his knees and scrambled for his closed bedroom door. The Bow Clansman threw the blanket off of his face and flew toward David. David grabbed the lamp on the bureau next to the door and threw it as hard as he could. It hit the pale-skinned man, and he tumbled from the saucer. The saucer dropped like a rock to the floor.

David opened the door and slipped out shutting it behind him. He grabbed his wallet and keys from his dining room table and ran out of his apartment.

As he climbed into his car, he saw the Bow Clansman fly out his bedroom window on the saucer. The Bow Clansman dived at him as he climbed into the Corolla. David pressed in on the horn and held it. The loud noise startled the Bow Clansman, and his shield plummeted to the ground. The Bow Clansman hit the ground and rolled. David hoped he was knocked out, but the man rolled into a squatting position and scrambled for his saucer.

David started the car and backed out of the driveway as quickly as he could. Brad Harrison, who owned the house and lived on the ground floor, opened his window and yelled at David. The Bow Clansman climbed on his saucer and flew off in the opposite direction from David. David wondered if Brad had seen the pale-skinned man, but he doubted it. Brad didn't even look in the direction of the Bow Clansman.

David ignored Brad's yells and turned onto Center Street. Someone was bound to call the police. What would Sheriff Harding think when he saw David's messed up bedroom? Would he think David had been attacked or would he continue thinking the worst of him?

David pulled onto the highway heading south towards Blanding, but where was he going? Should he drive to Provo? He didn't want to risk putting his parents in danger. Besides, that was the first place Sheriff Harding would look for him.

There was only one place he could go where he had felt safe. There was only one place where there was someone who understood what he was going through.

An hour later, he passed through Blanding heading south toward Mexican Hat. He would pick up Highway 163 there and head into Arizona. He just hoped he wasn't taking his trouble to Oraibi.

CHAPTER 41

David drove into Oraibi around sunrise. Already some of the 150 or so people who still lived in the pueblos were beginning to stir. He saw a trio of men walking toward the edge of the mesa to take the trail to the fields below where they managed to make fruits and vegetables sprout from the desert. Smoke poured from a dozen different chimneys as women prepared the morning meals. A group of young children walked across the road holding full buckets of water in each hand. Sarah had told David that water had to be drawn from a spring that was a mile away.

David climbed out of his car and stood still as if absorbing the atmosphere of the town. Why did he feel so safe here? The fact that the Bow Clan couldn't seem to find him here was only a part of the reason. The other part had to be because these people knew of the secrets beneath the earth. They could return to him what he could not remember.

David felt a hand on his shoulder and turned around. "I wasn't sure you would return here, David," Ethan said.

"I finished my business in Blanding."

"Ah, the funeral." David was surprised word had gotten around as to why he had left, but then again Oraibi was a small town. "Sarah will be happy to see you back. With Adam gone, she has been alone too much. She needs a man."

David shook his head. "It's hard to imagine Sarah needing anyone. She seems too independent."

"She has a strong will and a smart mind, but that doesn't mean she can't love. Her soul seeks its mate just as anyone else's. I thought at one time I might be that mate, but she rejected me. Kindly, of course, but she still rejected me. I think now she may have found that mate, but perhaps, neither of them knows it."

David touched his hand to his chest. "Me?"

Ethan smiled. "You could do much worse, but I doubt you could do better. I love her, David. I may always love her, or my soul may find its own mate someday. Either way, I wish to see her happy. If not with me, then with the one she has chosen. If I'm right, and it is you, I congratulate you. Come by my rooms tonight, and we'll drink to your happiness and to mine."

"I'd love to, Ethan, but I don't drink. I'm Mormon," David said.

Ethan laughed. It was a deep belly laugh that reminded David of someone playing Santa Claus.

"We'll drink pop. I have Diet Dr. Pepper and Diet Sprite." He patted his trim stomach. "It is better for the body. But alcohol? I would never drink it. My father drove his truck off the mesa and killed himself while he was drunk. I treasure my life more than that."

"Then I would be happy to come by," David said.

Ethan slapped David on the shoulder. "Good. I will see you tonight. I have to go into Winslow now."

"You don't work in the fields?" David said.

Ethan shook his head. "I make jewelry. I can't sell it in the fields. I sell some at the Cultural Center. The rest I sell in nearby cities. Each person works at what he or she is best."

Ethan started to walk off. He waved goodbye to David. "Tonight then after the meal time."

David returned the wave. When Ethan had gone, David walked over to the pueblo where Sarah lived. He knocked on the door to Sarah's rooms.

"Come in," he heard Sarah say from inside.

He opened the door. Sarah was kneeling in front of the fireplace prodding the logs to encourage the flame to grow. She looked over her shoulder and saw David.

She jumped to her feet and ran over and hugged David. "David! I didn't think I would ever see you again."

"Something happened to me in Monticello."

Sarah let go of him and stepped back. "What?"

David thought she looked tired. Then he remembered she had been up all night watching her grandfather's body.

"The Bow Clansman attacked me. I got away, but he made a mess of my apartment." David sighed. "Sheriff Harding already thinks I killed Terrie, and now this. I don't think I'm going to be very welcome in town when I go back."

Sarah gasped. "How did it happen?"

"He crashed through my bedroom window on that flying-saucer thing of his. I managed to get away, but trying to figure out what happened won't make the sheriff happy."

Sarah sat down on the ground next to the fire. "Will you seek to outrun the Bow Clan for the rest of your life?"

David wondered if that was possible. They would eventually track him down if they wanted to bad enough. He had no doubt of that. "Is it possible?" he asked.

Sarah shrugged. "I don't know. I didn't really believe in the old legends until those men attacked our camp and killed my grandfather."

"Is there anyone else in town who may know about the Bow Clan?"

"Everyone knows something. Perhaps Peter would know the most. He's a medicine man, but much of my grandfather's knowledge came from his visions he received in the kiva. They may have told him a different story than the legends."

Adam had seemed to place a lot of faith in his visions. Maybe that was the place for David to start looking for answers.

"Can I go to this kiva that Adam went to? Since I seem to be psychic, maybe I can receive a vision there that will tell me more about the Bow Clan and what to do."

Sarah shook her head. "This is a special kiva. Only the elders ever go there. No women or whites are allowed inside."

David sat down next to Sarah. "But this is important."

"I agree, but I can't change the rules of the village."

"Then who can?"

"Peter could, but you would have to convince him that there is no other way to learn what you need to know."

"Can you take me to meet him?"

Sarah nodded.

Sarah knocked on the door to Peter Kwa'ni's rooms. A man, David assumed it was Peter, opened the door. He was short and heavyset. If he had been white, David might have thought he was a snowman. He wore a fancily embroidered vest over a white shirt. His pepper-gray hair was held back with a blue bandeau. The man's eyes focused on Sarah and then quickly darted to David. David thought he saw the man barely nod his head. David smiled.

Peter stepped back from the doorway. "Come in. It's not often my wife, and I have guests. Have you eaten?"

"Yes," Sarah said a bit too quickly.

Peter cocked his head slightly to the side. "I see this is not a social visit then. Is someone sick?"

Sarah shook her head. "No one is sick, Peter. We've come to speak with you."

Peter motioned to the chairs in the room. "Sit, and we will talk."

Peter waited until Sarah and David had sat down before he took his own seat.

"This is David Purcell," Sarah said. Peter's face showed no signs of recognition. "He is a man who was lost in a cave in Utah for five weeks. He was recently found, but he has no memory of the time he was lost."

"You believe this man is the man Adam saw in his visions?" Peter asked as he stared at David.

"No, he is the man. My grandfather said so himself. My grandfather's visions were correct, Peter. He wasn't crazy," Sarah said.

Peter sighed. "I wish I could believe that, but Kuskurza has long been a dead world, and with it, the Bow Clan and the dark kachinas."

Sarah leaned forward in her chair. "But they aren't dead. I have seen them myself. The Bow Clan wants to kill David, and they are just as my grandfather described them." Peter still looked skeptical. "And they are flying on pa´tuwvotas."

Peter was silent for a long time. He rubbed his hands together in his lap. When he finally spoke, he said, "This is serious." Peter looked at David. "Adam feared for your life. He thought you would know how to keep the dark kachinas and the Bow Clan in Kuskurza. The fact that they have tried to kill you supports this." He looked at Sarah. "And Adam? Was he murdered by the Bow Clan?"

Sarah nodded. "David knows he needs to remember what happened to him in the cave. With your permission, he would like to go into the sacred kiva to see if he will receive the same visions my grandfather received there."

Peter's face showed his surprise at the request. "But no white man has ever been there. If too many people were to know its secrets, we would be in great danger."

David decided to break his silence to speak on his own behalf. "I can understand how you feel, sir. My people also have sacred temples where only a select few are allowed to go. I won't make you believe that going into the kiva is the only way I'll remember. I may remember in the next hour what I have forgotten, or I may never recall it. But I'm afraid that the Bow Clan will find me before I can remember. The Bow Clan has already killed three people trying to find me. I can't fight what I don't know. If I do know something that will stop them, then what happens if I die before I remember?"

CHAPTER 42

David looked up from the dark hole at Peter. The middle-aged Indian motioned for him to descend. David stepped onto the ladder and slowly climbed down. It looked dark inside the kiva, and it reminded him too much of descending into the cave.

Sarah moved toward the ladder, but Peter held out his hand to stop her.

"Only David. This is still a sacred kiva. I cannot violate all our traditions," Peter said.

Sarah nodded and stepped back.

"Be careful," she told David.

David smiled and continued down until he reached the bottom. The kiva was dark, but not nearly as dark as the cave. Not only was there was still light coming from the opening, but a small fire burning. Peter stepped off the ladder and stood beside David.

"You are the first white man to be inside this kiva. We don't place such strict restrictions on other kivas, but this one is a special place," Peter explained.

"How so?" David asked.

Peter took hold of David's elbow and led him across the room past the fire. He stopped in front of what looked to David to be a hole plugged by a large rock or it might have simply been a rock partially exposed by digging.

"This is why we hold this kiva so sacred. Other kivas have ceremonial sipapus, but it is said this is the true sipapu. Through this hole, our ancestors emerged into the Fourth World. It is not a shallow hole as a ceremonial sipapu would be. Beneath this stone is the path to Kuskurza."

"Why is it plugged up?"

"Long ago, my people lived in fear that the dark kachinas might return and destroy their new world as they had caused the destruction of Kuskurza. Because of this, the old Hopis sealed the sipapu so the dark kachinas could not escape. This kiva was built as a watchtower. From here, the Sun Clan can watch the sipapu in privacy. The kiva is kept especially sacred to keep out the curious. Only elders who know and respect the legends are allowed entrance here.

"Our population was long ago decimated by smallpox and then the white man's technology. The first took many of our people away physically. The second took them away spiritually. Very few now remain to tend this kiva and make sure the sipapu remains closed."

"Was Adam one of those who watched the sipapu?" David asked.

Peter nodded. "Once he began to receive his visions, he feared what was

180

beneath this stone. He would always put his foot on the stone to make sure it was still solidly embedded in the earth whenever he entered the kiva." Peter paused. "Sit on the bench, and we will meditate and see if Taiowa will favor you with a vision."

David sat on the wooden bench and leaned back against the cool stone wall. Peter sat down next to him and did the same.

"Close your eyes," Peter told him. "Do not try to focus your thoughts on any one thing. Taiowa will show you what he will show you."

David closed his eyes and concentrated on relaxing his body. The heat from the fire lulled him into semi-consciousness. The top of his head itched, but he did not scratch it. At first, he saw blurry images in his mind. After a few minutes, the images focused and he saw a world within a cave. It was nothing more than a large chamber. Along the edges of the chamber, he saw numerous pueblos. However, it was the pyramids in the center that captured his attention. He saw five of them; one large one in the center, and a smaller one on each side.

The focus tightened on a group of people working in one of the many fields nearby the pyramids. David saw himself standing in the middle of one of the fields. He was dirty, and his suit was in tatters. He was holding some sort of weapon that looked like a metal rod with a large bulb on one end. A Sun Clansman stood on either side of him. He could see two other pale-skinned men. Both of them were dead. One was dressed in the black-and-red tunic of the Bow Clan. The other dead man was a Sun Clansman. He had a gaping black hole in his chest just like the man David had seen in the cave when he was younger.

David watched himself lower the muzzle of the weapon as he stared at the empty spot between one of the pale man's legs. The first Sun Clansman lowered his tunic, which seemed to break the trance David was in.

"You are just like Masani," David said motioning to the dead Sun Clansman. Masani was the Sun Clansman who had found him in the cave after he had fallen. He had healed David with Kuskurzan medicine and brought him back to the Third World only to be killed himself by a Bow Clansman. Seeing the murder of his savior, David had managed to kill the Bow Clansman.

Nearly all the slave men are like this, the stranger said in David's mind. He waved his hand. *Come we must leave now. The Bow Clan will come.*

With the weapon, David motioned the man to start walking. "You lead. I'll follow. If this is a trap, you'll be the first to die."

Do not speak with your mouth. We do not understand your words. Think what you want to say. We can understand that. The pale man turned away and started walking.

David looked at the second man and thought, *I want both of you in front of me.*

I will not be commanded by an Outlander, the man told David.

He took a step toward David. David held his ground in front of the stranger. He held his arm straight out and pointed the metal rod at the stranger. The man did not stop but continued forward. He lunged forward and yanked the weapon from David's hands. The stranger flipped the rod over and placed it in David's hands so that the bulbous end was closer to David's body. The narrow end of the rod was pointed at the stranger.

If you are going to threaten me with a langher, then make sure you know how to use it, or you will kill yourself. David blushed but tried not to let his thoughts betray his humiliation. *To use it, you must twist the heavy end, and flip the switch.*

David looked at the weapon, then at the pale-skinned man. He was tempted to fire the weapon at the stranger, but he wondered if that was what the stranger was hoping he would do. What he wouldn't have given for one of the M-16s he used during his training exercises in the Army Reserves at that moment. He tried to remember how the Bow Clansman had held the weapon when he killed Masani, but he couldn't. David's attention had been focused on the spear he had thrown at Masani's killer.

Come now, or we will leave you here to die, the stranger said. Then he turned and began walking toward the edge of the vast chamber.

The stranger ran until he had caught up with the first man who had not stopped walking even when David threatened the second pale man. The two men mumbled to each other and laughed. David knew they were laughing at him and he felt foolish.

He ran to catch up with the two strangers.

I am David, he said when he stopped running. *Masani found me in the caves. He rescued me from the Bow Clan and helped heal my legs. He wanted to take me to meet someone named Ma´saw.*

The second man spoke without turning to face David. *We know who you are. Masani sent us his thoughts as soon as he entered Kuskurza. We were coming to meet you, but we were too late to stop the Bow Clansman. I am Polanque. The other is Scinaro.*

They walked without pause to the edge of the huge chamber. David guessed that it would have taken a morning to walk the same distance on the surface. The Sun Clansmen didn't seem to tire. David did, and his legs ached. Apparently, they still weren't totally healed from his fall, but he didn't allow the pale men the satisfaction of seeing him show any weakness.

Nestled in among the small alcoves in the walls were large pueblos much like those the Anasazi had abandoned in the mountain caves many centuries ago. David wondered if these people were related to the Anasazi.

At the pueblo they were walking toward, four ladders led up to the first level of rooms. However, instead of climbing the ladder to enter the pueblo, they walked around to the side and into a small canyon with high walls. David silently followed.

A short distance into the canyon, it ended. David looked around wondering what would happen now. His hand tightened around the langher in case he had been led into a trap.

Scinaro pulled a long-blade knife from his waistband, and David raised the langher. Scinaro looked at him and shook his head. He turned the knife so that the pointed edge of the blade faced up, and he jammed it into a crack between two rocks. As he pushed down hard on the blade, the rock wall behind Scinaro rose until it had reached the height of David's waist.

"Whoa," David whispered.

No, levers, Scinaro thought with a smile. *Go through.*

Polanque bent over and slipped over to the other side of the wall. David slid under the wall. As he straightened up on the other side, the wall slid back to the floor.

What about Scinaro? David wanted to know.

He must warn the slaves. When the Bow Clan discovers the body of the one you killed, they will attack the slaves.

I'm sorry that others will die.

Polanque shrugged. *It does not matter. If it had not been this incident, they would have found another reason.*

Polanque led David through a maze of passages lit by torches with no flames. Instead, the torch heads seemed to glow with an interior light. Polanque knew exactly where he was going. He looked to David to be a wisp of smoke. His thin, white body glowed in the dim light and glided through the passages. He didn't waver in indecision at the junction of passages. They passed many open passages that were equally well lit, but Polanque passed them by.

Where do the passages lead that you don't take? David thought finally when his curiosity got the better of him.

Death. They are traps to keep those who do not know the way away from the pueblo. I take you to the pueblo of the Sun Clan. It is a great hidden pueblo, and it must always remain so. If the Bow Clan were to discover the pueblo, they could kill all the Sun Clan and steal our stores of food and weapons, Polanque explained.

David nodded that he understood. He did not. Why did the Bow Clan hate the Sun Clan? Polanque, Scinaro, and Masani were of the Sun Clan. Were they the good guys or the bad guys?

The passage they were walking through ended abruptly. Off to the side was a ladder leaning against the wall. David looked up. The tunnel continued straight up further than the light from the flameless torches could penetrate the darkness.

Polanque began climbing the ladder and David silently followed. David wondered how long it had been since he had been sealed in the maze with Polanque. His body was weary, and he needed to sleep. He hadn't slept since just before he and Masani had entered Kuskurza.

When they reached the top of the ladder, another pale man waited at the entrance to another series of tunnels. Polanque spoke to the man in whispers occasionally glancing over his shoulder at David.

Finally, Polanque turned to them and thought, *You will rest for a cycle. When Ma'saw returns, he will speak with you.*

David offered no argument. He would be glad for the rest. How will I know where to go?

We will meet again. I must prepare an exploration group now. Polanque pointed to the short, stocky man at his side. *This is Teron. He will take you to a room.*

Polanque turned and quickly left at a trot. Teron watched him go and then turned to David. Teron looked at David from head to foot and shook his head.

You are the lost white brother. So the Fourth World truly does exist. Why is Polanque worried? He should be overjoyed at your discovery.

I have killed the Bow Clan, David thought.

Teron laughed. His low-pitched voice echoed through the tunnels. *You have not killed the Bow Clan. The Bow Clan still lives just as a manatus will live even with seven legs.* David didn't know what a manatus was, and he wasn't sure he wanted to find out.

Teron led David down the passageway until he came to a room divided from the tunnel by a curtain. Teron pulled back the curtain and ushered David into the room.

When Ma'saw wishes to see you, he will call. Do not hope, though. Ma'saw meets very few. I have yet to meet him myself.

Teron left the room. David turned around slowly to see what the room looked like. It was lit by a single flameless torch, which sat in the center of the room. The walls were bare and carved from stone. Metal spikes had been driven into the wall, and a soft material had been stretched between the spikes to form a hammock. David sat on one of the hammocks, then lay on it.

When he awoke later, it was neither light nor dark in the room. He hated the poor lighting in Kuskurza almost as much as he hated the total darkness of the caves.

David was still alone in the room, but someone had set a plate of fruit on the floor in front of the torch. David did not like the fact that he had slept while a stranger had entered the room. The person could have been an enemy, and David would not have been awake enough to defend himself.

Rolling out of the hammock, he sat down in front of the plate. It was filled with what looked like vegetables and fruit, but there was no meat. He picked up a long, ribbed piece of what he guessed was fruit and bit into it. It was sweet and juicy. His stomach reminded him that it had been a while since he had eaten. David finished eating the fruit, and then he went on to eat four other odd-shaped pieces of fruit.

He thought the fruit and vegetables were quite delicious, and they compared in taste to other foods he had eaten on the surface. He peeled a round piece of fruit and began eating the white pulp inside.

As he ate, David realized how badly he wanted to get back to Blanding. He needed the sun and the rivers.

The curtain parted, and Polanque stepped in. David jumped to his feet prepared for whatever might happen. He was still not entirely convinced Polanque was a friend.

You have rested and eaten. That is good. Ma'saw is here, and he would speak to you. Follow me.

Teron did not think Ma'saw would meet me, David thought as they stepped into the passageway.

Teron is not Ma'saw.

Polanque again led the way following the maze of tunnels with undisturbed surety. When they stopped, they were standing next to a wall with no exits or doors. Polanque picked up a rock from the ground and pounded it against the wall once. He paused, then struck the rock against the wall two more times. He paused again and then hit the wall once more.

The wall slid up as the wall next to the pueblos had.

Levers, David said proudly.

Polanque smiled as he ducked inside the room. David followed. The walls of the room were covered with large maps drawn on skins. David could not guess what sort of animal skins they were. Maybe the manatus. Most of the maps seemed to depict the passageways in the tunnels. None of them appeared to agree in what passage lay where, but they all had a large central chamber in the middle and smaller lines radiating outward. A few of the maps showed lines and rooms within large triangular shapes. David guessed these were drawings of the stone pyramids.

Across the room, a man stood with his back to David studying one of the maps on the wall. His white hair hung in two braids at his waist. His shoulders were wide, but sloped. He wore a vest made of a dark material David did not know and pants made of an animal skin.

The wall touched the floor with a dull thud, and the man turned around. He was older than David had expected him to be. Even from across the room, David could see the deep wrinkles in his face and hands. He did not seem as feeble as many old people.

Welcome to Kuskurza, the old man thought. *I am Ma'saw.*

David nodded. *I am David.*

Ma'saw's eyes studied David. *David?* David nodded. *Is that your only name?*

Purcell, David told Ma'saw.

Ma'saw smiled. *Pahana.*

David shook his head. *No, Purcell.*

Ma'saw nodded. *Pahana.*

David dropped the subject not wanting to get into an argument.

I have been told of what you did in the fields, Pahana, and I am curious. Why were you not killed by the Bow Clan?

I fell into a cave and broke my legs. Masani found me and made me eat something that healed my legs. He knew the Bow Clan was coming after me, so he carried me to safety.

Ma'saw nodded as he approached David slowly. Ma'saw sat on the floor and beckoned for Polanque and David to join him.

Taiowa was with you, Pahana. By saving you, Masani has brought us both our lost white brother and a breeder, Ma'saw thought.

A breeder? David repeated.

A man who keeps his parts and is able to father children is a breeder. There are few breeders among the Sun Clan. You are only the fifth.

Are you a breeder? David asked.

Ma'saw cocked his head to one side and smiled. *I have my male parts, but I am too old to breed.*

How old are you?

One-hundred-and-forty-one seasons.

David gasped even though he didn't know how long a unit of time "season" was in Kuskurza, but it sounded like a long time.

Ma'saw chuckled at their amazement. *Do not be startled. I am not yet old among my people. If I am not slain, I may live another sixty or seventy seasons. The oldest Sun Clansman lived to be 256 seasons.*

Is Ma'saw your title? David thought.

The old man shook his head. *The first Ma'saw was left behind in Kuskurza to guard the dark kachinas. The twin sons of Taiowa gave him the responsibility of keeping the dark kachinas imprisoned so they would not destroy Tu'waqachi. After a time, the dark kachinas started to regain their power, and they created more people to be their slaves. Ma'saw led some of the slaves away to form the Sun Clan to oppose the Bow Clan and the dark kachinas. When Ma'saw grew old, he passed on his name and his mission to a deserving warrior among the Sun Clan. The second Ma'saw gathered the rebels and began the construction of this hidden pueblo.* Ma'saw held his hands over his head and waved them around. *When his time ended, he gave his name to the most deserving member of the Sun Clan. When my time ends, I will give the name to Polanque, and he will become Ma'saw. As long as the dark kachinas exist, so must Ma'saw and the Sun Clan.*

Who are the dark kachinas? David asked.

They are spirits, evil spirits. They treat our people as slaves. They continue to use the Bow Clan to inspire fear. The Bow Clan think and act as one person. They communicate their thoughts without words, which is a skill we also have, but for some reason, a Sun Clansman cannot read a Bow Clansman's thoughts or vice versa. The mission of the Sun Clan is to lead the people of Kuskurza to the surface in the same way the twins sons of Taiowa led our people to the surface long ago.

I could show you the way to the surface, David thought excitedly.

I value your offer, Pahana, but I do not think you know what you say.

But I do! I remember the entrance I came through, and I remember the landmarks I saw along the journey to Kuskurza.

But many of those landmarks will no longer be there. Do you see all these maps? Ma'saw pointed to the various maps around the room. *These are the maps that show the structure and traps of the caves. No two agree. These maps are all outdated. There seems to be only one path to the surface. If that path is ever discovered, the dark kachinas quickly change it with their magic. They can close tunnels, make new ones, cause water to spring from the ground, or create deep pits. They seem to be able to sense whenever someone is in the passages. They then send the Bow Clan after them. Our exploration parties must work quickly when they are in the passageways, or they are slaughtered by the Bow Clan. We continue to search for a permanent path to the surface, but we have not found it. And now our exploration parties are far between. I am surprised Masani made it close enough to the Fourth World to find you and then find the way back to Kuskurza. The dark kachinas are becoming careless as their power grows. Hopefully, that will be their downfall.*

Why not send many teams out at once to search for the entrance? David proposed.

Our numbers are few. Even with breeders, there are no women to breed with. Our numbers increase simply because the dark kachinas must maintain slaves to work the fields and perform other labors. We seek out the slaves that are unhappy with their conditions, and we bring them into the Sun Clan.

Where do the slaves come from?

The dark kachinas keep the women in a breeding area. Some are selected as sacrifices for the dark kachinas. Others are used for breeding. The rest are killed. The Bow Clansmen are all breeders. They mate with the women to produce children. The female children are trained to birth children as their mothers do. The males are separated into Bow Clansmen and slaves. The slaves have their male parts removed and are given to other slaves to raise. Occasionally, a male will not be mutilated through the sloppiness of the Bow Clan, and the slaves will have a breeder. Now that you have found Kuskurza, our cause will be strengthened. You are proof that the Fourth World exists and can be reached.

Ma´saw's face went out of focus, and David wondered what was happening. As he regained his vision, all he saw was the ground rushing toward him as he fell off the bench and collapsed on the floor.

CHAPTER 43

"David, are you all right?" Peter asked as he grabbed David by the arm.

Yes. Yes, I'm all right, he tried to answer with his thoughts. When he realized Peter couldn't hear him, he said, "I'm fine."

Peter wiped David's face with a wet cloth. The cool water felt refreshing on David's skin, and it helped bring him to his senses.

"Walk slowly, and I'll help you climb out of here."

David shook his head. "No, I can't go now. I'm starting to remember things, but there's more to remember. I have to remember everything," David insisted.

"But you've been down here for over four hours."

"Really?" David staggered to his feet. He put one hand on the wall to keep himself from falling. Then he fell back onto the bench. "I have to remember. It's too important to stop now."

"You're acting like Adam. The visions drained him. People thought he was crazy."

David smiled. "I think you're trying to scold me, Peter, but comparing me to Adam is actually a compliment."

David leaned his head back and closed his eyes. He tried to relax his body, which wasn't too difficult under the circumstances. He was exhausted. He could understand how the visions would have drained Adam. It didn't take as long for the visions to return this time.

Like before, he saw all of Kuskurza – the temples, the slave pueblos, the fields, and the slaves working in the fields. His vision focused on the people, and David saw himself raise his head slowly without stopping his tilling. He was wearing the green tunic of a slave like everyone else in the fields. David looked around the field. All around him were others quietly tending the fields as if they were slaves, but David knew now they weren't. The slaves had readily agreed to stay in their pueblos for the work cycle when Ma´saw told them the Sun Clan would work in their place.

The Sun Clan slowly moved in the direction of the eastern stone mountain next to the central temple. Among the disguised Sun Clansmen was Ma´saw. When he dropped his hoe, that would be the signal for the small groups of Sun Clansmen to attack the Bow Clan overseers dressed in their red tunics with black trim. David looked at the imposing mountain of stone and wondered for the first time if the plan he had proposed would work.

He had been the one who presented the idea to Ma´saw, and he would be the one to take the responsibility if it failed.

The idea had occurred to David when he had heard Ma´saw address the Sun Clan. He had been standing in the corner of the meeting room that was tightly packed with men who wanted to be in the presence of Ma´saw when he spoke. David had stood in the corner of the room unable to see the legendary leader. David gave up trying and crossed his arms over his chest and relaxed.

Ma´saw stood in the center of the large room speaking. *Brothers, the exploration team Polanque sent out three cycles ago is dead. They were trapped in the caves and killed by the Bow Clan. Their bodies have been hung on the central temple as proof to us of the dark kachinas' supremacy.* Disappointed mumbles could be heard among the all-male group. *Our numbers are now fewer than they have ever been. The dark kachinas have not increased the number of slaves for many cycles. Until the time comes when our numbers are greater, there can be no more exploration parties, and no more attacks on Bow Clan quatis. We must focus our efforts on recruiting more slaves to our cause. It is the only way the Sun Clan will grow."*

David shook his head slowly, but he said and thought nothing. It would not be wise for him, still considered an Outlander, to challenge the leader, especially in front of so many witnesses. Besides, he had been in Kuskurza only a short time. There might be circumstances of which he had not yet been made aware.

Ma´saw spoke for a short time longer on how the Sun Clansmen would go about recruiting slaves to the cause of the Sun Clan. When he had finished, the men filed out of the room to go about their normal business. Their heads hung low as if they had been defeated in battle. David stayed behind while all the others left. Ma´saw had moved to the front of the room and was studying the maps with Polanque. The leader turned and saw David.

Ma´saw flashed a weak smile at David. *I can see you did not like what I said, Ma´saw thought.* David nodded slowly. *What in particular is troubling you?*

If you allow the Sun Clan to rest and grow stronger, so will the Bow Clan. But for every slave that becomes a Sun Clansmen during this rest, the dark kachinas will gain four or five Bow Clansmen. By waiting, the Sun Clan only becomes weaker, not stronger.

Polanque stepped forward, and for a moment, David thought the powerful-looking man might strike him. *You have been here only three cycles, Outlander, and you propose to instruct Ma´saw, who has been in Kuskurza all his life, how to lead the Sun Clan?*

Ma´saw laid his hand on Polanque's shoulder. *Let him speak. We should never grow so confident in our abilities that we cannot consider another opinion. Pahana comes from a different world, Polanque. He sees things in a different way than either the Bow Clan or we see them.* Ma´saw turned to

David and waved his hand. *Continue, please.*

David took a deep breath. *You can't just sit still and hope for things to change. We must attack the Bow Clan's weak points so that the balance will turn in our favor.*

What do you see as the Bow Clan's weak points? Ma'saw asked.

The same as the Sun Clan's. You both need more men to gain dominance over the other. Right now, the Bow Clan has the women and so they have enough men for their needs and they stay in control. The Sun Clan is forced to wait and choose from those men the Bow Clan considers slaves. If the Sun Clan had the women, the Bow Clan would not be able to replace their slain warriors.

Ma'saw nodded. *I agree with what you have said, but how does the Sun Clan regain the women?*

You have many maps showing the interior of the central temple. You must know where the entrances are, and you probably know where the breeding center is.

Polanque jumped into the conversation. *But we do not have enough men to attack the mountain.*

A well-planned attack when there are few Bow Clansmen in the temple will make the men you do have enough. Send a small group of men far away from the central temple to create a disturbance. They can attack the Bow Clan and run and hide. They can do whatever's needed to make the Bow Clan call for more men. It will keep many Bow Clansmen away from the temples.

We will consider this, Ma'saw told David.

David knew better than to press this point. He bowed to Ma'saw and left the room.

Now he stood bowed over the red vegetation still surprised that Ma'saw had accepted the plans of a stranger so quickly. He waited for the signal from Ma'saw to move into the eastern temple. There were fifteen quatis of men that would enter the eastern mountain. Each quati was composed of ten Sun Clansmen. Another group of one hundred would remain outside the pyramid to defend those inside.

Polanque had still been skeptical of the plan even after it had been finalized and approved by Ma'saw. Not because he believed it wouldn't work, but because of his nature, he was a cautious man. Ma'saw told him, *I will not live to see the results of our labors here, but you will, Polanque. I do this so that you will have the men you need to defeat the Bow Clan and lead our people to freedom. At first, there will be only four breeders, for I am too old to father children. But in the lifetime of the four, they will breed hundreds of children each, and their children will breed children. By the time you are as old as I, you will have many warriors to command. We cannot kill the Bow Clan by trimming their leaves, Polanque. We must strike at their roots.*

Ma´saw dropped his hoe. The nearest Sun Clansmen to the few Bow Clan overseers not chasing the diversion rose up and stabbed sharp spines of stone into the sides of the overseers. Quick kills of the overseers were critical. No telepathic warning could be allowed to be sent to the other Bow Clansmen. When the overseers collapsed, the Sun Clansmen fell upon them and placed the overseers' uniforms on themselves. The Sun Clansmen disguised as overseers stood up and acted as the guard in case another Bow Clansman might wonder where the overseers had gone.

When this had been completed, Ma´saw picked up his hoe. That was the signal for the first quati to move into the central temple. David hurried toward the temple barely refraining from running.

The temple towered over David, and he forced himself not to look up as he scurried toward the entrance. The two Bow Clan guards inside the doorway were dead. They had been killed along with the overseers.

The passages inside the stone pyramid reminded David of the passages within the hidden pueblo. They were twisting and dark, dimly lit by flameless torches. David saw few entrances, but he guessed the dark kachinas might use hidden doorways just as the Sun Clansmen did.

David and the other nine men in his quati sprinted along the passageway following the attacking quati that had entered the pyramid before them. The silence of the 150 men moving through the passages was unnerving. Though each passage was lit, David, in an odd thought, wished he were in the dark again. He would have felt safe from the view of the Bow Clan.

Their final destination was the top three levels of the stone mountain. There they would find the rows of small cells that held the women who bred the men of Kuskurza. They would also attack a fourth level that was used as a maternity center and prepare the newborn children to be either Bow Clansmen or slaves.

The nursery and birthing room were on the first floor the Sun Clan reached. They swarmed onto the floor through two large doors at one end. On one side of the large room was rows upon rows of cribs. Most of them were filled with babies. On the other side were tables. On some of the tables were women in the midst of birth. The women screamed as the first Sun Clansmen burst onto the floor, but if anyone had been listening, they would have thought the screams normal for a woman giving birth.

The Sun Clansmen plucked the children from the cribs and held one baby under each arm. When they had taken two babies they rushed out the doors to take the children back to the hidden pueblo.

The women in the middle of giving birth were being attended by older women past the child-bearing years. The older women, while they did not resist the Sun Clansmen, insisted that the women giving birth couldn't be moved. Polanque took control and told the women that those who could not be moved would be killed. If the plan were to work, there could be no women left in the mountain. The older women reluctantly agreed. They helped the women giving birth from the tables to something that resembled a gurney and pushed them toward the doors at the end of the floor.

The remaining quatis of Sun Clansmen pushed into the upper levels of the mountain. They charged through the doorway leading to the women's chambers and found themselves in a series of hallways opened upon by many doors. The men spread out so that one Sun Clansman was in front of each door.

One Bow Clansmen left his room early and was quickly killed with an arrow through his eye.

Ma´saw dropped his arm, and the Sun Clansmen rushed into the rooms. When David threw open the door to the room he stood in front of, he saw a nude Bow Clansman atop an equally naked woman. The Bow Clansman rose off the woman and reached for his langher, which was in the pile of his clothes. David raised his langher first, twisted the bulbous end, and slid the switch forward. A giant spark struck the Bow Clansmen in his head. It set his fine, white hair on fire even as it cracked his skull.

David's stomach churned at the sight and smell of the dead man's flesh burning. He had not believed a weapon could be so deadly. The woman screamed, and David told her to be quiet.

Help! Help! she yelled in his mind.

She rushed forward and began beating on David's chest. She tried to scratch his eyes, but David held his arm out and kept her away from him.

Be quiet! We are freeing you from the Bow Clansmen, David told her.

I don't want to be freed! she screamed telepathically as she tried to scratch his eyes again.

Polanque ran past the door then stopped and came back. *Pahana, hurry up and take her out. We have to move fast.*

She doesn't want to come, David thought as he pushed the woman back.

Polanque looked at the woman, then raised his langher and fired. The spark hit the woman in the chest leaving a gaping hole that showed the charred edges of her ribs.

David's eyes widened as he turned to Polanque. *Why did you do that?*

She would not have helped us. She has given herself totally to the Bow Clan. She would have betrayed us given a chance. She was an enemy, was Polanque's answer.

Polanque grabbed David by the arm and pulled him out of the room. He ran blindly along with the others as they retreated from the mountain. A few of the women kissed and hugged the Sun Clansmen as they ran. A pair of Sun Clansmen warned everyone to be as quiet as possible as they passed through the lower levels. They wanted to avoid as much conflict as possible. Their goal was to get the women safely to the hidden pueblo without getting into a massive battle that might cost them some of their men.

As the Sun Clansmen passed out of the pyramid, the women were handed green tunics much like those of the slaves. This would hide their features from all except those who came too close.

David was amazed at how smoothly things ran. He had expected more fighting, but the Bow Clansmen were too confident of their superiority. They were lazy and careless, and they had been caught off guard. The entire attack had lasted no longer than a half an hour. What had disturbed him was he expected to find more women; only sixty-nine had been rescued. Polanque assured him that was the only breeding center, so what happened to the other women?

When all the Sun Clansmen returned to the pueblo, Ma´saw took in the results of the raid. Two men counted all the women and children that came through the entrance of the pueblo. Ma´saw called the Sun Clan together in the meeting room and thought, *You have fought bravely today, and the Sun Clan are many now. We will need to build other pueblos where the Sun Clan can live and the women can be hidden from the Bow Clan. The Bow Clan will seek retribution. We must be ready to fight great battles and die, as we were ready this cycle. If we do, we will prevail in the end, as we did this cycle.*

David's vision faded, and he saw the fire burning inside the kiva. It had ended. Remembering how much time Peter had said had passed before, David looked at his watch. It was a quarter until eight. He shuffled slowly across the floor and climbed the ladder to leave the kiva.

He remembered everything now, perhaps too much. He could see why he would have wanted to forget some things. His mind had not only blocked out this most-recent incident but the earlier one as well.

When David climbed out of the kiva, it was dark outside. There was a little bit of activity around the plaza, but most people were in their rooms. David walked to Sarah's pueblo and knocked at her door.

There was no answer. Then he realized she would be in the canyon watching over her grandfather's body. This would be the last night of her vigil.

He walked over to Ethan's rooms and knocked. Ethan's face beamed when he opened the door and saw David.

"David, come in. I'll get the pops."

"Can we drink it on the road? I need a lift to the canyon where you dropped me off the other night."

Ethan nodded and took a six-pack of Diet Sprite from a tub of water, which kept the soda cool. Once they were on the road and had started drinking their sodas, Ethan said, "I hear you've been in the sacred kiva all day.

Peter must truly believe Adam's visions to allow you into the kiva."

"I remember everything that happened to me down there, Ethan," David said. "Perhaps too much."

"I would think you would be happy, but you don't sound too happy," Ethan noted.

"I'm happy I can remember, but now I can no longer avoid the issue. If I don't do something soon, the dark kachinas will be freed, and they will destroy this world."

CHAPTER 44

After Ethan dropped him off, David climbed the steep path up the side of the mesa and sat down on the ledge next to Sarah. She said nothing to him. The silence between them seemed comfortable, not awkward. He yawned and leaned back against the side of the mesa.

His stomach growled loudly, and he laid his hand on it to quiet it down. The pop he had drunk in Ethan's truck was beginning to eat at his stomach; the acid in the soda making him feel hungry. He realized he hadn't eaten anything since he had stopped in Tuba City for a hamburger last night on his way to Oraibi.

Sarah reached into her bag and handed David a piece of bread that reminded him of pita bread.

"Have you been in the kiva all day?" she asked.

David nodded as he chewed a piece of the bread. It was dry and hard to eat. David wondered if it was supposed to taste like that or if Sarah just wasn't a good cook. He swallowed the piece he was chewing wishing he had some water to wash it down with.

"I can remember everything now. My mind was purposely blocking out the memories because I didn't want to face up to them. That's probably why I got so angry with you and Adam the first time you two came to see me. I was reacting to the fact that Adam was challenging the wall I had built to protect me," David said. He reached over and held Sarah's hand. "Adam was right about everything, Sarah. He wasn't crazy."

"What happened to you in Kuskurza? What is it like?" she asked.

"It's about the size of a large city, but there is a lot of open space. In the center are five temples. The dark kachinas are imprisoned in the central temple. The Bow Clan lives in the surrounding smaller ones. Slaves live in pueblos around the edges of the chamber. Between the center and the edges are fields and rivers.

"When I fell into the cave, the Bow Clan would have killed me if they had found me, but I was rescued by a man named Masani. He was from the Sun Clan. They are former slaves who believe in Taiowa and the Fourth World," David told Sarah. "I helped them. They called me Pahana."

Sarah looked surprised. "Pahana? Are you sure?"

"Yes. I think they just couldn't pronounce my last name right."

"But David, Pahana is a mythical Hopi god. He's the lost white brother who will deliver us to freedom."

David nodded. "That makes sense. They thought I might be able to help them leave Kuskurza."

David fell silent. He remembered how so much of the Hopi creation stories Adam had explained to him in the hospital had paralleled Biblical beliefs, and now it also seemed the stories closely matched Mormon beliefs. The Hopi had seen a white savior and were waiting for his return on this continent.

"Adam would have been happy that you remember everything," Sarah said.

David detected a hint of melancholy in her voice, and he wanted to pull her close to him and hold her. He remembered what Ethan had said this morning and hesitated. Things were happening that might take him away from Oraibi. Would it be fair to ask her to go, too? He had only made Terrie sad when he took her away from Blanding. Was it right for him to take Sarah away from her home?

"What will happen now, David? Is this world in danger?" Sarah asked.

"I'll have to return to Blanding. Somehow I have to convince Sheriff Harding or maybe the cave team that there is another world where those cave passages end. Maybe they can use explosives to seal the passages permanently. If they could get some spotlights down there, they might be able to control the dark kachinas, but eventually, they would find a way to be free. The Bow Clan might sabotage the floodlights, or they might break down on their own. The only way to stop them is to seal the passages. Besides, if Taiowa couldn't kill them, neither can we. All we can do is imprison them again," David thought out loud.

"But the Sun Clan thinks you can save them. What happens if you can't?"

David shrugged. "I don't know. Then I guess they wait for the real Pahana."

"What if it's you?"

David laughed. He couldn't help it; it just slipped out. He was far from being Christ or even Christ-like. Sarah looked serious, though so he explained himself. "I'm no savior, Sarah, I'm just a klutzy guy who fell into a cave."

"You're psychic. That's special. And you've faced the Bow Clan twice when no one else in this world has ever even seen them."

"That still doesn't make me Pahana."

David looked at Sarah. She was staring up at the moon.

"What will you do now?" he asked changing the subject. He didn't like comparing himself to Christ because he came up short.

Sarah shrugged. "I don't know. I have the rooms here in Oraibi. It is something."

"But is that what you want?"

"No. I have tried to be a part of this world, but I'm not. I think I must have lived too long among the whites. The only reason I've stayed this long is because of my grandfather. He was my family, and I loved him. But now all that's left is his body. His spirit has left Oraibi. He had lived here all his life. If he could leave, so can I."

David felt his heart beat faster. Maybe there was a chance. Maybe Sarah wasn't like Terrie.

"You said something the other night about not knowing love, but you just told me you loved Adam."

"I was talking about romantic love," Sarah told him.

"Why haven't you ever been in love?"

Sarah was silent for a long time, then she said, "I have been, but the feeling wasn't returned. When I was sixteen, I fell in love with a white boy I went to school with. I thought he loved me, too. He only loved me until the day after we made love, then he turned his attentions to someone else. Then word got around school about me, and suddenly, there were a lot of boys who said they were in love with me. They treated me like a squaw. They didn't love me, and when I got smart, I stopped loving them. Not long after that, my mother left me here."

David shifted away from Sarah, and he felt her stiffen. She looked at him angrily, and said, "Am I too dirty to touch now?"

David shook his head. "No, but I thought ... It's just that the way you talked about those boys treating you that you might feel the same about me. I don't want you to think that I'm using you to help me through this."

David saw the tears form in the corners of her eyes. They were quickly followed by others until she was sobbing. David watched her unsure of what to do. Then he moved closer to her and put his arm around her.

"Sarah, will you come back to Blanding with me? I'm going to need help convincing Sheriff Harding about Kuskurza and the danger down there."

Sarah raised her head. "Of course, I'll come."

"Afterward, I'll need you to go to Provo with me. Can you go?" David asked innocently.

The confused look on Sarah's face almost made David laugh, but he managed to maintain his control.

"I suppose. But what's in Provo?"

"My parents live there. There's a woman who's very special to me that I want them to meet."

Sarah smiled and kissed David.

PART III

Kuskurza

"Looking about them, they saw they were on a little piece of land that had been the top of one of their highest mountains. All else, as far as they could see, was water. This was all that remained of the Third World."

Book of the Hopi

"And the earth was without form, and void; and darkness was upon the face of the deep. And the Spirit of God moved upon the face of the waters. And God said, Let there be light: and there was light. And God saw the light, that it was good: and God divided the light from the darkness."

Genesis 1: 2-4

CHAPTER 45

After Lou stripped out of his scuba gear, he started the ten-mile hike back to chamber one. He complained that he was tired and wanted to climb into his sleeping bag and rest, and he let everyone know it. Christine called for him to wait up, but he ignored her and continued walking. Although she was angry with him for leaving on his own, she knew how exhausted he must feel. She was partly responsible for it. Earlier, when they had been doing a vertical descent down a chimney on the other side of the sump, her pin had slipped from the cave wall, and she had fallen to the end of her safety cord. It had been Lou who had supported her weight until she had found her footing again.

"I'll keep an eye on him," Alex said as he started off to catch up with Lou. Christine heard Alex yell to Lou, "How about when we get upstairs, we drive into Blanding for something harder than the beer Gary keeps in the refrigerator? I think I saw at least one bar in town."

Lou said something, Christine couldn't hear, and then both men laughed. She turned her attention back to repacking her scuba gear so she could leave with Billy Joe. She didn't like having the team split up in pairs, but when Lou set his mind to something, there was no stopping him. The whole purpose of having four people exploring the cave at once was that if someone was hurt, one person could stay with the injured person and the other two could go for help. That way no one was ever alone.

But now they were divided. She wasn't sure why it bothered her since little had happened during their exploration. Besides her near fall, the most dangerous thing that had happened was when Lou got caught in the sump. Of course, that didn't mean the caverns weren't dangerous.

The exploration on the other side of the flooded sump hadn't yielded anything except more tunnels and the chasm. They had seen no indication of a natural opening yet, and Christine wondered if there would be. Instead of leading toward the surface, the gap went even deeper, and the tunnel continued on the other side heading south. If there was a natural entrance to this cave system, they were moving away from it. At the rate they were descending, they might eventually break the old record of 4,369 feet set in the Gouffre de la Pierre St. Martin in France. Think of it! Over four-fifths of a mile below the earth's surface. They were over 1,500 feet now.

Come to think of it, there might be other records broken by the time these caves were fully explored. Flint-Mammoth Cave's 180-mile claim to be the longest cave system was certainly in jeopardy.

Today they had managed to explore and map about three-quarters of a mile of passages on the other side of the sump in addition to the half a mile she, Alex, Lou, and Billy Joe had mapped yesterday.

Christine tied the final flap on her backpack shut and hefted it onto her back. Billy Joe was already standing and waiting for her.

"The last of the gentlemen," she said.

"Think nothing of it," he replied exaggerating his already pronounced southern drawl.

"You know we're going to have to set up another camp on the other side of the sump to do overnight explorations. We're losing too much time hiking back and forth between the surface camp and the passages we're exploring each day," Christine said.

"You're..." Billy Joe started to say before his eyes went wide.

Christine spun around and saw two, tall, pale-white men rising out of the water of the sump. They weren't wearing any scuba gear so they must have swum through the sump quickly. Their clothes were made of a shimmering black-and-red material Christine had never seen. It reminded her of silk. Each man also carried a metal pipe with a knobby end.

Christine backed away a step from the men. Whoever they were, they didn't look friendly.

The first man silently lifted his metal pipe and twisted the knobby end. It made a sound like thunder and then what looked to Christine like a giant electrical spark flew out of the end of the pipe. It hit Billy Joe in the center of his chest. He grunted and collapsed on the ground. His body jerked a few times and then lay still.

Christine started to scream, but the second man jumped forward and clamped his hand over her mouth. The taste of the stagnant water on her lips and the sight of Billy Joe lying on the ground with a hole in his chest made her feel nauseous.

Two more pale-skinned men rose out of the water. The first man pointed down the tunnel that Alex and Lou had walked into, and the second pair of men ran off into the darkness.

They were going to kill Alex and Lou just like they had murdered Billy Joe! Christine tried to scream again wanting to warn her friends, but the pale man's grip was too tight. She couldn't even open her mouth enough to bite his hand.

Christine heard the clap of thunder that seemed to accompany the electric sparks from the metal pipes, and she heard one person scream. She was sure it had been Alex. Even screaming, his voice was deep. After a minute, the second pair of pale-skinned men returned. The pale-skinned men dove back into the water and disappeared.

If Christine hadn't been so frightened, she would have laughed. Even in the midst of the danger, she couldn't help but think all of this looked like a science fiction movie. However, this was real and instead of laughing, she started to cry.

The man holding Christine stepped into the water dragging her with him. He grabbed hold of the guide wire Gary had strung up two days ago to lead the divers through the sump. Christine knew what he was going to do. She took a deep breath and prayed she would be able to hold it long enough.

If she lived, she would finally find out where the caves ended.

CHAPTER 46

Peter leaned back against the wall of the sacred kiva. This room had always been a place of meditation and worship for him. Despite the danger it represented, it was even a place of safety for him. And now, it had also become his place of mourning.

His friend Adam was dead.

This had been the place where Adam's death had started even though it had ended in Utah. This was where Adam had received his visions that led him north. If Sarah and David were to be believed, and there was no reason not to believe them, then the Bow Clan was in Tu´waqachi. All the precautions taken by the old Hopis had failed. The Bow Clan had found another way to the surface. If the Bow Clan had found their way to the surface, could the dark kachinas be far behind?

Adam had been right. Something David had done while he was in the caves had upset the balance between the Third and Fourth Worlds. David had angered the dark kachinas enough that they had sent Bow Clansmen into Tu´waqachi to kill him.

Peter closed his eyes and inhaled the smoke deeply letting it ease the tension from his body. Was he even worthy to be in this kiva? Adam had been pure of heart and had received visions of the danger. David had been worthy and had recalled his lost memories. Wasn't Peter worthy to receive a vision to understand what was happening?

Taiowa, Peter prayed to himself, *what can be done to restore order to the Fourth World?*

Now that the Bow Clan was loose upon the world, how long would it be before the dark kachinas were free and unleashed on the land? Did it even matter what the Hopis had done to keep the worlds separate?

His own grandfather had told him the story of the Bow Clan when he was much younger. It was not one of the legends the Hopi told the white anthropologists, even when those scientists were their friends. Very few people even outside of Oraibi knew the purpose of the sacred kiva. This was a Hopi problem, and so it was the Hopis' responsibility to solve it.

Had they failed?

After all these years of faithful duty, had faith finally given way to disbelief?

During the time the Hopi nation was confined to the small area called their reservation, a man had wandered into Oraibi. If this had been another Hopi, not much attention would have been paid to him. Even if he had been a white man, he might have gone unnoticed, for there were many white men who came into the villages on the three mesas. But this man's skin had been pale-white like milk.

He staggered into the town plaza shielding his face from the sun with his long fingers. The medicine man had been called for to administer to the man, but no one approached the stranger. Everyone was afraid of him because of his pale skin and white hair. He was like no one the Hopis had ever seen.

The medicine man had approached the strange man and spoke to him in the language of the Hopi. The pale-skinned man replied, and they were able to communicate. Not with words, though. The pale-skinned man had sent his thoughts directly into the medicine man's head.

The medicine man led the strange man into a room where it was dark and cool. The pale-skinned man lowered his arm, but he still had to squint even though there was little light in the room. His eyes were quite large and round.

As the medicine man and the stranger had communicated, the pale-skinned man told the medicine man about the Sun Clan. They were a splinter group from the Bow Clan who refused to follow the ways of the dark kachinas. They believed in Taiowa and wanted to live in Tu'waqachi. The stranger had been part of an exploration party trying to find the sipapu, but the party had been attacked by the Bow Clan. He had escaped their attack and gotten lost in the caves. While he was trying to find his way back to the Sun Clan, he had found the sipapu.

When the medicine man had asked where the sipapu was, the white-skinned man said there was a hole in the ground near the edge of the mesa. That is where he had come from. He was very anxious to return to his people through the sipapu and lead them to safety, but he was too weak to go very far.

The medicine man knew about the sipapu. Oraibi had been built to guard it, but nothing had ever come through the emergence hole. Many had even begun to doubt the old legends because the white men told the Hopis their beliefs were superstition. Now all the Hopi would know the truth about the legends.

The medicine man prepared a drink for the Heroz - that was the pale-skinned man's name – and left him to rest. After a few days, Heroz recovered from his wounds, and was ready to return to Kuskurza. Most of Oraibi watched him disappear into the hole near the edge of the mesa.

Once Heroz had gone, the medicine man advised the town to seal up the sipapu and hide it from view. If Kuskurza's Sun Clan would not keep the dark kachinas imprisoned, then Tu'waqachi's Sun Clan would. Neither the Bow Clan or the dark kachinas could be allowed to emerge from the sipapu. Now that the Hopis knew the legends were true, even greater steps needed to be taken to protect the Fourth World.

The strongest Sun Clansmen in Oraibi had hammered the large stone into the sipapu. Then they had built the sacred kiva around the hole to hide it from view. As the years passed, all but the faithful forgot about the incident. Fewer people visited the sacred kiva because other kivas were closer in town.

Peter was jolted out of his remembrances by the sound of screams. He sat upright and listened. He heard nothing. He stood up to walk to the ladder to leave the kiva, and he heard the screams again. Only they were not coming from anywhere outside the kiva, and not from anywhere inside the kiva either. They were coming from inside Peter's head.

He listened to see if he could understand any of the words, but he could not. All he heard were screams. Was he receiving Adam's visions now?

CHAPTER 47

Jared laid down his copy of *USAToday* and yawned. Gary looked up from the microwave TV dinner of dry roast beef and foul-tasting carrots and peas he was eating.

"Enjoy your boredom, Jared. Tomorrow you and I are back in the ground," Gary said.

Jared stretched. "By the way, where are the others? It's almost nine," he said as he looked at the clock on the microwave oven.

"Nine?" Gary set aside his fork and glanced at his watch. "You're right. I wonder where they are? I expected them back an hour ago."

"Maybe we should go down and see if we can find them," Jared thought out loud.

Gary considered the suggestion and nodded. "Better grab the first aid kit, too. We might need it if they ran into trouble. Lord, I hope there wasn't a cave in." That was only one of the many things Gary could think of that might have delayed his four friends from returning.

He grabbed a specially packed knapsack from a shelf in the closet. He opened it up and dumped a coiled, fifty-foot ladder from the bag. He slung his own knapsack over his shoulder, scooped up the ladder, and followed Jared out of the RV.

At the edge of the hole David had fallen into more than six weeks ago, Gary anchored one end of the ladder to the ground and dropped the remainder into the hole. He heard it smack the floor of the cave and then the nylon cords tightened. The nylon loop they usually used to enter the cavern was inside the chamber. Gary could have raised it and used it to lower themselves into the caverns, but since both he and Jared were going into the passages, there would have been no one left to operate the winch to raise them back to the surface.

After they had climbed to the bottom of the ladder, Gary and Jared turned on their headlamps.

"Where were they exploring today?" Jared asked.

"On the other side of the sump."

Jared tried to suppress his shudder. "I sure hope one of them didn't get caught underneath. You know how dangerous that place is. I'm surprised Lou would go down there again."

"I don't think all four of them would have gotten caught. One of them would have gotten out to come and get us."

Jared sighed and rubbed the back of his neck. "I sure hope they're on this

207

side of the sump. I don't want to have to go in after them."

They turned off the main passages to the smaller line of passages running through chamber four. After chamber four, the group walked through chamber seventeen. This chamber was nearly filled with a mountain of boulders they had to climb over to get to the other side. Three hours after entering the caverns, they had seen no one enter the passageway that led to the sump.

Although Gary said nothing, he shared Jared's concern that something had happened at the sump. He had hoped to meet the others on the way back to the entrance. Then they would be able to laugh about Gary and Jared's obsessive worrying, but they were nearly at the sump and had seen no one. If only one, two, or even three of them had been hurt, someone would have still been able to come to chamber one and call for help. Why hadn't they seen or heard anyone yet?

Jared paused and took a deep breath. "Do you smell that?"

Gary took a deep breath. Another smell tainted the usual musty smell of the caverns. Gary tried to place the scent but he couldn't. It was sweet and thick. Gary's stomach churned, and the roast beef he had eaten earlier threatened to rise.

"What is it?" Gary asked.

Jared shrugged.

"Let's keep going then," Gary said. "I'm starting to get worried."

"You're just starting? I've been worried since we climbed down here," Jared said.

They continued down the passage with Gary in the lead. He stopped suddenly when he saw a boot. Jared looked over Gary's shoulder and saw the boot lying just inside the circle of light cast by the headlamp. Gary took a hesitant step forward and illuminated the calf of the coveralls.

He took another step forward and illuminated the chest, shoulders, and finally, Lou's head. His eyes were wide open and staring unblinkingly at the ceiling.

Gary threw off his gloves and kneeled down beside Lou to feel for a pulse at Lou's neck. There was none. He was dead.

Gary ran down the passageway toward the sump with Jared.

"Christine! Alex! Billy Joe!" they both yelled.

There was no response to their calls but their own echoes.

Then Gary saw Alex sprawled on his stomach just as dead as Lou. He rushed to the side of the tunnel and threw up his dinner.

Billy Joe's body was at the edge of the water. His hand floated in the pool of still water. A black hole replaced his chest.

"Where's Christine?" Jared asked from behind Gary.

"Christine!" Gary called.

She had to be alive. She just had to. Gary didn't know what he would do if she were dead. She had to be alive.

Gary shook his head. "What the hell happened here?"

"I don't know," Jared spoke rapidly in a panicked tone, "But I know what we smelled earlier. It was burnt flesh. Look at Billy Joe."

Gary stared at the corpse at the water's edge. In the center of Billy Joe's chest was a black spot about the size of a saucer. The actual hole in Billy Joe's chest, Gary saw when he leaned closer, was small. The rest of the black area was scorched cloth and flesh. Gary pinched his nose and backed away.

"It almost looks like someone lit a fire on his chest or shot him with a blowtorch," Jared said.

"Where's Christine? We found the other three. If she escaped whatever killed them, we should have run into her."

Both their gazes shifted to the water at the same time. Gary pulled a powerful flashlight from his belt and shined it over the water. No body was floating on top of it. It was only a small, and all too brief, relief.

The water suddenly exploded upward in a large spout. Gary backed away as another spout of water exploded closer to the edge of the shore this time.

Gary saw two divers rise out of the water. Divers came out of the water. A jagged streak of electricity flew from it and hit Jared in the chest. He screamed, clutched at his chest, and fell. Gary didn't have to take a second look to know his friend was dead. He remembered too well what Billy Joe looked like.

Gary turned and ran back down the tunnel toward chamber seventeen. Behind him, he heard a rock explode near where he had been standing. He only hoped he could outrun whoever was behind him. Then again Alex and Lou hadn't gotten too far. Had they been running or had they been caught by surprise?

He ran down the passageway and jumped over Lou's body. He scrambled on his hands and knees up the mountain of boulders. Halfway up, he slipped and slid back three feet among a small avalanche of rocks. Part of the mountain exploded above him, and he held his hands up to his face to protect it from flying shards of rock.

He rolled to his side to go around the side of the mountain. As he did, his flashlight shined briefly on the two pale men at the entrance to the chamber. One of them fired another lightning bolt at him as Gary rolled around the side.

CHAPTER 48

Sarah kissed David goodbye at the door to his apartment. It was their first kiss, and it was as exciting as if it had been her first kiss. It was almost like she thought everything would work out somehow.

Wouldn't they? Sarah wished she could be certain.

She was sorry that the evening was ending. She and David had talked almost constantly on the long trip back to Blanding. However, once he passed by the sipapu, David had fallen uncomfortably silent.

"Don't worry," Sarah said when she pulled away. "We'll find a way to convince Sheriff Harding."

He still looked exhausted from the long trip back from Oraibi, and she knew she was tired. Because she had had to watch her grandfather's body, her sleep schedule was totally fouled up. She needed to get back on a regular sleep pattern so that she could think straight.

David smiled and kissed her again. "You're not going to sleep next to the highway again, are you?"

"Yes, but it's all right. I'll be all right."

David took out his credit card and handed it to her. "Go to a hotel and just sign the credit card slip 'Mrs. David Purcell.'"

Sarah handed the card back to him. "I don't need a hotel room. I've got a tent and blanket, and I know how to make a fire. What else do I need?" It wasn't that she actually wanted to sleep out in the desert, but she didn't want to feel indebted to David at least not until she was certain how things would work out.

"You need a locked door to help keep the Bow Clan away from you if they decide to finish what they started last week. You can't stay out there alone. If you don't want a hotel, you can stay here." Sarah stiffened and pulled away from him. "I don't mean...I'll sleep on the couch. I just don't think it's safe for you to be out in the open with the Bow Clan running around."

Sarah sighed and leaned forward and kissed him again. Then she took the credit card. "I'll stay in a hotel."

David watched Sarah walk down the stairs to the driveway. She paused at the door and turned back to wave to him. He waved back, then closed his door.

Sarah headed for David's car, which was parked on the street. As she reached into her pocket for David's car key, she heard someone running toward her. For a moment, she thought it might be David rushing to tell her something she had forgotten. She turned and thought she saw a ghost, but it was a man. A very pale-white man in a black-and-red tunic. He had his hands outstretched and was reaching for her throat.

Sarah's swung her fist holding the keys sticking out between the fingers. The charging man ran right into her fist. As she swung, the keys tore into the man's cheek. She hadn't lived in the white man's world without learning a few tricks about defending herself. She saw blood on the pale man's face. At least it was red blood and not some odd shade of pink.

The Bow Clansman screamed and grabbed his face. His momentum carried him right past her, and he fell into a gardenia bush at the corner of the driveway and the sidewalk. Sarah started running toward she car as fast as she could.

She fumbled with the lock on the Corolla's door trying to unlock it. The Bow Clansman ran toward her again.

Sarah opened the car door and jumped into the driver's seat. She tried to close the door, but the pale man pulled at it from the outside. If she let go of the door and tried to scramble out the other side, the Bow Clansman would pull open the door and grab her before she could get out the other side.

"Help!" she screamed.

She hoped David would hear her, but she would have been happy to see anyone at that moment.

The pale man yanked the door hard and wrenched it from her grip.

"Someone help!" Sarah screamed again as she tried to scramble into the passenger's seat and get out the other door.

The Bow Clansman reached into the car and grabbed Sarah by her calf and began to pull her back across the seats. Sarah kicked at him, but her kicks didn't seem to hurt him.

Then suddenly the pale men screamed and fell in between the open door and front windshield. He staggered, then regained his balance and turned to see what had struck him.

Sarah saw David through the window holding a bat and waving it at the Bow Clansman.

"Get back to the Third World, you devil!" David yelled in Hopi.

The Bow Clansman backed away from the car with David following him.

"Go back to Hell where you came from!"

David swung the bat. The pale man ducked, and the bat smashed into the back window of a nearby pickup truck. As the bat passed over the man's head, he rushed at David and tackled him. David dropped the bat and grabbed at the man. Their hands were locked around each other's throats with each man trying to choke the other. The pale man lifted David's head off the ground and repeatedly slammed it back against the ground. David tried to push him away, but he wasn't strong enough.

The Bow Clansman let go of David, and Sarah screamed when she saw David lying still on the ground. The Bow Clansman approached her cautiously. She was too terrified to try to run anymore. Besides, what good would it do? David was dead. Her grandfather was dead. There was nothing to hold her in either the white man's world or the Hopi's world.

The Bow Clansman grabbed her with his left hand. With his right hand, he touched his bleeding cheek. Then he backhanded her across the face.

Sarah's vision blurred and then went black as she passed out.

CHAPTER 49

The first thing that David realized when he regained consciousness was that his throat hurt. Every time he breathed in, he felt pain that encircled his entire neck. He got his hands underneath himself and rose to his knees. He swayed unsteadily, but he didn't fall.

He wondered why no one was on the street. It had been crowded with people when Terrie was killed, and she had lived on the edge of Blanding. David lived near the center of Monticello.

The Bow Clansman was gone at least. Had something scared him off? Why hadn't he killed David?

"Sarah," David called in barely more than a whisper.

He staggered to his feet and looked around. The door to his new car was open, but Sarah was nowhere to be seen.

The Bow Clansman had taken her!

David staggered to his car and climbed in. As he sat down inside, he saw Sarah. At first, he thought she had simply appeared from a hiding place and was coming toward him, but then David realized he was seeing through the eyes of the Bow Clansman again.

Sarah was alive, but she looked terrified as the Bow Clansman dragged her toward a hole in the ground. He was taking her to Kuskurza to serve as a breeder since there were very few women with the Bow Clan any longer. And David was the reason why. He was the one who had convinced Ma'saw to raid the breeding chambers and recapture the women.

David had to get to Sarah before the Bow Clansman took her to the central temple. Once there, he would never be able to get her out. She would be at the mercy of the dark kachinas.

David started his car and roared down the road heading for the entrance to the cave on Highway 191. He hoped he would be in time.

CHAPTER 50

Gary paused running through the cave and doused his flashlight beam. Had he heard them, whoever they were, pursuing him? A flashlight beam illuminated the wall near him, and he ducked back. How had they gotten in front of him?

He heard a woman grunting. Had there been a woman among the group that attacked his friends? He couldn't remember, but he thought they had all been men.

Maybe it was Christine. He shook his head. No, Christine couldn't have gotten in front of him. And besides, this woman's voice was deeper than Christine's.

Gary stayed hidden between two stalactites. As long as they didn't see him, he was happy.

He waited for the noises to pass, then he continued on trying to make as little noise as possible. In another two miles, he entered the main passages; the ones with which he was most familiar. He ran as hard as he could from chamber four to chamber one. He hadn't run so fast since his high school days when he had been on the track team. He didn't even worry about tripping in some small hole. He just ran all out.

Gary jumped onto the nylon ladder and was scurrying up it before it even stopped swaying. His feet slipped off the rungs three times because he was so tired, but he managed to hold on long enough to regain his footing. Gary prayed the pale men wouldn't catch him on the ladder. He'd be a sitting duck for those lightning bolts they shot.

He pulled himself onto the ground outside the caverns. He was out of breath, but he couldn't stop to rest. Pushing the button on the front of the truck, the winch began rolling in the nylon rope. Gary ran back to the edge of the hole and started pulling up the ladder as fast as he could. He had only pulled up a few feet of the ladder when he felt a sharp increase in weight that would have jerked him back into the hole if he hadn't let go of the rung he was holding.

Gary didn't even have to look into the hole to know what had happened. One of the pale men was on the ladder and climbing toward him. They must have doubled back and found the path he had taken.

Gary pulled out his knife and began sawing at the nylon. A yellow bolt of lightning flew out of the hole. Gary kept cutting. As a second bolt struck the edge of the hole, Gary cut through one of the two nylon ropes of the ladder. He immediately began cutting at the second nylon rope. A third yellow bolt flew from the hole as Gary cut the final cord.

The three feet of the ladder that showed above the hole quickly disappeared. He fell back on the ground and tried to catch his breath. He hoped he was having a nightmare that he would wake up from soon.

"Mr. Morse?"

Gary rolled away from the sound of the voice. He rolled himself into a crouch, and he held the knife ready to charge whoever had startled him. Then he saw who it was. David Purcell.

"What are you doing here?" Gary shook his head. "Never mind. I've got to grab my gun and get back down there. Christine may be in trouble."

David stepped closer to Gary and grabbed him by the shoulders. "Calm down. I know what's going on down there. I think we can help each other if you calm down."

Gary took a deep breath. "What do you mean you know what's going on down there? I saw it, and I don't even know what's going on."

"I remembered what happened to me when I was lost down there."

Gary spoke quickly, his voice bordering on the edge of hysteria. "Two pale-skinned men came out of the water by the sump. They killed Jared. Billy Joe, Ryan, and Lou are dead, too. They were dead when Jared and I got to the sump, but Christine is still down there."

"The men who killed your friends are part of a group called the Bow Clan. They attacked me at my apartment a little while ago and kidnapped Sarah," David said.

Gary gasped. "Then it was a female I heard."

"What are you talking about?"

"I heard a woman trying to scream in the caves, but I thought she was one of the people who killed my friends, so I didn't do anything. I didn't know she was your girlfriend."

"I need you to show me where the pale-skinned men came out of the water. I've got to get Sarah away from them before they get her to the central temple."

"What happens at the temple?" Gary wanted to know.

"She'll either be raped by the Bow Clan or killed by the dark kachinas. I hope it will be neither if I'm quick enough."

Gary didn't know what a kachina was, but he could tell by David's tone it wasn't anything good.

"If they've got Christine, they'll do the same thing to her, won't they?" Gary asked.

David nodded. Gary turned and ran towards the RV.

"If we're going down there, we'll need some protection, and you'll need to wear something heavier than that T-shirt. There are some clothes in here. Get changed into a pair of coveralls fast. I'll gather the other things we'll need," Gary said as he seemed to regain his senses.

"Pack some food, too. It takes a long time to get where we're going," David advised him.

"How long?" Gary wanted to know.

"About a week."

Gary's mouth fell open. He didn't know why he was surprised. He had always suspected the caves might be the longest in the world, but one week! That was unimaginable, even for him.

While David changed into coveralls and boots, Gary quickly packed two backpacks. He filled one with light sticks, two pistols, a box of ammunition, a detonator, and five pounds of plastic explosives, they used to seal dangerous caverns. Into the second, he dumped canned and dried food along with some Milky Way bars for energy.

David saw what the first backpack was filled with and said, "It looks like we're preparing for war."

"Aren't we? I saw what they shot Jared with. I don't want to be caught off guard. And if this central temple is as bad as it sounds, I don't want it left standing when we leave."

Gary was so angry he could barely keep from screaming. All his friends were dead. He had led them here for an adventure, and they had wound up getting killed. He wanted revenge, but more importantly, if Christine was alive, he wanted to get her out of there. If he could do that, he would never go back down in a cave again.

"We don't really have a choice. Things would only be worse if we blow it up," David said.

He shouldered his pack and shoved the pistol into one of his pockets. Gary carried his pack outside, and David followed. He lowered David into the caverns on the winch rope. Then he slid down the rope controlling his speed through leg pressure on the nylon rope and using a hand-over-hand grip.

"They were right behind me a few minutes ago," Gary said when he let go of the rope. "They may still be nearby. You had better keep your pistol ready. We may need it."

CHAPTER 51

When the Bow Clansmen came to take Christine from the stone room that had served as her cell for the past few hours. She knew she would not return. Christine could see it in the eyes of the other women as they watched the two Bow Clansmen lead her away. She walked between the two men and watched as a few of the women cried. Others simply looked at her then looked away as if she didn't exist.

Christine had expected something like this would happen to her. She considered it a blessing because she would gladly die as long as she didn't have to stay in this hell any longer. Six hours was already too long. She couldn't even understand the language of these people. They spoke like Indians, but they looked like albinos with their white skin and white hair. And this gigantic chamber they lived in resembled the Mayan cities in Mexico near the center and the cliff dwellings of the Anasazi at the edges.

It was an anthropologist's dream and nightmare at the same time.

The men who had captured her had taken her directly to one of four small pyramids near the center of the chamber. They had carried her down a hallway lined with doors. The men had ripped her coveralls off of her, and she thought she was about to be raped. Instead, one of the men had opened a door and she had been thrown into a small room about the size a bathroom. Except for the small opening in the door, there were no windows, and the walls were made of stone, which was exceptionally cold on her bare skin. A globe that looked like an electric light dimly lit the room. The room was empty except for a thin mattress lying on the floor.

Only a few minutes after Christine had been thrown into the room, the door was unlocked, and a man stepped inside. Christine covered herself with her hands as the man looked up and down her body. When he took off his clothes, Christine started screaming. She fought him as hard as she could. She hadn't worried about being hurt or killed because she knew she was never going to see the sun again. She had scratched and bit the man, but in the end, he had succeeded in raping her. When he finished, he stood up and left without ever having said a word.

A few minutes later, another man came, and the whole scene repeated itself. And again, a short time later. Christine fought them every time they came. At times, she told herself to stop fighting. It wasn't worth the trouble and the extra pain it caused her, but then she told herself it was either a lot of pain now or less pain stretched over years. It wasn't a hard decision for her to reach.

She would not allow herself to become a slave, and so her captors had quickly decided to take her away to wherever they took those people who resisted. She didn't struggle when they came to take her from her cell. It didn't matter where they were taking her.

She was glad it was nearly over.

The first Bow Clansman opened a large door at the end of a hallway within the largest pyramid. The two men leading Christine stopped walking and pushed her into the dark room. She managed to maintain her balance to keep from falling. She turned as the doors closed but did not try to rush toward them. They obviously meant to leave her in here.

With the doors closed, the room was absolutely dark like a cave. At least her cell had had a little light. Judging from the size of the door, she guessed the room was large. It had to be as large as the doors, and they had been larger than her cell. She turned around in a slow circle wondering what was supposed to happen to her here. Were there other people in the room with her? Other people who had resisted becoming slaves?

"Hello?" she called out. "Is anyone else here?"

No one answered, but she thought she heard a faint scraping sound in the distance.

Christine could feel the immensity of the room around her, and it disturbed her in the same way large chambers sometimes have a reverse-claustrophobic effect on spelunkers. She moved toward the door so that she could feel the wall and have some way to orient herself.

Something moved near her, but in the dark room, there was no way to see what it was. The darkness itself seemed to be moving, but there was no breeze that she could feel. The darkness swirled around her feet and tickled her ankles. When she tried to step out of it, it felt like she was stepping out of mud. It seemed to hold onto her refusing to let her move.

The room no longer felt large. It was small now, very small. Christine reached out to touch one of the walls, and something bit her arm. She jerked her arm to her side and backed away.

Something was in the room with her. Some sort of animal.

"Don't scream," she whispered to herself. "Don't scream. They're probably listening to you right now, and a scream is one thing they wouldn't need a translator to explain."

She took a deep breath and sucked on her lower lip.

The darkness moved up her legs. Suddenly, she felt sharp pains all over her calves and thighs. Gulping down a scream, she tried to run.

She couldn't. Her legs were stuck to the floor.

Christine bent over and tried to push away whatever was attacking her legs, but when she swung her fists, she hit nothing but air. Yet, her legs still hurt.

Then the bites started on her arms. She stood straight up and screamed, not caring whether they thought she was a coward or not. The bites on her arms continued, though. They moved from her arms up to her shoulders and neck.

Christine knew she was bleeding. She could feel the blood running down her arms as the bites increased in intensity. Touching her left arm with her right hand, Christine felt the deep gouge that had once been part of her biceps.

She felt a pain on the side of her neck and screamed again. She clamped her hands to her neck and could feel her blood pulsing between her fingers. She tried to run again, but her legs still felt stuck to the ground.

As she fell to the floor, she thought to herself, *This is what one of Dracula's victims must feel like.*

Christine prayed she was dying. She thought she wouldn't be able to live with all her blood pumping out of her neck. How fast was it pumping out? An ounce a minute? Two? How many pints did the average human woman have? Eight? How long would it be before she lost all her blood? Her mind fogged over, and she couldn't concentrate.

It hadn't taken these people long to kill her. She was glad that they didn't have much patience. She was a coward at heart, and she wasn't sure she would have been able to sustain her resistance through much more pain.

There were worse places for a spelunker to die than in a mysterious cave. If she had to die anywhere, she was glad it was underground just like Floyd Collins. Except he had had a nation to mourn his death when he was killed in a cave-in. Who would remember her? The Bow Clan had killed all her friends except Gary and Jared.

Gary. Gary would remember.

She felt something ripping open her chest, and she screamed for the last time.

CHAPTER 52

Kel'hoya switched on the flashlight he had stolen from the Outlanders and shined it around the chamber. He didn't recognize this chamber, but he knew if he continued to go forward, he would eventually find the path to Kuskurza. He had chosen to come this way because he didn't think David would follow him, if he lived, which Kel'hoya doubted. He would not take any chances, though. He was too close to success now. He would find favor with the dark kachinas once again when he presented this woman to be used as a breeder.

He called to the Bow Clan with his thoughts. *Your brother has returned, and I have brought a gift for the dark kachinas,* he thought.

If his thoughts didn't reach the Bow Clan, he was sure his presence in the caves would be detected, and the dark kachinas would send the Bow Clan to investigate.

He continued to broadcast his thoughts, but it wasn't until he climbed a steep pile of rocks that he saw the Bow Clansmen. They had been closer than he thought they would be. Four of them in full uniform stood at the base of the rocks. Kel'hoya stopped walking and waited for them to approach him.

Brothers, he thought to them. He almost spoke, but he remembered he was of the Bow Clan and the Bow Clan communicated by thought.

We do not recognize you, one of the Bow Clansmen told Kel'hoya.

I am Kel'hoya.

What is the gift you spoke of for the dark kachinas?

Kel'hoya momentarily forgot his embarrassment and yanked Sarah to her feet beside him. *This is a woman from Tu'waqachi. She is strong and will bear many strong warriors for the Bow Clan. She and others like her can replace the women freed by Pahana, Ma'saw, and the Sun Clan.*

We will take her.

Kel'hoya held up his hand. *No. I wish to present her to the dark kachinas when I ask their forgiveness.* He started walking down the slope dragging Sarah behind him. She tried to pull away from him, but he was too strong. *Let us hurry back to Kuskurza. I miss my world. I have much to tell the dark kachinas about Tu'waqachi.*

Two Bow Clansmen raised their langhers. *You will not be returning to Kuskurza. You do not look like an Outlander, but we have been told you are not of the Third World.*

Do I look like an Outlander? I am of the Bow Clan, and I must report to the dark kachinas.

The two Bow Clansmen fired their weapons at the same time. The electric bolts hit Kel'hoya in his chest and stomach. He screamed out loud and in his mind at the same time. His arms flew out to his sides, and he tumbled down the rock slope, dead before he reached the feet of his brothers. The Bow Clansmen standing below clenched their eyes shut as if it would keep out Kel'hoya's screams.

Sarah took advantage of their momentary distraction and scrambled back up the hill. At the top of the hill, she could see the lights of the Bow Clan as they raced to catch her. She rolled over the top of the pile and into the darkness beyond. She moved slower in the dark, but she didn't mind because as long as it was dark, the Bow Clan weren't near.

She felt her way along the wall trying to find a dark crevice she could hide inside. A bright light spotlighted her, and she tried to sprint out of the light like a scared rabbit. She wasn't fast enough. No matter which direction she moved in, the light seemed to be there, and the edge was always out of her grasp.

Then she heard the Bow Clansmen walking towards her.

As soon as David set foot on the cave floor, he was afraid. It had been one thing to remember what had happened to him from the safety of the kiva. It was quite another to remember it while he was in the caverns. The memories of his five missing weeks rushed at him with such force he was staggered. He saw the Bow Clan firing their langhers at him. They seemed like unstoppable mechanical soldiers. He remembered his blind run through the caverns as he tried to find a way out. He felt his fear of not knowing if anyone was behind him or not. He had forgotten all of it, and now that he remembered it, he wished he hadn't.

"Are you all right?" Gary asked him as they moved toward the edge of the chamber.

David nodded. "Just having some bad memories."

"Yeah, I know what you mean. I think I'll have nightmares for a long time after all of this is over."

Sarah saw the pool of water and kicked at the Bow Clansman holding her. She knew they planned on going under the water. She wasn't sure how long she could hold her breath. She hoped it would be long enough.

The first two Bow Clansmen dove into the water. Sarah could see the light from their crude flashlights as they moved around below the dark water.

When their lights disappeared under a rock, the Bow Clansman holding Sarah dragged her into the water. Her mind tried to tell her it must not be far to the surface if the Bow Clan could hold their breaths and go through.

The Bow Clansman pulled her deeper into the water. Sarah kicked one of them in the shin, but he didn't yell as she expected him to do. He slapped her on the side of the face and pushed her into the sump. Sarah tried to keep her head above the water, but she knew it was a useless battle. Just before her head went under, she took the deepest breath she could.

Once under water, she kept her eyes closed. She doubted she would have been able to see anything in the dark water anyway. She simply let the Bow Clansman guide her through the water. She didn't struggle because she didn't want to use up the little air her lungs were holding.

Her chest wanted to burst as her oxygen was gradually used up. She had once heard that the human body would not allow a person to breathe in water. Drowning victims actually died from suffocation, and then the water entered their lungs. Sarah felt that she was only moments away from finding out if that was the truth or not.

Her head pounded as her blood rushed through her skull. She wondered if suffocation hurt.

Then her head broke the surface, and she gulped hungrily at the air as she scrambled onto the dry bank.

Sarah sat with her back against the wall of the tunnel. At least she knew there was one direction she did not have to worry about the Bow Clan coming from.

The four Bow Clansmen formed a semicircle around her. They stood in various postures staring at her. They looked at each other with odd expressions and laughed, but their stares always returned to her.

Sarah wanted to cry. This was worse than it had ever been living in the white man's world. She could feel the tears forming behind her eyes, but she thought that crying would only encourage the Bow Clan. She focused her willpower on herself and ordered herself not to cry. It worked, but she knew her hold on her emotions was fragile and would break at the slightest touch.

One of the Bow Clansmen stepped forward and reached out to touch Sarah's black hair. On pure instinct, Sarah slapped his hand away.

The corner of the Bow Clansman's lip twisted up in an almost animal-like sneer. He grabbed Sarah by the hair and yanked her to her feet. Sarah screamed, but instead of crying like she thought she would do, she felt anger.

The Bow Clansman squeezed her breast through her wet blouse and smiled. Then he ripped open the shirt exposing her dark skin. He paused for a moment to stare at her skin.

Sarah knew she was only seconds away from being raped. She might be able to discourage one man, but if all of them wanted to take part, she wouldn't be able to stop them. But she could stop some of them. She wouldn't make it easy for them, especially since she expected they would kill her anyway.

The Bow Clansman's hand dropped from her breast, and his finger started down her stomach. Sarah jerked her knee up hard hoping all of the Bow Clan's anatomy was like a typical male's.

The Bow Clansman screamed and doubled over. He grabbed his crotch and rolled around on the sandy floor of the cave. He kept his eyes shut, but he couldn't keep the tears from streaming from the corners.

The other Bow Clansmen laughed and pointed at the one on the floor. Sarah pulled her blouse together and waited for the other Bow Clansmen to attack her.

But they didn't attack. They just continued watching their comrade rolling on the floor in pain. When he finally managed to stand up, he quickly wiped the tears from his eyes. Turning to Sarah, he glared at her.

Sarah watched him raise his hand, and it was almost like she was looking at something in slow motion. She saw the fist coming toward her, and she was powerless to move out of its path. The Bow Clansmen hit her on the side of the face knocking her head back against the hard stone wall.

Sarah tried to fight back the encroaching grayness that threatened to overcome her. She knew it wasn't the cave's darkness. She was on the verge of losing consciousness. Her legs went weak, and she slid helplessly to the ground.

The Bow Clansman pulled the odd metal rod from his waistband and pointed it at her. Though Sarah didn't know what it was, she had seen the same weapons kill the Bow Clansman who had forced her into the caves.

The three Bow Clansmen who were watching stopped laughing. If Sarah had been able to direct her gaze beyond the end of the metal tube pointed at her face, she would have seen the worried looks on the faces of the other Bow Clansmen.

They grabbed their companion and raised the arm that held the weapon so that it pointed away from Sarah. He struggled slightly as they pulled him away from her.

When they released him, he turned and started walking down the tunnel.

Another Bow Clansman turned to follow him. A third Bow Clansman grabbed Sarah under her right arm and hoisted her to her feet. Then he pushed her through the tunnel in front of him.

Sarah wanted to run, but she knew that if she did, she would not avoid being killed a second time. She would have to wait and see what they had planned for her.

CHAPTER 53

Gary's flashlight revealed the fifty-foot pool of black water that marked the beginning of the sump. He shuddered when he saw Billy Joe's and Jared's bodies lying sprawled on the ground. Gary looked away and tried to concentrate on the sump.

David unshouldered his pack and walked up to the edge of the water. Gary stayed back. He couldn't help but remember the Bow Clansmen rising out of the water and the destruction they had brought with them, especially when much of that destruction lay nearby.

"How far is it to the other side?" David asked.

"About 200 feet. I laid out a guide line when I made my first dive a couple of days ago, but your Bow Clansmen must have cut it from the other side when they went under," Gary said as he held up the frayed end of the guide line he had pulled from the water.

"Will that stop us from getting to the other side?"

Gary shook his head. "It won't stop us, but it will slow us down a little bit."

"Once we go through here, we might not be able to get back," David commented.

"What do you mean? We don't even need the tanks. It's short enough that we can hold our breath and make it through."

"The Sun Clan told me that the dark kachinas can close and open the passages to keep the Sun Clan from reaching the surface."

Gary shook his head. "You're talking about major geologic events. How powerful are these kachinas?"

"More powerful than you or I, but they are not all powerful. They have their weak points," David said.

"If they don't want the Sun Clan to reach the surface, why even keep an open passage?"

"The Bow Clan still needs to breathe air and the only way to do that is to have two open passages to allow air to flow through their world." David pointed to the sump. "Anyway, if we swim through the sump, they may close the passage behind us, and we would be stuck just like the Sun Clan. So if you don't want to go, you don't have to. I can make it myself from here."

Gary was tempted to stay behind because he had no desire to meet something that could open and close cave passages. Thinking about the Bow Clan was bad enough, but this was almost too much for him to handle. Yet, the only way he could help Christine was to accompany David to the end of the caves and hope he would come back out.

"I'll understand if you don't want to go on," David said. "I was hoping we would find Sarah before we reached this point. They were only an hour or so ahead of us. They must have run the whole way or flown on those flying disks that they have."

"Well, obviously, they did beat us here," Gary said waving the cable.

"We're going to have to go into the water after them," David noted.

Gary shook his head. "It's not that easy, David. Cave diving is dangerous. Very dangerous. The diving caves in Florida kill about eighteen people a year. It's not something that amateur cavers should do."

"I'm not an amateur. I've been diving in Lake Powell," David said.

"But..." Gary started to explain.

David grabbed Gary by the shoulder. "Don't argue. I'm not holding you responsible for my safety. Just tell me how to get through to the other side, and you can go back and warn the sheriff. Every minute I waste gives them another minute longer to get to Kuskurza, and I have no desire to see that place again. I want this over before then."

"If you get hurt...," Gary started to say.

"Then I get hurt. I'm going through one way or the other. Either you can tell me how or I can find out for myself."

David let go of Gary and stripped to the waist. The cool cave air instantly raised the goosebumps on his skin. He checked the submersible pressure gauge on a set of twin eighty-cubic-foot tanks. There was still enough air for a short dive and the return trip. He strapped the tanks onto his back.

Gary sighed and checked the gauges on another set of tanks.

"I told you you don't have to go," David said.

"I know. Shut up before I change my mind. You're not the only one going after someone he cares about. Besides, while you may know about Kuskurza, you don't know about caves," Gary told David.

"Well then, don't preach to me. Let's go. I've got to find Sarah," David said as he inserted his mouthpiece.

David pulled his mask down over his face. He looked at the underwater caving helmets sitting on the ground. He picked up one with a pair of waterproof flashlights mounted to it.

With a disgusted grunt, Gary took off his shirt and put on a buoyancy compensator jacket. Then he hefted his own pair of tanks onto his back.

David looked at Gary and smiled.

"Don't be so smug about it," Gary said. "I still don't think you should go, but I also think we need to stay together."

When they had suited up, Gary said, "Okay. Here's what we need to do. This is going to be a short dive, nothing fancy. Keep one hand on me at all times. I'll lead. If you have any problems, communicate by grip. Pressing forward means go. Squeezing means stop. Pulling means come back. Try and stay as far away from the bottom as you can. There's plenty of silt down there, and we don't want to stir it up. The passage is narrow, and I don't want our visibility obstructed. It's going to be a tight enough fit even when we can see the widest spot to fit through. Got it?" David nodded. "Okay. Let's get this over with."

Gary inserted his mouthpiece and turned on the regulator. When he stepped into the freezing water, he shivered. He had forgotten how cold the water was. If it hadn't been for the mouthpiece, his teeth would have chattered against each other. He'd wished they'd had time to put on their wetsuits. This had better be a short dive. If they stayed underwater too long, they might die from hypothermia. Everything was happening too fast. They needed to slow down and plan. For once in his life, he wasn't too anxious to see what was at the end of a cave.

David followed Gary into the water. Gary turned on his flashlight and stepped off the ledge he was standing on. David hopped off the ledge and sunk into the water.

The lights lit up the sump about ten feet in front of them. Although they were barely kicking their flippers, the water was dirty with silt. It was a sign that someone who hadn't been careful had gone through the sump recently and Gary thought he knew who it was.

Was Gary really going to see an underground city? Although his mind rebelled at the idea, it also excited him. When he was fifteen, he had read *Journey to the Center of the Earth* in his English class. He had been fascinated with the thought that Atlantis had been sucked up by the earth and was still basically intact underground. That book, more than anything else, had gotten him interested in caving, and he had never gotten over his fascination with the story or caves. Finding a city like Atlantis underground would be like playing a character in the book.

Gary dove deeper trying to go under the roof of the cave. The passage narrowed and he turned sideways so that he could get through the choke. As he slid between the narrow rocks, he saw something wedged in the crevice. He slowed his movement and grabbed the object as he passed by.

It was a glove. A small glove. He turned up the inside tag and saw "C.S." written in permanent marker.

It was Christine's glove.

Those...people had her. What would they do to her and Sarah? David seemed to think they would be used as breeding stock like a prized steer.

Suddenly the idea of blowing up part of the cave didn't seem like such a bad idea after all.

CHAPTER 54

Gary hated the water. Not water in general, just this water that filled the passageway through the cavern. If by some stroke of luck they did manage to find Sarah and Christine, they were still going to have to get out of the caverns without getting themselves killed. That would be very hard to do if they all had to put on their scuba gear again while they were being pursued. It would take too much time.

David let go of Gary's calf and shot to surface ahead of him. Gary could see his body treading water. Gary allowed himself to slowly float to the surface. The entire dive had taken about four minutes because Gary had laid out another guide rope to help them get back through quicker.

As his head broke the surface, the two flashlights on his helmet illuminated the shore. Half a dozen pale men stood there. They looked just like the men Gary had seen kill Jared, except that they were wearing yellow tunics with black trim, not black with red trim.

Gary grabbed for the pistol he had tucked in the waistband of his pants. He had sealed the gun in a waterproof bag before diving into the sump. He brought the pistol to the surface and pointed it at the men on the shore. It would be useless to try to take it out of the bag. He didn't know how much time he had before the men on the shore attacked them.

If the men knew the pistol was a weapon, they certainly didn't seem afraid of it. They didn't even move at the sight of the gun. It would be like shooting targets in a fun house.

As his finger tightened on the trigger, David's hand slapped the pistol below the surface of the water.

"They're good guys," David said in answer to Gary's unasked question.

Gary and David slowly climbed out of the water and stood in the center of a ring of half a dozen Sun Clansmen. David moved slowly because he wasn't sure if the Sun Clansmen trusted him, and he didn't want to startle them into action. As the Sun Clansmen stared at them, David motioned for Gary to take off his scuba equipment.

David stared back at the Sun Clansmen waiting for something more to happen, but nothing did. He wondered if they even recognized him.

David's skin dimpled, and he shivered in the cool air of the caverns. He reached into his waterproof bag and pulled out a towel to dry off with. When he had finished, he was still cold but at least his teeth weren't chattering. Somehow it just didn't seem right to let his teeth chatter in front of the Sun Clan.

Gary still looked overwhelmed by everything that was happening. His face was pale, and his brow kept wrinkling as if he was mulling over some critical question. He had unbagged his pistol even before he had taken off his tanks. The pistol was shoved into his waistband, and Gary kept his hand near the butt.

"Why don't they say anything?" Gary whispered in David's ear.

"You wouldn't understand them if they did. They speak an ancient form of the Hopi Indian language. Let me concentrate for a minute and see if I can communicate with them like I did before," David told him.

In truth, David wasn't sure if concentration was the key to communication with the Sun Clan. It had happened so naturally before. Masani had touched the center of his forehead, and David had suddenly heard Masani's voice in his head.

David held out his forefinger and walked toward the nearest Sun Clansman. He didn't know which one was the leader of the group, but he assumed he should be able to communicate with any of them. The Sun Clansman backed away from David's touch. David smiled and tried to touch the man's forehead again. This time he succeeded.

As he made contact, he thought, *I am a friend of Ma'saw.*

You are Outlanders. How do you know Ma'saw?

David took a step back. If things went as they had before, he would be able to maintain communications without direct contact with the person.

Masani helped me. He helped me escape the Bow Clan when I was lost in the caverns. He took me to Polanque, and Polanque took me to Ma'saw. I helped organize the raid into the temple to reclaim the women from the Bow Clan.

Masani is dead.

I know. I am sorry, but I killed the Bow Clansman who murdered him.

It is a risk the Sun Clan takes.

It might be, but that didn't stop the man from hurting, David noted as he saw the pained expression flash across the man's face. He wondered if the Sun Clansman and Masani had been friends.

"Are you talking to them?" Gary asked. David nodded. "Ask them if they can help us find the women."

The Bow Clan has taken two women from us. We have come to find them. The first is called Christine. She has blond hair, green eyes, flat-chested, and round hips.

Christine is dead, a different voice said inside David's head. *I saw her body displayed on the central temple before I left with the Sun Clan. The dark kachinas killed her.*

"What's wrong?" Gary asked when he saw the look of disappointment on David's face. "Haven't they seen her?"

David wondered if he should tell Gary the truth. "They've seen her. She's dead, Gary," David said to him.

Gary's shoulders sagged, and he put his hands over his face.

The dark kachinas displayed the woman's body to tell the Sun Clan that the Outlanders are no match for the dark kachinas. Is that true? one of the Sun Clan asked.

David turned to Gary. "They want to know if we can defeat the Bow Clan and the dark kachinas."

Gary nodded. "Tell them we can kill them if we have to. They're only human."

David relayed the message, and all the Bow Clansmen smiled. Then David described Sarah and asked if they had seen her.

The Sun Clansmen shook their heads.

One of them said, *If the Bow Clan has her, they will take her to the central temple.*

Can you take us there? David wanted to know.

Two of the Sun Clansmen shrank away from the circle.

It is the central temple. We cannot take you there. It is too dangerous, someone thought.

Your people attacked it and stole back the women a short time ago.

That was a smaller temple. Sarah will be where the dark kachinas dwell, and once there, she will die.

Can you show us how to get to the surface? someone asked. *We have come a long way to find a path to a new sipapu where our people can exit. You are Pahana. It is said you will deliver us from Kuskurza.*

We cannot return to Tu'waqachi until we find Sarah, David told him.

I have told you we cannot take you. It is too dangerous.

David wished he knew which voice belonged to which Sun Clansman. He wanted to stare into the eyes of the ones who were afraid and see if they were actually afraid of the central temple or if they just wanted to continue their explorations before the Bow Clan found them.

Take us to Ma'saw, David told the Sun Clansmen.

CHAPTER 55

The Bow Clansmen dragged Sarah through the poorly lit hallway. She saw no entrances or exits anywhere along it, only the massive doors she had been dragged through and the equally tall doors she was headed toward. The ceiling was nearly twenty feet above her head. It reminded her of a massive chamber in the caves.

The Bow Clansmen stopped in front of the ten-foot high doors and pushed one open slightly. Then with a rough push, they shoved Sarah inside.

The door had closed behind Sarah before she was even able to stop herself from moving forward. She turned quickly and ran back to the door. She felt along the wall for a doorknob. Even if she found it, she guessed the door would be locked, but she had to try nonetheless. There wasn't a doorknob that she could find. She couldn't even feel the seams that marked the edge of the door.

Sarah turned around and leaned back against the door. The room she was in was pitch black like a cave when there were no lights. How big was the room, she wondered. And why had she been thrown in here? Was it some sort of punishment? Solitary confinement?

She started to feel her way along the wall wanting to know how big the room was and if there was another entrance. She had only walked a few feet when she stopped.

She wasn't alone in the room. Something told her that someone else nearby. She was tempted to call out, but anyone she met would certainly be an enemy, so she remained silent.

Then she felt the weight around her ankles. She looked down and didn't see anything. Or at least she didn't think she saw anything, but something was there. She could feel it. It moved in the darkness. It was like the darkness itself was moving.

The shadows! It was like the shadows in the cave when she first went inside them with David. The shadows had taken on a solidity. All she had to do was turn on a light and the shadows would disappear, but here there was no light to turn on here.

What would happen when there was nothing to stop the shadows? She tried to move away, but her legs seemed glued to the floor, and all she could do was stand and feel the darkness slowly work its way up her legs.

Then she remembered her matches. She always kept a book of matches in her pocket to light the lanterns in the pueblo. Sarah patted her hip pockets of her jeans and felt the reassuring bulge. She wondered if they would still be wet from being pulled under the sump. That had been at least a day ago. It was hard to judge time when she had needed to keep her balance on the flying disk the Bow Clansmen used. Her clothes had dried out already. She just hoped the matches had, too.

The darkness had climbed to the middle of her thighs. She felt something sharp like a needle prick her calf, but she managed to contain her startled yelp.

She pulled the matchbook out of her pocket. At least they felt dry. She struck the first match, and it flared then fizzled out. Sarah was disappointed, but she had felt the darkness back off for the moment the flame had burned.

The darkness was at her waist now. She felt two more needle pricks on her buttocks. She suppressed a yell both times, but when she felt something bite her thigh, she screamed.

She struck another match, and this one stayed lit. It cast a dim light that reached no more than a foot into the darkness before it faded.

The darkness stopped moving, and something yelled. It was hard to tell where the yell came from. It seemed to echo from everywhere at once.

Now at least she had something to defend herself with no matter how small it might be.

CHAPTER 56

The dark kachina screamed in pain. Light! Light! How could the light enter his chamber consecrated to the darkness?

It was the woman! She had brought the sun inside with her to kill him. He retreated into the darkest corner of his chamber and waited for his death to come. Soon the room would brighten as the twins returned with Taiowa's light. It would be just as it had been before.

The twin sons of Taiowa would enter Kuskurza and drive all the darkness from the Third World. Pahana would free the Sun Clan. The power of the dark kachinas would wither, and they would be driven into the darkest recesses of the central temple. Only this time, there would be no place to hide. If the twins entered the chambers of the dark kachinas, the dark kachinas would surely die. There would be no place to hide from the light. He and the others would be imprisoned for another millennium or worse yet, they might die.

Then the dark kachina noticed the light, although it brought much pain when it touched him, it was weak and small. It was brighter than the light in Kuskurza, but it was small, very small. It cast out the darkness for only a small area, not even enough to expose the woman's entire arm.

The woman had magic, but only a feeble magic. It was not a magic powerful enough to kill him if he was careful.

The woman spun the light around trying to illuminate all sides of her at once, but it was impossible. She knew her magic was weak and she could not fully compensate for the weakness.

He moved in closer, but he was careful to stay out of the range of the light in case the woman might turn quickly and catch him in the glow of the light. As she turned away from him, he moved in quickly and bit her shoulder. She screamed and dropped the light. It went out, and the dark kachina allowed himself a sigh.

He turned his attention entirely on the woman. She had run away from him, but there was no way she could escape him. There was only one entrance to his chamber, and it could only be opened from the outside. The woman was his to consume.

He surrounded her and pressed in on all sides of her body. He did not want to give her a chance to create another light. He could feel her heartbeat quicken as her fear increased. He could feel her chest heaving as she struggled with each breath. He released her, and she leaned against the wall taking deep breaths.

232

He watched her for a minute as her eyes darted blindly around the room never seeing him even though he stood directly in front of her. She started to try and create another light. He reached over and bit her right hand. She screamed and ran along the edge of the wall. The dark kachina laughed and let her run. She would tire herself, and she would be no further away from him.

He would toy with her awhile longer and then he would kill her. He bit her thigh this time, and she began to cry. She pulled away from him, but she did not run. She realized it was futile to try and escape from him.

He watched her feel around on the floor for her light maker, but it was far from her reach. He was untroubled by her search.

He felt something. A warning, but it was dim, too dim. The Sun Clan were in the caverns again. How long had they been in the caverns without the dark kachinas sensing them? They were returning from an exploration. He could tell that from the way they moved.

The dark kachinas should have known before now. Where there was no light, the power of the dark kachinas was supreme. How could the Sun Clan have ventured so far within the strongest domain of their power?

The dark kachina stopped and sent a message to the other dark kachinas. *The Sun Clan is in the caverns. Where have they been?*

To the barrier, came a reply.

There are two more returning than there were going, another told the Lord.

Is it the twins? he thought with more than a hint of fear.

We cannot tell, but they seem the same as the Sun Clan.

Kill them all.

Yes, kill them.

It was agreed. The call went out to the Bow Clan. Those in the caverns would die.

CHAPTER 57

The light in the large room was dim but bright enough to see without having to turn on a flashlight. The Sun Clansmen led David and Gary into it. The man sitting on a stone chair at the front of the room signaled for the Sun Clansmen to leave.

"Who's this?" Gary asked David.

"His name is Ma´saw. He's the leader of the Sun Clan," David replied.

Ma´saw was as white as the other people of Kuskurza. He wore a loose tunic over his thin body made of the familiar silky yellow-and-black material of the Sun Clan. His head rested on his interlaced fingers.

Ma´saw said something that David did not understand.

David closed his eyes and tried to project his thoughts. *Can you understand me?* he asked.

I understand, a deep voice replied in his head. *Our lost white brother has returned once again. It is good that you have not forgotten us, Pahana. Have you come to lead the Sun Clan to Tu´waqachi? We have been awaiting your return.*

We know the way, yes.

Ma´saw raised his head expectantly. *Will you lead us there?*

Yes. Ma´saw smiled. *But first, my companion and I must find a woman who was taken from Tu´waqachi by the Bow Clan.*

Ma´saw's smile fell. *If the Bow Clan has taken her, she is lost. Forget about her. She is dead.*

I did not forget about the women of Kuskurza when I was here before. How can you ask me to forget about this woman I have grown to love? If she is dead, as you say, then I must see the body. Somehow David knew that Sarah wasn't dead, at least not yet. Maybe he could sense her life with his psychic ability, or maybe he was just hoping he wasn't too late this time. He had failed Terrie. He had failed Adam. He wouldn't fail Sarah.

Perhaps the dark kachinas will display her body. Perhaps they will not. It does not matter. Will you lead the Sun Clan to Tu´waqachi? It is your destiny.

As I promised, I will lead them, but I am not finished here yet, David told the Sun Clan leader.

Ma´saw stood up. *The Fourth World is our destiny. We have lived up to the teachings of Taiowa. Now it is time for us to venture out to Tu´waqachi and take our place once again beside our brothers.*

David crossed his arms over his chest. *What makes you think the Sun Clan deserves to venture onto the surface?*

It is our destiny...

David cut him off. *No. Show me that your people are worthy to live on the surface. Show me that you are truly no longer of the Bow Clan. Would Taiowa have you abandon the woman of the one you ask to lead you to your destiny?* David advanced on Ma´saw and stood in front of him. He wanted to grab Ma´saw's tunic and shake him, but he restrained himself. Ma´saw might think David was attacking him and call for help. *Help us find the entrance to the central temple and the woman. Then we shall lead your people to the Fourth World.*

Ma´saw studied David for a minute in silence. *If we lead you to the central temple, you will be killed, and we will have no one to lead us to the surface. The central temple is an evil place. Even the Bow Clansmen are afraid to enter it. They only do so if they have to.*

We can't return to the Fourth World until we know the fate of the woman.

Ma´saw considered this. *If you wish to die, so be it. I will lend you one quati. No more. I will not send good warriors to die on a fool's mission.*

That will be enough, David answered without knowing how many men would be needed, but he was in no position to ask for more.

The group of twelve men stopped at the edge of the massive stone structure. Gary slipped his bulging knapsack from under his tunic and set it on the ground in front of him.

David wondered if Sarah was really somewhere within this pyramid. And if she was, was she alive or had she been killed like Christine? A lot could have happened in the week it had taken them to reach Kuskurza. It depended on how much faster the Bow Clan had reached Kuskurza with her. David felt Sarah was alive, but was it only because he wanted her to be? According to his watch, it had been seven days since he and Gary had entered the caverns to try and rescue Sarah. If she and the Bow Clan had been traveling at the same rate as he and Gary, Sarah should have arrived only a few hours before David and Gary. Certainly no more than a day earlier. Sarah had to be alive. She had to be. He couldn't be late this time.

The nearest entrance is around this corner about thirty sans along the wall. There will be guards, a voice said in David's head. He still wasn't sure who was addressing him since all of the ten Sun Clansmen were staring at him.

David turned to Gary. "The entrance is around the corner. He says there are guards."

Gary slid on his stomach the few feet to the corner of the structure. He kept low as he looked around the corner. He could see two guards standing about forty feet away from the corner. They stood straight and unmoving like statues.

He looked back to David and whispered, "There's no cover anywhere near them. No way we can sneak up on them. They'll see us coming as soon as we step around the corner."

David glanced at the langher one of the Sun Clansmen was holding. *Can I use that?* he asked.

The Sun Clansmen glanced at the langher, then David. *Yes, but you cannot shoot the Bow Clansmen with it.*

Why not?

To get within the range where the bolt from the langher would kill would place you in the open. The Bow Clansmen could just as easily kill you if you are too slow.

David sighed and stared at the pistol in his waistband. Gary had given it to him when they left the hidden pueblo. He pulled it out.

"That's going to make a lot of noise," Gary said.

"So? They won't know what it is. Besides, we're going to have to make a lot louder noise sooner or later."

Gary shrugged and pulled his pistol out. "I'll take the one further away. You take the one closer."

David nodded and squatted down next to Gary at the corner.

"Aim for their heads. We can't give them a chance to send out a telepathic warning to the others," David said.

"That makes for a lot smaller target, and I'm no marksman," Gary replied.

"Yes, but it also makes for a lot fewer targets later on."

David braced his arm against the stone wall and took aim through the metal sights. The Sun Clansmen clustered around them to watch what would happen.

"On three," Gary whispered. "One."

David took a deep breath and held it.

"Two."

He sighted the nearer Bow Clansmen through the pistol sights again.

"Three."

David squeezed the trigger.

Two of the Sun Clansmen yelped at the sound of the two mini-explosions. The Bow Clansman nearest David grabbed his head and fell. The second Bow Clansman turned to face them.

The Bow Clansman fired his langher. The yellow bolt of electricity fell to the ground about six feet in front of David. He jumped back, pointed the pistol at the Bow Clansman and fired again. A red spot blossomed on the Bow Clansman's head, and he fell in a heap on the ground.

The quati of Sun Clansmen smiled at the sight of the dead Bow Clansmen. One of them reached out and touched the barrel of Gary's pistol, but quickly pulled his hand back when he felt the hot metal.

Others will come, one of the Sun Clansmen told David. *The one who fired the langher had time to warn the others. We must work quickly.*

When David told Gary this, Gary snatched up his knapsack and started running along the edge of the wall. He stopped between the two dead Bow Clansmen. He felt along the wall for the seam of the doorway.

David tried not to look at the dead Bow Clansmen. He had never killed a man before. Then he remembered the speared Bow Clansman from his first time lost in the caves.

Gary found the seam and he pulled a large ball of what looked to David to be orange Play-Doh modeling clay out of his knapsack. David realized it was plastic explosives. Gary took the ball out of the plastic bag and kneaded it in his hands. After he broke off a piece the size of a golf ball and jammed it into the seam of the pyramid, Gary put the rest of the explosive ball back in the bag and took out two black boxes. He stuck the smaller of the two boxes into the orange ball and ran a pair of wires from the small black box back to the corner of the pyramid.

"Better tell them to get out of the way. There's going to be a lot of stone flying through the air in few moments," Gary said to David.

David relayed the message to the Sun Clansmen as Gary hooked the wires to the larger black box he was still holding. The Sun Clansmen quickly ran from the side of the pyramid to the corner where David and Gary were squatting.

When the last of the Sun Clansmen ran around the corner, Gary flipped the switch on the box.

David heard the sound of the explosion first. A loud "poof," quickly followed by a thundering "boom." The pyramid shook so fiercely, he thought the whole thing would collapse in on itself.

The pyramid exploded. Just like in his dreams. Then he remembered what had followed the temple exploding. The dark kachinas.

Gary turned to him, and said, "Let's go."

Sarah could tell she was alone. The air felt light, not as thick as it had when she had been attacked, and the darkness didn't seem to be quite as dark. It had been a long time since she had felt another presence near her. She wasn't sure how long, though, time moved at a different pace in total darkness. Whatever had been attacking her seemed to have tired and left her alone.

The floor shook slightly or at least she thought it did.

She touched her shoulder where the thing had bitten her. It didn't feel moist, so she doubted she was bleeding.

Sarah felt around until she felt the cold surface of the stone wall. Then she began her search for an exit.

In the distance, she heard a shuffling noise moving closer to her. Was the thing in the dark coming after her again?

The rumbling in the floor grew louder and more violent. Sarah steadied herself against the wall and wondered if this was what an earthquake felt like underground. The floor pitched to one side. She staggered, but she managed to keep herself from falling.

Off to her left, a thin line of dim light appeared in the darkness. She didn't know what it was, but she knew it was light. She ran for it.

When she reached the crack of light, it had grown larger. She realized it was the crack around the door she had been thrown through by the Bow Clansmen. The quake had broken the door's tight seam.

Sarah leaned on the door wondering if it was open or if the quake had jammed it so it could never be opened. The thought scared her. How long could she live in the darkness with that thing that had bitten her?

Where was it anyway? Was it staying away from the light? She hoped so.

Sarah looked around wondering if the thing was watching her from the darkness. It was scared of the light apparently. Even her matches had hurt it, and this light was much larger, though not any brighter. She would be safe here.

The door moved slightly, and Sarah threw her whole one-hundred-and-ten pounds against it. She felt a brief pain in her shoulder, but then the door flung open sprawling her into the hallway.

She was in the light again! She was safe from the thing in the room. It wouldn't venture into the lighted hallway.

Sarah looked down the hall in the direction the Bow Clansmen had brought her. She glanced over her shoulder into the dark room wondering if whatever was in there would come after her. She climbed to her feet and started running.

CHAPTER 58

Gary didn't like the silence that the explosion left behind in the large chamber. It reminded him too much of the silence in the caves, and even though this place was part of the caves, it was nothing like the caves. He kept a tight grip on the pistol. It was a standard police revolver that he had brought on the trip as protection against night-time prowlers around the camp site. The prowlers hadn't come from around the campsite, though. They had come from beneath it.

He had expected to run into an army of Bow Clansmen once he walked into the central temple, but there was no one. Furthermore, there were no sounds of anyone in the central temple approaching them. It was like the place was deserted. David had told him that the Bow Clan was afraid of this place, but he expected to find more than just two guards protecting it.

The Sun Clansmen hesitated near the entrance afraid to enter the hallway.

Gary turned to David and said, "Tell them to get in here. We need to know where to go. Those Bow Clansmen aren't going to wait for long."

David nodded and turned to the Sun Clansmen. Gary waited anxiously to receive an answer. David grimaced as he apparently carried on a silent argument with the Sun Clansmen. Finally, the pale men began to move through the rubble ahead of Gary.

David followed closely behind them. He walked so fast that he had to keep stopping to wait for everyone else to catch up. The Sun Clansmen seemed all too willing to allow David to take the lead.

Gary turned a corner in the pyramid and heard a humming noise. David speeded up his pace to a slow jog. Gary wondered what the Sun Clansmen were telling David. Gary purposefully slowed as he tried to place the sound. He was sure he had heard it before.

It sounded like electricity running through overhead wires.

"David, stop!" Gary yelled.

David glanced over his shoulder. Then it was as if he ran into an invisible wall. His body flattened against the unseen surface. He jerked wildly and then he fell to the ground.

CHAPTER 59

David felt pain. Every nerve in his body cried out at once as he fell. He supposed hitting the stone floor hurt him, but it was so minor compared to the other pains he felt that he was barely aware he had fallen.

A familiar voice whispered to him somewhere in the back of his mind, but it was drowned out by the pain.

His heart raced until it felt like it would explode from his chest. Then it began to slow, too slow. He thought he could feel all the blood in his body stopping.

Was there a poultice the Sun Clan could push into his mouth this time that would heal him and stop the pain? He doubted it.

"David."

David sighed at the sound of his name. Sarah spoke to him in her melodic voice. He hoped she was all right wherever she was. He didn't want to think of what would happen to her if he and Gary couldn't free her.

"David."

His mind floated free from his body in much the same way he felt right before he had his visions of the Bow Clan. David followed the passages of the central temple to a spiraling passageway that descended into the ground. He followed the tunnel deeper into the ground. He didn't know how the tunnel could go any deeper. They had entered the central temple on the bottom floor. There must be more levels of passages beneath Kuskurza.

"David."

Sarah's voice beckoned him in the opposite direction, but he resisted. There was something down here he should see. He could feel it pulling at his mind.

The curving passage turned into a straight hallway at the bottom of its descent. David stopped and hovered above the floor. He could see the rows of flashlight-like torches illuminating the hall, but at the other end, there was only utter darkness. There were no torches within the darkness. No light to tell him what lay at the other end of the hallway.

Sarah ran down the hallway toward him. He didn't understand why she was running. Nothing was behind her. Then, as David watched, the furthest pair of torches blinked out. The darkness was moving toward the surface. It was like India ink, obscuring everything as it rolled over it.

"David!" she screamed.

David felt his body rise slightly and then he was rocking. His pain receded somewhat. He felt a hand brush back his hair and his heart raced. A splash of cold water hit him in the face. His eyes snapped open. He had a few moments of blurriness, and he panicked thinking the blindness he had been expecting since he was rescued from the cave had finally come. Then the images melted together, and David saw Gary standing over him.

"What happened?" David asked.

"You nearly died. You ran into some sort of electric wall and almost fried yourself."

David pushed himself into a sitting position. His arms shook, and he nearly fell back. "You tried to warn me, didn't you?" he asked Gary as he vaguely remembered Gary's shouted warning.

Gary nodded. "I recognized the sound, but too late."

"No, not too late. I slowed down enough, so I didn't run full force into the field. If I hadn't, we wouldn't be talking now." David paused. "The explosion freed the dark kachinas."

"If they're as bad as you say, we've got to get out of here now," Gary said.

David put his hand on Gary's arm. "You wait for me outside the temple. I'll be out in a minute."

"Why? You need someone to help you get out of this place. You can barely walk."

David pushed himself to his feet. He swayed a little, but he managed to stay standing.

"I know where Sarah is. I have to help her, the dark kachinas are after her," David said.

"What can you do? You can't help her run. She'd have to help you, and that would only slow her down when what she needs now is speed."

"If it was Christine in danger, would you try to help her?" David challenged Gary.

"Well, yes, but..."

David pushed Gary away and started up another hallway. This one wasn't booby-trapped with an electric field. He staggered more than ran, but he eventually began to recognize the passages from his vision.

"Sarah!" he yelled.

His voice echoed down the hall, and he waited to hear a reply. When it came, it sounded far away, but it was definitely Sarah. He ran on until he nearly ran into her.

"David," Sarah said grabbing him by the arm and continuing to run. "It's after me. We've got to get out of here."

David looked over Sarah's shoulder and saw the darkness approaching. He shuddered at the sight. It seemed like a giant tidal wave of black water slowly rolling toward him and Sarah. And it was much closer to Sarah than it had been in his vision. It was gaining on her. If they couldn't find some way to delay the dark kachinas or find a burst of speed within themselves, the dark kachinas would overtake them in another minute.

David pulled free from her. "Keep running! I've got an idea to slow them down."

Sarah ran off a few steps and then stopped to wait for David. He reached into his backpack and tossed the light sticks to Sarah. "Bend these until you hear a snap. Then shake them until they glow. Lay them out around the corridor." She started to say something, but he said, "Just do it!"

David pulled the two powerful flashlights from his pack and switched them on. He looked up and saw the darkness was only a few feet away from him. Taking a deep breath as if he were going to dive into a pool, David ran into the darkness waving the flashlights.

Behind him, he heard Sarah scream. Then he heard something else scream, and it wasn't Sarah. This was higher pitched and drawn out like fingers scratching a blackboard.

David spun around flashing the lights everywhere he could. The darkness seemed to try and retreat from around him, but he ran with it keeping himself in the center of the darkness. He swung the flashlights like swords, and he hoped they were cutting into the dark kachinas like a sword would.

He felt something bite him on the back, and he spun around. Something hit his hand and knocked one of the flashlights from his grip. It spun off into the darkness and disappeared.

David gripped the remaining flashlight with both hands and swung it around himself. How long had he been in the darkness? One minute? Two minutes? Was it long enough for Sarah to throw all the light sticks out? It had better be. He wasn't sure how much longer he could last.

Something hit him in the back of the knees. He fell forward, the remaining flashlight flying from his grip. He didn't wait to see if he could recover it. He rolled in the direction where he thought he had entered the darkness.

He rolled over some small objects on the ground, and then he could see the light, and he was out of the darkness. David felt a hand on his face and saw Sarah. He managed a smile and the look of concern on Sarah's face changed to a smile.

"Where'd you come from?" David asked.

"There was an earthquake, and it let some light in the dark kachinas' chambers. It nearly shook the whole place apart."

"That was no earthquake. Gary blew a hole in the temple," David told her. "Are you hurt?"

Sarah shrugged. "A little, but I'll get over it. What about you? Are you hurt?"

David pushed himself into a sitting position. His arms shook, and he nearly fell back. "I'll be fine."

He looked over his shoulder. The darkness had stopped at the edge of the light cast by the light sticks. It seemed to churn and surge, and with a scream, it passed the first light stick. The dark kachinas were determined to be free, and the light from the stick wasn't bright enough to hold them back.

"We've got to get out of here. That won't hold them for long."

Sarah nodded and helped him to his feet. Together, they ran toward the hole that Gary had blown in the outside wall.

When Gary saw them come out of the central temple, he smiled. "Now let's get out of here."

"There's a problem," David said.

"Another one?"

"The explosion didn't only open up the temple, it freed the dark kachinas. This was their prison. The light from Kuskurza will hold them off for a short time, but it may not be as long as we would hope. If they get free, they'll destroy the Sun Clan."

One of the Sun Clansmen screamed and pointed behind David. David turned and saw the ink-black darkness creeping toward him. The dark kachinas had managed to get past all of the light sticks.

Gary aimed his pistol at the darkness and squeezed off three shots that sounded like thunder in the temple. The blackness recoiled slightly. David guessed it was more from the muzzle flashes than the bullets. The darkness continued forward. The Sun Clansmen turned and ran. David pushed Sarah to follow them.

David turned to Gary. "It's the dark kachinas. We've got to get out of here. Bullets won't stop them, but we can outrun them. I have an idea that will hopefully buy us a little time. I'll need your help."

Gary hesitated an instant and then shoved his pistol into his waistband. He grabbed David around the waist. David slung his right arm around Gary's neck, and they stumbled as close to the pyramid as they could.

"Will they stay inside the temple?" Gary asked.

"I don't know," David told him.

As if in answer to his question, the darkness began to ooze through the opening in the side of the pyramid. It reminded David of an oil leak his Camaro had once had.

"Use the light!" Sarah yelled. "It hates bright light!"

"Give me a flashlight," David asked Gary.

Gary reached under his tunic and pulled out his flashlight. David took it, aimed it at the black blob, then turned it on.

A shrill yell sounded through the large chamber. David took a step forward, and the blob backed off. David kept walking forward. The blob would scream, then retreat, tucking itself back into the hole in the pyramid. When David had reached the edge of the pyramid, he set the flashlight down on the ground so that it shined into the pyramid. He couldn't tell if the circle of light cast by the flashlight was a natural circle of light or if the black blob was pressing the limits of the light.

David started to back away. He stopped and pulled a hand-held battery-powered lamp from the pack and switched it on. He set the lamp on a rock just outside the pyramid next to the flashlight. A little extra insurance. They should have at least seven more hours, no more than fifteen, to get started. After that, the batteries would die, and the dark kachinas in the pyramid would be free.

David tried to run back to Gary, Sarah, and the Sun Clansmen. His legs were still shaky, and it was not easy. When he reached Sarah, he gave her a quick hug and turned to Gary.

"Let's get back to the pueblo," David said. "We have to warn the others, and we need time to prepare."

"Prepare for what?" Gary wanted to know.

"The Bow Clan will come after us. Just because we trapped the dark kachinas doesn't mean they still can't control the Bow Clan. They've been doing it for centuries."

Hours later, when they finally reached the entrance to the hidden pueblo, David wanted nothing more than to sleep, but he knew there was no time. His skin still tingled from the electrical charge, and he wondered if the electric field had caused permanent nerve damage, not to mention the bruises and bites he received from the dark kachinas.

He looked over his shoulder and saw a small black patch slowly growing and swelling in the center of Kuskurza. It nearly covered the largest of the pyramids. The dark kachinas had escaped.

In front of the blackness, David could see hundreds of pale-white men racing toward the pueblo. The blackness they might be able to outrun, but not the Bow Clan. There would be a battle.

Ma´saw met them at the hidden wall that allowed access into the pueblo. He looked at Sarah and then over her shoulder.

He said something David didn't understand. Then he thought, Pahana, what have you done?

We must all leave now. All of the Bow Clan are massing against you, and the dark kachinas have joined them. You wanted to go to Tu´waqachi. The time is now.

Taiowa, we need you, Ma´saw thought.

CHAPTER 60

A silent, telepathic shout went through the hidden pueblo telling the Sun Clan to prepare for an attack by the Bow Clan. No one was sure how long they would have before the assault by the Bow Clan and the dark kachinas began, but they knew the attack would come. The arsenals were opened and the men, and even the women, were armed with langhers, jotas, takles, and bows.

David was happy to see that the Sun Clan was willing to fight for their freedom even in the face of incredible resistance. He could not imagine defeating spirits so powerful that it took Taiowa to beat them before.

Ma'saw divided the Sun Clan into four groups. He sent the first group outside the false wall to act as a diversion from the hidden pueblo. This would give the rest of the Sun Clan time to start their evacuation from the hidden pueblo into the caves. The diversion group was also tasked by Ma'saw to cause as much damage to the Bow Clan as possible before the warriors reached the pueblo. David warned them to stay as far away from the dark kachinas as possible because their weapons would be useless against them.

The second group took up their position just behind the false wall to provide assistance to the diversion group when they began their retreat back to the pueblo. The third group stood guard at the entrance to the hidden pueblo to destroy the ladder and seal the entrance once the last of the Sun Clan had retreated into the pueblo. The final group had the job of disarming any traps in the cave passages set by the Bow Clan so there would be no hindrances as the Sun Clan left the pueblo and headed for the surface.

Ma'saw assigned David and Sarah to the second group. Gary was assigned to the fourth group to help lay out the path that the Sun Clan would follow to the Fourth World.

There were nearly 200 Sun Clansmen in David and Sarah's group, enough to fill the passages of the maze and form a human barrier to face the Bow Clan. David had wanted Sarah to go with Gary because he thought it was safer for her, but she insisted on staying with him.

David watched the decoy group, led by Polanque, march under the false wall. Polanque nodded to him as he passed David in the maze.

May the power Taiowa strengthen us, Polanque thought.

God's speed, replied David.

Polanque's group would take the heaviest losses. They knew it as they left, but they did not show their fear of dying or their doubt that they would return. The wall slid to the ground as the last man passed under it, and David settled down to wait along with the rest of his group. Many of the people in his group were armed only with bows, arrows, and spears. The more lethal weapons in the arsenal had been given to everyone in the decoy team so they would at least be evenly matched with the Bow Clan. The remaining weapons were spread among the remaining groups. David was one of the fortunate who had been handed a langher. He also had his pistol, but the weapons wouldn't help much against the dark kachinas. The decoy group would light fires, but those would eventually burn out. The sparks from the langhers might delay the dark kachinas, but they appeared and disappeared as fast as the lightning bolts they resembled.

After he had waited for what seemed a long time, David began to grow anxious for the coming attack. The attack was imminent, and he just wanted to get it over with. Sarah sat next to him nervously plucking at the string on her bow. Some of the other Sun Clansmen were pacing in small circles within the tightly packed group while others simply laid down and slept. Some wanted to leave the maze and join Polanque's group. The majority, however, decided to obey Ma'saw's orders and wait for their time to fight.

When the wall finally slid up, it startled everyone. Bright flashes of light shot back and forth across the dark sky. A few stray flashes of lightning slipped under the wall and into the maze. One Sun Clansman screamed and fell to the ground clutching his shoulder where his arm had been attached only moments before.

A handful of Sun Clansmen scurried under the wall. The front line of the second group lay on their stomachs and fired under the wall at the advancing Bow Clan. The Bow Clansmen screamed as they died, but they continued to charge the wall as the dark kachinas directed them. David tuned out the noises and tried to concentrate on a single Bow Clansman at a time as he fired, instead of the group. He took careful aim with his langher and fired each bolt with the intent of killing a Bow Clansman.

Polanque stood outside the wall providing covering fire with a jota while the remaining Sun Clansmen in his group retreated under the wall. When he stood alone, Polanque fired three more shots of a thick, blue, liquid poison, then knelt down to slide under the wall. A bolt from a langher hit him in the neck, and he fell on his face. Someone near David grabbed Polanque by the arm and pulled him inside the wall.

Remembering how the lever mechanism in the rocks worked, David thrust his knife into the crack between the two rocks and reversed the process he had seen Scinaro perform almost two months ago.

The wall dropped quickly crushing three Bow Clansmen with it when it fell. There was a heavy silence in the maze after the screams of the crushed Bow Clansmen died off. No one spoke. A few women cried, but they did it softly so as not to disturb the silence.

The silence was broken by a pecking sound that sounded like someone chipping away at stone. David listened intently as the sound grew louder. It was coming from the false wall, and David was afraid he knew what it meant. The sound intensified until a tiny bit of rock flew from the wall leaving behind it a small hole. In the next instant, a bolt from a langher flew through the hole with a whine.

The Bow Clan was destroying the wall.

Keeping his head low, David ran to the hole and stuck the end of his langher through the hole and fired. He didn't even look where he was shooting. He only wanted to show the Bow Clan that the Sun Clan had not given up. After this shot, he chanced a look outside the wall to take aim. The Bow Clan had backed away from the wall. David fired again and was rewarded with a direct hit on one of the closer Bow Clansmen.

Another hole appeared in the wall, and someone else following David's lead manned the hole and began firing stone darts from a takle. Within a few minutes, there were a dozen holes in the wall all plugged with weapons firing back at the Bow Clan.

The Bow Clan's fire finally began to wane. David couldn't tell if it was because they were losing men or if the Bow Clan realized that for every hole they punched in the wall, they allowed another weapon to be fired at them.

By the time someone relieved David at the hole, the Bow Clan had begun their retreat. David started back through the maze to the hidden pueblo. It would be his job, and Sarah's, to help Gary lead the way through the caverns to the Fourth World. Halfway back to the hidden pueblo, David heard the Sun Clansmen near the wall cheer, and he assumed the final Bow Clansmen had retreated for the time being.

David didn't have to tell them that the Bow Clan would return soon. They knew that this was the final battle for Kuskurza. Either the dark kachinas would kill the Sun Clan or the Sun Clan would reach the safety of the Fourth World.

After a while, the Sun Clansmen near the wall started their own retreat back into the hidden pueblo. It was time to run for Tu'waqachi.

CHAPTER 61

Flameless torches lit the cave passages to nearly the brightness of morning; a morning on the surface not one in Kuskurza. Every Sun Clansman carried a flameless torch, and they all had them turned on. The collection of lights would keep the dark kachinas away from the group, and the Sun Clan would only have to deal with the Bow Clansmen. Most of the male Sun Clansmen were at the rear of the migrating mass to fight the Bow Clan when they caught up with the Sun Clan. The women were near the front of the group hurrying as fast as they could following Gary, Sarah, and David through the caverns. Some of the women were armed, but most carried the meager supplies they were able to gather in the few minutes Ma´saw had given them to prepare for the evacuation of the hidden pueblo.

It surprised David to see the Sun Clan had used an evacuation drill. Ma´saw had created it centuries ago when the Bow Clansmen had nearly overrun another hidden pueblo.

Three quatis of Sun Clansmen led the group through the tunnels in case of an attack from the front, but that was doubtful. Sarah, Gary, and David jogged through the caves at the very front of the group along with Ma´saw.

"We'll never be able to outrun them," Gary said between breaths. Running with a heavy pack was exhausting, and he hadn't slept in over a day.

"There's too many of us. We can't move fast enough, and the longer we run, the quicker we'll tire out," Sarah added.

David communicated their thoughts to Ma´saw when the Sun Clan leader looked at him oddly.

Some will die, but the Bow Clan will not follow us to Tu´waqachi. Nor will the dark kachinas.

"The Bow Clan will. They've already been on the surface when they tried to kill you. I won't allow the Bow Clan to get out of the caves. Not after what I've seen them do," Gary said when David translated Ma´saw's thoughts.

Ma´saw didn't reply.

"You don't seem to be concerned about your people being slaughtered," Sarah said.

Ma´saw stared at Sarah while David translated. When David finished, Ma´saw looked hurt.

I do care for my people. My heart feels each death, but for every Sun Clansman who dies, I still have many to care for. If I were to mourn each death, then many others would suffer. I cannot change what will be. It seems throughout our history that every few thousand seasons either a great exodus or slaughter must occur. It must be this way, or there would be no room in Kuskurza for the Bow Clan, the Sun Clan, and the slaves. In the days of the first Ma'saw, there was a great exodus of people to the surface. In the time of the eleventh and the twenty-ninth Ma'saws, there were great battles that killed nearly one-third of all the people in Kuskurza of both Sun Clan and Bow Clan. It is only in the past few seasons that both the Sun Clan and the Bow Clan have reached their former strengths. Now, it seems it is time for another great battle, but I have chosen to lead my people on an exodus. Whatever happens, many souls will be free in a short time.

An incomprehensible yell passed through the crowd racing from the Sun Clansmen closest to Kuskurza to those closest to the surface.

What is it? David asked Ma'saw.

The fighting has started.

"What's wrong?" Gary asked frantically.

"The Sun Clan has started fighting the Bow Clan. We've got to move faster if we're going to get anyone out of here," David told him.

"We can't. We still have to go through the sump. That will slow us down to a stop, and there's no guarantee everyone can hold their breath long enough to get through. We can use our tanks to help anyone who can't make it at first, but it's still going to be slow going. What happens if someone gets caught in that crevice? It will seal off the passage just the same as if the dark kachinas did it," Gary said.

"We can't let the Bow Clansmen out of these caves, and especially not that...that thing," Sarah said frantically. David knew without more description that Sarah meant the dark kachinas.

David nodded his head fiercely. "I know. I know. But we can't leave all these people down here. We'd only be trapping them. We might even be killing them."

David was torn. He felt he owed it to the Sun Clan to help them escape Kuskurza since the Sun Clan had not only saved his life and healed his broken legs, but they had helped him escape from Kuskurza to the Fourth World. But there was no way he would be able to get everyone out of the caves and seal off the entrance and the dark kachinas were only free because of his interference.

David turned to Ma'saw dreading what he had to do. *Ma'saw, do you know who I am?* David asked.

Ma'saw looked puzzled. *You are Pahana.*

David shook his head. *No, I'm David Purcell. I'm just an Outlander.*

But you are from Tu'waqachi.

Yes, but I'm not Pahana.

But you are delivering us from the dark kachinas.

David frowned as he told Ma'saw, *No I'm not. I can't. The Sun Clan is too large to get to Tu'waqachi without also freeing the dark kachinas. I can't do that.*

But it is our destiny.

David shook his head. *Your destiny was to keep the dark kachinas imprisoned until Pahana returned, but I'm telling you I'm not Pahana. You and the Sun Clan have to fight the Bow Clan and imprison the dark kachinas. It's not yet your time to leave Kuskurza.*

Ma'saw started crying and David felt like the world's largest heel. But the dark kachinas couldn't be allowed onto the surface. Too many lives were at stake. Ma'saw should understand; he had had to make similar decisions. These were the type of command decisions that the Army Reserves had tried to teach David to make, and he had always hated them.

When will we be free, Pahana? Ma'saw asked. *When will you return?*

David shook his head. Ma'saw still didn't believe him. The Sun Clan leader still thought David was a Christ-like god. How could David make Ma'saw understand?

Should he even try?

I will return soon. The time for the reuniting of our peoples draws nearer, but Tu'waqachi is not yet ready to receive you. And here, Kuskurza must be reclaimed in the name of Taiowa. As you fulfill your mission from the Creator, I will fulfill mine, David told Ma'saw.

How? What must we do?

Show your hearts true. Fight the Bow Clan. Use the flameless torches to force the dark kachinas into the temples again. Conquer the evil, and then I will return.

Ma'saw nodded reluctantly. David reached out and laid his hands on Ma'saw's head. Silently praying in his head so that Ma'saw could hear his words, David blessed the Sun Clan leader in God's name with strength and wisdom to endure to the time that Pahana would deliver the Sun Clan from Kuskurza. When David removed his hands, Ma'saw hugged him.

Thank you, Pahana, we will await your return.

Ma'saw turned and rushed back down the passage to lead his people into battle. He was quickly lost among the crowd of Sun Clansmen.

"They'll be slaughtered," Sarah said.

"No, they won't. They're doing God's work or Taiowa's work; however, you want to address him. They will win in the end. Light and faith will be their banner to victory."

A stray langher bolt hit the wall above David's head bringing him out of his daze.

"Do you know where you want to set the charge?" he asked Gary.

Gary nodded. "If we set a series of charges along this passageway, we could create a blockage they would never get through."

David knew Gary meant "they" as the Bow Clan, but it also included the Sun Clan. If they trapped one, they trapped both.

"Do you have enough explosives and detonators?"

"I'm going to run a series," Gary said as he pulled the plastic explosives from his backpack. He pulled off a chunk and positioned it in a crevice. He pushed the detonator box into it and attached the two wires. He ran them about twenty yards down the passage and pushed another piece of explosive into the cavern wall and armed it. When he had used up his explosives for five different detonations, he trailed the remaining wires off and attached them to the detonator he had used at the central temple.

From the other end of the cavern, everyone could hear the fighting growing closer. There were screams of pain and explosions of electricity. Rocks tumbled, and feet pounded the ground. There was not much time left.

"Everyone, get down and cover your ears," Gary ordered.

Everyone did as they were told. Gary flipped the switch to arm the detonator.

"Here goes," he said.

He pushed the button, and nothing happened.

CHAPTER 62

Gary covered his ears expecting to hear a thunderous explosion like he had heard when the pyramid exploded. *This if for my friends*, he thought, and for a brief instant, he pictured the bodies of Alex, Lou, Billy Joe, and Jared sprawled by the sump. His mind wouldn't allow him to imagine Christine's destroyed body displayed on the outside of the central temple.

Instead of the thunderclap, Gary heard a muffled curse from David.

Gary opened his eyes. He could hear the yells and screams from the fighting Sun Clan down the passageway. He saw flickering light from flameless torches and weapons.

"Nothing happened," David pointed out.

"I know," Gary snapped. "I must have pulled one of the first contacts loose because I was hurrying. I'm going to have to run down there and reattach them. Take this." He handed David the detonator, "Be ready to flip the switch."

He stood up and started jogging back down the passage. When he reached the first explosive charge, he saw where one of the contact wires had pulled free from the detonator box. As he spun the wire around the exposed metal post, he chanced a look at the fighting that was going on further down the passage.

He could see a mass of people moving around with arms and legs flailing. One man fell and was trampled beneath the crowd. There was no way to tell the good guys from the bad guys except for the color of the tunics they wore. How many of them would die in the explosion?

"Come on, Gary!" David yelled. "They're getting close."

Gary wanted to yell back that they already were close. The back end of the Sun Clan was only a dozen yards away. He turned to start back when a stray langher bolt hit him in the calf.

He felt a searing pain in his leg as he fell. He looked behind him and saw the fighting had moved even closer. In a few minutes, they would be past the first explosive charge, and then, even more Sun Clansmen would die. The problem was they weren't only men; there were women among them, too.

"Gary!" Sarah screamed.

She started to run toward him.

"No!" Gary yelled waving his hand for her to go back.

David jumped forward and grabbed Sarah to keep her from running into the passage.

"Gary, look out!" David called.

Gary looked back. One of the Bow Clansmen was charging him. Gary rolled onto his back and kicked out with his uninjured leg. He caught the Sun Clansman in the crotch. The man grabbed himself and fell to the ground moaning.

Gary rolled on top of the Bow Clansman and closed his hand's on the man's thin neck. He tightened his grip.

"This is for Christine, Jared, Alex, Lou, and Billy Joe," he murmured to himself like a chant.

The Bow Clansman's face actually began to show some color and Gary heard himself laugh. The pale man stopped struggling, and Gary rolled off him.

"Come on, Gary!" David called. "We can't wait any longer."

Gary looked at the backs of the Sun Clan. They were too close now. By the time he reached safety, the Sun Clan would be between the charges. They would definitely be killed then. Gary stood up and instead of staggering away from the fighters, he ran toward them trying to push them to the ground.

"Gary!" David yelled.

"Blow it up!" Gary shouted over his shoulder.

Gary jumped on the nearest Sun Clansman's back forcing him face down on the ground. He stood quickly, grabbed a woman and shielded her with his body.

He should have heard the explosion by now. Why didn't they just do it and get it over with?

He heard a sharp crack. Quickly followed by another and another and another and another. The hard burst of air blew him off his feet and against the side of the chamber. His head slammed against the wall and everything went dark.

CHAPTER 63

David fell forward pushing Sarah away from the last explosion of rock. He doubted it would do any good if the cavern caved in around them, but it was the only thing he could think to do.

Something fell on his legs. He grunted from the pain, but then he felt nothing as his legs went numb. Rocks rattled and bounced off each other. He threw his arms up to protect his face from the rocks.

When the rocks settled into an uneasy silence, David said, "Sarah, are you all right?"

He heard her cough and knew she was at least alive. "I'm fine. A little banged up. David turned on the flameless torch Ma'saw had given him for the retreat and shined it in Sarah's direction. Dust was in the air obscuring his view, but he could see her hazy form sitting against the far wall. She was holding her knees drawn up to her chest.

He turned the flameless torch in the direction of what had once been the path to Kuskurza. He saw nothing but a wall of rock in front of him.

He tried to sit up, but he couldn't roll over. Something was pinning his legs. He groaned.

"David, what's wrong? Are you hurt?" Sarah said.

"My legs are pinned under some rocks. I can't move."

Sarah scurried over to his side. She took the flameless torch from his hand and moved down to his legs.

David saw her try to move one of the rocks. She grunted, but the stone refused to move. David could have told her as much. He had tried to pull his legs free, but couldn't. He was pinned down.

"You're going to have to go ahead without me and bring back some help," David told Sarah.

"But you don't have any food or water. It will be days before I can get back here with help. You could die before I get back," Sarah said.

"Well, I can't go with you."

"We could..." Sarah stopped talking and scurried back to David's head. "The rocks disappeared."

"What are you talking about?"

"I suddenly couldn't see the rocks."

David twisted to the side and looked at the wall of rocks pinning his legs. Although Sarah was shining the flameless torch on the wall, there were no rocks to be seen. How could that be? He could feel the weight of rocks on his legs.

The dark kachinas.

The dark kachinas had no form. They could slip through the cracks in the rocks like water or smoke. A physical obstruction wouldn't stop them unless it was sealed with some sort of mortar. Of course, right now, there was no cement around.

David took the flameless torch and shined it on the wall moving the beam back and forth.

"Sarah, you've got to go and get help quickly."

"I don't want to leave you."

"You've got to. The dark kachinas are coming through the rocks. Unless you get some help and bring back some more flashlights, they'll kill me. I can't run away from them this time, and this torch won't last forever." He grabbed her arm. "You can do me more good if you get help than if you stay here with me. I can hold them off for a while. Hopefully, it will be long enough for you to get help and get back here."

"But it will take a week to get back to the RV, and who knows how long it will take to convince someone to come back with me," she argued.

"Then you buy the flashlights and picks and shovels and come back by yourself. We'll have to do this ourselves. You've got to go."

"No she doesn't," said a voice from behind David.

CHAPTER 64

Sarah spun around. She rubbed her eyes because she couldn't believe she was seeing the five Hopi men standing in front of her, but Ethan was holding a torch. He smiled at Sarah's look of surprise.

Peter stepped forward from the group and knelt down beside David. "Are you hurt? Do you feel any pain?"

"No, I don't feel anything," David told him. "How did you get to us?"

Peter pulled a plant from his pouch and made David chew on it. After a few moments, his mouth seemed to go numb, and the rest of his body soon followed. David wondered if this was the same plant Masani had given him to eat after he had fallen into the caves.

"I had a vision inside the kiva. I saw the dark kachinas escaping, and the Sun Clan running, and I saw you in trouble," Peter explained.

"But how could you get all the way to Utah and then be able to follow our path through the cave?" Sarah asked.

"We didn't have to. We entered the sipapu in the sacred kiva. We allowed our ko´pavis to open and Taiowa showed us the correct path to follow. We could not let you perish after everything you have done to help the Hopi."

Peter waved to the others. They moved closer to the wall and began freeing David's legs. The brightness of their lights drove the dark kachinas back even further so that the rocks could be seen.

"But the sipapu in the sacred kiva is sealed by a huge boulder. I saw it when I was inside," David said.

"It was sealed by a large boulder. The Hopi sealed the sipapu, and they opened it again," Peter told him. "We will take you back to Oraibi. I'll look at your legs there. You may have to go to the hospital in Winslow if the injury is too severe."

"He's free," Ethan announced.

"Can you move your ankles and legs?" Peter asked David.

David tried, and his legs did move, but the effort hurt him, and his face looked almost as white as one of the Sun Clan's.

"We'll have to carry you out," Peter said.

Another Hopi Peter called Joshua laid out a large piece of canvas with handles on each side of it. Then he and Peter lifted David onto the canvas so that he could easily be carried.

As they lifted him up, David said, "We should leave as much light here as possible. It will keep the dark kachinas back for a while, but then they will come after us. How far away is the sipapu?"

"About four days travel," Ethan said.

"You have to seal the wall so the dark kachinas can't get through," David said. Or the Sun Clan, he sorrowfully reminded himself.

"That won't stop them," Peter said.

David shook his head. "Yes, it will, and it will last. It may not last long in the eyes of the dark kachinas, but it will be centuries before any gaps occur that they might squeeze through. And don't forget the Sun Clan, either. If they still live, they will imprison the dark kachinas until Pahana returns to lead them to freedom."

I'm free while they have to put their lives on the line for a world they don't even know, David thought. I hope Pahana returns for them soon.

As if reading his mind, Sarah held David's hand. "You did the only thing you could do, David."

"I lied to them."

"They'll survive. They always have before, but for now, it's finally over," she said.

David nodded. "Not for them it's not."

Sarah looked back at the well-illuminated wall of rock. "Do you think Gary is still alive on the other side?"

David shrugged. "I don't know. I'm not sure he would want to be alive in that world. He seemed to have his mind set on destroying it. I only hope the real Pahana returns soon. The Sun Clan needs him."

"He will."

CHAPTER 65

David sat alone on the bench in the sacred kiva. The fire glowed brighter than usual in the center of the room. It was allowed to burn with open flames now, rather than simply red coals. He was alone in the sacred room. He shifted his body and winced. His ankle still hurt even though it was in a cast. One of the rocks had snapped his leg just above the ankle.

David stared at the open sipapu just waiting. He half expected to see the darkness in the hole overflow into the kiva as the dark kachinas escaped from their newest prison. The seal the Hopis had added to the stone wall had held so far. At least no dark kachinas had flowed onto the earth, and David prayed none ever would.

Peter had ordered that the fire in the kiva always stay lit. He was obviously not as confident in the seal's ability to hold as everyone else seemed to be. Either that or he was being extremely careful.

As David watched the sipapu, a man's head appeared out of the darkness. Ethan climbed out of the caverns and sat down next to David.

"How's it going down there?" David asked his friend.

"I've never heard so much praying or seen so many kachina dolls. Even if the dark kachinas do slip through the wall, they won't go anywhere. The land is blessed, and the other kachinas will guard the way."

"That's good to hear."

"Do you go back today?"

David nodded slowly. "Don't remind me."

"Why go if you don't want to?"

"It's not that easy. Right now, Sheriff Harding is probably investigating more murders than the county has had in the past five years, and he suspects I had something to do with them. He's going to want to solve these murders quickly, and I don't want him pinning them on me. I have to convince him that I'm innocent, but he would never believe the truth if I told it to him."

"Then don't," Ethan said.

"What?"

"If he can't prove anything against you, then you shouldn't worry. He'll either accept the truth or find some way to 3explain it away."

"David. David, are you down there?"

It was Sarah calling him from outside the kiva.

"I'm here," he replied.

"The truck's ready when you are," she told him.

David looked around one last time. "I'm ready."

He hobbled over to the ladder and struggled up it. He had to hold tightly to the ladder and hop from rung to rung on his good leg. When his head appeared above ground, Sarah helped him get out. Ethan followed David out of the kiva.

Together, Sarah and David hobbled into the plaza where Ethan's red pickup truck sat. Sarah helped David into the passenger seat, then climbed behind the driver's wheel.

David looked over at her and smiled. She smiled back and made his insides feel warm. Ethan waved goodbye to them.

David thought about how surprised his mother would be this weekend when he introduced her to his future wife.

ABOUT THE AUTHOR

J. R. Rada is a pen name for award-winning writer, James Rada, Jr. He has written five books of fantasy and horror. These include *A Byte-Size Friend, Welcome to Peaceful Journey, Kachina, and Kuskurza.*

He works as a freelance writer who lives in Gettysburg, PA. James has received numerous awards from the Maryland-Delaware-DC Press Association, Associated Press, Maryland State Teachers Association and Community Newspapers Holdings, Inc. for his newspaper writing.

If you would like to be kept up to date on new books being published by James or ask him questions, he can be reached by e-mail at *jimrada@yahoo.com.*

To see James' other books or to order copies on-line, go to *www.jamesrada.com.*

DON'T MISS THESE BOOKS BY
J.R.RADA

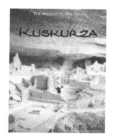

KUSKURZA
Contains "The Path to Kuskurza" and "White Indian" as well as a sneak peek to "Kachina." These are stories of the ancient gods of the Hopi and Third World in which they lived before emerging in this world.

A BYTE-SIZED FRIEND (HACKERS #1)
Chris Alten was a 13-year-old athlete until a car accident kills his father and leaves Chris confined to a wheelchair. Depressed, Chris meets a new friend online who makes him interested in life again. It turns out the new friend is a computer program, though. Then Chris discovers that the cyber-terrorists who killed his father are searching for program, and Chris must decide if helping an artificial friend is worth risking his life.

WELCOME TO PEACEFUL JOURNEY
Welcome to Peaceful Journey Funeral where the journey from life to death can be anything but peaceful. The viewing rooms bear the names of heavenly glory as found in the different religions of the world, but it is a long-forgotten religion that controls Peaceful Journey. Owner Bruce Godsey tries his best to be comforting to mourners, but he has seen a lot more than he can admit.

Made in the USA
Middletown, DE
22 September 2024